CRACKED
ICE

KD CURETON

Cover Design: Katelyn at Design by Kage
Interior Formatting: Katelyn at Design by Kage
Editing & Proofreading: Funky Like Feathers

AUTHOR'S NOTE

I'm so glad you've picked up my book and can't wait for you to read it, but a couple of things to note before you get started. This is a DARK hockey romance, and though it isn't the darkest of the dark, there are themes in this book that should not be repeated, tried, or emulated in any way. This book is about flawed characters with real-world issues but NOT real-world solutions. It is acknowledged several times in the book that one of the MCs has mental health issues, but those issues are not resolved in a way that should be celebrated or imitated. Also, you will see some BDSM themes throughout the story, but this is not a how-to instruction manual and none of the things mentioned are based in fact. There IS such a thing as limits, and there is NO such thing as "safe phrases". For more content and trigger warnings, please view the back of the book. Now, enjoy the game!

stalk·er /stôkər/ noun

1. a person who harasses or persecutes someone with unwanted and obsessive attention.
2. a person who hunts game stealthily.

To all the girlies who's love and dedication might be a little intense, you are not a stalker—you just have a big heart.
And to the dirty little sluts who love getting filthy, you're not desperate—you're just extremely motivated. Enjoy the game.

PLAYLIST

FIRST PERIOD

'I Wanna Be Your Girlfriend' by Cameron Hayes
'Daddy Issues' by The Neighbourhood
'Normal' by Silent Child
'Good Girl' by Thomas LaRosa
'Bad Guy' by Falling in Reverse ft. Saraya
'Heaven' by Julia Michaels

INTERMISSION

'Ocean Eyes' by Billie Eilish
'Boys Like You' by Tanerélle
'In My Head' by Mike Shinoda
'Anxiety' by Doechii
'Pretty Boy' by Isabel LaRosa

SECOND PERIOD

'Hostage' by Billie Eilish
'Like A Dream' by Thomas LaRosa
'Chills-Dark Version' by Mickey Valen, Joey Myron
'Issues' by Julia Michaels

'Taste' by Ari Abdul
'100 Ways' by Austin Hull
'Aphrodite' by Sam Short

TIME OUT

'Jump' by Silent Child and PatrickReza
'Prisoner' by Raphael Lake, Aaron Levy & Daniel Ryan
'Static' by Sleep Theory
'Playing With Death' by NOT A TOY
'Voices In My Head' by Falling in Reverse

SECOND PERIOD

'Middle Of The Night' by Loveless
'Show Me' Black Atlass
'Body' (Slowed and Reverb) by Rosenfeld
'Desire' by Nic Dean
'A Little Bit' by Ella Boh
'Bad Things' by MGK and Camila Cabello
'Sweet but Psycho' by Ava Max
'The Devil In I' by Nikki Idol
'When the Night is Over' by Lord Huron

INTERMISSION

'Where Are You?' by Elvis Drew, Avivian
'One Track Mind' by Thirty Seconds to Mars ft. A$AP Rocky
'Tip Toe' by PatrickReza

ZAMBONI BREAK

'Who To Blame' by blurblur
'Say Yes To Heaven' by Lana Del Rey
'Head Over Heel's' by STARSET
'Super Villain' by Stileto & Silent Child

THIRD PERIOD

'Toxic' by Omido ft. Rick Jansen
'Caramel' by Sleep Token
'Go to Hell' by Nikki Idol
'Do It For Me' by Rosenfeld
'Good Girl' by Burt, Beneld, Omido
'BEG' by gonedark
'GOD Complex' by April Jae
'You Put A Spell On Me' by Austin Giorgio
'Little Girl Gone' by CHINCHILLA
'Not Afraid Anymore' by Halsey
'Twisted Nerve' by Bernard Herrmann
'Confidence' by Pre Kai Ro, Oliver Davis, Super Beats
'We Found Love' by Rihanna ft. Calvin Harris
'Dangerous Night' by Thirty Seconds to Mars

OVERTIME

'FREEFALL' by NOTHING MORE ft, Chris Daughtry
'Apartment' by Bobi Andonov
'X' by Kxlly
'For Your Love' by Cera.uno
'Use Me' by Makk Mikkael
'Someone You Loved' by Lewis Capaldi
'Before You Go' by Lewis Capaldi
'Jokes On You' by Charlotte Lawrence

SHOOT OUT

'Dark Paradise' by Lana Del Rey
'The Night We Met' by Lord Huron
'NEVER EVER' by Omido

FIRST
PERIOD

CHAPTER ONE

SYDNEY

"THIS MIGHT BE EXCESSIVE. Even for me," I mumble, chewing nervously on the flesh of my thumbnail.

I'm aware it's a disgusting habit, unbecoming of a young lady of my stature. I can already hear the phantom notes of Dad's voice scolding me, reminding me that I'm *too pretty* to carry myself in such a way, as if the nervous tick hinders my ability to be beautiful, but I no longer register the pain of the bite. These days, I chase it. Anything to distract me from the anxiety settling in my chest so I can focus on the goal in front of me.

Except, the goal changed. It changed out of nowhere and set me on a course from which I can't deviate. For so long, figure skating was my one true love, but now, my heart is calling for something else, *someone* else. It's like I'm being pulled against my will, sucked into a black hole and broken down on a cellular level. It sounds terrifying. Feels that way, too. I suppose falling for someone always is. But there's an excitement there as well, one you feel when you're on the verge of discovery, the unknown, or death. I haven't quite determined where this new path leads. All I know is its destination, so I'm taking the leap and committing to the jump.

Trepidation coils in my gut and my teeth sink into my thumb so hard I reopen the perpetual wound made sensitive from constant gnawing. The metallic taste of copper pricks at my tongue, but I ignore it, swiping my tongue to lick away the blood and continue biting at the sore flesh. I will my feet to move faster, picking up my pace so as not to encourage the impulse to turn around and forget I was ever here. I'm not ready to let go yet, to let *him* go. My blond ponytail tickles against my neck—the frantic bobbing, incessant with every hurried step as I speed-walk toward the roaring hockey arena.

It feels weird walking through the front doors and not going to practice or a competition. Turning right versus left toward the east wing is awkward and foreign. Muscle memory dictates I go to my left, toward my own rink, but that's no longer where the path leads.

The atrium is rather empty as I pass. The obnoxious squeak of my sneakers echoing off the concrete walls grates in my ears. The steady tempo indicating just how fast I'm walking. With the game about to start, there's hardly anyone left in the seating area. The lingering staff and stragglers stand around to watch the TVs but that's about it. For a moment, I consider standing with them, to watch the game from behind the safety of television screens. But if I were going to do that, I shouldn't have bothered coming in the first place. There's a reason I stepped foot back in here, and it wasn't so I could stand elbow to elbow with strangers cheering on guys playing with their sticks, so I force myself to keep going.

I pass the school's trophy case and my favorite vending machine for the last time. I push through the swinging doors with the broken hinge that screeches every time it opens. I watch the air conditioner blow the school banners, causing them to billow above me for the *last* time.

The building is huge, and the hockey side is grander than what I'm used to on the figure skating side. For however long I considered this place home, it's bittersweet as I breeze past all its glory and shine for a final time. I'm still several sections away from the actual rink and, though my toned legs are pushing as fast as they can, I don't feel like I'm making any progress. My destination only seems farther away. If *that's* not a huge metaphor for the state of my life, I don't know what is. I'm closer than I realize, mere moments away from the most critical juncture of my life.

I keep my head down, but the farther I walk, the more people I encounter and the louder their voices grow.

"What is she wearing?"

"Is she a figure skater?"

"I wonder what she's doing here?"

"I didn't know there was a figure competition here today, too."

"Look at her outfit."

Nettlesome whispers surround me, but I do my best to push past the noise.

Distorted shadows reflect off the shiny gray concrete floor as I draw closer, taunting me with its mocking reflection. The big blue bow in my hair is comically disproportionate in the shadows. I look like Minnie Mouse, if Minnie Mouse were a recently disgraced figure skater.

I can feel the accusing stares creep over my body before they shift and dart away. I cease my thumbnail chewing long enough to flash a smile to those who stare, flicking my ponytail over my shoulder and holding my head up high again. Disgraced or not, perfection was something I always strove for. No point in switching it up now. I can't let them see me sweat, even if they are oblivious to my true discomfort. I can deal with being the center of attention, even if the attention is bad. What I *can't* deal with is being the butt of a bad joke, which is what this is starting to feel like. I catch another glimpse of myself mirrored in the tall windows as day gives way to night.

I did it again.

I know I did.

I took it a step too far like I always do. It'd be one thing if I was simply wearing my skating competition outfit, but nope, I couldn't leave it at that. I had to go above and beyond, go the extra mile, *like I always do.* God, why am I like this?

I dig my pointer finger into the wound on my thumb, picking at the cut. The dull stinging sensation settles me once more.

Part of me believed the more I looked like myself tonight, the less likely *he* would suspect me. I was sure I'd never been caught but, with my luck as of late, he'd know it was me immediately. I figured if I was going to commit to coming straight here, I might as well *try* to look the part. There was no reason to linger on the humiliating ostracization from my team, possibly the entire U.S figure skating collegiate organization. This *is* a big game. Everyone should be showing school spirit, right?

Wrong. Everyone is in fact *not* decked out in glitter and hair streamers.

And here I thought I looked hot. I thought I was making lemonade out of lemons when it seems I was making Bloody Marys.

Soft snickering catches my attention, accompanied by not-so-subtle finger pointing. I swivel my head to the right, spotting a group of friends in plain t-shirts and jeans. They eye me suspiciously, like I've grown a second head or have extra appendages growing from my abdomen. I turn away only to see a group of older women dressed in jerseys and leggings for the rival team. They look just as confused, and my cheeks burn from the fabricated grin stuck to my face. I no longer have the energy to smile, not genuinely. Yet, I do it anyway. Force of habit, I guess. I'm always performing, and a perfect smile will sell the show every time.

It's taken everything in me to be here and not break down in tears. Because I'm *here*, instead of *there*. Today was my last shot at greatness, my *last* chance to achieve glory, and I fucking blew it. I didn't just lose focus, I lost my goddamn mind.

And still…I came here.

Of course you did.

But now this is a chance to do what *I* want for once. So, I won't let the last two hours taint what I'm trying to accomplish now. I've lost something important to me, something I chased my whole life and now I'm going to lose the *person* I've been chasing the last three months, who captured my attention before I've ever even had him.

So again, no, I won't let their burning stares and snickering get to me.

A little boy no older than seven points at me like I'm infected with cooties.

Yeah, that is a whole lot easier said than done.

"Oh, hey, Sydney, is that you?" shouts a girl from my *ethics* class of all places, waving me down from up ahead like she's trying to hail a cab.

I try pretending I don't hear her but she's drawing more attention by calling my name a second time, then a third. I can't very well walk right past her like I don't see her without raising further suspicion, can I?

She plants herself in my path, leaving me no other choice. "Sydney!" she yells, her arms still flapping despite forcing me to walk right up to her.

"Hey . . . you. What's up?"

I'd never bothered remembering her name. She was nice for conversation in class, but our interactions started and ended there.

"What are you doing here?" Her eyes squint as she points to my outfit. "Shouldn't you be—"

"Oh, I . . . uh, couldn't afford the entry fee this time," I lie, trying to be casual about the whole thing, though my perspiring forehead gives me away easily.

Why is it so hot in here? Isn't this an ice arena?

The excuse sounds stupid the second the words leave my mouth.

"You . . . what?" That scoffing sound she's making is laden with a hefty dose of disbelief. There's not much a Sinclair can't afford, least of all an entry fee.

Her mouth contorts. But then she's gasping as if I've just revealed something important to her, though I've not said a word. For all my practice, all my sweet-talking and sugar-coating I so easily fall into, I have nothing left to say or give.

"Are you okay?" She asks, reaching out to...console me? I blink at her abnormally large hands that reach for mine and subtly tuck them behind me.

She either doesn't notice or ignores my slight against her, leaning in instead and lowering her voice. As if anyone can even hear us over the abysmal rendition of the national anthem blaring over the speakers. "Look if you're, like, in any trouble, you don't have to worry. I won't tell anyone." My brows scrunch at both her closeness and her words.

The hell?

I'm still wracking my brain around the awkward one-sided conversation when it finally hits me. Ohhh. She's speculating that I've somehow gone bankrupt in the last twenty-four hours.

"That..." my lips part to tell her the truth but then clamp shut. That...might've been preferable actually. If only this were a matter of money instead of matters of the heart. I ultimately forgo correcting her. Best to let her think whatever she wants. Everyone else does.

"Um, well, gotta go," I say, shifting my eyes around the rink as if looking for friends, not that I have any at this point. "I'm running late. See you later. Bye."

"Well, wait I—"

I scurry off before more questions can be asked of me. She'll learn the truth sooner or later, and by then it won't matter, because I won't be here.

A minute later, one of my professor's TA's tries to wave too when they recognize me, but I'm not one to make the same mistake twice. I promptly ignore them. Optics be damned.

What's left of my thumbnail goes right back to its place between my lips as my manic muttering continues.

Fan-fucking-tastic!

"Congrats, Sydney. If you wanted his attention before, you're definitely going to get it *now*," I mutter.

The sudden onset of delirium is still not enough to convince my feet to stop moving toward their goal. The bright red skaters costume I've been sporting, complete with bedazzled sequins and glitter spray, should be reason alone to turn around and forget this whole thing, but—as is my nature—I stubbornly proceed.

When I put this outfit on a few hours ago I was a competing collegiate figure skater. Flash forward and I'm a bedazzled freak at a hockey game. Funny how quickly things change.

Though, if I'm being honest with myself, it wasn't all that quick.

I'm no longer a collegiate figure skater, which means I no longer have a scholarship, which means it's *over*. How I managed to get kicked off a team I worked my whole life to be on is beyond me. How I managed to get swindled by my own father is another issue entirely.

I gotta hand it to him though, Dad moved quick. My program was set to start at three o'clock today. I was confronted by Coach at two o'clock. Expeditiously escorted from the ice by two thirty. During what should have been *my* moment of glory, *my* program music playing and *my* name being called, I was being interrogated by the ethics committee. Though it pained me to do it, one phone call to my father and an hour later all conjecture, questions, or suspicion was killed on the spot—but so were my chances of ever coming back from this. My namesake may have been saved by Dad, but in the end he's the one who'd truly won. *One* private car and *two* hours later, my dad had arranged my transfer, broken my apartment lease, enrolled me into his internship, and confirmed my complete surrender. By the time I'd arrived back at Bellemere it was a done deal, my time at Belle U was finished and all before my sophomore year.

So I had my driver course correct and bring me straight here. *One last time.*

For a moment, the pain manages to register, my teeth digging in a little harder than I mean for them to. I yelp, pulling my thumb away on reflex. I try to shake off the pain, but it's in vain. It sticks to me like a visceral beacon, a blaring red warning sign that says, "Beware of the girl with the broken heart." The second the pain dissipates, my bleeding thumbnail goes right back in my mouth, as I speed past the uncomfortable watchful eyes of sports patrons.

Excessive, indeed.

I could have at least gone home and changed. Why didn't I do that again?

Because you knew you wouldn't come back otherwise.

Oh, right, I'd run.

@therealLucifer
Online

Vere you in the arena last nig

Seen

Who the hell is this?

Seen

CHAPTER TWO

SYDNEY

THIS IS MADDIE JAMESON's tenth birthday party all over again. I had been so excited about the prospect of a real princess-themed birthday party, I showed up in a handmade pink princess ball gown. It had been made special by my nanny with hand-stitched lace and my own embroidered handkerchief. My hair had been professionally styled and topped with a real diamond-encrusted tiara that I begged my father to have made by the family jeweler. Needless to say, I was dressed so lavishly, I wasn't allowed to play with the other girls. To make matters worse, Maddie Jameson was so jealous, she purposely spilled her Kool-Aid on my princess gown and never invited me to her birthday parties again.

Joke's on her though, my parties were infamously better.

However, the same feelings I had back then are the ones I'm plagued with now.

A chill slithers up my spine at the memory, or maybe it's the chill of the arena as I draw ever closer.

Get it together, Sydney. You don't have time to wallow.

My bloodied thumb slips from my lips a final time to swing at my side as I stride forward. The crowd thickens and I have to weave around more than walk ahead. My heart pounds and I press my hand to my chest, forcing it to calm down, but it fights back, thumping against my palm like we're high-fiving or some shit. I've performed in front of a crowd of thousands, yet the sheer idea of talking to the guy I like is causing me to scratch at my skin—or rather bite at it.

9

The plan was simple: watch the game, fake some kind of run-in with him, then live happily ever after. But the more I let that thought take root, the sicker I feel.

What is wrong *with me?*

Today was going to be the day I was finally going to talk to him. Though, if this is my body's reaction, I might be hoping for too much.

A flash of all my other failed attempts to speak to him spring to mind, but I shake it off.

No, this time will work. It will. It has to.

But then my phone is ringing and whatever hope I had a second ago is immediately dashed. I answer on reflex, knowing ignoring it *isn't* an option. Letting it ring more than twice is an even worse alternative.

"Hi, Dad," my voice trembles.

"What is that noise? Why is it so loud?" He questions me.

I rush to cup my hands over the speaker, but it's already too late. I elbow the people in my way to make it to one of the alcoves lined between the restrooms. Ducking behind the columns, I smash the phone to my ear.

"Yes," I hiss. "I'm here, I'm just . . ."

"Why aren't you home packing, Sydney?" my father accuses, not allowing me to get a word in edgewise, even if I did have a suitable answer.

My eyes close on a sigh. I didn't even make it to the rink before I was caught.

"Umm . . ." *Smooth, Sydney. Real smooth.* "I just needed to make a quick stop. I'll be heading home soon. I promise."

"What kind of stop?" he asks, bypassing regular socio-normative greetings entirely and straight into interrogation.

No, *'Hi, Sydney, how are you?'*

Or *'Hello, daughter, are you feeling alright after I completely upended your life?'*

I've no clue why I'm even surprised. The conversation never goes that way.

"I asked you a question, Sydney. What kind of stop did you make?" he asks again.

I take in a deep breath. "I came to the arena to get the remainder of my things."

It's not my best lie, but it's partly true. What's the thing people say? The best lies are wrapped in truth.

"What for? You won't be needing it." His voice is stern, leaving little room for rebuttal.

"I know, but I was asked to clear it out and it was better I do it myself, so they won't have to cut the lock off and throw it all away. At least this way I can donate the skates to someone worthy," I counter, knowing any one of the girls would gladly snatch up my skates if I left them.

He chuckles, but it's his public relations laugh. The kind that holds no real sense of joy in the expression. He might as well be yawning. *That* would be less offensive.

"Worthy? Honey, they're figure skates, not investment bonds. The only thing you need to be doing right now is making sure you're ready to go by ten tomorrow morning."

There are so many ways I want to respond, but ultimately sickening desperation wins out. If I could just get him to see reason.

I clear my throat.

"What if . . . What if I talk to the coach again? Maybe I could get the—"

"We had a deal. And a Sinclair—"

"Always honors a deal," I finish for him. "Yes, I know."

"Exactly. I commend you for holding out all this time. Genuinely, I do. I'd expected you to falter long before now but you proved to be far more formidable than I'd initially given you credit for." My heart skips at what—from him— is the closest thing to high praise I've ever received. "However . . ." The guillotine drops. "I've let you play fairy princess for long enough. I spoiled you and let you pursue your frivolous hobbies, but it stops now. You couldn't hold up your end of the bargain and, what's worse, you almost let our good name get tainted with your antics. It's time to come home. You'll have a couple weeks to get settled, but then you'll start your internship at Sinclair Enterprises and claim what's yours."

Mine? There is no mine. It'll never be mine.

"But if I could just—"

"In the meantime I've set up some dinner dates for you. We need to refocus on expansion and securing you a suitable match that will ensure our future. Now more than ever."

"Please, Dad. Just let me—"

"Forget all of this and put it behind you." He brokers no room for argument. But inside, I am screaming. I didn't want to put it *behind me.*

My life at this school was supposed to be my *future* and the life I put *behind me* was the one with him and those god awful people. Going back meant I was going to be reduced to being a glorified honeypot meant to seduce and trick his competitors. And these dates to find me a 'suitable match' was just another deception. He didn't care if I actually liked the guy, only that they helped him garner more power. And apparently he never cared what my plans for the future were because this has been nothing more than a foregone conclusion to him.

The worst part is he hasn't raised his voice once. He doesn't have to. His words are sharp enough all on their own and I'm used to the cut.

"But—" I try again, my unyielding nature one of the few traits we share.

"But nothing," he says. "You failed. My expectations were clear and more than fair if you ask me. I let you go to that school. I paid for your housing, gave you an allowance, funded your lessons." He ticks them off one by one, keeping meticulous record of all his 'charity.' "What more could I have done, hmm? If it was so important to you, you should have remained vigilant. Instead, you let yourself lose focus over what you *claim* mattered most to you. This was a consequence of *your* error."

"I *was* focused," I argue. "I applied everything you taught me, and I *earned* my spot on the team."

"You did . . . and then you lost it."

His choice of words are no accident. They're a slap to the face after everything I worked so hard for. "Accept it and move on, Sydney."

I can feel his disapproval through the phone. It snakes through the line and winds around my neck. Like a noose, it grows tighter and tighter, until I'm struggling for breath.

"I told you . . . I . . . I didn't do what they're saying I did. It's all a *big* misunderstanding. I can fix this. I can—" I choke out.

"You should have thought about that sooner," he states.

I should have, but my thoughts weren't on the consequences, they were on *him*.

"Dad, please," I whisper, too choked up to say more.

Dad sighs and I can hear the faint tiredness in his voice. I'm tired too.

"What have I always taught you?" He doesn't let me answer. "In life, you don't get do-overs. You don't get to make mistakes without enduring a cost. This is the cost, Sydney. So, pay it, and don't ask me to change my mind again."

Though his words are heavy, his voice is soft and unassuming. They're spoken with the weight of a father who only wants what he thinks is best for his only daughter. I knew this would be his stance. Once he enters an agreement, there is no changing his mind.

My lip quivers, threatening tears, an automatic response to his harsh words, but I'm not actually processing the pain. It doesn't hurt anymore.

"Are we clear, Sydney?" His voice lowers, his warning tone sounding closer to my ear than his earlier speech.

The lump in my throat swells and I'm forced to swallow it before I speak again. "Yes, we're clear." It's a weak rasp and I'm embarrassed by how immature I sound. I don't sound like a champion, I sound helpless.

"Good. I'll see you in the morning."

And just like that his sour mood's forgotten. He only sounds like this when . . .

"Yeah, see you—" He hangs up. "Later."

I stand there for a full minute, letting his words slice me open and bleed me out before a deeper pull tugs me forward again.

I thought my dad had been exaggerating when he said boys were distractions. But in all the years I'd hoped my dad was wrong about something, this was the one that hurt the most to admit he wasn't entirely wrong about. Fourteen years of dedicated, hard work just blew up in my face and what am I doing? Working out a way to talk to my crush.

The only thing I can think about is how I'm going to finally work up the nerve to speak to the star hockey player I've been obsessing over the last few months. It was his distracting presence that led to my downfall to begin with. Before him, boys weren't hard to ignore. *Winning* had always felt better than any childhood crush.

But there was nothing childish about *this*. This felt like cardiac arrest. Like my heart wanted to physically rip itself out and hand itself over to him as tribute. This was like nothing I'd ever experienced before.

Maybe if I had any real experience with emotionally competent caregivers, a supporting father, or even a present mother, I wouldn't be some freak who doesn't know how to properly handle genuine feelings for someone. I'd be able to manage introducing myself like a normal human instead of thinking of elevator pitches. I'd like people for who they are instead of for what they could do for me or how they could best serve me in the future. I'd show up to a sporting event without creating a spectacle.

Jesus, it's no wonder I've never had a boyfriend. I understand now that it was a larger part of Dad's master plan to ensure I stayed above the rest and as far from normal as possible.

I sigh, deep enough to be audible to those around me. Cursing under my breath in response to more stares, I shake my head and square my shoulders. It'll be fine. I *am* normal. I'm a *normal* girl who likes a *normal* boy and all I have to do is say "Hi." It's not that hard.

I'm clearly *still* mumbling to myself like a crazy person because a little girl blinks at me, staring in either abject horror or morbid curiosity. Her small arms are wound tightly around the man's neck in front of me, their hair a matching dirty blond color. Her dad, if I had to guess. Her eyes squint in accusation, her expression wary, as her head flops to the side, resting on his shoulder. The blond pigtails in her hair, held tautly by glittery blue scrunchies, splay over her face, providing perfect cover for her eyes and protecting her from my return stare.

I search around briefly, ensuring no one is looking, before I make a weird face at her, forcing my eyes to cross and sticking my tongue out. She giggles, squeezing her father's neck tighter. Her smile is bright even as she holds on for dear life. The man's shoulder shakes, suggesting he's laughing too. Perhaps at her random head lock and laugh attack, but he appears unfazed. His hand comes up to pet her on the head, ignoring her viper grip as he gently sweeps her pigtail back into place. It's obvious he doesn't mind the tightness of her hold. As he strokes her hair, her giggles settle, and she rests deeper into the crook of his neck.

There's a sharp pang in my chest at the gentle gesture, a heaviness that grips my heart and squeezes unexpectedly. Her small hand waves at me before they veer off down a different path, presumably to a different section. I consider following them, wondering if their destination is better than mine, but I have my own path to follow.

Why couldn't my relationship with my dad be like hers?

I would have liked going to a hockey game with my dad at that age. Hell, even now at nineteen. But as made evident from our little chat, that wouldn't go well. It wouldn't be as comforting as they'd made it look either. We'd inevitably bump heads, but at least it'd be something.

It's not as though the little girl looked anything like me, but, right now, it's hard to not draw parallels. Once upon a time I went everywhere with my dad, I still do. They're not places that'd allow any real father/daughter bonding, but even still, I can't recall a single time where he held me like that. No comforting hugs or gentle words of encouragement. Maybe if I had a strong, dependable shoulder to rest my head on, things wouldn't have turned out this way.

My eyes sting, but I blink away the incoming tears. I'll be back with Dad before I know it, right back where I started. No point in ruining perfectly good makeup with needless tears.

I start walking again. For now, this is where the current path leads. This is where *he* is.

I've never been to a hockey game before. I've never been able to summon the courage to see him or find the time to go. Yet, here I am, on the worst day of my life, all tricked out in the school colors, ready to risk everything and throw caution to the wind.

I'd be appalled at myself if I wasn't already so hopeless. If the teasing shadows are anything to go by, I still look good, giant bow aside. Even Dad could at least be proud of my efforts. After all, "a Sinclair always makes an impression."

Though, I can't shake the feeling that this impression might be more grandiose than I originally intended. It's bad enough I came straight here, it's even worse I'm risking getting caught. Jesus, I didn't need to gift wrap myself in a *literal* bow to get his attention. I'm not even sure I *want* his attention. But that's what happens every time I look at him. I lose all sense of rationale and control.

My ears perk at the sounds of blades cutting against the ice, followed by more cheers.

I bounce on my toes. The long-awaited entrance is finally within my reach. The air grows colder and the smell of saturated fats from stale popcorn, day-old hot dogs, and melted plastic cheese press upon me. I can't believe I'm really doing this. I mean, I *actually* can't believe it. It smells gross and everything looks sticky.

There's exactly two things I know about hockey. The first: Number 66 is the reason for the success of the Bellemere University Titans. *Even if he is the reason for my demise.*

I can already hear his name being chanted like an incantation as I draw closer to the opening. A weird mixture of relief and determination flood me simultaneously. I'll finally get to see him play. I'm giddy just thinking about it. This is the first time I get to see him in action. Unfortunately, I'm quite literally late to the party and no amount of running will get me any closer with the hordes of people currently in the way of the long staircase that leads down to the lower-level seating. It's a long shot, but if I'm going to be forced to sit in the stands like a commoner, I at least want a good spot. I'm sure if I actually *were* here with my dad, we'd be in the box seating above. But I'm here for one reason only: to watch Number 66 play.

I'm brought to an abrupt halt by the backs of strangers, forced to wait for others as they shimmy between rows toward the inconvenient middle seats. I take a step back, still cast in the comforting shadows of the corridor, a final attempt to regain my senses. The need to turn back and let this silly obsession go is ever present. No one needs to know I was ever here, least of all, him. But this is my last chance. I can't let a moment like this slip. It was a miracle I managed to snag a ticket at all. I'm half convinced the only reason I did is because the ticket counter girl knows me. She seemed aware this was out of the norm for me when she handed me my ticket. Hell, she might've even felt pity for me because she knew the truth. I'm not supposed to be here.

My feet shuffle forward as the crowd presses on. Now, fully inside the arena, I'm temporarily blinded by the lights. I'm almost rendered deaf from the roars and screams of excited patrons already buzzing with energy from the first five minutes of the game. *Shit, it's started.*

@therealLucifer
Online
ere you in the arena last nig
Seen
Who the hell is this?
Seen
SYDNEY

CHAPTER THREE

SYDNEY

MY EYES DANCE WILDLY over the sea of foam fingers and signs, before finally spotting an open seat. My ticket is for the nosebleeds but that one is a prime location with a center view of the arena and right off the aisle. It's just... nestled between two shirtless dudes who have painted their entire torsos blue and white, faces included. Great. *And here I thought I was being over the top.* Jesus, I'm used to being cold on an ice rink, but they've got to be freezing. Their rosy cheeks and sweat-glistened mid-sections suggest the total opposite. They look harmless enough, like the typical college guys at a sports game. But they obviously started drinking early and are among the loudest of screaming fans.

"Woooo! Let's Go B-U!" The one with a B painted on his back shouts into the open air.

"B-U! B-U! B-U!" This from the other one with a U on his back.

They're fairly attractive, so at least they have that going for them, though their attractive qualities are quickly overshadowed when they start barking and howling like dogs. We're the Titans, not the Bulldogs, so the barking makes no sense. I try to shield myself from the second-hand embarrassment, but it's like watching wild animals in their natural habitat; it's fascinating.

They bump chests and high five, transferring some of their color onto each other. I wait for their bro fest to die down before I can be certain the seat between them is available. I glance at my ticket for my seat again, then scan the area once more before settling on the only option worth taking. *I want* that *seat.*

"Hi, um, is anyone sitting there?" I point my bright blue nail in the direction of the free seat nestled between them. They both turn in unison to look at it as though they hadn't realized its existence before now. I fidget with the hem of my skirt, a healthier alternative to my usual flesh biting. When their attention turns back to me, I feel as silly as I look. The blue and white streamers and hair ribbons atop my head paired with my red outfit make me look like I'm cheering for goddamn Team USA or something.

"A pretty girl like you can sit anywhere she wants," the guy farthest from me speaks first.

It takes considerable effort not to roll my eyes. Instead, I offer him a flirtatious smile, and bat my glittered eyelashes, making sure to look down and away as I play coy. I tuck a few nonexistent wisps of hair behind my ear for no other reason than to draw attention to my face, before I look up and let them dive into my baby blue eyes, lined in cerulean blue eyeliner to match. *Too easy.* Yes, I may have overdid it with the team spirit, but it hardly makes sense to complain about it now, especially when it's working in my favor.

"Is that so? And if I want *that* seat?" I drawl out, poking in the seat's direction again, my voice higher pitched and breathier than usual to sell the show. It's not like they would know the difference between my real voice and the lie. Their mouths drop open, and I swear the one currently eye fucking me drools. My performance is well rehearsed and perfectly timed. What's a couple of hockey fans to an entire judge's panel?

"That one's taken . . ." he says.

My smile stays in place, but my chest falls, unexpected defeat hitting me square in the gut and reopening the fresh wound of rejection.

"But this one has your name written *all* over it."

His hips rut upward, humping the air in front of his crotch, and I'm forced to pretend my giggle is because of his charm and not his ridiculous suggestion.

"You don't say?" My tone is teasing with just the right amount of unsurety. As far as he knows I could be flirting or I could be shy, maybe even a little naive. Both work in my favor, but the key is not making it obvious. I was taught to win by any means necessary. If that means I have to use my feminine wiles to win them over, so be it.

A hand slaps him in the chest.

"Don't mind this idiot. The game brings out the neanderthal in him." His friend next to him speaks, the one I felt comfortable enough to approach in the first place and who's attention has been a little more evenly split between the game and my tits. He smiles down at me with kind brown eyes. His gaze over my figure is less blatant than his friend, before he positions himself away, stepping out into the aisle to allow me through. I stand there with my arms folded while I reevaluate my choices. Nice though he may appear, it doesn't seem he's willing to give up his aisle seat for me.

"Our other friend couldn't make it, so it's all yours." he presses, his arm stretched out in a gentlemanly manner, encouraging me to sit. I'm not sure if he's aware of my hesitation or if he's legitimately a nice guy, but, either way, I fold.

"Thank you."

I shimmy past his wide frame and my smile melts into something a little more genuine. The victory is sweet, but made better by the fact I won't have to be sandwiched between *two* assholes. Except, the moment my ass lands on the hard plastic seat, my ponytail shakes and the asshole of the two takes it as an invitation to poke at the bobbles in my hair.

"Nice outfit," he says, breathing entirely too loud in my ear.

I withhold my eye roll, opting instead to adjust on the hard blue plastic folding chair. It proves fruitless, the damn thing tries to flop closed every time I move. The discomfort is only made worse by his salacious perusal of my body. I look ahead, over the ice, faking deafness so I don't have to talk to my new seat buddy, but I can feel his eyes burning a hole in the side of my face as he waits for me to acknowledge him.

I don't.

Until he reaches up to play with my curls. I snap sideways to face him, keeping my hair out of his greasy reach. *Shit.* Now that I'm facing him, I can't pretend I didn't hear him.

"Huh?" I ask, scrunching my face as I twirl the ends of my ponytail, ensuring it stays far away from his grasp.

He repeats, louder this time. "I said nice outfit!"

His glassy eyes move up and down my body, lingering on my legs and then my tits before he resumes semi-normal eye contact. I obviously heard him the first time, but it's the assumption written on his face right now that has me ready to run back home. Fuck this, I *should* go home. This guy is gross. Like an idiot, I didn't consider that I might draw the attention of douchebags with this getup. At least, not in *that* way. God, maybe I *am* naive. My efforts were to blend in, but all I've been doing since walking in here is standing out.

He leans in closer, smelling of cheap beer and stale nachos.

"Um, thanks." I lean away; the performance no longer needed now that I've gotten what I wanted.

"Hell yeah, loving the team spirit!" Whoops his friend to my right, oblivious to his comrade's weak attempt at flirting and my unusual choice in outfit. I suppose when you're shirtless and painted half blue you don't have much room to judge.

"Yeah," I try to feign interest. "Big fan . . . of hockey." *Of him.*

My smile is tight-lipped. I might as well be cheering for Team USA. The Belle U Titans *are* undefeated, after all. As sad as it is, they're probably the closest thing to an Olympic team I'm ever going to see now, so I might as well soak it all in and go all-out, right?

Go Titans.

I settle in, immediately working to seek him out, my eyes straining to search for his jersey number.

Come on, Number 66, where are you?

I'm trying to follow the game, but my eyes aren't used to following so many uncoordinated movements. The buzzer sounds, causing me to jump. The flirtier of the two beer bros takes the opportunity to continue his fruitless attempt at conversation, but my heart doesn't bleed for him.

"So, what's a girl like you doing over here?" The guy turns to me with his head tilted.

I look at the hopeless flirt in confusion.

A girl like me?

"Where else would I be?" I ask with a blank stare.

I turn in my seat, briefly worried that I did all of *this* only to end up seated in the opposing team's section or, even more worrisome, that he somehow knows what happened and who I really am. No, he doesn't seem the type to have ever been to a figure skating competition and the whole arena is packed with Titan fans. These two appear to be the die-hard type. Between them, I no longer feel overdressed. Even shirtless, they take the cake with the body paint, matching Mardi Gras beads, and beer helmets they busted out about five minutes ago.

"His fan club typically sits over there," my annoying seat neighbor says, drawing my attention as he points to the crowd of girls with their signs up and tits out, the number sixty-six painted on their exposed cleavages. "Seems like that'd be more your speed, no?"

I take it back.

The die-hard fans are in that direction. Well, die-hard fans of *him* at least.

"What makes you say that?" I ask, feigning confidence I don't feel.

He points at my face, circling the air around me with his index.

"You certainly *look* the part," he says.

My cheeks heat from embarrassment, remembering the same number painted on their boobs is painted on my cheek.

Is *that where I belong?*

I shake my head. No. I may not be the typical hockey fan, and I may not be here for unselfish reasons, but I sure as hell don't belong down *there.*

I laugh him off, pretending his observation doesn't sting. But either this guy lacks total social awareness or he's the obnoxious type who finds enjoyment in making others uncomfortable.

"Yeah, well, there weren't many seating options, and this is a sold-out game," I snip.

And yet, some kind of way the girls he pointed out have all snagged seats directly next to the home team's bench. They must have gotten their tickets early or saved seats. I'm hard-pressed to admit I'm envious of their commitment to the cause, but I hate the sight of my competition having the upper hand. I try to shake the discomfort as I stare at pretty brunettes and exotic redheads with their painted blue lips and coordinated WE LOVE YOU signs. Logically, I know there's no point in being jealous. I would have never thrown myself in that viper's pit. Not on purpose, anyway.

"Aw, come on," he pushes, unwilling to let this go. "You don't need to lie. All the girls want Morningstar's dick."

He says it like it's a matter of fact. Like the sky is blue or the grass is green.

"Not me," I deadpan.

His expression is smug; his brow cocked upward with a lazy grin spread across his face.

"You sure about that?"

"Yes," I hiss.

He chuckles. "Bullshit! Have you met the guy?" My stomach drops at the very idea. *I want to.* It's the whole reason I'm here. "I bet you'd change your mind and run down there right now if you saw what he looks like."

I refocus my attention on the ice.

"Sounds like you're the one that wants his dick," I grumble.

He laughs harder. "Nah, I don't swing that way babe, but I know a handful of guys who'd definitely suck that guy's cock if given the green light."

My head whips back toward him.

"Seriously?" They'd suck him off just because they were a fan? Or is it because he's that good looking? I suppose both is reason enough.

"Yeah, so you see, I find it kind of hard to believe you're not secretly a closeted bunny," he taunts, his arms resting behind his head while he gets a kick out of teasing me.

"I told you. I'm a fan of . . . hockey," I grit.

I can barely get the word out. Hockey isn't exactly an everyday term for me.

"So are they," he juts his chin back over to the group of girls. Despite my better judgment, I follow his trajectory again. My gaze intensifies as I stare down each and every one of them.

A growl lodges itself in my chest, but I remain the ever-poised 'good girl' I'm expected to be.

"Good for them. I think it's good for team morale to have such dedicated fans, don't you think?"

Hand me my award for world's greatest actress.

My eyes sweep the arena with a careful eye this time before I return to Mr. Obnoxious beside me, challenging his apprehensive stare.

I should have known better.

Every girl in this arena is sporting his number. Almost all the signs, t-shirts, and beanies either have his number or his nickname: Morningstar. Rage simmers beneath my skin, itchy and hot. I want it out. My nails dig into my palm to break inside and release the uncomfortable feeling, but no matter how hard I press, it remains. I *hate* losing.

What do they have that I don't?

I'm not particularly keen on coming off as some desperate puck bunny. The one *other* thing I know about hockey—their fan girls are called puck bunnies. I mean, to each their own, but I'm a Sinclair, I don't *do* desperate.

I prefer the term 'extremely dedicated'.

"Right," he drawls. "Welp, it makes no difference to me."

He leans nonchalantly in his seat, his foot resting on the back of the one in front of him. Most people are leaning forward, eyes focused on the game, but not him. This guy is more than entertained with getting under my skin.

"Could've fooled me. You seem rather *invested* in my seat choices," I quip.

His face twists in what I can only assume is supposed to be an attractive smirk, but his eyes are too squinty, and half his face is drooping, the alcohol in his system doing little to aid him.

"Nah," he grins. "I'm just happy to get my pick of his leftovers."

His eyes flick to my chest and then back up.

I grind my molars, working hard to remember he's just some drunk guy I sat next to. I can ignore him. I don't owe this asshat anything, I shouldn't even honor his stupidity with a response.

Luckily, I don't have to.

"Stop fucking with her," the nice one to my right defends. "If those puck bunnies knew anything about Morningstar, they'd know he spends more time on the ice or in the Sin Bin than he ever does on the bench. He might spend a little time over there in between shifts, but when the puck drops, his eyes are on the ice. Always."

"The Sin Bin?" I ask, confused by the terminology.

"Oh, yeah, big ol' hockey fan," mutters Asshat.

We both ignore his sly comment.

"This cage right here." He points a few rows below us toward an empty box-like cage.

My nose scrunches at the barbarism, the idea of *him* locked in a cage doing funny things to my already volatile emotions, but I force a neutral expression, not wanting to expose my feelings to this guy.

"Trust me, this is the better view," he continues.

I refocus on the ice and a second later I finally see him. The one they call Morningstar, Number 66. It's only the back of his head, but it's an unobstructed view of my sole reason for being here. Inky black hair peeks from beneath his helmet, slick with sweat and pasted to his slender neck. I practically swoon at the sight of him. My entire world is crumbling apart, yet seeing him still manages to be the highlight of my day. It's hard to keep up with him, he's so fast, but I do my best to not lose sight of him again.

Three months ago, you couldn't have paid me to go to a hockey game. But three months ago, I still had a dream to pursue. Now there's only him and I'm determined to see him play one time before I go. Even now, my consciousness begs me to turn back and go home, a sixth sense warning me that I don't know what I'm getting myself into. Pursuing a guy they've nicknamed Morningstar doesn't exactly evoke a sense of security. Nor does it scream good decision making. But, not for the first time, I don't listen.

I've grown quite adept to danger. I perform dangerous jumps over solid ice every day. And in this case, there's a hell of a lot less risk. By morning this place will be in my rearview mirror, and whatever first-time crush I had will be a meaningless blip in the history books of my life.

The puck bunnies scream his name and he bops his head in their direction, acknowledging their obvious love for him. I swear to God, some of them *do* swoon while others fan themselves as though we're in a sauna and not an ice hockey arena. My eyes roll and my thumb bleeds again with the way I'm going at a particular hangnail. Since backing down is *not* an option, the question now becomes how do I toe the line of blending in and showing school spirit versus crazed fangirl who wants to ride the nation's top center forward's cock like it's my brand new BMW? I have a deep and unsettling inclination that when it comes to Number 66, that line is particularly fine.

CHAPTER FOUR

SYDNEY

"*Lucien 'Morningstar' Morrow, folks!*" The announcer's voice blares over the loudspeakers.

I've never seen a more graceful skater. He's by far the most beautiful skater I have ever had the privilege of watching, even with the blood dripping from his split lip. His strong jawline, striking golden eyes, and tousled dark hair peeking from under his helmet give him an alluring, rugged charm. The way his muscles move effortlessly under his jersey, combined with his confidence and charisma on the ice, make him utterly mesmerizing. I'd always thought my performances were captivating, but they don't hold a candle to his talents. I find it hard to believe that others don't see what I see in him.

In the months I've spent watching him, I've learned that people don't see Lucien because they're not looking at *him*. Not really. They're looking at the mask he wears, the facade he puts on. They're blinded by his flirtatious winks and attractive smiles. Three months ago, I would have called him normal, but now I'd bet money on him being as far from it as I am. Whether that's by choice or a happy accident, who knows. But I'm determined to find out.

His footwork is flawless as he fakes out his opponents and scores a goal. I've never been more enthralled by guys shuffling a disk across a slab of ice with a stick before. I practically bounce in my seat with joy.

I can see him perfectly from here.

Seems the sweaty dude next to me fist pumping the air was right after all—this *is* the better view. I'm almost grateful to have met these guys, despite their odd appearance and behavior. Gym bros who chug beer

29

and watch hockey aren't my usual crowd, but these two aren't *so* bad. They definitely aren't the worst. And though I don't feel as out of place among them, I am done deluding myself. I am *still* out of place.

I don't belong here, not anymore. I'm not sure I ever did. I came to this school because they had the best collegiate figure skating team in the nation. Without being a member of the team, it's just a regular college to me. A regular college with a subpar business program that my dad has never approved of. He made himself clear and there is no going back on my word.

The deal is signed, sealed, and delivered. Quite literally. He filed it with his assistant when I was only seventeen. Succeed as a figure skater or admit defeat and leave the program. He'd been serious when he said it. The glint of challenge in his eyes proved that and I agreed to it anyway. I had believed I was so beyond reproach that there was no way I wouldn't succeed. How wrong I turned out to be. I knew nothing. Supportive father that he is, he had said he wanted to give me something to fall back on in the event of failure. Well, I failed spectacularly. I let it all slip through my fingers. I let myself get distracted and allowed someone like Lucien Morrow to steal my focus.

I should probably hate him for that, or resent him at the very least, but I can't bring myself to do it. It's the first time I have a goal outside of figure skating: talk to him.

I was supposed to be competing in my own competition today, but here I am, watching Lucien instead.

I'm momentarily distracted from that goal when someone equally irksome causes my phone to buzz in my hand.

Bradford 7:30 PM

> Hey, if you want, I can pick you up instead of your dad. If I use the jet, I can be there as early as tonight.

Having him here is the last thing I want. I'm trying to savor what could have been and keep whatever good memories I can before I have to leave here tonight. Bradford can wait.

> I appreciate the thought, but that's okay. I'm just gonna focus on packing up everything here and then maybe I'll catch up with you when I'm back.

> I could help you pack. The quicker you're packed, the more alone time we'll have.

I scoff.

Of course. He doesn't really want to save me from my father's wrath or even help me pack. He wants the time and excuse to have me alone so he can finally fuck me. I've got to give it to him; he's been committed to the long game for some time now. Currying favor with my father and catering to my whims. That, or he really fancies himself in love. I really hope it's the former and not the latter. I don't think I'm wrong, but I'd hate for him to be in love with me.

I'd told myself I was falling for Lucien, but into what, I wasn't sure. The truth is I've never known love, not in the traditional ways others have, so how am I supposed to give it? With Lucien, I flew right past love and into obsession. My body never responded to Bradford's hints at intimacy, but I came to life at the very thought of Lucien. Even sitting here right now, I'm turned on. If I think about him too hard, I'll grow slick between my thighs and my clit will ache for a friction only he can abate.

I force my attention back to Bradford just to stave off the immediate lust I feel for Lucien. I'd been willing to sleep with Bradford, if only for the sake of being unburdened by my virginity. I'd thought maybe it would feel good, and I could understand what the fuss was all about. Bradford was cute and he wasn't the worst option, but every time I try anything with him my pussy rebels. I'm not prudish, nor am I so innocent and naive that I don't understand the way it works, but sex has never been on my radar. It's never seemed appealing. For the longest time, I thought something was wrong with me. I could go with it or without, but intense wanting lit my body on fire the moment I learned what true desire felt like. Finding Lucien ruined me, because now, sex is all I think about.

More specifically, it's the *type* of sex I think about. Watching him made me realize the reason I never understood the appeal was because of how it was portrayed to me. The kind of sex I want is *not* the kind that most people have. I crave something much darker, more forbidden. Something I can't imagine Bradford *ever* being able to give me, but Lucien could. He fits the profile of one willing to do anything in the pursuit of pleasure.

I can't believe it's taken me this long to watch a single game. We shared an entire arena, and yet, it was in these recent months that I ever acquired a modicum of interest in hockey. We might both compete on the ice, but our worlds don't collide as much as one might think.

The day I found Lucien skating on his own, everything changed. Everything I thought I knew about myself cracked and splintered as it fell to my feet. It was the first time I thought I belonged here. More importantly, I belonged with *him*.

That night was supposed to be like any other, and had it not been for Tiffany, it would have been.

Something about seeing him that day initiated the countdown to the demise of everything I had managed to build, and I savored every second of that doomsday clock, even when it hit zero.

But now I can't do that anymore. Can't exactly stay late and watch him if I no longer have a reason to come in the first place. I'll be leaving soon, and I'll no longer have the opportunity to sit and watch him, to imagine what it'd be like to touch him, to have him touch me, to wrap my legs around him and feel him break me. This is it for me.

I knew Lucien had talent, but I didn't understand how *much* talent until now. We're halfway through the game and Lucien has been killing it, scoring two of the three goals they have already.

"If he scores another one, he'll have a hat trick," the one I've nicknamed Asshat squeals. My two new companions slap me on the shoulder like I'm one of them, giddiness sparkling in their irises as Morningstar carries them to certain victory. I have no idea what that means, but I clap and shout all the same, knowing it's obviously a good thing.

I watch closely at the next play as two guys try to trap him against the wall. He moves to guide the puck to the goal, but as soon as one of them tries to slam him, Lucien skids to a stop, spraying ice into the air and making the dude slam himself into the wall instead. Without the additional player in his way, Lucien shoots the puck to another Titan, but the same opponent who was blocking him before is back on him, not leaving his side. He follows Lucien around the ice even when he doesn't have the puck.

I'd assumed it might have been like basketball, where you defend your assigned man, but this seems a little different. Lucien looks noticeably upset, but he's still on fire, skating up and down the ice like he was born to it. It's a tussle for who secures the rubber disk but he finally gets it back then races for the net, slapping the puck in with a deafening crack. Another goal for us!

"Hat trick, yes!" whoops my nice companion to the right, more like an excited kid than a grown college student.

"Fucking hat trick. Morningstar is the fucking GOAT! He's going to kill it in the NHL," yells Asshat. "That's my boy! Oouu!"

If anyone's a closeted bunny, it's him.

I scream, elated and clapping my hands, happy to see him succeed and win the hat or whatever, but the excitement is short-lived.

The crowd starts booing and yelling.

Wait, what's happening?

I stand up to look around, my eyes first catching on the score. It's 4-2, the goal counted. We're winning. I look around again. Everybody is still on their feet and screaming.

What the hell is going on?

Looking down at the ice again, I see why everyone is in such a tizzy. A fight has ensued, several actually. Jesus, they were just in the middle of a game. They should be celebrating, but now the whole rink is in an uproar. My eyes frantically search the faces of everyone brawling, looking for the only player who even remotely matters to me. I lose him in the chaos, but then I spot the unmistakable black hair, his legendary jersey number, on top of one of the opposing team players, pummeling his face. Both of their helmets have come off and drops of sweat drip from Lucien's dark, saturated hair as it sways violently with each blow. I bite my lip, a little floored to see his full face without obstruction.

His eyes are alight, a wild expression glowing amid his amber irises. Pure determination, worthy of a top athlete in the heat of battle, reflects on his face. I recognize it. The metaphorical mask he constantly wears—the one set even deeper than mine, that hides the true him and keeps his fans oblivious to his true talents—falls like cheap fabric, disintegrating into thin air and leaving nothing behind but the real monster beneath. I lean forward, engrossed in the unabridged version of Lucien Morrow.

His jersey pulls back, stretching so far across his broad chest it looks ready to snap. People grab at it to yank him back, but he presses forward, unhindered. He hasn't noticed that it's his own teammates who are trying to pull him off. Lucien finally pulls away, elbowing them off, not relenting, not letting up. Not even when the injured player stops moving. He keeps going, roaring loudly as blood coats his fists, spatters onto his face, and leaks to the ice.

The other team works in tandem with the Titans, trying to drag their teammate free from Lucien's grip, but it's no use. He's too strong and too focused on his kill. They all look like they're trying to remove a meal from a lion, pulling in opposite directions to free them from one another, but it's clearly not working. He won't be robbed of his prey.

Relief sweeps through the crowd when one of the refs not engaged with breaking up the other brawls comes in to finally put a stop to the madness. Goodness, what the fuck was taking them so long? People are getting hurt. Though I guess only one person is suffering any real damage.

Hand over heart, I let out a breath, but then Lucien turns to the referee, wrenches off his helmet and head butts the ref so hard blood pours from the ref's face. More chaos erupts. Lucien didn't even give the ref a chance to speak. I gasp, my hands clutched at my metaphorical pearls, squeezing the neckline of my costume as I stand there stunned.

I can't believe he did that. I knew hockey was a violent sport, but at no point did I think it was *this* violent. Not even the referees are safe apparently. The refs struggle to get the other players under control, leaving Lucien too open to do what he wants: hurt.

Lucien's eyes are more gold than I've ever seen them, ablaze with a fury I've only ever seen one other time. But it's the disassociated expression on his face that has my fingers twisted in my skirt. I've seen Lucien angry, or so I thought, but that time was nothing like this. It's not just anger I see, it's pain.

The ref stumbles back, falling onto the ice as he holds his face and screams out. When the majority of those on the ice shift focus to helping the ref, Lucien takes the opportunity to turn his bloodied face back toward his original prey. I recognize him as the player who kept following Lucien around on the ice. A couple of the guy's teammates manage to get his seemingly lifeless body to his feet. They're on either side of him with his arms limply wrapped around their necks.

It's evident the skates are the only thing alleviating his weight and he's very much still unconscious. It's hard to see if he's even breathing. His face is so mangled and swollen. My stomach churns from the sight of him, but Lucien *isn't* the type to leave a job undone. For some insane reason that only makes me fall deeper for him. Unfortunately for me, perseverance is a quality I find incredibly hot.

Lucien lunges for his prey from behind, sending all the other players holding him up back down to the ice. Oh God. He's not going to stop. He *needs* to stop, or he'll kill the guy.

An empty, crazed glint settles in Lucien's eyes that tells me he sees nothing and no one but this poor kid, and still, he's ready to land another blow. But something in me *knows* he can't take another hit.

Adrenaline pumps through my veins, thick and bitter like acid. My palms secrete sweat, even as I rub them vigorously against my clothes, but I can't eradicate the heat, can't quench the burn. My skin buzzes, a weird feeling between panic and excitement sparking within me, igniting me all over like electricity. I grip my hair, trying to ground myself at the horror that's unfolding.

This could ruin everything. This school won't even notice when *I'm* gone, but *him*? Everyone will feel the loss of him. If he loses it right here, it could spell the end of everything he's worked for. Just like me. I can't let that happen, I need him to stop.

Stop.

The words snake their way out of my throat before I even process what I'm saying or why I think it'll change anything. But it rips through me anyway.

"Lucien, *stop!*"

I scream it so loud, so resolutely, I'm thrown off by my own strength. The words cut through the arena like butter. It's almost eerie how clearly it penetrates the other noise, echoing from the tips of my toenails to the ends of my hair. Time slows, or maybe I'm so wired it only feels that way. The voices around me quiet, the jeers and hollering cease, and just when I think another explosion of violence is about to erupt, it doesn't.

It's unlikely he heard me, but all the same, his face slowly turns toward me, and our eyes lock. For the first time ever, he *sees* me. Those golden-amber eyes meet mine and I'm frozen. The already cold arena feels like it plummets to arctic temperatures. My hands grip the back of the seat in front of me so hard my knuckles drain of color. The pounding in my chest feels like it might explode. Fear claws at my throat and I will myself to calm down. The look on his face is devastating.

It's fine, he's not looking at you.
He clearly is.
There's nothing to be scared of.
That's absolutely not true.
He won't hurt you.
He definitely will if he finds out who I am.

My eyes widen at the realization he really *is* looking right at me, and breathing becomes that much harder. I can see everything that lies beneath that wicked stare. His objective hasn't changed; it's altered. He has a new target: me. His crazy eyes lock in on me and it all becomes transparently clear-he's dangerous.

I squeeze my thighs together.

He's a danger to my body, mind, and heart, and I'm drawn to it like a moth to flames.

My lips slowly curl into a smile, to grin wide and show him my teeth, show him how happy he makes me. If he's happy, he won't hurt him. Yeah, that's right. He'll calm down and look at *me* some more. But my smile crests and breaks like a crashing wave when I search his eyes.

His chest expands and retracts while a mixture of blood and sweat trill down his face to his uniform, staining his white jersey and blue numbers. I tuck my lower lip behind my teeth, biting down at the sight. The corner of his mouth twitches as his tongue darts out and licks his lips. Even with the fear suffocating me, and his display of unbridled violence and pure determination to end the guy beneath him, wetness gathers between my legs. My pussy salivates with a hunger I've never felt before.

He's looking at me. Right at me.

I stutter a breath at my reaction, clenching my thighs to abate the sudden ache of desire. An ache that spreads through my middle and takes over my good senses. Though one could argue my senses were never all that good to begin with.

He's terrifyingly beautiful. Shivers crawl their way up my spine the longer his eyes hold mine, seeping into my bones and wracking my body with chills, but I only find him that much more enthralling.

His fist is still clocked back, ready to enact his final blow. But he holds it the same way he holds our eye contact, challenging me to blink lest he continues his assault. I accept that challenge.

"Stop." I whisper it this time, more like a prayer, knowing he can't hear me, but willing him to stop anyway. I don't blink, even as his stare hardens. Even when he breaks first to roam the length of me, my eyes don't leave his. I let him drink his fill; confident he has no clue who I am.

Time resumes, and for a second, I think he might ignore my prayers and beat this guy's head in anyway, but he chooses to honor our silent agreement. Lucien smiles a crimson grin and spits the accumulated blood onto the ice near the knocked-out players before allowing himself to be dragged off the ice and tossed to the sidelines by a different set of refs.

Typically, he'd be thrown in the cage near me, the 'sin bin,' but he's not being given a penalty or slap on the wrist. He's being thrown out of the game. The crowd is noticeably upset. At who, I'm not exactly sure, but I'm too busy tracking Lucien's movements to give the crowd another thought.

I watch as he grabs his stuff and heads through to the locker room doors. That heady danger rolling off him like a cloud of smoke. When he disappears around the corner, my body immediately unlocks. *I need to get to him.*

I turn on my heels to leave but the two guys I so happily sat between aren't as easy to get past as they were to get through.

"Excuse me," I call out.

They're too busy grumbling about bullshit calls and "*what was Morningstar thinking?*" to notice me.

"Excuse me," I try again. But again, their attention is stolen as they focus on the medical team on the ice retrieving the limp body of the player Lucien beat up. He looks like he was torn to shreds by a dog.

"Excuse me!" I repeat, louder this time.

"Look, can't you see we're having a moment for the fallen, he's hurt!" yells the seat neighbor who'd been sweet, angrily pointing at the bloody rink and unconscious player.

The fallen? He didn't die in battle. He was massacred . . . in front of everyone.

I scoff, surprised it wasn't Asshat to speak up first, and his eyes narrow at my unsportsmanlike conduct.

"Does it *look* like I care?" I snap, eying him up and down with folded arms.

He appears shocked by my callous outburst. There's a low-churning guilt that wades in my subconscious from the sneer that follows, but I push it away. He was nice to me, and he let me have this great seat to begin with. Even Asshat became tolerable somewhere around the second period, but now they're both an obstacle and it's the Sinclair way to get rid of obstacles. I don't particularly enjoy being unkind, but it seems the most efficient way to garner any respect around here. God, I hate when my father is right, but he would be proud.

"Now get *out* of my way," I seethe.

I barely give him time to comply before I push past him and run after Lucien, my guilt abandoned. I can't lose Lucien, not yet. But when I burst through the corridor doors after him, he's already gone.

LUCIEN
@BladeSpinner
Online
In life?
Seen
Haven't decided yet.

CHAPTER FIVE

LUCIEN

WELL, THAT WAS UNEXPECTED. The girl, not the fight. The fight was inevitable.

But the girl . . . the girl was a pleasant surprise.

There aren't too many people who can get me to stop when I get like that. I learned a long time ago how to accept the chirping as just a part of the game. I had to adapt. I can't very well kill every hockey player who chirps, but Jake Anderson, well, he just had it coming. I never understood why people assume that they're not in any danger of being hurt simply because there are spectators around. Nine times out of ten they won't protect you, not if it means risking anything themselves. And I'm not one to go back on a promise. I don't make idle threats.

If *I* say you're dead, then you are.

If only he'd never talked about my family. My very *dead* family. Even being forced to acknowledge their absence is enough to set me on edge. I gave him the chance to stop, but he didn't take it. On and on and *on* he went about how they're never here so they must not love me. I must be a disappointment and a failure to be so alone.

It was an odd thing for him to be so obsessed with me that he'd notice something like that. For a moment I considered that *he* might be my stalker. Especially with the way he droned on, but that's not Jacob's style. He doesn't have it in him. I knew that the moment I saw his beady fucking eyes. They lacked conviction, absolution. There was no way he was the one who'd been following me. My stalker is special. They get me in a way no one ever has and they wouldn't provoke me like this. In fact,

I know they wouldn't. That's not what makes the game between us so fun.

No, *that* piece of shit, Jake, wanted me to hurt and he didn't understand me not one bit. If he did, he showed no signs of awareness. There was no kinship between me and the dickhead whose blood now stains the ice.

I did warn him though. That's got to count for something.

I *tried* to ignore his antics, to focus on the game. He just wouldn't stop talking.

My fingers drag across my scalp, ruffling my hair as I recall the events leading up to everything. I'm more agitated than I thought. I pace up and down the row of lockers, trying to reign in my temper, but I'm not sure it's working. It was the final nail in his coffin when that motherfucker told me, *"Go home and cry to your mommy about what a loser you are because you're going to lose tonight."* Yeah, lose my fucking mind. But that wasn't what made me snap. No, those last parting words he uttered are what earned him the public crucifixion. *"Oh, that's right, you can't."*

I *can't.*

Can't. Unable. A physical impossibility that no matter how much I fucking wanted to, I couldn't make plausible.

If he only knew how deep that very desire ran. I would do *anything* to hold my mom again, to cry in her arms.

But that's not the way the world works. This life doesn't freely offer do-overs.

My pacing stops, and clarity returns to me once more.

It's not nice to pick on orphans.

He learned a valuable life lesson tonight: actions have consequences.

I suppose the consequences of *my* actions are that I'm thrown out of this game.

Ah, well, you can't win 'em all, I guess.

I strip off one layer at a time. My bloodied jersey. My pads. I keep my mouthguard in though, chewing agitatedly on it while I untie the string of my breezers. These padded shorts make me feel like my balls are in a straight jacket. With my shirt off, I feel less restricted, untethered, and a thousand times lighter.

I interlace my fingers together and stretch them outward. There's a chilled silence in the air, one broken by the cracking sound of my finger joints popping. I roll my neck from side to side, letting those joints pop as well. Nothing like a good fight to really get your blood pumping. I'm on cloud fucking nine right now. Seriously, I feel like I can fuck the president, free climb a volcano, surf a tornado, or some other impossible shit. I bring my hands up, inspecting my fingernails and note the blood that's not only under my nails, but spilling from several of my split knuckles.

Well, that's unfortunate.

I flex my hands while I make my way over to the mirrors lining the communal sinks. Blood trickles down my fingers, trailing a path behind me toward the bathrooms, but I leave it. Loose skin hangs from my shredded knuckles, but it's nothing a little ointment can't fix. There's something rather important that's more deserving of my attention.

Gripping the ceramic edge of the sink, I stand too tall in my skates to see myself in the mirror. Forced to lean over, my head bows for a better look. Pink droplets clink against the bottom of the bowl, echoing in the near-silent space. I raise my head, taking a good look at the rest of the damage. I roam the reflective surface in minute detail, making sure to take in the full picture. My gaze catches on the empty benches reflected behind me.

More droplets leak into the sink basin, drawing my attention, this time a deeper red. Oh shit, look at that, I'm bleeding. Cool. Ah, wait . . . no, shit, that's somebody else's blood. I swipe at my face with the pads of my fingers and the blood smears away.

Well, damn.

Smearing it around, I rub the viscous substance between my fingers, losing myself in thought before flicking on the water. I let the cool water pool in my palms, splashing it on my face to clean off the blood and sweat. It stings a little. Hope flickers in my chest, and I look up to find I do have *some* light scratches on my forehead. They're barely worth the fight if you ask me, though I'm pretty sure that was from the headbutt, not the actual fight. I cherish my small battle wounds all the same. Shifting my face from side to side, I check to see if there's anything else worth noting, but it seems I'm still intact. I don't know why I'm surprised; he barely got a hit in before he passed out. Nothing's broken and my teeth are still solid.

I take out my mouthguard, toss it onto the pile of discarded items and chomp my teeth loud enough to click, before taking one last look at my hands. I'll have to wrap the knuckles, but I should be good to go after that.

Walking back over to the bench in front of my locker, I whistle my favorite little tune—the iconic intro of Kill Bill because that movies a fucking classic—as I take off my skates. I take my time unlacing the strings, whistling louder as the ominous tune echoes.

"You know, you were the last person I expected to see at my game tonight," I say aloud. "You don't usually come to see me play."

There's no response, but I continue. I had expected them to be shy at first.

"Hmm...so what's your plan here? Watch me undress? Sneak up on me? Gotta say, it's kinda rude to sneak up on people. Bad manners and all that."

I tug the skate strings one by one. "But then again . . . you've been very bad lately. Haven't you?"

To the average person it would seem quiet, but I'm not an average person and neither are they. They've been here the whole time.

I let out a deep sigh.

"Well, now you're just being an asshole. It's not nice to ignore people when they're talking to you. It's impolite."

I hear the softest breath and pause, resting my forearms on my knees while I await their answer.

"If I have to come find you, I won't be so polite. *Trust me,* you won't like it when I'm mean," I warn.

There's a stillness in the air, a thick fog that's settled in the space around us. It expands, trapping us until there's no escape for either of us—not that I want to. I'm undoing my laces on the other skate when she finally gathers the courage to walk around the corner and embrace the inevitable.

One sharp blue eye peers from around the wall and then another. I lean forward to get a better look, and excitement grips me by the balls. She takes tentative steps toward me but stops several feet away. Presumably to maintain distance, but what's done is done. She's right in front of me.

Look at that, it seems there might be a God after all. I knew I had a little stalker, but no way in hell did I think it'd be someone as beautiful as her. I've had some committed fans, sure, but never have I met someone bold enough to follow me in here.

Such an interesting girl.

She's a bold one, too. The smell in here is foul and she's gulping air by the lungful.

I prop an elbow on my knee and rest my face in my palm, taking in her features piece by piece.

"*So* . . . whatcha doing here?" I coo, as though she's a lost puppy wandering into a lion's den. "Came to surrender?"

She stands there speechless, like she's not entirely convinced any of this is real.

That would make two of us if I weren't so overly familiar with hallucinations and this isn't one of them. I've never felt more sure about anything in my life. For once the world around me appears crystal clear. I sit up and pull off the last skate, throwing it over my shoulder, not daring to draw my eyes away from the girl in the tutu standing in front of me. The skate hits the metal lockers behind me at an awkward angle, causing a loud clanging noise that reverberates throughout the locker room. She jumps back, startled. I level her with a stare that's meant to discourage her from utilizing those flight or fight instincts, but the look she gives me in return makes my cock rage and my skin tighten in anticipation.

She's going to run.

For the first time in years, I'm tempted to pray in hopes I resemble the predator who's about to devour her, because that's exactly what I am—and now she knows it.

My tongue licks across my teeth, tracing the edges as I watch her track the motion. I fail to contain my growl, wanting nothing more than to lunge forward and attack, but I remain still, waiting.

Her breathing picks up, and I can see the slightest tremble in her limbs. I arch a brow in warning.

I dare you. Go ahead. Try to run.

Her body vibrates with the need to flee. To be anywhere but where she is right now while I'm itching for her to take the chance. I haven't been this excited by a girl in a long time. I'm even more excited that *this* girl and my stalker are one and the same. *Who fucking knew?*

Most people would be scared they had a stalker, or at the very least concerned, but not me. I was intrigued. Our meeting has been a slow, gradual build up that was always going to result in us facing off. Gotta say, I never expected it to be someone like *her* though.

There's something about her that begs to be caught, yet her eyes flick to the door like she can't escape fast enough. I can see her calculating how many steps it would take to reach it, how much time she would need to fully escape me, but despite her pointless calculations, her eyes reflect what she and I both already know. She's come to the resolution even if she can't accept it. There's *not* enough time and *not* enough steps—but she tries anyway.

She fucking goes for it, and I breathe a brief sigh of relief, loving that she didn't make this too easy on me. That's my little stalker. Taking one step back, she pivots to run, her sneakers squeaking against the floor tiles like she's about to burn rubber, but unfortunately for her, she's too slow. I'll give it to her, she's a skilled sleuth, but speed isn't her strong suit. I pounce before she can even turn away.

"Oh, no, you don't," I whisper in her ear.

My arms wrap around her waist, sealing her back to my front. She squirms, but I'm spinning us around and trapping her against the lockers before she can escape. Her hair slaps across my face and her scent wafts in my nostrils as she fights me with all her strength. Her body twists and she pushes against my chest but the brief contact only turns me on.

Both of my arms come up, caging her between my hard dick and the cliché obstruction. Her struggling isn't helping matters one bit and my cock is loving it a little too much. But the second my hands land on either side of her head, she stills, knowing she's caught.

Fucking finally.

My eyes drop to her mouth and the most adorable whimper escapes her plush pink lips. I tilt my head, watching her, my hair tickling the deep-set crease whittled into my forehead as I take her in. I swipe it away from my eyes for a better view, and again, I groan. It's deep and guttural and now it's my turn to vibrate with need. The need to possess her, to keep her high on a pedestal where she could never be brought down, belonging to me and only me.

At last, we meet.

I've thought for months about the day I'd catch her, it's been the only thing outside of hockey occupying my thoughts day in and day out, and now that I have her in my sights, it confirms everything I speculated. She's a lot like me.

@BladeSpinner
Online

What do you want

In life?

Seen

WTF No

Haven't decided yet.

CHAPTER SIX

LUCIEN

Her mouth opens to speak, but nothing more than a broken squeak comes out before it clamps shut again.

Who knew stalkers could be so cute?

Her pretty honey blond hair is innocently curled and her sky blue eyes sparkle with both dark and light hues. *How appropriate.* They remind me of cracked ice, like a frozen-over lake filled with fissures and fractures, etched into the orifices of her face. I could drown in those frozen eyes. I could get trapped beneath the ice and never come up, she's *that* beautiful. It's unreal.

My palms itch to touch them, to roam my fingers over the thin membrane and ensure they're real—not contacts or an illusion. Her pupils dilate the longer I stare into those eyes, promising their existence to me. It's at that moment I decide, she's worth not killing. Quite the opposite actually. She's worth killing for. She's too goddamn pretty, like a pretty little princess doll. A porcelain figure that I could so easily break if I'm not careful.

Sweat drips from my hairline, coating my skin while she drinks me in for what feels like the first time. She's seen plenty of me, though.

Our bodies have never been in such close proximity, and our skin has never touched. I've never been close enough to breathe her aroma—like coconut and fruit. Unfortunately, I don't smell half as good, yet she sucks me down like I'm oxygen itself.

Her lips part to speak again, but if I didn't know any better, I'd say she was experiencing shock.

At this point, killing her would be more accidental than purposeful. It's entirely possible I'll crush this butterfly before she ever gets to fly. Those delicate wings of hers could crumble beneath my touch the moment I get my hands on her. The instinct to hold onto her and never let go is so strong. And the emotion guiding me is foreign. I've never wanted something this bad.

Her lashes flutter while she attempts to speak for a third time.

In the time I wait for her to say something, the itching of my palms becomes almost unbearable, craving the feel of her skin. I'm dying to touch some part of her, to cement her physicality with some sort of contact. I need to touch her, hold her, squeeze her. The desire is so intense, my hands shake against the metal.

It's a risk I'm willing to take. But I won't break her . . . yet. It's too soon.

In my defense, the only reason I considered killing her in the first place was because I thought she was going to kill me first. I mean, she's been stalking me for months at this point, so it's a logical assumption. She's never spoken to me and never came to games or team practices. She just stared at me from hidden locations, and only when I was alone. Occasionally, she smiled at me from beneath a dark hood like she knew something I didn't. She hid herself well too, not too many people are capable of that with me.

Honestly, good on her. She managed to achieve what others barely live to see. I mean, I knew she was there, but she always remained *just* out of reach. I never got close enough to see her up close, especially not *this* close. I wasn't even sure my stalker was a girl until she showed up here.

What was I supposed to think? Her behavior absolutely gave 'I want to wear your skin' vibes, not puck bunny vibes. Now here she is at a game, sporting my number on her goddamn face, dressed to the nines in school spirit and standing right in front of me. I think it's kismet. Nothing but fate could make this possible.

"Um, hi," she finally says. I blink, not expecting those to be her famous first words.

"Hi," I respond, something between an amused laugh and a questionable scoff hidden behind the singular word.

The corners of her pouty lips tick upward in a nervous smile and I'm unable to hold back anymore. I reach out to touch her, tracing my bloodied knuckles down her supple cheek. Red streaks trail in their wake down to her jaw. *She's so soft.* She sucks in a stuttered breath. Those peculiar eyes of hers growing wider, but I don't miss the way she's looking at me, like she's memorizing me. It's then I see the truth. This is as surreal for her as it is for me. Our first time face-to-face.

"I was wondering when I'd finally get to meet you," I breathe, entranced by the proximity of this very real person standing before me. For a second there I almost worried the doc was right and that it was all in my head, but here she is standing in all her glory.

Seeing my blood streaked across her face makes me want to see what other bodily fluids I can smear on her skin.

"Excuse me?" she asks, her voice a shaken whisper.

My eyes flick from her cheek to her lips. Well, seems the little stalker princess *does* have manners.

"You're different than I thought you'd be," I state, somewhat absentmindedly, as I reach out and pull on one of her curls. It *boings* when I let it go, and I chuckle. "So fragile and small." I tilt her chin up. "I thought you'd be . . . scarier."

It's hard to reconcile this flawless girl in front of me with the one who relentlessly tracked me down. For the better part of a week, I seriously considered she might be part bloodhound or that I was being tracked by something otherworldly.

She jerks her face away.

"I don't know what you're talking about," she rasps, before clearing her throat.

"Well, you're *her*, right? The girl who's been following me, sneaking into my private practices, watching me? *Messaging* me? You're *her.*"

She better hope she is. I've been waiting for this day for months, when I could finally play with the person crazy enough to stalk a demon like me. If this girl turns out *not* to be my stalker, well, let's just say, killing might be back on the table. I would think my real stalker wouldn't be too happy about her if she wasn't. They might hurt my new plaything.

"I didn't—" she shakes her head rapidly. But there's a twitch in those cracked-ice eyes peering up at me like I'm personally responsible for the sun setting and rising. I fucking love it.

"It's not what you think. I'm not . . ." she tries again.

I know it's her, and yet it's not her, not in this moment. Right now, she's a scared damsel, frightened and confused, or she's pretending to be. I'm not sure which. Something tells me it's the latter, that this is all an elaborate act.

Her hair has a sheen that you only get from constant maintenance at a salon. With the exception of her hair, her scent is expensive like leather, cashmere, and exotic florals. Real diamond studs are lanced through her pierced ears. Her teeth are blinding white with perfect pink gums, and her skin is as smooth as glass, not a single open pore or blackhead to be found. She's too perfect a creature to be the same one who left creepy gum figures around and sent those disturbing messages. But she is, there's not a doubt in my mind.

"Don't lie to me," I sing-song as I step in, pressing our bodies together. "I have a particular distaste for liars."

If this is going to work, she can't lie to me. The rules of the game insist we play fair. We can't do that if the players are liars.

"How . . . how did you know it was me?"

I shrug. It's a bit hard to put into words. I've had years to turn what most people might consider extreme paranoia and hyper-awareness into a blade so sharp nothing gets past me unscathed. Usually. She's been the exception. I never saw her coming.

"Same way I knew you followed me here." I lean my head down, nudging her hair line before taking a long whiff of her hair. "You—smell—so—*sweet,*" I groan.

"I—uh, thank you?" She licks her lips and shifts beneath my hungry gaze, but it doesn't escape my notice that she's no longer searching for the exit.

I nod my head once, acknowledging her, before taking the flat of my tongue and licking up the side of her heart-shaped face right over the #66 she has painted there. I really like that she's wearing my number on her face. It's cute. The other puck bunnies paint their tits and flash me their chests, but I much prefer this.

I hum in satisfaction. "You taste sweet, too."

"What the—why?" Disgust temporarily replaces her fear, and she raises her hand to wipe it away, to wipe *me* away. I snatch her wrist, pressing it to the locker.

"Nuh uh uh. There will be none of that. You're not allowed to wipe me away, not now that I've marked my territory."

I drag her other wrist up on the locker, pinning them both in my grasp so that her arms are suspended above her head. This should keep her from getting any more funny ideas.

You can never be too careful with these stalker types.

I smile down at her face that's now covered with my blood on one side and my saliva on the other, and hell if she didn't just get more beautiful.

"I'm not—" she cuts herself off.

"Go on. Finish what you were going to say. You're not . . . what?" I goad.

Mine?

I dare her to finish that sentence.

"That's what I thought. So, tell me, to what do I owe this pleasure? Did you come here so you could watch me some more or did you actually have intentions for me?" I waggle my brows, hoping it's the latter because I *definitely* have intentions for her.

She bucks beneath my restraints, her bouncy tits bumping me in the chest. Fuck, we're going to have so much fun.

"Let me go," she growls. She says it like she's used to people following her commands. "Let me go right now or I'll . . . I'll scream."

"Aw, well, don't threaten me with a good time," I croon.

"I mean it. I'll scream for help."

"I'm not gonna stop you. Go ahead. Scream." I grin, the acoustics in here are perfect for blood-curdling howls.

Unfortunately, she doesn't scream, nor does she appreciate me calling her bluff, but she does try to get away by kicking me in the balls.

"Fucking hell, Princess," I wheeze.

"Oh no, I am so sorry. Are you—"

"I almost came," I laugh. "Do that again." She bucks against me again, trying to take advantage of the opening she's created.

"What's wrong with you? I thought I really hurt you," she admonishes.

My dick *does* hurt, but I'd gladly endure any discomfort for this delightful interaction.

"Only in my dreams could you ever hurt me."

She has no idea the monster she's awakened.

"I—" She shakes her head. "I can't be here right now. I have to go."

She tries to pull away from me again, but I nudge my throbbing dick against her thigh, pressing her deeper into the wall of lockers.

"No, no, no, we're just getting started," I coo. "You're not going anywhere. Not until you tell me exactly what you're doing here."

Her lips seal closed and those cracked-ice eyes start to darken. My erection, barely affected by her attempted mutilation, instantly stands at fuller attention, jutting between her thighs as I fixate on her lips. Her jaw tightens the moment she realizes, but her face remains stoic, pretending she's unaffected.

Such defiance.

"I can force your mouth open if you'd like," I warn, tapping my finger to her lip.

She shakes her head in protest, but those still aren't words. I went months never knowing what her voice sounded like. Never hearing the cadence of the siren song from which those lips coerced my deepest, darkest secrets. She does not have the *option* of staying silent now, so I squeeze her wrists until words fall out. Squeals of pain tumble first, but I keep the pressure until I get what I want: answers.

"Ahh, okay, okay fine. I *was* here to check on you, but now I'm seriously regretting that decision. You obviously have brain damage because who *licks* somebody they just met?" she blurts. Innocent little thing looks almost apologetic, but we both know she's not.

That's it? That's all she has to say for herself?

I burst out laughing in her face, resting my forehead on hers and letting out my fit of giggles.

Oh, now we're having some fun.

I pull back.

"Who follows some guy she *barely* knows into the men's locker room? Even if you've been stalking me, it seems kinda reckless to lock yourself in here with me, no?" I cock my head in question.

"I'm not a stalker," she huffs. "And what are you talking about? I'm not locked in."

"Oh, really? Try leaving."

She looks toward the door, then back at me. She tries to wriggle her wrists from my hold, but I keep my grip solid. I hold her wrists one-handed while she squirms like a fish on a hook. It's amusing to watch her fight so uselessly. Finally, she tries dropping her body, hoping the weight will release her from my hold, but she weighs a buck thirty when wet . . . if that.

I smile at her feeble attempt. This almost makes getting kicked out of the game worth it.

More huffs of frustration exit those pretty pink lips as she tries to bounce her way out from under my fingered chains.

Never one to waste an opportunity, I spin her limp body around, pressing her front to the lockers, her backside nudging my cock as she tries to squirm free. The new position allows me unfettered access to peer down and admire her ass. It's round and soft, but firm at the same time. She's fit. I'm guessing by the getup she's wearing, she's a figure skater, but that only makes me even more curious because if she *is* a figure skater and she goes to this school, then she especially has no reason to be here.

I'm pretty sure they had a competition in Seattle tonight. I only know that because they had to borrow the team bus to get there and Coach was none to happy about sharing resources. Which means *I'm* her reason for being here.

She doesn't *look* like a stalker, but she doesn't appear to be a typical puck bunny either.

"Get off me!" she growls again.

Yeah, no, definitely not a puck bunny.

I, of all people, understand how deceiving looks can be, but there's something about her that warms my blood and sends electric shocks straight to my cock. It's not just her mouth or her eyes, though those are both very high on the list of things I'm attracted to. It's her fucked up little head that ultimately wins me over.

Using my other hand, I wind her silky ponytail around my fist, pulling it back so she's forced to look up at me, but then something truly unexpected happens . . . she moans.

Well, that's interesting. She was growling at me a second ago and the second before that she was disgusted. She's full of surprises. Our text conversations have never been overtly sexual, but at least this confirms that her obsession was more of a sexual nature than a murderous one.

I bring my mouth closer to her throat, my lips a hair's breadth away from her goose-bumped skin.

"No," I growl back right before biting into her neck. Shrilled gasps escape her lips and tears well in her eyes, but I don't release her right away. I bite down harder.

She hisses between clenched teeth and gives a weak cry.

I am loving the symphony of sounds this little stalker makes. The anticipation of hearing what she will sound like when she comes sends a thrill that tickles the undercarriage of my balls. I love that I caught her. I grind my hips against her and something between a whimpered moan and a squeal parts from her mouth next.

Yeah, good luck ignoring me now.

I'm so fucking hard I could stab her with my cock and we'd probably both still cum. I *know* she can feel me. Hell, she might even thank me for it if I shove my cock inside right now, but I hold back as best I can. If I really want to have fun with her, I'll have to bide my time.

I release my mouth from her neck with a popping sound and smile in delight when I see the indented marks along her bruised cream skin.

"Your skin marks so *beautifully*," I croon.

"You bit me!" she yelps.

"Yeah, I know," I lick along the bite to soothe the sting. "There. All better?"

"Oh God, you're completely insane," she whines but there's no animosity in her tone. If I'm not mistaken, that's admiration I hear.

"You have no idea," I whisper into her ear.

More goosebumps rise across her skin, and I notice the shiver that skates across her body. Her breathing changes and she presses her body against mine. She's turned on and it only makes me that much more curious. She's a *horny* Little Stalker Princess.

"Stop it," she pleads, that superior authority all but gone now, but I don't think that's what she really wants at all. I can practically hear her pussy crying out for me. Why deny what we both want? Why go through all the trouble of stalking me if she's not going to enjoy the spoils of catching me?

"Stop? But I haven't even begun."

It's freaking adorable how wide her eyes just went, like she's already picturing what *real* effort from me would feel like.

It would blow your fucking mind, Princess.

"Lucien, *please* . . . I'm begging you. Let me go." My name is a prayer on her glossed pout. And if I was even considering letting her go before—which I absolutely wasn't—I'm *definitely* not letting her go now.

Aww, don't worry, Princess. I'll teach you how to beg properly.

"But we have so much to talk about," I muse, relaxing my grip on her hair and petting her more gently. It's like I said, I don't want to break her yet. There'll be plenty of time for that later.

"Like what?" She cranes her head back to look at me, brows furrowed. I stifle a laugh. I don't think my Little Stalker Princess meant to get caught today, but she's clearly not a very smart stalker if she thinks we don't have a fuck-ton to discuss.

"For starters, why'd you stop me from beating up that player? Better yet, how?" I ask.

My perception skills are top-notch but picking her out of a crowd of hundreds goes beyond even my skill set. I heard her so clearly, or at least

I felt like I did. And when our eyes locked I knew then she had to be something special. That we were bound by something unexplainable. I knew then that she'd be mine.

"How? I don't know *how,* I just . . . you were gonna kill that guy," she scolds, attempting to turn the tables.

I cock a brow at her.

"Eh, that's a little dramatic, don't you think?"

"Dramatic? They carried him out on a stretcher." Her words screech annoyingly in my head. Ugh, I can tell she's one of those people who 'cares' about other people who wish her harm simply because they're a 'person'.

I sigh. "He should have fought to win then."

"He was no match for you," she shoots back.

That excuse is even worse than the 'we're all people' excuse. Just because I was the better opponent doesn't mean he wasn't worth fighting.

"How's that saying go again? 'Play stupid games, win stupid prizes.' Next time he'll know better than to provoke an opponent he can't win against."

She rolls her eyes, exasperated, but I'm already loving our little back and forth.

I want to continue playing with my new toy, but shouts and buzzers erupt from the arena.

"Aww, man," I complain.

"What is it?" she panics, perking up even though she's still trapped beneath me.

I stifle my amusement and settle for moving quickly rather than offering any explanations.

"I'm going to need you to be very quiet."

"Wha—"

I yank her back a little rougher than I intend. She hisses in pain but I don't have time to be any gentler; not that I would anyway. Opening the locker, I shove her inside. I know she's ready to thrash and curse, but I can't have that right now.

"Not a sound, Princess," I warn, closing the locker in her face before she can protest. Not a moment later, the locker room floods with loud cursing and groans. *Shit.* I'm guessing we lost. The room fills quickly with everyone on the team and immediately jerseys start coming off. Mine sits neatly folded, blood on it and all, but I chuck it into my bag with the rest of my gear before it can draw more attention.

I turn my back to the locker I've stuffed her in, standing guard. Wouldn't want anyone discovering my new toy before I've gotten the chance to play with her.

I strip off my breezers and grin, knowing she can see through the grate in the locker and feeling her eyes graze across my backside. It's like nails dragging down my skin and I can't wait to see what kind of pain this hellion can inflict. Better yet, how much she can take because I'm going to enjoy every sound that falls from her lips.

SYDNEY
@therealLucifer
Online
ere you in the arena last nig
Seen
Who the hell is this?
Seen

CHAPTER SEVEN

SYDNEY

I WANT TO SCREAM.
I *should* scream.

From frustration. From anger. From excitement. But the second his pants drop from his hips, the desire to make any noise at all leaves me entirely, replaced only with the need to lick every inch of him just like he did me.

I actually can't believe he did that. I can't believe I *let* him. Though I don't think stopping him was an option. A kick to the dick didn't even faze him and, admittedly, his unorthodox disposition did little to change my feelings. He consumed the very fiber of my being the moment I was within reach.

Lucien Morrow is nothing like I thought he'd be, and yet everything I knew he'd be. Lethal. Dangerous. All-consuming.

I should be upset, right? A normal person would be upset. But I'm not. What does that say about me?

My panties are soaked, though I *know* I shouldn't be turned on right now. Even still, my heart races, and my knees threaten to buckle. I'm locked up, bound to his will and completely at his mercy.

He's filthy and vile, and flecks of blood still linger on his neck and ears...but he's also talented and cunning, and fucking beautiful. He's breathtaking. I'm utterly powerless to him, and it feels *amazing*.

For the first time he *saw* me, and all I could sense in him was adoration.

It was shocking because he was so apathetic when I found him. The only concern he'd shown was when he looked at his knuckles, which haven't been wrapped and still drip blood everywhere. I could feel the warm fluid when he stroked my cheek, so soft and lovingly. I bring my hand up to cup my face, still feeling the blood on my skin and the tightness of my cheeks from where some of it has started to dry. I've never had anyone touch me like that.

I want him to do it again.

I've never had anyone lick me in my face or bite me in a first encounter either. But that singular act of stroking of my cheek made me feel...sentimental.

I had been prepared to walk away when I'd seen he was fine, but then...I couldn't. Not yet. When he started talking to me, *actually* talking to me, I just couldn't. I almost leapt in his arms the moment our eyes locked again.

I had assumed he was talking to himself, much like he'd been doing while he examined himself, but he called me out. He spotted me right away.

How did he do that?

I guess I could have ignored him and slipped out anyway, but there we were, in this space. This moment where I could finally just talk to him and it seemed as good a time as any.

However, standing in this locker is seriously starting to make me question my own sanity. Though the view of his ass is certainly soothing the discomfort. I could yell and knock against my prison like a normal person, but unlike my recent decisions suggest, I'm not stupid.

And as we've established, I'm not normal.

Making my whereabouts known is going to present more questions for me than it will him and I'm on thin ice as it is. So I'll wait patiently for them to leave and forget all about this little encounter with Lucien Morrow. Even though my heart is screaming for the exact opposite. It begs me to never forget and to keep a memento commemorating this occasion.

Shame the blood has to wash off.

I'm chewing on my thumbnail again when a stout middle-aged man storms into the room, slamming the door open so forcefully the locker walls shake. I press my palms to the cool metal and try to remain still, taking only shallow breaths.

"Morrow, what the *fuck* was that!" shouts the hard-bitten man in a Bellemere-blue button down I can assume is the coach. "How many times have I told you? How many? Keep your emotions in *check*! Do you have *any* idea what you cost us? What you cost *yourself*?" his coach spits, heading right for Lucien.

If it were me being yelled at, I'd be shrinking in on myself, but Lucien stands tall. He's a powerful force to be reckoned with even wearing nothing but compression shorts that hug his ass like they were painted on.

"Was I actually supposed to be keeping count? Because I gotta say, you're putting me on the spot here," responds Lucien.

"You think this is fucking funny?"

"Not at all, sir. Mental math is really hard for some people."

A snicker bubbles out of me before I can stop it, and I slap my hand over my mouth. Lucien doesn't look my way, but his back tenses and I'm certain he heard me. *Shit.* I'm probably going to get in trouble for that later. My eyes roll at the idea.

Get in trouble? Seriously? I'm an adult woman. He can't do anything to me. But my heart pitter patters all the same. Even if it's punishment, he'd be touching me.

The coach pinches the bridge of his nose, exasperation evident from his premature wrinkles and splotched, reddened skin.

"I've warned you, time and time again, but this time you've gone too far," the coach breathes.

I'd heard of Lucien's violent streak before, how he'd gotten kicked out of games, gotten into multiple fights, spent more time in the penalty box than he did on the ice some games. But this was my first time seeing it first-hand. I'd assumed people exaggerated. That they stretched the truth to fit the Morningstar brand. But I was wrong.

"This time was different," Lucien grits, his voice sounding darker, angrier. He doesn't sound at all like he did a second ago. He sounds haunted.

"Oh, you're right about that. This time *is* different. You have no idea how badly you just fucked up, kid."

"So, what's the fucking problem? He'll live. If he couldn't take a punch, he should've kept his fucking mouth shut or, better yet, tried for a less violent sport," Lucien snaps.

"Not everyone is your enemy, Lucien!"

"If you're in my way, you're my enemy," Lucien growls, taking a step toward his coach. And though I can't see his face, I know what his eyes are doing. I can see the fear written on the coach's face. See his teammates jerk to attention, ready to stop whatever daring move Lucien makes next.

The coach straightens his shoulders, remembering his authority as he clears his throat.

"Well, this time you chose the wrong enemy. That was Jacob Anderson, the school president's son." He pauses, searching for a reaction in Lucien. When he doesn't give one, the coach sighs. "Look, kid, I like that killer in you. You got good instincts. You're fast and ruthless. You've got talent, but you lack control, and that is what's going to be the end of you. This time you really fucked up. The Andersons are not people whose bad side you want to be on. I can't protect you this time."

Everyone stands still, absorbing the news.

"You *didn't* hear what he said." Lucien's voice is flat.

"I don't *care* what he said, Lucien!" The coach explodes. "You sent him to the goddamn hospital. You might've crippled him. His father is not going to let that go. And the ref! You attacked an NCAA official. They're talking about keeping you off the ice for the remainder of the season. This could mean suspension from the team. Expulsion from the school. You might not ever get to play again; do you get that?" The coach flails his arms with each statement.

Lucien's quiet, but the message hits home. His tattooed back tenses and his muscles ripple across the landscape as he works to reign in his temper. He appears more tightly coiled than me, and I'm literally stuffed in a locker. I want to reach out, to let him know it'll be okay, but I have no idea if it'll be okay. In fact, I'm almost certain it won't be. I don't particularly associate with the Andersons but I know what people like them do to those who cross them. It's what my own dad would do: protect the family name.

I move a hand to the locker door, foolishly wanting to provide him comfort, when my phone starts buzzing in my bra. I fish my hand between my boobs but in a haste to grab it, I accidentally knock my elbow against the locker.

Shit.

I angle the screen up, greeted with Bradford's profile picture staring back. I stab my finger against his face to shut it up, my fingernail taps unhelpful as I brace myself for the inevitability of my capture. Instead, Lucien speaks.

"I'm sorry, Coach," he grits.

The silence in the aftermath of Lucien's apology is deafening. No one in the room can decide which sound to acknowledge. The sound I made in the locker was small, but it's his apology that seems to be the more startling occurrence.

The coach is the one who breaks the awkwardness, huffing a derisive laugh.

"No, you're not, so save your fake-ass apologies for when you'll actually need them. And believe me, Morrow, you *will* need them." He turns away from Lucien and I can feel the heat of Lucien's rage. "As for the rest of you, go home, get your rest, but come Monday morning . . . you can thank Morrow here for the world of pain that's going to come from practice."

"Uh, *morning*, sir?" one of the players inquires.

"Yes, Chauncey, *morning*," he reiterates.

"But some of us have classes," another player explains.

"Did I fucking stutter? You *all* have practice! All day. No excuses. No breaks. Your asses are mine or you can be out like your buddy Morningstar here." He points angrily in Lucien's direction and at least a dozen angry eyes pierce him like daggers. I can feel everyone else's disdain and resentment. It serves him right, but I can't seem to get my heart on board with the feelings of everyone else. I know how that ire burns the skin. How it sears into your bones like a hot iron that you have no choice but to endure and take for the sake of the *team*.

Instead of condemning him, my mind can't help but conjure all the ways that I can make Lucien feel better. Many of which involve me naked and contorted in ungodly positions yet to be invented. Hell, I'd even settle with just wrapping my body around his back like a koala. It's the only line of sight I have, and I want nothing more than to comfort his expressive back, even if it is adorned with a tattooed depiction of Hell.

I probably shouldn't feel so melancholic about his feelings. I genuinely don't think they're capable of being hurt, but his poor back definitely has feelings. It needs to be rubbed and cuddled and—

Oh my God, stop romanticizing his back, *girl.*

I don't.

I continue to personify his back as though it is its own separate entity from him while I patiently wait for this psychopathic heartthrob to release me from this locker prison. It takes longer than I could've imagined, but over the next however many minutes the voices grow lighter and the weight of hatred in the room dissipates. Then everything is quiet for a long, *long* time.

As the silence starts to settle, the locker door wrenches open, making me jump. My body bounces off the walls as I clamor about like a fish out of water.

I'm caught so off guard, it takes me a while to realize that my new friend, "Lucien's back," has disappeared and the real Lucien stands before me again. And damn it if I thought I was a fan of his back. I'm an even bigger fan of his front. He's *still* shirtless.

He's not insanely large, but what he lacks in bulk, he more than makes up for in solid, lean muscle covered in tattoos and scars. Suddenly the back tattoo makes a lot more sense. He's a demon spawn born from Hell and, my god, could he wreck me if I'm not careful.

I can't blink. And when my eyes finish roaming his body, I'm met with an amused stare. Leaning back into the locker, I find that I feel safer in here than in front of him. I gather what's left of my determination. I'm not letting him trap me again. But then again, would that be so bad?

If only I'd met him sooner, maybe things wouldn't have to be this way. Who am I kidding? It was always going to be this way.

I take a cautious step forward to exit the locker, thinking I can just make a run for it. But as fate would have it, I've lost all feeling in my legs from the lack of blood flow, so I fall . . . right into Lucien's arms.

His skin is warm to the touch, and his hold is more careful than when he shoved me in the locker, but I stop breathing entirely when his fingers grip my chin and force me to look up at his sinful grin.

"You did *such* a good job, Princess."

Holy hell, if that doesn't make me wet all over again.

"I did?" I ask, my voice almost imperceptible.

"Yes, you did," Lucien all but whispers.

He taps my nose with the tip of his finger, like one would a pet, but I'm too lost in his favor to care. I'm speechless. Those simple words of praise strung together cause me to beam with the impregnable force of a solar flare. *I did good. He said I did good.*

I'd managed to calm my raging hormones some twenty minutes ago after my legs went numb, but now they're back with the strength of a thousand suns and fuck me if now I don't have to run away just to keep from jumping him. I scoot away to test it, to see if I'm still 'locked in' with him, but he doesn't make a move to stop me. I stare at him warily before lifting a wobbling leg to stand. He moves with me and I sigh, fearing he won't let me go afterall, but all he does is help me up and brush me off. Rubbing my ass to remove the nonexistent dirt.

"Well, this has been . . . lovely," I deadpan. "But I'm leaving now."

I make my way to the exit, moving as quickly as I can without bursting into a full-blown sprint, but he seems resolved to remain in his spot. Part of me hopes he won't let me, that he'd force me to stay with him, but I know better now than to hope for anything more than what fate is willing to give me, and it's not him.

My footsteps slow of their own accord as I'm about to close the door, wanting to savor this last moment with him. It wasn't exactly the introduction I'd always wanted, and it was far beyond the realm of normal, but it certainly won't be one I ever forget. Despite the craziness of it all, I'll cherish this moment forever.

"See you around," he teases, his smile wide with mischief and playfulness. I don't smile back.

"No . . . you won't," I tell him, right before the door closes, and I disappear for good this time.

INTERMISSION

INTERMISSION

SYDNEY

Three months ago

*C*HOOSING THIS SONG WAS *a mistake, I think right before I fall.
Do figure skaters even make money?*

I grunt at the sting of ice on my knees as I struggle to peel myself off the ice and stand again.

If you can't even succeed on the collegiate level, how am I supposed to believe you can make a career out of this? You're better off coming home, finishing your business degree, and claiming your seat at the table.

My father's words ring in my head.

"No, no, no, dammit!" I slap my hands against the ice, intensifying the pain.

The chances of you making it to the Olympics aren't marginally high. You had your chance and look what happened.

"Fuck!" I scream into the empty air. The pain, my only solace. The rink, as abandoned as my spirit. And the echoes, my reverent audience.

I fall again and again before I'm forced to take a quick break, lest I pass out in the middle of the rink. In an effort to hydrate, I chug enough water to drown then move back into position. But before I can start the music again, my phone chimes with a message.

Bradford 8:30 PM

> Are you coming home for Spring break?

Heaving the deepest sigh possible, I grip my phone tighter.

"Not if I can help it," I mutter even as my fingers fly over the keys to respond.

Sydney 8:31 PM

Depends on my training schedule.

Bradford 8:31 PM

They make you train over the break? Lame.

If you want to be taken seriously as a competitive figure skater, you absolutely train over the break. You train harder than anyone else, for *longer* than anyone else, until you're the best. Which is what I'll be—the best. I'll be even better than before.

Sydney 8:32 PM

It's a competitive sport.

Bradford 8:32 PM

Wouldn't you rather come hang out with us in Aspen?

By 'us' he means the same other five legacies whose mommies and daddies hang out at the country club together. I wish I could say our parents are 'friends,' but the wealthy don't have friends, they have business associates. They don't have 'parties,' they have networking events. And they sure as shit don't have fun, they siphon joy out of the nearest living life source and feed on the collected misery of others.

Sydney 8:35 PM

Totally! If I can get away, I'm so there.

Yeah, I know. I talk a big game, but this is the only life I know. If I'm not training, I have nothing better to do, so I might as well spend my break in Aspen with Bradford. It's important I get used to spending time with him since, knowing Dad, he'll probably be my husband one day. Might as well get used to faking it with him.

Bradford 8:35 PM

Great. Can't wait to pick up where we left off
winky face emoji

I grimace, remembering the point where we left off. My pussy still burns from the way he hammered his bony fingers so hard I thought he was trying to start a fire. Honest to God, I thought that was how I was going to lose my virginity. Alas, it's still intact, scientifically speaking.

Sydney 8:37 PM

Me neither. Maybe this time I'll return the favor.

God, I'm hopeless. Why am I even getting his hopes up? I've seen his dick—he texted me a picture—and it's nothing to salivate over. I'd rather get this routine down than go to fucking Aspen to suck his mediocre dick and get carpet burn of the clit again, or rather the labia, since he couldn't *find* my clit. I'm getting irritated just thinking about it. Had he had any idea what he was doing, he might have broken my hymen.

Bradford 8:37 PM

Damn, baby, you're killing me. You're going
to make me come just thinking about you
wrapping your lips around my cock.

Jesus. And he's going to make me gag just thinking about it—and *not* in the good way.

Sydney 8:37 PM

Smirk emoji

Bradford 8:37 PM

What are you wearing right now?

Aaand that's where I draw the line. I step back onto the ice, restarting my routine. This time without the music. I need to focus on the fundamentals again and quiet all the fucking noise. Dad's voice in my head is hauntingly clear, a whisper I can't seem to ignore.

Why do you fight this so much? Do you have any idea how grateful anyone else would be in a position such as yours?

My ankle twists and I'm forced to go with it, conscious not to go against the bend and break it. I drop with a hard *thwack*, bracing myself in the nick of time with my hands. The ice is cold against my bare palms, but I shake off the pain radiating from my wrist, ignore the fact that my hip will be bruised in the morning, and get up to try again. The same thing happens, and this time, I don't get back up so quickly. Sitting up, I sniffle, the cold finally getting to me.

I've been out here for hours. My hair is matted with sweat and sticking to my skin. I hang my head, giving myself one more moment of self-pity. I'll do it. I'll get there. I'll be the greatest there ever was. But first, I could desperately use a shower, I brush my hands together and stand again. Time to admit defeat and go home.

Click

"Hello?" I call out.

Soft giggling

"Who's there?" I hate that my voice sounds weak.

More giggling

"You guys, if this is some sort of prank, it isn't funny." Okay, at least my voice didn't crack.

The sound of a door slamming kick starts my heart, and I jump almost ten feet in the air. *That's one way to stick the landing.* I huff a breath, the cloud billowing into the air as I stand in the middle of the rink. Alone. I give it a minute before I'm dumb enough to go toward the noise. I find out too late the *real* dumb decision was not moving faster. Teetering on my skates, I scurry to the exit and press against the push bar on the door. It clicks with every thrust, but the door doesn't budge, it doesn't open.

"Son of a bitch," I grumble.

My eyes roll as I try to keep my emotions in check. More like daughter of a bitch, because this childish stunt has Tiffany St. James written all over it.

"Ocean Eyes" by Billie Eilish plays on my phone.

My headphones drown out thoughts, leaving the serene voice of my girl Billie. A shower did wonders to calm me down, but Billie Eilish is doing the rest. Back in normal clothes, I head out of the arena.

What a fucking bitch.

Tiffany, not Billie.

Of course, it wasn't enough that she beat me in last month's competition or knocked me out of the running for the singles championships. She wants my complete humiliation. I can almost respect her position on the matter. After all, we're not so different.

I'm *technically* still in the running, and that makes her anxious. Even though I came in fourth, I can still compete if one of the other placements gets sick or injured, or can't compete because of grades or something. Anything can happen, and even though the chances are slim, they *are* viable options. So, like any respectable athlete, I haven't relented on my training. If I'm given the chance, I'll win for sure . . . a fact that apparently worries Tiffany.

It almost makes me smile but tonight's practice was rough. If I could just get this move right. I'm not coming out of my spin fast enough to pivot into the jump I need. I'm not generating enough force to make the height, and the song choice isn't helping matters either.

Maybe if I lose a few more pounds . . . or change the song?

My teeth click as I nibble on the small piece of flesh near my hangnail.

I can't let Tiffany beat me again.

I *deserve* to win. And not because I'm a Sinclair. My dad's money doesn't help me here. I may be on the top of the food chain back in California, but in these Washington mountains, I'm no one. As much as that annoys me, I actually prefer it. I'd rather be here as a nobody than a somebody back home. I'd rather struggle as a figure skater than be another pawn on the Sinclair chessboard. That's why I've worked so hard to create my own destiny. I want to win my own game, not my father's.

I take my time walking out of the arena, checking all the side doors on the way out, just in case. I'm headed toward the exit on the hockey side of the building since that door's always open. Those keys are held by the janitorial staff for the whole arena, not just the figure skaters' side so I should be golden.

I marvel at the expanse of the space and the quiet echoes of my footsteps as I trudge forward. This town lives and breathes hockey, so everything is bigger and shinier on this side. I can tell it's impressive, though some of the lights are busted. They flicker and buzz, straining to light the path ahead. If I didn't already reach my scare quota earlier tonight I might be frightened, but as it stands, I'm only mildly entertained with how anti-climatic this all is. Now if it were me, and the roles were reversed, if *I* was enacting revenge on Tiffany, I wouldn't have stopped at just locking her inside and leaving. Oh no, *that* lacks imagination and follow through. Honestly, where's the creativity?

If I really wanted to prove a point, I'd ensure not only that this was her only way out, but that she had no means of contacting help. I'd create a true sense of danger, maybe sneak up behind her in the dark and bind her to the shower faucets while she was naked in the locker room. Or ominously appear at the end of the hall in a mask holding a knife. I dunno, make her pee herself from fear and record it so I'd have evidence of her humiliation. Use it to blackmail and keep her in line or use it to force her to drop out of the running for the competition altogether. See, that's her problem.

She lacks conviction.

She doesn't know what it's like when the stakes are truly high. It's one of the first few useful things Father taught me. When I have a goal, I *commit* to it. But before I can make it out of the building, my phone starts buzzing.

Group Chat
Bellemere Figure Skating team

Tiffany 9:13 PM

Don't forget you guys we have a 4 o'clock practice tomorrow. I've locked up for the night, so I'm headed home. Tootles, see you guys tomorrow.

Regina 9:14 PM

Thanks for the reminder, bestie.

Bria 9:15 PM

We'll be there.

Hannah 9:15 PM

I'll be a little late. I have a dentist appointment.

Kieran 9:15 PM

Toats McGoats

Shane 9:16 PM

Ay Ay, Captain

I scoff. She's not even Captain.

Sydney 9:16 PM

OMG really? That explains why I can't get out then. You must have accidentally locked me in.

Tiffany 9:20 PM

Aw, no. I'm so sorry. You must have been in the locker room when I locked up. I had no idea you were still there. I've already left for the evening, but do you need me to turn around? I can come back and let you out, maybe give you a ride home if you need it?

I knew it.

> No worries. I'll just leave out the main entrance. No need to go out of your way or anything.

> Okay then, be safe. And, Sydney, have a good night.

Yup, she's just petty. Amateur.

I'm almost at the entrance when the bright light shining out of one of the arena entrances catches my attention. I've passed several and they've all been off, adding to the dark, ominous hallway vibe, but not this one. This one suggests it was left on intentionally. A flicker of hope shimmers that she might have grown a backbone and will address her concerns like a rational human being. But when I remove a headphone and listen for noise, I'm met with the sound of scraping ice and . . . slapping?

The slap is so hard, I flinch. It sounds like a person was struck. Tiffany deserves to be slapped that hard, but I realize that it's not the sound of a person being hit but an object. I hear it again, this time I'm sure it's the sound of two objects clacking together.

My feet guide me closer toward the source where I see far below there's someone playing hockey alone. I'm not even sure how that's possible, but I'm pretty sure that's what he's doing. There's a dummy goal person set up in the net and various black disks positioned in numerous places around the ice. It looks like he's running drills, but there aren't any coaches or teammates around.

I spin around to leave him to it, my body already halfway out the door before I see it. That move. I turn back around, taking another step forward to see better. The rink and the main floor entrance are illuminated, so I'm safer in this midsection where neither sources of light reach me. I watch him again, waiting for him to repeat the movement. It doesn't happen right away, but after a minute or two, I see its flawless execution. I plop onto the steps in disbelief that just happened.

He's a hockey player for Christ's sake, but I sit there and watch him do it again and again, perfect every time. He's not actually committing to the jump, but he's definitely doing some sort of combination between a double loop jump and a pirouette. The power in his spins could easily allow him to do the jump. Instead, he propels forward, spinning around his imaginary opponent and sinks the shot past the dummy. The more I watch him, the more I notice other little spins and mini jumps. I notice the power, the speed. I marvel at the artistry and commitment to his craft.

Tears prick my eyes, a flood of emotion overtaking me. He's not out there performing any crazy routines or dangerous jumps, but even he is better than me.

How can that be? I want it so badly. I work for it. I live for it. I breathe it. Why the fuck aren't I that good? I made it all the way to qualifiers before, so why can't I do it again? And why the fuck can't I get my dad's voice out of my head?

I grip the follicles of my hair, my head hunched over on my lap, ready to boil over and scream, but all I do is cry. Silent tears fall onto the cold concrete step below me. I'm still shrouded in darkness, and he still skates, unassuming of my presence.

I stay a while longer until he's all done, despite the sounds of his skates cutting into the ice, lulling me to sleep. I didn't track every goal, but I'm sure almost all of them went in, if the net full of pucks is to be believed.

He chews on his mouth guard as he maneuvers his makeshift course. There's an intensity in his eyes that appears dark and angry, but I can't see the color, only the tension in his face. It makes his features so sharp I can barely make out the full picture. He doesn't seem real from up here. I'm squinting to get a better look when my phone buzzes against the concrete floors. I panic, reaching for it to see my dad's face on the screen. I missed check-in. I had no idea I stayed so long. It's almost ten.

Jesus. I really am tired.

I look over my messages and see another one from Bradford.

Bradford 9:56 PM

You naked yet?

Ugh. I stand to sneak away, stealing one last look over my shoulder before heading out one of the darkened corridors.

LUCIEN

Lucien 8:17 AM

Hey, were you at the arena late last night?

Cap 8:17 AM

No. Was at family dinner with my parents, remember?

Lucien 8:17 AM

Oh yeah, I forgot about that. How'd it go?

Cap 8:18 AM

Same as always.

Lucien 8:18 AM

Fuck 'em.

Cap 8:18 AM

You would say that about my FAMILY.

Lucien 8:18 AM

Sorry?

Cap 8:20 AM

No, you're not, but it's all good. Why'd you want to know if I was at the arena last night?

Lucien 8:20 AM

No reason. You wanna come over later?

Cap 8:25 AM

Not tonight. I'm in the library. Got a huge test I have to study for. Counts for like thirty percent of our grade and he made his office hours at an ungodly time so no one would think to ask him for help.

Lucien 8:25 AM

Sucks to be you.

Cap 8:25 AM

Fuck you.

Lucien 8:26 AM

Aww, don't be like that. It's not my fault someone wasn't more careful with their class selections this year. I could have told you Professor Jones was an asshole. Mathieson is way better.

Cap 8:26 AM

Middle finger emoji

Lucien 8:26 AM

Careful. You know hostility is my love language.

Cap 8:26 AM

Two middle finger emojis

Lucien 8:27 AM

Well, now you're just being a tease.

New Follower Request

@BladeSpinner

Hits Accept

"Hi, can I help you?" asks the girl behind the Bean Cup register. I notice just in time it's my turn before the guy behind me has a fucking aneurysm for having to wait two seconds.

"Yeah, let me get uh . . ." I start.

The man huffs a breath of annoyance so hot it could melt the polar ice caps. Jesus, this guy needs to give me ten feet. His nervous energy is making me nervous, and I don't do well when I'm nervous.

I try again. "I'll get a, uh, chamomile tea with honey and a peppermint leaf. Actually wait, do you guys have those fresh-baked pistachio cranberry muffins, are those in season yet?"

"Aww, no, you're a couple weeks too early. But we should have them in stock by the end of the month," she offers, pointing a finger to where the shelves behind her stand lined with delicious baked goods and pre-packaged to-go orders.

"Damn. Okay, those things are fucking delicious."

She smiles, her cheekbones pushing up her glasses.

"Yeah," she says, shifting her weight. "They're by far our most popular this time of year, but we still have the pumpkin creme Danishes with honey toasted almonds if you're interested in that."

"I don't know," I sigh. "I kind of had my heart set on the muffins."

"Are you guys going to discuss pastries all damn day, or can I order a coffee?" the man behind me fumes. My shoulders flinch, sharp annoyance pricking at my mind and the immediate desire to make him move claws at my insides.

The cashier girl stutters, embarrassment tinting her cheeks as she looks away from his hard stare. Poor thing looks to only be a freshman, probably using the money from this job to pay her way through, like most students. Bellemere might be secluded, but it's not cheap.

"I-I um . . . will—" she attempts to calm the guy, but he doesn't allow her to respond.

"Do you mind hurrying it up here?" he barks back at her.

"Do you mind not breathing down my *fucking neck*?" I grit.

The guy scoffs as though I've offended him. As though *I'm* the one in the way of his breathing air. I haven't had enough therapy to deal with this rationally and he's pushing my goddamn buttons way too early in the morning.

"Look," he spits. "Just order your fucking pastry so the rest of us can get to work."

I peer past him at the long line of people dawdling on their phones before focusing my attention back on him. Majority of the people in line are other students because it's a fucking college campus. In a *college* town. And we're at peak start time for 9 A.M. classes.

I doubt he's rushing me to get to work, but I give him the benefit of the doubt. Facing back to the cashier, I ignore him and ask the cute girl, "Is there any way to get that warmed?"

"Well, we could warm it up, but honestly, I think the creme filling would melt too much, so it's probably better to—"

"Come on! Hurry it the fuck up," the man grunts, as he fumbles with his watch.

She flinches, rearing back at his forceful tone. She somehow manages to compose herself in time.

"Sir, I'm going as fast as I can. Please wait your turn," she asserts, pushing her glasses up and straightening her shoulders.

"Not fast e*nough!*" he barks.

Her shoulders slump again.

I grit my teeth, already coming down from my zen morning. I finally managed to have a decent night's rest, and this tub of lard is ruining my peaceful morning. He's a burly motherfucker, resembling one of the mountain men around here, thick beard and plaid shirt to boot. It reminds me of a lumberjack, which makes me think of axes.

Huh? Well, it's an option.

"Dude. Seriously. Calm the fuck down," I snap.

I don't know who the words are more meant for, me or him, but I can already feel myself climbing out of my skin, shedding the temperate persona. It doesn't help that he hasn't moved a millimeter out of my personal space.

"Oh yeah? And what are you going to do about it if I don't?" he challenges.

I mean, the options are endless. There are *so* many ways to make one hurt.

But who is the adult here? I'd roll my eyes and laugh if his obvious animosity weren't directed at me right now. Even more so if his hostility toward the girl weren't so apparent.

"You really wanna know?" I challenge back.

"S-sirs," she clears her throat. "I-I'm going to have to ask you both to leave if, you know, you can't control yourselves."

I stare daggers at the man standing an easy five inches from my face before resolving I really want that fucking Danish. Maybe the sugar will help ease the foul taste this guy is leaving in his wake.

"I'm sorry. You were saying?" I snap my fingers in remembrance, facing her once again. "Oh, yes, you were kindly letting me know something about the Danish? Something about the icing melting?"

I flash her a grin and she blushes, scooping her brown hair behind her equally red ears, and pushing her glasses up.

"I was just . . . well, I was just saying I think they're better not warmed because the, um, cream filling can get, uh, runny if it's too warm." She gets more and more red at her own choice of words. She swats the air while I stare at her, blushing harder when I bite my lip. "That's all. But, you know, it's totally your choice. Whatever you want." Her throat clears and she bats her doe eyes at me. My personal annoyance eases when I see she's less upset by the fucker still embedded in my asshole, he's so fucking close. God, it's setting my teeth on edge.

"You've got to be kidding me," I hear the guy grumble, practically whispering his bitter nothings into my ear.

The cashier girl doesn't notice though. She's smiling at me now, ready to offer me all the pastries I want if it means I keep standing here smiling at her. Being attractive helps keep me and all my fucked-up baggage under wraps, but it's only effective to the men and women attracted to me in return. It makes things worse when you have assholes, like the gentleman behind me, who grow angrier when you're the more attractive, better mannered, and just all-around better person getting what they secretly want. Maybe he's in a bad mood because he wants the pistachio cranberry muffins too.

"I'll take your suggestion, uh . . . Mary," I finally read her badge. She starts scrawling a name on the cup and I decide to keep flirting with Mary, if only to distract myself from the explosive temper I'm keeping at bay.

"Aren't you gonna ask me for my name, beautiful?"

She's tomato red now and her freckles pop even more against the color. Her big brown eyes gleam behind her thick lashes hidden behind the glasses but beautiful, nonetheless. She's cute in an adorable chipmunk kind of way and it *has* been a while since I've gotten laid, but unfortunately for my dick, Mary will be calling out for God before we ever make it past second base. One look at her and I can tell I'd break her in fucking half and snuff out whatever bright light still burns in her innocent eyes.

But . . . maybe just a taste.

"Oh, no need, everyone knows who you are, Morningstar."

"So, you're a fan?" I grin.

"Uh, yeah, I go to all the home games. You're . . ."—she pauses her scrawling—"you're pretty awesome."

I like how red her blush is, I wonder what other colors she could turn. It varies from person to person. There are all sorts of shades I've yet to see.

"Oh my God. If you're done sucking his dick, the rest of us would like a goddamn coffee order."

My fists clench and my teeth bare, but I keep my head down, breathing through the discomfort, the pressure that builds until I have it, until I taste it: vengeance. I want it more than the fucking Danish at this point.

"Hey, Mary," I add. "You know, speaking of, you mind throwing in a large coffee for me, black? Make sure it's extra hot."

"Oh, uh, sure it'll be . . ."

I hand over my card, my head hanging low between my shoulders as I breathe in and out. In and out.

In and fucking out.

Yeah, fuck peaceful, give me carnage.

LUCIEN

The jerk from earlier takes forever to leave the cafe. I'm even more annoyed now because my coffee has cooled a few degrees more than I'd like, but damn if Mary wasn't right. The pastry was fucking good. I'm licking the last of the crumbs from my fingers before I follow the rude motherfucker to his car. Who the fuck *drives* here? He made the conscious choice to come to a college campus to get coffee and be upset that it took longer than anticipated? Shame. Walking might have saved him.

It's unsurprising that he doesn't hear me walk up behind him. The moment he steps in the car, I open the other side, not giving him time to react.

Grabbing him by the beard, I throw my weight over the center console and straddle his lap. He flails, spilling his fresh coffee down his chest.

"Ah! Fu-shit, what are you doing?"

"You want your fucking coffee so bad?" I ask. "Here. Drink up."

I release his beard, pinching the hollows of his cheeks to force his jaws open, then shove his head back into the headrest. Taking what's left of my coffee, I pour the piping hot liquid down his throat. He tries to shake me off, wriggling side to side, grabbing at my face and pushing at my shoulders, but I work out every fucking day. I will not be overpowered by some weak man who needs to bully pretty cashiers and ruin my perfectly good morning.

The more he squirms and cries, the better I feel. The more he screams and pushes, the harder I hold him down. He pushes back, barely gaining an inch, but it's enough. My back presses the steering wheel, tapping the horn. I force him back, quickly scanning the parking lot to make sure no one heard. I only see people off in the distance walking to their classes or other breakfast spots.

Despite the physical strain, my tension releases. His tears fuel me up, the smell of dark roast and despair bringing my cortisol levels back to optimal. And even though the red haze reappears, blinding me with rage, and bleeding out all my hatred—I've never felt better.

The man sputters and gags, not only from the burns, but because now he's drowning, unable to swallow faster than the rate I'm pouring.

"St—" he garbles.

I think he's trying to say something. If only I cared what that was.

He's so busy coughing up his lungs, he's too weak to hold me off anymore. Though he wasn't doing a good job beforehand either. Getting the drop on him was too easy.

I crack my first real smile of the day. "You wanted to know what I was going to do about it, remember?"

"Ple-ase," he rasps.

"You should be more careful of what you wish for."

Coffee gone; I resort to punching him in the face. With his head pinned, the impact is immediate, his cheek already swelling and the skin splitting. It's quick, effective, and, oh, so satisfying. Once, twice, thrice, until I'm uncontrollably roaring in his face. I hadn't realized how loose of a thread I was hanging by today.

"Please . . . stop," he whimpers, blood streaming from his face and his mouth swollen from second-degree burns.

I don't want to stop. My bloodlust isn't satiated. He's not bleeding nearly enough for me to feel good about stopping, but I suppose the punishment should fit the crime. Maybe he's learned his lesson, and I *should* stop.

"Y-you won't get away with this," he slurs.

I blow out a long breath. "And just when I was conside letting you go."

"I . . . know . . . who you are," he pants.

I lean in closer.

"You have no idea *who* I am," I growl.

I wait for the moment it clicks for him, watching his eyes when he realizes. I am not the person on his TV screen, or the boy on those sports posters sold around town. The person he *thinks* he knows, is not who faces him now.

I wrap my hands around his throat, and he struggles to suck in air again. His eyes start to bug, though not from lack of air—well not *entirely* from lack of air—more likely from the firm erection that's pressing into his stomach.

I laugh. "Oops."

He stares down in horror even as he gasps for air.

"Oh, I wouldn't worry about that. I would never sully my dick by fucking the likes of you. But your miserable screams do get me hard." I grin. "Scream for me again. Go on, do it."

He couldn't scream if he wanted to, I haven't let go of his throat, but he tries anyway. I let go, deciding I want nothing more than to hear his agonized screams. Instead, he hacks and coughs. I hold his jaw away so he doesn't get his filthy germs on me.

"So disappointing," I muse.

I'm about to punch his teeth in so he can choke on those too when I hear my phone ding. He's too weak to fight me back, especially in the close quarters of his Honda Civic, so, I opt to take a breather and check it.

@BladeSpinner

Someone's coming.

My back straightens and the hairs on the back of my neck stand at attention. My focus sharpens and the haze lifts but when I peer at the road, no one's there. I look at the username again, my other hand back around this guy's throat to keep him quiet in case he decides to scream for help and the 'someone' nearby hears him. I'm not sure if it's necessary, but the more I stare at the screen, the more I note it's no one I recognize.

I look out the window again, the glass fogging up from all the mouth breathing and hot coffee. He's huffing out breaths at a pace faster than what's considered normal breathing. That's probably not a good thing.

Fuck, this idiot better not die . . . at least not here. I let go of his throat, and once again this piece of shit starts coughing on me. I swear to God, if he gets me sick . . .

I'm still not satisfied, but I'm in loads of a better mood, so I reach for my empty coffee cup and open the driver's side door, casually stepping out. All's right with the world again . . . at least for now.

I press a hand on the roof of the car and lean forward.

"You breathe a word about this, I won't just burn your tongue, I'll burn your whole goddamn house down with you still in it. You understand me, Jerry?"

"You're . . . fucking crazy!" he whines, tears streaming down his face as he trembles. Shaking like a leaf in the wind. *Beautiful.*

I grin. "You flatter me."

He snivels and my grin drops. Erased like it was never there.

"I better not ever see you at my coffee shop again, Jerry."

"M-my name's not . . ." he splutters.

"Does it look like I give a shit about your real name?" I bark.

He shakes his head, cheeks jiggling with every protest.

"Good. You have a good day, *Jerry*. I know I will." My smile returns, bright and full. Softly closing the car door, I stretch my back, strolling back onto the street and whistling my favorite tune until I hear my phone dinging again.

@BladeSpinner

> Well, that wasn't nice.

@therealLucifer

> Who's this?

@BladeSpinner

> Your friendly neighborhood Spiderman.

@therealLucifer

I was always partial to DC comics.

Now, seriously, who the fuck is this?

@BladeSpinner

You seem the type.

@therealLucifer

Who is this?!

@BladeSpinner

Guess.

@therealLucifer

What?

@BladeSpinner

I said guess.

@therealLucifer

How the fuck am I supposed to do that?

@BladeSpinner

I feel like you're not very familiar with the concept of guessing.

It's when you take a shot in the dark and see what happens.

@therealLucifer

You obviously don't know me very well. I don't take shots in the dark.

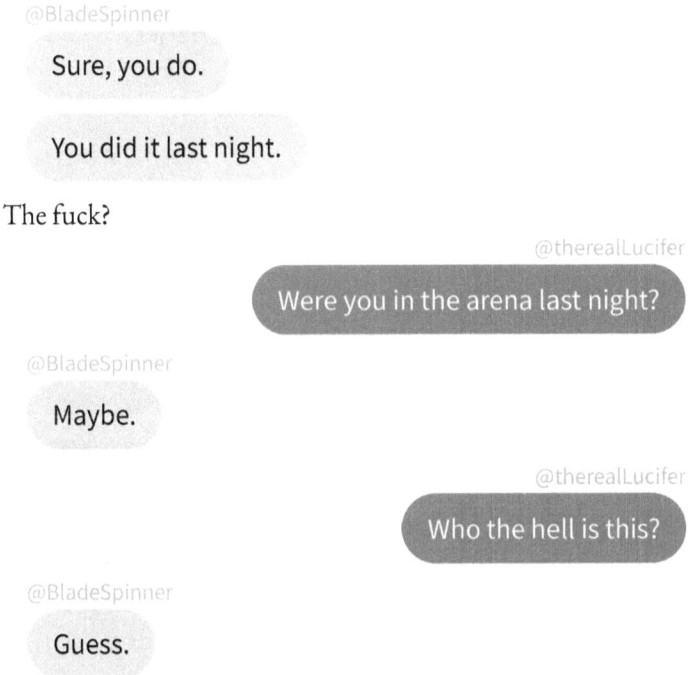

@BladeSpinner

Sure, you do.

You did it last night.

The fuck?

@therealLucifer

Were you in the arena last night?

@BladeSpinner

Maybe.

@therealLucifer

Who the hell is this?

@BladeSpinner

Guess.

I squeeze my phone. I'm both intrigued and pissed off. This had better not be anyone from the team. I've only just managed to get my good mood back and this fucker is trying to ruin it again.

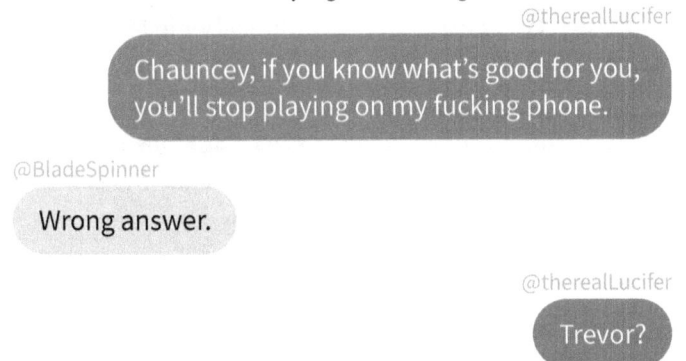

@therealLucifer

Chauncey, if you know what's good for you, you'll stop playing on my fucking phone.

@BladeSpinner

Wrong answer.

@therealLucifer

Trevor?

@BladeSpinner

That's all the time we have now, folks. Better luck next time.

@therealLucifer

Seriously?

@BladeSpinner is offline
Blocks user
@BladeSpinner has been blocked
@user00_00 message request

Somebody's a sore loser.

Deletes message

"What the hell?" I mumble, looking around to see if I recognize anyone acting out of the ordinary or being suspicious. There's only regular, unsuspecting passersby who don't even spare me a second glance. At least, not more than usual. After blocking the second username too, I head home to my on-campus dorm, the one I stay in when my mood is off. Typically, I'd go on a run right about now, but being among the public isn't feeling like a smart move. What I did was reckless. I could have just gotten his license plate number and tracked him down later. Broad daylight was a little bold, even for me. But, fuck, I needed the release.

I make it to the dorm and shut the curtains, immersing myself in the dark for a minute, standing amid the silence until my skin grows hot. Until I'm sweating. Until my eyes are so screwed shut, the headache starts to set in right around the same time the visions do.

Glass shards spread over the ground, lining the street, leading to the body of a young boy. The boy comes to consciousness only to be met with a crumpled

vehicle that looks a lot like the car he was just in, except he's not in it now. He's outside of it, in the cold with a scraped knee and glass in his palms. He looks at the car and . . .

My eyes flash open and I rip open the curtains, flooding the room with fresh light. The shining sun chases away the dark visions. Flopping onto the bed, I peer at my empty, cold pillow. I shift to stare at the ceiling instead, the view less melancholic and pathetic.

Grabbing a game controller, I sit up, opting to skip my classes for today to play some video games and blare my music until the sun sets. Until the RA is banging on my door to tell me that it's lights out. Until the nightmares inevitably return.

SYDNEY

My fork stabs into the eggs on my plate. It clinks against the glass at a steady beat, coming away with yolk on the tips, only to drive right back into the imploded center. My eggs lay murdered, ripped to shreds with no hope for survival after the twentieth stab wound. Clearly, I have no interest in these eggs anymore, but they make perfect substitutes for eyeballs. I fling some of the golden goop around the dingy ceramic plate and a bit gets on the printout of Lucien's schedule.

Dammit.

I pull a flimsy paper napkin out of the metal box on the table and wipe at the paper.

This thing cost me $500 from the lady in the Admissions office. I'm not about to let it get ruined by egg guts.

"Not a fan of the eggs?" asks the Bean Cup employee I've grown to loathe.

I glare up at the waitress whose unique sandy-brown tresses are annoyingly whimsical even on this cloudy day.

"No, *Mary*. They were a little . . . *soft* for my taste," I spit.

She peers down at the mess I've made, her discomfort evident in the pinch of her brows. *Good*.

"Oh, um, I'm sorry." Her lips poke out and her unpainted fingernails tap at the tip of her cupid's bow. Shit, even I have to admit she looks adorable. "I can ask the kitchen to make you some more?" she offers, her tiny left shoulder tilting into a small shrug.

Fuck, she's sweet, too. She's making it difficult to stay mad at her, and for good reason because there should be no reason *for* me to be mad at her. I've dealt with the constant disdain of members of my own team, believing I stole my place here or bought it, and have never *once* cared

CRACKED ICE

enough to be mad at them. I don't like *all* of them and make no move
to be their friend or anything, but I genuinely don't care enough about
them to have any strong feelings either way.

My mind keeps wandering through all the reasons I can try to be mad
at Mary. Does Lucien think she's prettier than me? Of course, he's never
actually seen me, so . . .

Staring back at his schedule, I try to figure out how to look accidental
when running into him since we don't share any of the same classes or
even classes in similar fields. His are all science stuff. I mean, Advanced
Bloodstain Pattern Analysis? That doesn't exactly overlap with Intro to
Business Law.

"Did you want more eggs?" Mary asks again.

I totally spaced out.

"No, it's alright. Don't bother," I answer with a tight smile, despite
my growing sense of hatred.

It's game day today and everyone is wearing sports gear. Even Mary
here is donning a Belle U Titans hoodie over her regular shop uniform.

Mary hugs the empty tray like it's her support blanket.

"Maybe I can offer you a muffin instead. They're fresh," she beams,
her bubbly attitude kindling for the burn in my chest. I consider her offer
for a second, internally dying to try the muffins Lucien seemed so excited
about that day, but I'm distracted by the bright blue sixty-six written on
the back of her hand in marker with a red heart around it. I stare at it,
wondering if it's possible to chop the offensive limb off with my butter
knife, but think better of it.

My attention gets pulled to Lucien at the smoothie joint across the
street. He goes there on Fridays for a protein shake. I can see him from
here, but he won't sit long because, according to this handy dandy
schedule I managed to snag, he has class in fifteen minutes. I doubt
Virgin Mary even notices his proximity. Or maybe she does, and she's
been waiting for him to walk in and talk to her again.

She flirts with him every time he comes in, throwing in free cookies or
giving him extra stamps on his reward card. Ugh, I bet she's a Satanist
and plans on sacrificing herself so she can be reborn as his future bride

or something. I mean, I'm a virgin too, but you don't see me making any blood offerings or skipping around with hearts in my eyes.

That's because your *eyes have ice picks in them.*

"So, that's a *no* then?" Mary startles me back to reality.

"I'm sorry, what?" I ask, realizing I totally spaced out again.

"On the muffins?" she clarifies.

"Oh, yeah, no thank you." I wave her off.

They're poisoned. Yeah, that's it. That's how she got him to like her, there's a love potion in the pistachio muffins.

"Alrighty then. Well, just pay up front when you're done." She turns to leave.

"Just pay up front when you're done," I mock her childishly in my head. *Pay?*

That's it!

"Hey, Mary," I blurt.

"Yeah?" she smiles, her super-cute freckles adding to her whole hot-girl-next-door act.

"Mind if I ask you a question?" I ask, genuinely smiling back for once this morning.

"Uh, sure, what's up?" she asks, her wariness of me intensifying, but I'm about to be her new favorite person.

"Why do you work here?"

The question's apparently funny enough she starts laughing, ending it off with an adorable snort that makes the urge to get rid of her stronger. Something so cute and precious is a threat to what I'm trying to accomplish.

"Why else?" She shrugs. "It pays the bills. Tuition isn't cheap, you know. I didn't make it here on scholarship like many of the athletes, so it's just been me trying to get by, you know?"

If she wasn't so oblivious, I'd think she was making a jab at me, but lucky for us both I have a scholarship *and* money.

"What if I told you I could help with that? Would you be interested?" I ask with a tilt of my head.

If I've learned anything, it's that there is more than one way to get rid of a body.

SYDNEY

After several days of not being able to find Lucien, he's finally back. Not that I think he's been specifically avoiding me but rather avoiding @BladeSpinner. Of course, it's far more likely he's not actually trying to avoid anyone but just moving about life in a way that doesn't happen to cross paths with my own.

I've been coming to this side of the arena at this exact time every night for the past week. I need to watch him a little more closely this time if I want to study his movements. Except every day I'd come here, was every day *he* wasn't there. I've gotten strangely close with Bernard, the janitor, who's been having to come ask me to leave. I had to play nice and talk to the old guy so he wouldn't immediately kick me out when he caught me waiting.

Bernard and Lucien *must* have some sort of deal they've worked out. I figured I could get the same one. I explained to him how I was preparing for my upcoming competition and he talked to me about all of his grandkids and how he still works to help them with school and other needs. I must admit, I've become fond of the old man and don't mind it so much when I have to talk to him instead of finding Lucien.

But tonight, Lucien is back on the ice, like he never left, cranking out moves I've never even seen before. He'd make for a great figure skater the way he moves with such fluidity, such raw power and control. He's better than Shane, that's for sure. It's like he was born to it, like he's one with it.

I watch in rapt attention as he weaves between pucks and skirts the edge of the rink with top speed and precision. Again, he's shooting the pucks, but my eyes stay glued to his skates, as I memorize his movements. With small alterations, I'm sure I can use the configuration to put more power behind my grand finish and achieve greater force and height. Most of us figure skaters would never admit to needing moves from a hockey player but this one, this one has talent bleeding from his pores.

It's no wonder everybody loves him. I *should* leave now to go practice, but instead I lean into the dark, shrouded in shadows, while I watch him practice. My chewing gum grows stale as I wait, so I pluck it from my mouth, playing with it as he runs more drills and giving my hands something to do. I shape and mold it as I try to figure out why he's practicing by himself. Pretty sure hockey's a team sport. Shouldn't he be out here with friends or teammates? I find the thought he's not, reassuring, that he might be like me, an outlier by nature. Someone, who despite their best efforts, deviates from the regularly scheduled program. If only, to have the space to be ourselves.

Bradford 8:39 PM

WYD?

Sydney 8:45 PM

At the rink. Wbu?

Bradford 8:45 PM

Thinking about you.

I roll my eyes and tuck my phone away, checking over the seat to be sure Lucien didn't see the blue light from down there, but he's still moving along the ice.

Assured that he's none the wiser to my presence, I stay a little longer, appreciating our time alone together.

The next day I catch him again and follow essentially the same routine—sitting in the same chair, playing with my gum—only this time I'm surprised by a notification on my way out the door.

@BladeSpinner unblocked

@therealLucifer

Were you at the rink again yesterday?

@BladeSpinner

Maybeee.

@therealLucifer

What do you want?!

@BladeSpinner

In life?

@therealLucifer

WTF! No, with me.

@BladeSpinner

Haven't decided yet.

@therealLucifer

You better not just be fucking with me.

@BladeSpinner

What if I am?

@therealLucifer

I'll make you regret it.

I can't help but giggle a little at his frustration. This is the most entertainment I've had in a while. I'm sure he'll find all of this funny when he finds out he let a figure skater get him this riled up. Who knows . . . I may never let him find out. Maybe *this* is the extent of it. I think I'd be fine with that.

I'm leaving earlier than I want, partly afraid I'll be caught if I stick around too much longer. I think I've got his movements figured out anyway, so all I'll have to do now is practice it. I know if I can get it right, Tiffany won't stand a chance against me at next month's competition.

Bundling my coat, I push out the door, leaving today's sculpted gum creation on the door bar. It looks like a little dagger with a foil hilt. I used the gum wrapper to make it look like an actual knife. It's kinda cool looking, if I do say so myself. Maybe he'll like it.

LUCIEN

It's been two fucking weeks and I haven't been able to shake the feeling that someone is following me. At first, I ignored it because I *always* think someone's following me, but this time it's not in my head. *Someone* has definitely been keeping tabs on me. At first I thought the puck bunnies were being extra voracious this season, or maybe—because I went viral again—people were being extra weird, but outside of a few extra dap-ups and smiles, nothing has been out of the ordinary from any other time. It doesn't help that the paranoia coupled with the insomnia is starting to fuck with me. I've had to cave twice and take those garbage pills that make my hands shake for two days.

"Name for your order?" the cashier at Bean Cup asks.

"Lucien," I answer. "Hey, whatever happened to the other girl?"

"What other girl?"

"You know? Freshman, cute, kinda mousy, light brown hair pulled in a messy bun with glasses?" I mean, who wouldn't remember her?

"Oh, her." His thoughts start to register. "I'm not sure. Last week she just quit. Out of the blue."

"Quit?" My eyebrows furrow.

"Yeah, right in the middle of a shift, too. It was super weird and inconvenient as hell, but she seemed sorry about it." He shrugged. "She said she'd picked up new courses over at the nursing school off campus and couldn't work here anymore."

"Oh. Cool," I sigh.

Well, there goes my option to get my dick wet. I knew I wouldn't be able to get my fill with her, but she'd at least been an option. Since she was an acquaintance, it meant I didn't have to bother getting to know her through traditional means. The only reason we'd even spoken was because she made great pastry suggestions, which is more than I can say for other puck bunnies who would no doubt already have me chomping at the bit to slit my own throat rather than hold a conversation with them.

But Mary seemed harmless enough. She was quiet and kind of soft spoken and, in a weird way, those things made her feel safe, even though she would be anything *but* safe with me. I admit, it may have been a little unreasonable for me to want something so innocent-looking to take my stress out on, but it had been a long time since I'd been tempted and, she'd looked appetizing enough. Good enough to eat. But I have no desire to chase her down. Out of sight, out of mind.

I hold my card out to pay.

But the considerably less tempting cashier reads the name on it. "Oh, hey, you're that Morningstar dude?"

I force a smile. "Yep, that's me."

I am not in the mood to be fawned over. I'm a chronic insomniac in need of a new plaything and whose potential prey has escaped.

"Oh. Um, don't worry about it then." He waves his hand over the machine, blocking access to the card reader.

I pause, the card centimeters from the machine. I slowly pull the card back, wary.

"Oh, uh, thanks, man."

He nods before he starts prepping my order in a trained, robotic fashion. He had been smiling, but his features lacked the telltale sign of pride from a good deed or job well done.

My brows pinch. "Is this because of the win last week?" I ask, unable to squash the niggling feeling that there was something fishy about this.

"I mean, probably," he says. "I couldn't say for sure. I just know someone came in and created you a tab. It was kinda badass. I didn't even know we did that, but yeah, you're all set, Superstar. Free coffee and pastries for life, I guess." He shrugs and turns back to making coffee.

But his statement only makes my hackles rise higher. "Did you see who it was?"

"Uh, no. I didn't set it up," he says, bobbing my bagged order in my face until I reach for it.

"Do you know who *did*?" I push, practically snatching the food from his hands.

"No, sorry man." He shakes his head. "From what I heard, they didn't come in person, but you know, now that I'm thinking about it, it would have been around the time the girl was working here."

Of course it was Mary. Yeah nope, still not tracking her down. I don't care that much, but it still seems a weird thing to do for me. How'd she know that would even be something I'd want? There are plenty of coffee shops around here. Hell, there's one right across the street. This just happens to be my favorite one. Though, I suppose it's a lot of people's favorite. Mary *could* have done it herself before she left, but then again, I doubt she'd spend all her job earnings on a coffee tab for me. Would she? That's a little creepy. I *like* creepy.

I'm halfway to class, still considering whether or not I want to track down Mary when I take my last sip of coffee. Pulling out my phone, I send out a text.

Lucien 9:08 AM

Did you create me a tab at Bean Cup?

Cap 9:10 AM

Why the fuck would I do that?

Lucien 9:10 AM

Uh, because you're my best friend?

Cap 9:10 AM

I'm your only friend.

You have 300 new notifications
Notifications start scrolling across my phone screen and they all have one thing in common: they're all from @BladeSpinner.

"Looks like you're not my only friend," I mutter.

I scroll through every notification. Every post on my page has been liked and favorited. I have more than thirty thousand followers, mostly Belle U hockey fans, since all my content is footage from my games, but @BladeSpinner hasn't left a single comment.

I scroll their page, unsurprised when I find there are no posts and they're only following one person: me. Their profile picture doesn't give anything away either. At least nothing I can use to learn anything about them. It's a picture of a gopher skiing down a mound of dirt that says Gopher Gold across the middle.

It's kind of funny actually, but I can't tell if they're fucking with me to be funny or if they want something. The wadded gum thing was weird, but it wasn't like it was poisonous. Maybe a little disgusting, but not an inherently bad thing. I doubt they expected me to eat it or anything, so again, what was the point? They asked me to guess, so maybe I know them or know *of* them.

Why are they hiding from me?

Oh my God! This one's alive. He's alive you guys!

Sweetie? Hey, sweetie, can you hear me?

Can you hear me?

Wake up.

Wake Up!

My head pounds as I jolt awake, my brain physically throbbing as if I slammed it through a window. I groan, pressing the heel of my palm to my temple. It always feels so real. Every time, it's like I'm right back there. I lay back against the headboards, staring at my hands. They're shaking. Balling my fist, I force myself to take a deep breath.

chime

I blindly reach over and grab my phone.

Unknown 2:13 AM

You awake?

Lucien 2:23 AM

How did you get this number?

Unknown 2:23 AM

shushing emoji

It's a secret

Lucien 2:24 AM

Dude, what is your deal? Why the fuck are you making this so weird?

Unknown 2:24 AM

I'm not being weird. You're being weird.

I huff a laugh, sitting up as I regard their text more closely, then choosing to respond over the alternative.

Lucien 2:24 AM

How am I being the weird one here?

Unknown 2:24 AM

You're talking to a stranger in the middle of the night.

Lucien 2:25 AM

So are you.

Unknown 2:25 AM

No, I know exactly who you are. It is you who does not know me.

Lucien 2:25 AM

Then tell me who you are.

Unknown 2:35 AM

I've changed my mind.

Lucien 2:36 AM

About?

Unknown 2:36 AM

I don't think I want you to know who I am anymore.

Lucien 2:36 AM

Why the fuck not?

Unknown 2:36 AM

I'm having too much fun.

Lucien 2:37 AM

You think this is funny?

Unknown 2:37 AM

Immensely

Lucien 2:37 AM

It won't be so fun for you when I catch you.

Unknown 2:38 AM

Good luck with that.

Padding over to the bathroom, I huff another laugh. What the fuck? Who has ever intentionally riled me up like this? No one. Everyone else is always, "Chill out, *Lucien*", "Calm down, *Lucien*", "Don't break his arm, *Lucien*."

I've been in a bad mood these days. Probably from the lack of sleep, but it's not getting any better. I'm two seconds from blowing either my own head off or someone else's. I know it, my coach knows it, Trevor knows it. My team probably suspects it, but I'm still performing during games, so no one's complaining, but this guy, whoever they are, is pushing me, poking the fucking bear. And for what? To see me snap? Because that's what I'll do if they don't fucking quit.

I'll snap, and then we'll see how brave @BladeSpinner really is.

LUCIEN

@BladeSpinner has tagged you in a post.

I open my phone to see a picture of myself slumped in my seat with a short message.

@BladeSpinner

I don't see how you haven't died of boredom yet.

What. The. Fuck?

My head whips in the direction the photo's been taken, but there's no one there. No one suspicious, that is. They must have considered I'd look that way first and posted the picture after they'd already left. Smart.

I lean forward, resting my elbows on my knees as I type back, hoping to catch someone in the act . . .

@therealLucifer

Is death something you desire?

I jerk my head back up. But no one turns around or looks toward their hands. It doesn't help that there are at least two hundred students in here. I should have paid better attention on who exactly was in this fucking class. That way I could spot the outlier, but I've been in a prison of my own mind this semester and I didn't have time for the frivolity of niceties. So, I have no fucking clue who's in this class.

I look at my phone again.

There's a long tentative pause.

@BladeSpinner

> **Sometimes.**

Well, at least they're honest. Death is something I could easily give, even though it's been evading *me* for years. If I wasn't already contemplating their murder, I think I'd feel bad that they feel that way. I don't wish that on anyone. But, alas, I don't feel anything close to that particular emotion. What I *do* feel is a kindred spirit of sorts, a camaraderie I don't typically feel outside of hockey. I message back.

@therealLucifer

> **Lucky you. Death and I are on favorable terms.**

@BladeSpinner

> **Wow, one who rivals even death. Impressive.**

@therealLucifer

> **Death has no rivals.**

@BladeSpinner

> **And yet you breathe.**

I'm not picking up any malicious intent around me even when the message implies otherwise. Though it's not like I'm being given much to go off of. My eyes scan the large auditorium-sized classroom but again there's no one acting out of the ordinary. The only thing out of the ordinary is me, having back-to-back text exchanges with a stage-4 creeper. I haven't had this much phone activity since . . . since *them*.

@therealLucifer

> **I was supposed to die once before.**

Why the fuck did I tell them that?

@BladeSpinner

> **Why didn't you?**

@therealLucifer

> **I was spared.**

The anger I'm constantly holding back must bleed out onto my features because the next message comes quickly.

@BladeSpinner

> **You don't seem too happy about it.**

@therealLucifer

> **I'm not.**

@BladeSpinner

> **I thought your terms were favorable.**

@therealLucifer

> **I didn't say I liked it.**

I search the rows again, even more curious to see who they could be, but almost everyone has their phones out, hidden in their laps. Or their laptops open, either taking notes or pretending to take notes. It makes it harder to tell who could be sending these messages. I consider blocking them again, but then another message appears.

@BladeSpinner

> **I'm glad you were spared.**

SYDNEY

It's at the tip of my tongue to ask him what he *does* like. He obviously fancies himself the quiet brooding type when, in fact, he's the furthest from it. I see the way he peacocks around here, fluffing his feathers and preening for his fans, but I wonder which is the real him? Is it the one who smiles and flirts with everyone he meets or is it the one who sneaks away to practice alone? Who is Lucien Morrow *really*?

I stand from my position in the risers above, careful not to fall or make noise as I smile down at him. I'll find out soon enough I suppose . . . *after* my own practice that is.

"One and two and three and four and—good, good, looking great, Sydney," my coach shouts over the ice. My grin grows wider, doubling in size when Tiffany's morphs into a scowl. Hannah, on the other hand, looks like she's about to be sick. My grin grows impossibly larger because if Hannah is getting sick, that could mean an opening in the roster. The once-happy expression dwindles though when I take into account she probably won't *still* be sick in six weeks. One could hope, but, unless it's something serious, it doesn't seem likely. Unless . . . it *becomes* something serious.

MANIFESTATION JOURNAL

DATE: JAN. 12, 2024

> Today I'm going to follow him to the bakery that he likes so much and talk to him. With that girl, Mary, out of the way, he'll see me and say, "Wow, that girl Sydney is so beautiful, she's amazing and super cool." He's definitely going to ask for my number and we're going to go out on a date where he'll wine and dine me and tell me how great I am.

Unfortunately, today is not the day I talk to Lucien D. Morrow. I want to. I yearn to cross the street, walk right up to him, and use all of my infinite charm to seduce him into doing . . . fuck . . . I don't really know. *Something* with me. Except, when I'm near him, I practically choke on air. It's nothing like when I have Bradford wrapped around my finger, he begs for my attention. Or even Dad's colleagues who pretend they're interested in my thoughts on political ties in the pharmaceutical sector, and how that affects the free-trade agreements.

No, the only thing *they* want to trade, is their left nut for even the chance to gaze upon my virgin cunt. A fact they're all aware of because my father flaunts it like it's the gold medal of all successful child-rearing adults to have a daughter as pure and innocent as his. They look at me like sharks who smell blood in the water.

They *want* to make me bleed. They *want* to fuck me. And one day, one of them will—it's just a matter of when, by force or otherwise.

If we were in historical times, they'd probably bid for my virginity, and my father, smart, successful businessman that he is, would probably consider the sale if it were a decent offer. I'm sure the deal would be lucrative. Sadly, I've grown so accustomed to their 'desire,' I no longer even flinch when they peek at my tits, unable to hold conversations with their eyes on me because, apparently, I'm so goddamn irresistible—but not to Lucien.

No, star hockey player and beloved Morningstar of Bellemere University can't even bring himself to notice me. I've brought down Fortune 500s with my purity schtick and yet I can't get Lucien to even *look* at me.

He can't see you if you're all the way over here, crazy.

I brush off the rational thought because my disinterest never seemed to be a problem for others before. No matter how hard I focused on my own goals, guys inevitably found ways to impose on me even when I wanted nothing to do with them. I have no idea how to act with things this way. How does one become the pursuer? Is that even what I want? To pursue? And what happens when I get it? We talk, we date, and then . . . what? I'm not so sure this is as appealing as I'm making it out to be.

I stare across the street for a little while longer. I couldn't bring myself to go to Bean Cup today, there's been no point now that I've gotten rid of Mary. Besides, this cafe has the better espresso shots.

The cute French-style bistro is much more my scene and sits conveniently across from Bean Cup. It's surprising they're both as successful as they are with the rivalry, but I guess they serve different purposes, so they both thrive. *This* bistro has the better espressos and food, but Bean Cup is more cost friendly and has the better baked goods. I see why he likes it over there. In recent weeks, I've learned he's a sucker for something sweet.

I stare out over the street where he sits, watching his knee bounce frantically. Sheesh, he needs to cool it on the caffeine if he's going to be so jittery. I watch the cars pass as they obstruct my view one by one. It grates on my nerves. I don't want any barriers between us. It's a simple street, but it may as well be miles of canyon with the amount of distance that rests between us.

I start to wonder what would happen if I stepped out into traffic, would I get his attention then? I mean, I know what would happen; I'd be severely hurt or killed, but then what? What would Father think? Would he be crushed?

I chuckle.

No, I'd *be crushed.*

Would he be heartbroken? I'd like to think so. I'm sure he would. I know Father loves me. He can stand to show it a little better, but I know I'm his crowning glory. The culmination of all his success. His pride and joy, if only I didn't figure skate. He'd probably raise all hell and burn this school to the ground, build condos on its ashes and charge triple the rent if he blamed them for my untimely death, intentional or not.

The bigger question though, is how would Lucien react? Would he see some dead girl in the street and keep walking? Would he try to save me? I think he'd be curious. Yeah, he seems familiar with the concept of death.

What was it he'd said? Oh yeah, that him and death were on favorable terms, whatever that means. Point is, he'd know I was a goner for sure, but I'd like to think he would at least wonder why I walked into traffic.

I chuckle into the China cup poised to my lips, barely stifling the giggle as others watch me. It's not funny . . . but then again, it's a *little* funny. It's a joke as old as time.

Why did the figure skater cross the busy road?

Because she wanted to get to the other side.

I snort a laugh again, unable to hide the sheer amusement of my own joke. More people look my way as though I've lost my mind. Maybe I have.

When I look across again, I see Lucien getting up to leave.

Oh shit.

I clink my cup back down, slap a fifty-dollar bill on the table, and am on the move once more. I wonder where he's going now.

One way or another, I'll get his attention.

SECOND PERIOD

@BladeSpinner
Online

What do you want

In life?

Seen

WTF No

Haven't decided yet.

CHAPTER EIGHT

LUCIEN

Present

I T DOESN'T TAKE ME long to find her. My Little Stalker Princess is *shockingly* easy to read. Someone who has the time to stalk typically doesn't have a lot of friends. And even if she had one or two, they're not the kind of friends to have come to the game with her.

When I saw her across the ice, she appeared to be by herself, and the fact that she followed me back into the locker room and got herself trapped in the first place suggests she had no one waiting for her. Someone *that* comfortable with being alone needs a place to ensure they remain that way, which means leaving the arena with a slew of people is out of the question, and if she stayed and waited out the crowd in a shimmery leotard no less, then . . .

Voila.

Here she is, skating on her own rink. And as predicted, alone.

I was right.

Though it didn't pose an extreme challenge, I'm still going to enjoy the spoils of my riches. I'm about to go down there and collect my prize when an idea forms. I'm going to take a moment to watch *her* for once. *Yeah*, I'm capable of exercising a little control, so I'll let her pretend she's safe and at peace, then smack her with my hammer of truth when she's done putting on her show. And by my 'hammer of truth,' I do mean my dick. I imagine her making a Thor joke and the immediate desire to hear the witty remarks from her DMs in person sets me on fire.

Silently taking the steps two at a time, I pick a seat in the middle, dropping my bag in the seat next to me. I'm a few rows up from the rink where it's still dark so she's none the wiser to my presence. . . for now. With no scheduled competitions and the team in Seattle, the only lights present on this side are the ones directly above the rink. Like a spotlight, only the illuminated circle is visible in the dimmed space. That would be fine, but unlike our side, the space isn't huge. She could spot me if she looked hard enough.

Beneath the spotlight, a small boombox sits in the middle of the ice with her where she poses like a ballerina, sporting a pair of glittery white skates. The music begins to play a slow, sensual ballad that sucks me in and trains my focus on the beautiful girl. I lean forward in my seat; my hoodie pulled back from my damp hair so I can get a better look. I can't wait to see how she skates and learn what the infamous @BladeSpinner can do.

The username is more clever than I gave her credit for. I'd assumed she had a thing for knives like me, but this makes loads more sense.

I'd never given much thought to the figure skaters before. Unlike other schools, we have separate rinks from one another in a top-of-the-line facility that rivaled some of the other professional arenas. They stayed out of our way and we stayed out of theirs. But sitting here, watching her in her natural habitat, there's no way she'll ever be off my radar again.

She pushes off strong at first, her body clearly honed to perfection to excel at the sport. Her long, lean legs are etched in muscle. They tense and flex, balancing the weight of her body throughout her movements. Ice shavings fall like confetti against her pale skin and though she looks cold, she skates like she's on fire, like she'll combust from the heat.

The song she's selected sounds sad at first, but it's a powerful crescendo, highlighted by her equally powerful motions throughout the piece. The speed she's generating alone is impressive, causing the wind to whip at her hair and thrust the skirt of her velvety red leotard up as she moves to the beat of the sultry song.

I'm captivated. I was too busy licking her face to notice what she was wearing in the locker room. It's a deep blood color. My cock jumps as the flaps of her skirt flit and brush across her backside, her bare ass playing peek-a-boo with my resolve, teasing and taunting me to come down and take a bite. I salivate at the opportunity laid before me. The opportunity to take and hurt. To lick my metaphorical wounds after a shitty night and bathe in her desperate screams for mercy, for forgiveness. I rub myself through my sweatpants to keep calm and tame the erection that threatens that thinly-lined resolve.

I'm ready to slam my hammer of truth into her pussy and hear her screams echo throughout this arena. She's not safe, the farthest from it in fact, but when I stand to make my way toward her, she stutters and falls.

She grunts in frustration, and I pause my descent down the steps, trying to work out the rational side of my brain that says I should probably check on her or something. Luckily, I don't have to force a decision.

She gets back up and tries her routine again.

Atta girl, show that ice who's boss.

I rewatch the private show she's put on, temporarily putting aside my thoughts of fucking her. This time, I don't allow myself to be distracted. I watch her face, noting how tight it is. Her brows are furrowed, deeply wrinkled and hardened in concentration. Her limbs are strained throughout her movements. She's choppy when she should be languid. Her smile is so fake, it's sad.

I lose my hard-on entirely and flop back down into a seat, watching to see where this train wreck goes. Perhaps it can be salvaged.

But she falls again.

Ouch.

I wince, envisioning the pain she must be experiencing, but not getting turned on by it. Her thigh smacked the ice hard on that last one and I can see the large area of skin turning pink from here. That's no way to bruise. I'll have to show her the proper way. *The way that leads to mind-boggling orgasms afterward.*

Twenty minutes have passed and I've long since made my way closer to the rink, moving to sit along the wall's edge after she almost broke her ankle when she didn't land her final jump. She tries the routine a few more times without the music this time, but I can tell she's reaching her limit and wearing herself out. My feet swing back and forth, watching with rapt attention as she fails each time. It's not the failure I'm enjoying, but rather her refusal to quit. *That's a positive sign.*

She starts her performance over three more times before finally screaming a defeated growl and driving her skate through the boombox. It sparks upon impact, screeching a high-pitched howl before imploding on itself and cracking. Whatever song was playing groans and skips until it's nothing more than an obnoxious hum. Then she lifts her foot up and thrusts her skate down one more time to shut it up for good. Just like that, my hard-on has returned with a mighty vengeance.

What a beautiful display of violence.

Looks like I'm not the *only* one who lets their emotions get the best of them. Right when I think I have her figured out, she manages to surprise me again. I guess that's just it though, isn't it? My Little Stalker Princess has been surprising me all day, acting out of character.

I didn't hear from her for *two* days, no ominous texts or random check-ins, and then she shows up out of the blue all cute and innocent at my game. Her aggression is the first honest expression she's made since we were back in the locker room. Her fear was real, her disgust—at least initially—was believable, but everything after has been lies.

Her breasts bob at a frantic pace as she tries to force additional air into her lungs, resting her arms atop her head as she stares up at the ceiling. Sweat trills down the soft curves of her reddened cheeks and hair that's slipped from her braid sticks out in swirled patterns along her hairline. Her bottom lip trembles as a silent curse whispers into the air.

"Shit."

Aww, fuck, she looks like she's ready to cry. My lip pokes out in a pout. Poor thing. I don't want a *sad* plaything. That's no fun. My Little Stalker Princess should be happy. After all, she got to meet the object of her obsession today. Doesn't that make stalkers happy? I mean, I guess I've heard the opposite too; that they get so disappointed in their obsession the only choice is to off them, but she's barely even *tried* to hurt me.

The kick to the balls she tried apologizing for doesn't count. Am I not worthy of psychotic behavior? Are we not the same? Surely the thought has passed her mind.

Bad stalker princess.

Now *I'm* sad that I was a disappointing victim, not even worth being happy about catching or sad enough to murder. That sucks. I should cheer her up.

"Why so serious, Princess?" I ask, doing my best Joker impersonation. Though, I suppose my best might have been too good because she practically jumps out of her skin at the realization I've been sitting here the whole time.

"God! What are you still doing here?" she shouts, her eyes bugged out in surprise. The light shining above barely touches me, the outer layer of light a thin veil she hadn't noticed until it was too late.

You'd think she'd be better at this game.

"You can't just pop up on me like some kind of Houdini!" she shrieks.

'Silly rabbit, tricks are for kids.'

The barked laughter that erupts from my chest comes out more maniacal than I intend. Her shoulder's flinch and I attempt to take it down a notch. I'm going to scare her off at this rate.

Yet she slowly skates toward me, not away.

"Well, most people call me Morrow—or Morningstar when I'm being particularly savage—but I quite like the sound of God. Do you want me to be your god, Princess?"

I drawl, though judging by the open-mouthed expression, she'd happily worship my cock if motivated enough.

A beat passes and she's still stunned into silence, so with a sly grin I ask, "Well, if I'm God, what should I call you?"

I hop over the wall and walk into the light, comfortable with the ice even in my boots. Her eyes blink, adjusting, but then she's staring at me, like she's seeing me for the first time.

"I . . . um,"—she clears her throat—"most people call me Sydney . . . but I'm guessing you're not like most people, huh?" She narrows her eyes at me, worry filling those blue pools that have magically lightened, the color appearing more ice blue under the bright fluorescent lights.

I crane my head up. And when she mimics the movement, I glance back to find it's the light from within that makes those blue orbs shine the way they do. She tries to seek for herself what's above us, her head tilted skyward while I stare at her profile. Her eyes are so fucking blue, like pretty blue marbles. If I could, I would gouge them out and add them to my collection—of marbles, not eyeballs—but either way, I prefer them in her pretty little head.

It's funny though, she didn't say no to me being her god.

"Sydney," I mull her name around in my mouth, savoring the syllables on my tongue. *I like the way it tastes.* "I'm *nothing* like other people."

"Yeah, I can see that."

I quirk a brow.

And she lets out a slow exhale, folding her arms.

Not sure what folded arms are going to do to protect her from me, but if it makes her compliant, who am I to stop her?

"So, you gonna tell me what you're doing here?" Her hip pokes out and she stands a little taller. Easier to do when you're on skates, but again, whatever keeps her talking to me.

"I could ask you the same thing."

Two days without hearing a peep from her and now she's acting as though meeting me somehow inconveniences her.

Oh, but I see how it is. I'm on *her* turf now. My little stalker is trying to assert dominance. Adorbs. Her ponytail has been tied into a braid since our time in the locker room and my palms itch to pull on the long rope of hair that reaches her lower back.

"I'm practicing . . . obviously," she says with a huff.

"I'm *watching* you practice . . . obviously," I parrot, my smile never leaving my lips.

She grimaces and I can't help but chuckle at the irony. "What? You don't like me watching you practice? Should I go back to hiding in the shadows, like you?" I point over my shoulder in the general vicinity of my earlier seating spot. "Peek around corners and secretly follow you to class? Ooo, or my personal favorite, wait until you're all alone then show up unannounced when you're at your most vulnerable? Huh,"—I shrug—"on second thought, I guess I am like you."

She bristles but still manages a snarky retort.

"Ha ha, very funny. It wasn't like that. I just . . ." She looks everywhere but directly into my eyes, moving from my mouth to the ice repeatedly. "I liked watching you skate, okay?" I don't bother reminding her that she stalked me even when I wasn't skating. Instead, I let her continue. She inhales sharply, eyes closed and fist balled at her side. "You're . . . really . . . *really* good."

When she finally does look my way, her eyes burn into me, sincerity and envy bleeding from her gaze. I'm both flattered and confused as to why she would be jealous of me when, stalker or no stalker, she skates like a beautiful ice princess.

"I'm *really* good at a lot of things, Princess, but I'm willing to bet you are too." I give her a salacious grin, hoping she picks up my meaning. It doesn't really matter if she does or not. I'm more than willing to prove my theory; Sydney looks like she'd happily go the extra mile.

"I guess," she fidgets, nibbling on the side of her thumb. I can see from here how red it is, likely bleeding the way she's going at it.

I send a warning glare her way, which she promptly ignores. If anyone is going to make her bleed, it's going to be me.

"So, you're a fan of watching me play?" I ask, taking a step forward.

Who knew my little stalker would be such a hockey fan? I didn't peg her as the type.

"I'm a fan of watching you *skate*," she clarifies, subtly skating back, ensuring I don't get any closer.

"Just skate, huh?"

I take another step forward, closing the distance between us again.

"Yeah," she snips, attempting to cut our conversation short.

This chick has some serious defenses up right now, and though they are paper thin, no doubt, they put up a nice facade. Her whole attitude screams 'leave me the fuck alone,' but her eyes scream 'don't ever leave my sight.'

No worries, Princess. I'm not going anywhere.

"What do you like about how I skate?" I ask, prowling across the ice in her direction until I'm right in front of her. I want front row seats when those defenses come down for me.

"I . . . like the way you move."

Just me standing here is overwhelming her and I'm dying to learn why. What could make someone as sweet and innocent looking as her go to the lengths she did just to follow me.

"And how do I move?" I press.

That bleeding thumb slips from her lips, and she licks at the corner of her mouth. My cock instantly raises its head at the sight of her little pink tongue. Even more so as I watch her drop the act and face me.

"Like you control the ice," she says.

I step in closer.

"And that's something you like?" I continue.

I know I'm a good hockey player. I've been complimented on my goal accuracy, my speed, even my ability to defend the net, but I've never been complimented solely for how I skate.

"Yes."

It's cute, the way she tries to sound annoyed, but I'm betting, despite her air of attitude, her feelings reflect my own. That this was a long time coming and all that curiosity we have built up about one another is finally being discovered.

"Why?"

I won't let her hide from me again. She no longer has pillars she can hide behind or crowds she can disappear into. It's just me and her on this ice.

"Because . . ."

"Because *what*, Princess?" I push more.

I'm going to peel back every layer she has until her every inside thought and feeling is known to me.

"Because *I* want to skate like that."

"Why?" I growl.

"Why do you care?" she shoots back, her voice louder, echoing in the vast space.

I ignore her yelling.

"Why, Sydney?" I push again.

"Because I want to be the one they adore! I want my competition to see me as a threat. For *them* to gun for *my* spot, not the other way around. I want to reign supreme and bathe in their defeat. And *then*, when it's all said and done, I want to hear the roar and claps and screams for *me* when I'm crowned the goddamn best. *That's* why!" She shouts, jabbing a finger to my chest, a fire burning in her eyes.

Holy shit, that was hot. That shit gave me goosebumps down to my toes. I knew there had to be a reason for my instant attraction. I mean, yeah, she's pretty, but I can't imagine it'd bode well for either of us if she really were a soft, meek, mild-mannered girl. I wouldn't just corrupt her, I'd *defile* her, ruin her for any that came after me. Hell, I probably will anyway, but at least now I think there's hope this little hellion can withstand it.

"Well, that's interesting, but the ice is not all that I can control. You wanna skate like me? You're gonna have to learn how to submit to the ice before you can wield control over it." I cock a grin at her and wink. "If you want . . . I can *teach you* to submit."

I swipe my thumb across her plush lips, smearing the gloss into a glittery smile of my own making since she's resolved to frown. She jerks her head away and I laugh.

"You look *terrified*," I say.

She scoffs, "You don't scare me."

Her defiant chin jerks up, but the tremble in her voice gives her away.

I chuckle again. "That's a lie, but I'm not talking about me. I mean when you skate. You look terrified." I reach out to stroke over her cheek that has been cleaned of my blood. Oh well, I'll just have to bloody her up again. Maybe this time it'll be her own.

"I'm . . . not scared. I'm concentrating." She swats my hand away. She's like a baby cub who hasn't found her roar yet. Maybe her monster only comes out to play behind a phone screen.

"Concentrating on what?" I ask.

"Not falling, my routine, executing my moves, hitting all my jumps. There's a lot that goes into figure skating. We're not out here flitting about for no reason!" she huffs.

"Woah there. Down, girl." I hold my palms up. "I'm just wondering why you worry about all *that* instead of simply skating. If you just skate—you won't fall. You'll execute all your moves and hit all your jumps. You'll be perfect."

"I *am* skating, and I *don't* need your help. I don't need to *submit* or take your advice or whatever the fuck you're insinuating. It's different. You play hockey, that's not the same. I'm not just going up and down the ice, waving a stick around, and punching people," she chides, waving her hands haphazardly toward the ice.

I throw out my hand, gripping her throat as I wrench her closer, forcing that heat in her stare to simmer down a notch.

"You know," I whisper into her ear, "you're downplaying it *a lot* for someone who's been watching me for months *just* to see me skate. You said you wanted to skate like me; *move* like *me*. Yet, when I give you some ways to achieve that, you insult me. That's not very nice, Sydney. I'm hurt." I lean back, taking in her new expression.

"I-I'm sorry. You're right. I'm getting defensive." She licks her lips. "I do that sometimes."

Another lie.

She didn't give bitchy vibes earlier. I must have hit a nerve, but so has she, and I'm not one to back down from a challenge.

I growl, "No, you don't."

Even after I blocked and threatened her she never reacted to me like this.

She squirms in my hold as she tries and fails to remove my hands from her neck.

"How would you know?" she spits.

"Because I know you. "

She scoffs, "You *really* don't."

"Oh, how quickly we forget," I jeer.

Her glower is adorable. I think I like this side of Sydney.

"That wasn't . . . that's not me," she explains, tripping over her words.

"Oh, but it is. It's probably the most *you*, you've ever been."

The roll of her eyes is fucking beautiful, especially with my hand necklacing her throat.

"You're incorrigible," she huffs, breathless as she gulps in more air that's getting harder and *harder* to come by.

The fact that she still has the energy to spew insults is commendable. I know bigger men who've folded by this point.

"And *you're* a little liar. Guess that's why they say never meet your heroes," I say.

"No, I'm not," she whines, bringing her hands to my wrist in case I decide to squeeze even harder, but she doesn't pull away.

"Oh, yes, you are. One look at you and I can tell you take a lot of shit lying down. But I can give you a *real* reason to take me if you're going to be down there anyway," I tell her, my tone a teasing threat.

Her pupils dilate and her blue nails pinch a little tighter into my skin, but I don't take my focus off her for one second. I wanna see it, those frosted orbs begging me to give her what she *really* deserves. She's not the only observant one among us.

I cant my head to the side.

"I'm willing to bet people look down on you. The way you skate. The way you walk. The way you carry yourself. You're probably used to a certain way of life." I eye her up and down. "Yeah, one look at you and I can tell you were *born* with a silver spoon between those pretty lips. I'm betting that silver spoon cost a pretty penny though, huh? You had to behave, move, and even breathe a certain way just to prove your worthiness of it. I'll bet anything when people turn their noses up at you, you just take it. You probably think it's easier to dish it back out, but only to those you're already convinced you're better than. Those who have nothing to give you in return, who give you their boot to kiss, *probably*, have all of your respect, don't they?" Her mouth drops open, aghast. "Mmm, I'm sure you'd look amazing licking my boots." I bite down on my lower lip just thinking about it. "Maybe you *do* get defensive, but I

KD CURETON

have a feeling when those *other* people turn their noses up at you, you just take it. Obedient Sydney. And now you're wanting to take all that frustration out on me. Am I right?"

I squeeze the sides of her neck a bit and those ice blues betray her. Of course she wants to take her frustrations out on me. I know because I want to take my frustrations out on *her*.

"Respect isn't bought Sydney, it's taken. So cut the shit and be nice to me. You're starting to hurt my *feelings*."

She opens her mouth in protest, but no sound comes out. It's her own lies she's choking on now.

The front she puts on, I've seen it a thousand times and it doesn't typically appeal to me. It's how I knew she had to be different. Silver spoon or not, Sydney works hard. Between figure skating and stalking me I've grown to admire her dedication, but her attitude reeks of superiority.

Her body quakes with shivers.

"Do I make you nervous, Little Stalker Princess?" I ask, stroking my thumb right over her windpipe, flirting with the idea of crushing it with one little push. "Be honest or there'll have to be consequences. You've lied to me at least three times now and I don't like it one bit."

"Consequences?" she rasps.

"Oh yes, liars get punished. And if you can't tell the truth . . . then you don't get to speak." I squeeze tighter, trapping the air in her lungs until I'm sure they're burning. "You're not a liar are you, Sydney? I hope this isn't a pattern of behavior for you. Honesty is *always* the best policy."

She shakes her head . . . Well, she tries to. I loosen my grip, allowing her to suck in a ragged breath.

I raise my brows expectantly, waiting on her to answer my question.

"Words, Sydney. I want your words," I coo.

Her stare hardens, challenging me even in the face of fear.

"No . . ." She clears her throat, sending vibrations through my fingertips. "I'm *not* a liar." Her next answer is louder and more confident. "And, yes, you *do* make me nervous."

My grin is wide with her admission.

"Good fucking girl," I cajole.

126

Her lips curve at the corners and I can't help but to wonder how good she'd be willing to be for me. But, of course, it can never be that simple with her.

"Permission to speak, *Master*?" Her obvious condescension—even as she's still trying to catch her breath—makes me laugh. Though her nickname for me makes my balls draw tight.

"Permission granted, Princess."

Her eyes roll in response, but I suspect its real purpose is to avoid looking at me. I know those panties are fucking soaked for me.

If she's even wearing any.

"Tell me why you're *really* here," she says.

I smile down at her. I'd think it was obvious.

"I'm not done playing with you yet."

CHAPTER NINE

SYDNEY

I FORCE AIR INTO my lungs with deep breaths.

Another.

Another.

I'll pass out if I don't. I wish I could say it's because he's squeezing my throat again but I'm not afforded such grace this time. The warmth of his hand around my neck is sending tingles down my back and goosebumps across my flesh, especially with that grin on his face. His smile is unlike the one on the game posters. It's different from the one he presents to screaming fans, or the one he flashes to the barista who knows his drink order. No, this smile is undeniably real. He's deriving true happiness from my despair.

The balance I thought I had, the stability I once captured on these skates, all but fail me now. I feel unsteady, precarious, with him touching me like this. Like he could take me down with a single breath.

His exhale against my cheek does exactly that, causing my knees to knock and my body to sway.

"Try not to pass out yet," he croons. "The fun is only starting. There'll be plenty of time for breath play later."

He winks, and my legs buckle.

Is this what I've been reduced to? A woman who faints because a cute boy breathed on her?

My fingers cling to his wrist, feeling his chilled skin against my fingertips, assessing his perfectly calm heartbeat. He increases the pressure the tiniest fraction and I do the same, my nails clawing into his flesh, anchoring myself to him. But he still doesn't let me go.

Even in skates, his six-three frame and imposing presence dwarfs me. With his hand wrapped neatly around my throat, my pussy throbs, and I can barely keep it together.

This is a scene plucked directly from my subconscious and all my late-night fantasies. And yet, I'm in such a state of shock I can't reconcile that this isn't fantasy at all, it's reality. That can't be though, because in reality it normally doesn't feel this good to be choked. In reality, I shouldn't want him to squeeze harder. In reality, he could kill me if he really put his strength behind it. And in *this* dimension of delusion, I'll happily let him.

"Where have you been?" he whispers.

It's a soft-spoken question, more to himself than me, but I can't bring myself to answer.

His eyes are un-fucking real, a golden amber that practically glows beneath stage lights. And they're roaming me, breaking me down piece by piece.

I swallow. Feeling bold, I slide my hand down his forearm, my nails dragging. He practically vibrates beneath my touch, his gaze holding mine.

"*Oh*, she has claws. Promise me you'll use them on me later," he coos. I lift my thumb to my mouth on instinct as I consider my options. "What's the matter, Sydney, cat got your tongue?"

If I stay quiet, will the moment disappear?

Will the fantasy bubble pop?

Will he hold up his end of the threat and punish me?

Fuck . . . I've known him for all of an hour, and in that time he's more than demonstrated his affinity, not to mention *ability*, to inflict delicious pain. He obviously can cause bodily harm but he absolutely can cause bodily pleasure if he so chose. There's a softness to him . . . deep . . . deep . . . *deep* inside that, strangely enough, tells me as much as he likes pain, pleasure isn't off the table. It's the dessert at the end of a three-course meal—and I'm ravenous.

My neck still aches from where he bit me back in the locker room. My eyes flutter close, thinking back to how I rubbed my fingers over the indentations of his teeth, and smiled at his parting gift. Now here he is again offering me more memories to take with me when I leave.

"Well, if you're not gonna talk . . ." he trails.

His hand leaves my throat and, for a second, I'm saddened by the removal of his threat. He takes my thumb from my lips, bringing it to his own and sucking it into his mouth. I go limp, words still failing me, because what do you say at a time like this? Thank you? It's the only thing that feels remotely appropriate.

Thank you for letting me have this one thing.

Thank you for not letting my last night here suck.

Thank you for showing me what desire feels like.

Thank you for making me feel . . . *something* these past few months.

I don't thank him though.

Instead, I struggle to hold back a whimper, swallowing it so that it sounds as though I fucking purred. What am I, a cat? I don't purr, I growl.

His mouth is warm and wet, and I can feel the textured buds of his tongue expertly swirling around my digit. He hums his satisfaction while his finger rests on the pulse point at my wrist. The direct line to my naive heart, giving away all my secrets. He eats it the fuck up. Sharp desire slices me to my core and more arousal immediately dampens my panties. It'll soak through if he doesn't stop.

Flattening my free palm to his chest, I push him away, my thumb popping audibly from his lips when he doesn't let up on his sucking.

Even though he's on the ice in regular boots, my push does nothing to move him. Instead, I'm the one forced to slide back, not far, but enough to create some distance.

He chuckles as he licks his lips, giving me a peek at the tongue that just wreaked havoc on all my bodily senses for the *second* time tonight. He's more dangerous up close than he ever seemed from a distance.

"Oh, Sydney, please don't think being in skates will save you from me," he says, casually walking across the ice with no fear of sliding or falling.

"Maybe if you were in skates too, I *would* be more worried, but right now it protects me just fine while I make my escape, thank you." My fingers press against my temples. "I need a minute to think."

My heart hammers in my chest. He is *so* barking up the wrong tree. I don't have time to play out fantasies tonight. I leave tomorrow.

"Listen, Lucien, I have to tell you—" He launches forward, sliding on his shoes. And with no way of stopping, he falls with me to the ice, purposely knocking me to the ground and pinning me in place. Sharp cold laces up my entire backside and I scream. I've done nothing but fall for an entire half hour during my practice, but this *hurts*.

"Now, what was that about escaping me?" he asks, his breath warm as he huffs in my face.

"*Ow!* Lucien! That hurt! Why did you—" I hiss from the cold when he rests his weight on me.

"Did you really think I would let you get away so easily?"

I didn't, actually. My feet just moved on their own accord. There's no way this doesn't end badly for me.

He tuts, gripping my chin and shaking my face.

"Why do you want to run away from me? Aren't you happy to see me?" His voice is melodic when he speaks. Every word a deceivingly sweet serenade. A pathetic love-sick whimper dislodges itself from my throat and he relishes the slip up. "Of course you are. So why are you being this way, huh? We were having fun, weren't we, Princess? I run; you hide. You used to be much better at this game. What happened?" he coos.

Reality came crashing down, that's what. In the virtual world we'd built, this *was* fun. But right now, this is reckless and stupid, and I feel like an idiot for letting it go this far.

I lick my lips, desperately trying to encourage speech.

"I-I shouldn't have messed with you like that," I admit.

"*No,* you shouldn't have." He leans forward, his lips brushing the shell of my ear. "But I'm *so* glad you did." He pulls back slightly, our faces a hair's breadth apart. "It's been years since I've been *this* entertained."

My body softens against him, deflating at his words.

Entertainment. That's what he saw this as. Nothing more. My heart constricts, but I ignore it. That traitorous organ has gotten me in enough trouble.

"It's cold," I stutter, my teeth chattering as I relay the obvious. "You need to get up. Someone could see us."

"You want me to warm you up?" His hard cock grinds into me and the heat he wanted to induce spreads over every surface like wildfire. I'm ablaze with the feeling of him against me like this.

"No, I said—"

His tongue sweeps across his bite mark on my neck, a teasing warmth I wasn't expecting.

My shriek echoes in the arena.

Shit. The noise is wrenched out of me before I can stop it. He feels so big. He's so hard and the aim of his cock against my center was accurate, rubbing directly over my sensitive clit. I've masturbated a lot over these last few months to various fantasies of this, of him, but I never thought in a million years my sweet nightmares would ever come true.

"You sound so pretty when you scream." He caresses his cheek up the side of my face, his breath tickling my lips. Squeezing my eyes closed, I try to calm my pulse, but the absence of one sense only heightens the others. His freshly washed skin permeates between us, something acidic or minty in his scent. I could get drunk off it.

I'm haunted by images of his tattooed back wet with soap suds dripping down the hellish landscape inked into his skin, rolling over the dips and crevices of his muscles. His nuzzling lets me feel his shaven face smooth across mine, our cheeks rubbing against one another like furless animals. I can practically feel my pussy purring. My eyes burst open at the realization that this is *not* helping.

"Oh God, please let me up. Please," I beg.

My hips buck to throw him off, but it's pointless, he's heavier than he looks. I thought my efforts were so I could get away, or maybe it was to get him to grind into me again, who knows, but that's exactly what he does. He grinds his cock between my spread thighs until I'm moaning again.

The heat of my front, a stark contrast to the cold on my back, drives me insane with pain *and* pleasure.

A dark, humorless laugh slips past his full kissable lips. "There's that name again. I always knew one day you'd worship me," he whispers, as though his godliness is a secret only we share.

"It's so cold. Please. Let me go," I cry out.

"I can't do that. Running away is against the rules and when you break the rules . . . you get punished." His hips roll into me once more while soft lips brush against the shell of my ear. Voice low and serious but still that hint of playfulness in his tone that suggests he would be more than happy if I *did* break the rules, if only to *inflict* said punishment.

"What rules? What are you talking about?" I preen, arching my back away from the cold ice as the chill seeps through my clothes. But he splays his long, thick fingers over my abdomen, shoving me back down, forcing my back flat against the ice as he sits up and straddles me. He leaves his hand there, his silent warning that I better not move again. I shiver but work hard to follow his command and stay still.

"To the game, silly. The rules are simple, be a *good* Little Stalker Princess for me. Can you do that?" He smiles wickedly as he strokes his finger with his free hand down from my lips to my chin, to the crevice of my breasts, down my torso, to my belly button, only stopping when he's right above my pubic bone where his . . . *oh my God*. Every nerve ending fires off at the touch of a single finger. I'm doomed.

"What does that *mean*?" I groan, as he lifts my skirt up to my stomach, forcing the exposed bare skin to sit directly on the ice. I don't know what kind of game he's playing, but it sounds so good, so deliciously sinful and too good to be true.

I've been tempted before by other men, hell, even by Bradford, but Lucien isn't like any of them. I want nothing more than to be wrapped around him, pinned beneath him, just as I am now. It's unbearable how badly I want him. But I can't sit here and be teased all night long. I have packing to get done.

He tilts his head, eying me warily.

"It means I finally have something worth playing with, so I need you to be a good toy. No running away and no breaking," he sing-songs.

A toy. He wants me to be his toy? One that doesn't break. A fuck toy more like it, but I have to admit that the sick part of my brain that likes his crazy-eyed demeanor—that demented area that wished for this, prayed for it—is shouting at me to be his shiny new toy.

"You want to play with me?" I breathe, my words choked as I try to get the question out.

The air between us is sexually charged and my breathless words do little to hide my own desire. This is not where I saw this going.

"Abso-*fucking*-lutely, I want to play with you. With your body. Your mind. Your entire fucking nervous system," he says.

A twisted rollercoaster of emotions circles through me before resignation finally settles in. What's one quick rendezvous? I'll be lost like all other toys in the next thirteen hours anyway so . . .

"What do you want to play?" I pant, his heaviness making me breathless.

"A game for keeps. I win, I get to keep you," he says, pulling at one of the ribbons in my hair until it unties.

"You can't keep me," I choke out, trying my hardest to keep the emotion out of my voice.

The ribbon slides between his pinched fingers as he strokes it from tip to end, admiring the length. It takes me too long to notice what he's doing, and by the time I do, it's too late. He snatches both my wrists and holds them above my head, securing the ribbon around them. I hiss a breath when he secures the final knot.

"We'll see about that. Now don't move," he instructs.

He squeezes one of my breasts and I gasp, "Hey, what are you doing?" His eyes flick to mine.

"Taking what I want."

So, he *does* want me, at least for now, and maybe that works for me because *now* is all I have anyway, right? Maybe this is a sign? But is he being serious or is the real game him messing with me?

"You want me?" I ask, somewhat surprised that he'd feel this way.

"So fucking bad."

"But . . . but we can't," I stutter.

"Of course we can. There's nobody here to stop me, and even if there was, there's no way I'd ever miss the opportunity to touch you like this." He traces the edges of my wrists, dragging down my arm to my elbow then following up to the curve of my neckline before settling below the swell of my breasts. I yearn to moan, to give in to the want, but I remain vigilant.

"We shouldn't."

"We absolutely should." He grabs my breast again and I have to clear my throat to keep the moans at bay.

"I *can't*."

"There's no such thing as *can't*. Only *won't*," he challenges.

He arches a brow, waiting on me to make the clarification. "Not in this case." Normally I'd agree with him. *Can't* is not a common word in my vocabulary but in *this* instance, I can't. I'll be in even more trouble with my dad if we're caught.

Instead, I say, "Someone could see."

"And I bet that makes you wet just thinking about it," he taunts.

Fuck, he's good. Even strung by my own hair ribbon and laid flat against a slab of ice, he has me more aroused than I've ever been. I'm burning with lust, the freezing of my back barely registering.

"We could get in trouble," I insist.

The corner of his mouth tilts in a devious smirk.

"I'm already in trouble, remember?"

He has a point. The same can be said for me. I'm already in trouble. I'm already being forced to leave my dream school, to leave *him*. I'm already being punished. I open my mouth to protest, but nothing comes out. I'm out of excuses and he knows it.

"Play the fucking game, Sydney," he urges.

I narrow my eyes.

"What's my reward if I say yes?" I run my nose up the side of his cheek, stopping at the shell of his ear. "What do I get if I win?"

He seems taken aback, like it should be obvious what I get out of this, but he has no clue what I really want.

More time.

"Orgasms," he says with a smirk. "Lots and lots of orgasms. I'm going to make you come in ways you didn't even know you could, and I'm going to hear you scream every time I do. It will be so painful but so, *so* worth it. How does that sound, Princess?"

I turn to look at him again, the rest of the world falling away when our eyes connect. It *sounds* too good to be true, but it's more than I'd expected when I came here. I nod, too fixated on his promises of orgasms and the tingle between my legs to do much else.

"That's my girl. Keep still," he warns, but I'm too hung up on the words '*my girl*' to heed it.

"Why?" I ask.

Why me?

"Because I need you to be still for this next part," he answers, avoiding my deeper meaning and distracting me by thumbing my nipple back and forth through the costume material. It hardens with the additional stimulation to the point of pain. They were already stiff from the cold, but now they're sharp points cutting through the fabric.

"No, why are you doing *this*?" I press.

Lucien Morrow is wanted and adored by many, but as much as I'm relishing this stolen moment with him, I can't help but feel somewhat tricked. Not by him exactly, but by the universe. Why give me the object of all my desires today, when no matter how bad I want it, it will be stripped from me by sunrise tomorrow? It's cruel and unusual punishment to be teased like this.

"Because. I am as obsessed with you as you are with me." His freakishly golden eyes stare into me, demanding focus and fealty. They say 'take what I'm giving you or suffer the consequences.' His pelvis grinds into me, showcasing his point and, despite the cold, I melt into him, giving him all that's left of me. The version of me that'll die right alongside this forgotten memory.

He grinds into me again and again and *again;* growing harder every second. Maintaining eye contact is becoming difficult, but I can't look away. I want to dream of these eyes, even when years have passed, and I'm stuck living a life I never wanted. I want to remember the time I *almost* had Lucien Morrow, even if it means he moves on the second I'm gone. His obsession doesn't rival mine. I'll be forgotten the moment he realizes I was no one special, but right now, he's mine.

"You—don't even—know me," I moan as my head lolls back and his hand draws closer to my pussy, smoothing down my torso to between my thighs.

"Sure, I do. You're my Little Stalker."

I growl.

"I *didn't* stalk you."

He starts rubbing slow, deliberate circles over my clit. All four fingers are meshed flat and firm over the swollen bud through my costume. I try to bring my legs up, to alleviate the discomfort, but he stops me, his harsh grip on my thighs, ensuring they remain open and exposed to him.

"Yeah, we're going to have to work on that. Don't follow dangerous people, Sydney." He circles harder and my back pushes against his hold to arch. My legs spread wider. "You never know, unassuming prey can easily become the predator."

My lust-filled eyes still manage to glare at him.

"I *didn't* prey on you. I only wanted to see you," I moan, heat spreading up my middle as his fingers massage my clit. There's simultaneously too much separation and not enough as the two ridiculously thin scraps of fabric between my pussy and his hand sweep over my pulsing core with agonizing vigor.

"I would have chalked it up to morbid curiosity, Sydney, honest to God, but you see . . ."—my pussy throbs against his touch—". . . you've been watching me for months, even outside of this arena." His fingers slide against the outer edge of the dress, and I clench in anticipation, desperately wanting him closer and craving his fingers to be inside. "You figured out my schedule." He inches closer. "Followed me around campus." Closer still. "Watched from far-away places." His thumb slides over my slit through the fabric. I want to rip this thing off and bare myself before him on this ice if it means he'll touch me *there*. "And I'm pretty sure you skipped your competition to come to *my* game instead."

That's technically not true. I didn't skip it. I was kicked off the team right before my performance, but I don't bother telling him that now. Not when he's rubbing my pussy and staring at me like that.

"If that's not stalking . . ."

He's not wrong. My obsession with him has gotten a *bit* out of hand, but I'd hardly classify myself as a stalker. I'm . . . a consistent voyeur. But I'm *not* a stalker.

His pressure on my clit doesn't let up and he increases his speed. I writhe beneath his hold as my orgasm draws nearer, the movement reminding me that I'm pressed against ice.

"I-I couldn't help it. I wanted to learn more about you." A violent shudder racks my body when he licks a trail of my salty skin from my chest to my chin. I'm not half as disgusted as I was when he licked my face. In fact, I find it hot as hell. Especially when he rubs my pussy harder, increasing the friction.

His fingers roll over my clit through the fabric and I crave closer contact.

"Hmm, what did you expect to learn?" He licks his lips. Watching, waiting for that moment I break apart under his touch.

It's not enough, but my body is reacting anyway.

"I d-don't know. I-I just thought you were someone worth knowing." My teeth chatter as the shivers become uncontrollable. My whole body is shaking from the biting cold of the ice and the incumbent orgasm he's soliciting.

He palms the bulge growing beneath his sweats, switching to his thumb to press against my clit that he's teasing while rubbing himself. I've soaked through the costume, but I only grow wetter when he pinches the sensitive bud between his thumb and index finger.

I whimper.

"And what do you think about me now, Princess?" he muses, moving his hands from his cock to lean forward again and hold my ribbon restraints as I shake.

"I *think* you're insane," I answer.

Certifiably.

"You're not wrong," he growls in my ear, right before he nips at my lobe, sending a pulsing signal so strong to my pussy I practically come on the spot.

More. I need more.

"*More.* Please," I beg.

"You like this, don't you?" he croons.

"Yes," I moan breathlessly, unable to control myself. My core tightens, my clit aching and throbbing. I'm stimulated all over.

"Oh shit, I'm going to come," I breathe.

"Already? But we were just getting to know one another." His expression is teasing as he continues his ministrations, but he doesn't change his pace.

I'm just as disappointed as he is, but I can't hold back anymore. It's been too long since I've had any kind of proper attention down there.

"I can't help it," I whine. "It feels too good— Don't stop— *Please* don't stop."

A wicked grin emerges on his lips and my pussy contracts in anticipation.

"Ahh, yes . . . yes. *Please* don't stop. Please. Please," I plead.

"I wouldn't dream of it, Princess. Now push your legs back . . . yeah, just like that. Wider. I want you nice and spread for me . . . yeah. Good fucking girl. Now come for me. Come on my hand like a good little toy." I couldn't be happier to follow his instructions.

I do *exactly* as he says, my pussy clenching at the idea of being used for nothing more than his pleasure. "Oh yes . . . yes . . . mmhmm, right there. Right. *There.*"

He leans over me again, deep enough that his head is right by my chest. His soft hair rubs against my neck as I lift, and my back bows to come harder than I ever have before. But when he bites my nipple, intensifying my climax to a new level I've never experienced, I lose it entirely.

Blood-curdling screams rip through my throat, echoing through the arena. My orgasm hits that much harder, elongating enough to make me weep and cry out his name.

"Lucien! Oh my god, yes! Lucien— Fuck, *please!*" I chant.

"That's it, Princess, let me hear you fucking scream." My body trembles from the force of my orgasm and I whimper at his praises. I've whispered his name countless times when alone in my room, but screaming it with him as my audience has never felt better.

"So beautiful," he moans against my chest, peppering kisses along the swell of my breasts. "Imagine what I could do with your clothes off."

Lucien and me? Naked?

"Yes," I pant, nodding without question.

I'm willing to do whatever, *be* whatever he needs me to be—for the next thirteen hours. That was nothing like what I'd been able to achieve on my own. I take my masturbation sessions seriously, but what we just did? I let out a breath. I'll do anything this man says if it means finding out what new heights he can conjure. I may have lost everything, but for now I'm going to focus on everything this game of his can offer.

@BladeSpinner
Online

What do ... want

In life?

Seen

WTF! No...

Haven't decided yet.

CHAPTER TEN

LUCIEN

AS SHE DESCENDS FROM her orgasm, I rest the flat of my face against her soft tits. They feel like squishy marshmallows against my skin, sticky and warm. The ice is more welcoming than hurting now that she's worked up a sweat. It cools my skin and tempers the urge to take more than I should right now.

I keep our bodies pressed to one another as we lay over center ice, our legs tangled, and my arm wrapped possessively over her.

She doesn't move or even complain.

Her heart is beating fast, thrumming against my cheek, and the rise and fall of her chest moves me to the rhythm of her exhales, as if we're of one body. I feel for my own heart, sliding my hand up her thigh, over her torso and to my chest, but it's beating a lot slower. My face scrunches. I want us to be in sync.

I suppose I can't expect to be as winded as my Little Stalker Princess here. I've barely done anything to work up a sweat. Long shifts in a contact sport like hockey will do that to you. I'll have to work on her stamina, but for now I'm going to need a little more patience.

"That was . . . *amazing*. Thank you." Sydney pants her appreciation like a sated puppy.

I pop my head up from her chest, staring down at her flushed complexion and lust-filled eyes. *Oh man,* that patience is thinning quickly. She *thanked* me and the appreciation shown in her eyes is enough to incite round two. Yeah, if we don't leave right the fuck now, I'm going to say fuck patience and have all my fun right here on this ice. I hop up and stand before her, looking down at my masterpiece. She doesn't get up right away, instead taking a moment to catch her breath. I take full advantage. Pulling out my phone, I snap a quick picture before helping her up and tucking my phone back in my pocket. I'm going to mark this moment as the day I caught my princess.

"Wait, did you just take a picture?" she asks, as she holds her bound wrists out toward me.

"Yes, I did," I answer, untying her ribbon restraint.

"What for? Delete it!" she gripes.

I hover my hand over the final knot, waiting before I pull it free. Bending my head down, I look her right in the eyes. "This way I'll never forget what you look like . . ." I drop my voice to a whisper, then tack on, "after you come for me."

I pull the final knot and her hands slip free. She wastes no time lunging for my phone, but she only manages to grab my very hard dick.

I grunt in satisfaction, and she panics, trying to pull her hand away, but I'm faster. I palm my hand right over hers.

"You wanna play with it?" I taunt, squeezing our fingers over my thickening erection, drawing out the discomfort and relishing in the pain of her grip over my cock.

"Oh my . . ." she gasps.

But her fingers remain pressed to my hard-on even when my hold loosens. She doesn't notice that I'm no longer controlling her movements when she squeezes again. I groan when her eyes fall to my mouth as I bite my lower lip. She gasps again when I move her hand down my length. Her eyes flick to where our hands are then back up. It's a quick glance, but it's enough.

I lean in closer, watching the sweat bead against her forehead and closer still to feel her breath skitter over my lips.

"If you're really good, I'll let you."

I keep my voice low, the instinctual urge to capture those lips between my teeth a strong presence I hadn't anticipated. I pull back from her and wink. Her throat bobs. *Well, would you look at that? She's considering it.*

"I— Uh— It's so . . . big." She looks at me wide-eyed, slightly panicked that she's admitted it aloud. A-fucking-dorable. There's an innocence in her timbre that makes my cock jump against her hand. She jerks back, frightened by the movement, but I grab her hand and put it back. I need her to feel the effect she has on me. I don't want there to be a doubt in her mind that I want her. Or that I won't succeed in making her mine.

"This is what you do to me." My cock presses through the thick cotton sweats against her palm. "And you're going to take all eight inches like a good fucking toy." Her lips part on a whimper. "By the end of the night, you're going to thank me properly and you're going to give me all those beautiful screams when I destroy you with it." I can't help but to giggle in excitement. "It's going to be so *fun!*"

I let her snatch her hand away this time and she promptly slips her thumb back between her teeth as she closes her eyes, attempting to bite back either a snarky remark or a moan. Neither is a deterrent. When they open again, she's a little calmer but much more *curious* looking. It's the curiosity that draws me closer to her.

She shakes her head, releasing her thumb.

"Are you like this all the time?" she asks. Though her exasperation doesn't go unnoticed, there's a blush and tentative smile decorating her face.

"Depends. What am I like, Princess?"

She raises her hand between us as she ticks off her list.

"So impulsive and direct . . . filthy and disgusting . . . dangerous and scary—"

"Oh, Princess, stop it. You're going to make me blush," I say, giving her my best fuck-boy smile.

"How charming," she deadpans.

"What can I say, it's one of my better qualities."

I give her another wink. I can be *very* charming.

"Oh, I bet the ladies just *love* you," she says. I know she's making another dig at me, but there's an undercurrent of jealousy in her tone that I love. It drives me to reassure my plaything that I don't do this with everyone, that she is *different* from all the others.

"Eh, I'm on most girl's no-fly list. I'm not exactly Prince Charming, despite my winning personality," I grin.

"Gee, you don't say. Can't imagine why." Her arms fold and she feigns an air of nonchalance, but her shoulders sag in relief and her stare is less pensive. Winning personality or not, she's as drawn to me as I am to her and that just makes her that much more worth keeping.

That's right, Princess, lay your claim on me.

"I don't always play so nicely with others . . . but I'll play with you. I can't promise I'll be nice, but it'll at least feel good," I say.

That gets a laugh out of her. "Oh my gosh, you really are something."

"As long as I'm something you'll let inside you, that's just fine with me," I answer.

Again, she rolls her eyes, but it doesn't have the desired effect on me. It only makes me think how they'll roll when her pussy's stuffed full of my cock.

"So, what? You scare me, lick me, bite me, and follow me here all because you want to *play*?" She arches a sculpted brow. "And by 'play' you mean you want to fuck me? Do I have that right?"

"No." Her face falls in obvious disappointment. "I had already decided when I caught whoever was stalking me that I was going to fuck them. All the stuff before was just foreplay." I tongue my lower lip, grinning when her eyes trail from my eyes to my mouth.

"Foreplay?" She scoffs a laugh. "Seriously? You thought what we were doing before was *foreplay*?"

I cock my head, letting my hair swoop from my face.

"Wasn't it though?" I goad.

"No."

"No?" I repeat. Pretty sure she was having the time of her life when she was provoking me with her messages.

She shifts her weight between feet, struggling to settle back into her confident stance from before.

"I mean . . . not at first. It was—it's not something I can easily explain," she says.

"Then don't," I shrug.

She scoffs again, unable or unwilling to accept this for what it is.

"So, you thought 'someone' was stalking you and your first thought was to fuck them?"

"Well, fuck them or kill them, but no worries. I decided in the locker room I wouldn't kill you, so we're all good on that front," I say.

Her face drains of color but there's not a thing for her to worry about. She's something *special*. I would much rather keep her than kill her.

Her eyes widen.

"Jesus Christ, you're being serious, aren't you?" She seems a little shocked for someone who spent her waking hours stalking me.

"What? You stalker types are *dangerous*. I was being cautious," I say.

Her cute fists ball at her sides and she stomps her foot petulantly, her skates scuffing the ice.

"For the last time, I'm *not* a stalker. And you couldn't have been that cautious if your only two options were murder or fucking."

I'd be all ears if she had a third option, but something tells me she doesn't.

I shove my hands in my pockets.

"I'm getting the feeling that you're getting really hung up on the killing thing . . ." I tilt my head as if the better angle will help me decide her point. "Or is it the fucking thing that's got you all hot and bothered?"

"I'm not hot and bothered," she says, even as a blush creeps across her cheeks.

Liar, liar, pants on fire.

"So, you *don't* want to fuck me?" I clarify. "Because I'm pretty sure you just came in your leotard from me rubbing your pussy through your clothes."

Pink hues spread all the way to her chest like wildfire. She shouldn't bother lying to me. Those fucking lies she tells won't save her anymore.

"Oh, *wow*. You're a cocky fucker, aren't you?" she teases.

"No, I'm a *painful* fucker. I like to incorporate pain when I fuck. But you *like* pain, don't you, Princess?"

I really need her answer to be yes or it's going to make playing with her next to impossible. I'd even settle for her having a high pain tolerance.

I'm far from gentle, a fact my little stalker is very aware of at this point, and she sought me out anyway.

"What makes you say that?" she breathes.

Aww, she's playing coy, how cute.

"Aside from the fact you came harder when I bit your nipples?" My finger brushes over her nipple, reminding her how good it felt. She shivers from the reminder, doing little to shake me off or prevent me from doing it again.

"Yes," she hisses. "Aside from that. That doesn't count. I was already . . . you know . . . in the middle of it." It's even cuter when she tries to deny it. She turns her body to skate away, but it only affords me the view of her ass, reddened from the time spent pressed against the ice.

"I can show you better than I can tell you," I muse.

"Oh yeah?" She whips back around. "And what if I don't want to play with you?"

I know she does, but insane or not, I'm a pretty nice guy. I don't mind giving her an out if she needs one.

I walk over to her.

"Tell me you don't, and I'll stop. *But* I find it kind of hard to believe that you'd spend months stalking me to watch me skate, learn more about me, let me rub your pussy until you come and then turn me down the second I want to sit you on my cock and fuck you until you're screaming my name. Just seems like a wasted opportunity if you ask me." I grin, quickly becoming a fan of how her body reacts to my dirty talk.

Her mouth falls open and I withhold the desire to fill it. She tracks my eyes on her mouth and clamps it shut. I still ache to fill her mouth and give her something she can swallow. I can practically feel the roll of her throat around me.

"It's not that, it's just . . ." Her eyes turn away from me and it's the first time since we've met that she's looked apprehensive, not scared per se, but worried.

"How about this? I'll make you a deal," I offer, folding my arms and widening my stance.

"A deal?" She perks at the option.

"It's more of a bet," I clarify.

Her eyes light up and I know I've got her in my clutches. My Little Stalker Princess *loves* a challenge.

"Okay, what's the bet?" she asks, a giddiness to her voice.

"Pick any game, right now, to compete against me. If you win, I'll leave you alone. But if I win, you come out to play. The *real* you. @BladeSpinner." Her face turns ashen at the mention of her EZgram username, but she schools her features.

"Any game?" she questions.

I nod.

"Of *my* choosing?" she presses.

"Yep," I say.

"My rules?"

I thrust my hands in my pockets to keep them from reaching for her.

"As long as they're fair, yes."

She beams, appearing happy with the conditions we've set.

"Fine. I challenge you to a race," she says.

I cock a brow at her. "You sure you wanna do that?"

I'm all for winning, but I always play fair. There's no way she's beating me in a race, on skates or otherwise.

She holds up a manicured finger. "I'm not done. I challenge you to a race *backward*. Three laps around the rink. I win, you let me go home and we never speak of this night again."

Her eyes gleam with pride, confident her victory will be easily obtained.

And that right there is exactly why she *won't* win. She's made the stakes too high—now I can't lose.

I walk back to the rink's edge, grabbing my skates out of my gear bag, and put them on only to return and see her face set into one of extreme determination. Her corded braid spills down her back as she rights herself, leaning into a stretch and rolling her ankles.

Is she really that set on beating me? Even if she *does* manage to win this race, she's still not getting away from me.

Her ice blue eyes are focused as she lines up at the starting line. She shakes her arms out and rolls her neck as she gets into position. That competitive look in her eyes both turns me on and pisses me off. She *wants* to win. She wants to pretend we never met and what? Go back to being anonymous? That's not happening, Princess.

"Remember, three laps. First person to cross *this* line wins," she points at the ice where she's created a makeshift line between the debris of the boombox she destroyed earlier and her bag.

Ugh so fucking cute.

"Hey, no hard feelings, okay?" I goad.

I line up beside her and grin, my mind already made up—I'm going to crush her.

She rolls her eyes and sets the timer on her phone. In five seconds, our fate will be determined.

Ding!

And then we're off.

Eat my dust, Little Stalker Princess.

"I want a rematch!" Sydney yells at my back as I retreat.

"Nope, all's fair in love and war, baby."

I smirk. There was no way I was going to lose. I *needed* to win this. She's not just going to walk away from me.

"How the hell are you so fast?" she pants, her chest bulging as she strains to catch her breath.

"Practice. Years and years of practice," I answer.

My time on the ice predates my hockey career, back when life wasn't so dark and brilliant color still existed. When there was laughter and warmth present on cold nights and frozen lakes.

"Best two out of three," she huffs.

"No." I plop against the bench seat and casually lean back, my arm propped against the benches behind me.

Truth is, she almost had me at the end. The only reason she lost is because she's easily rattled, and I wasn't above using that to my advantage. If I give her another chance now, she might beat me.

"A deal's a deal." I remind her, settling further in my seat.

She sighs, a bit peeved, but not wholly disappointed when her arms fold in on themselves again. It eases my own frustrations.

"Fine. How do you want to do this?" she asks.

"Well, for starters, I want to take you to a party," I say.

Her brow arches.

"A party?" Her arms unfold as she stands on the edge of the rink.

"Yes. A party," I confirm.

I start removing my skates and toss them back in my bag, officially solidifying my win.

"That was not what I was expecting you to say." Her shoulders slump. She grabs her skate guards off the ledge and makes her way over to me, though she keeps a strange amount of distance between us as she unlaces her own skates and takes a seat beside me.

I'm glad I decided to attend the party first. This girl has got to learn to relax. Did she really think I would go in straight for the kill? I suppose I did come off kind of strong, but I want to savor every second I spend with her by my side. I'll be taking my sweet, *sweet* time with my stalker princess.

"What'd you expect me to say? 'On your knees, let me fuck your throat until you can't breathe?'" I taunt.

She sets her skates to the side.

"I mean, yeah."

Jesus fucking Christ, this girl.

I quirk an amused brow while I adjust my cock in my pants and she quickly backtracks her statement, realizing what she's said.

"I meant, yeah, that's what I expected your lewd response to be," she corrects. "But, um, okay, yeah, I'd like to go to a party with you. What time should I meet you?"

Scooting in closer, I lean over, eradicating that space she's trying to keep between us.

"Look, I'm not always a demon, but if I'm being completely honest, meeting you couldn't have come at a better time. Today didn't exactly go as planned for me, but if you're my consolation prize then I'll happily play this game with you. So, let's go, before I change my mind and we go with the throat fucking instead."

CHAPTER ELEVEN

SYDNEY

"WAIT, WAIT, WAIT, WE'RE going to the party right *now*?" I ask, expecting the party to be a little later in the evening, *not* at this exact moment. I thought I'd have a moment of reprieve, but he seems set on not letting me leave his sight.

I scramble to gather the rest of my stuff off the nearby bleachers as he starts heading out, telling me we have to get going.

His large duffle bag is already slung over his shoulder as he waits for me by the exit.

"Hurry up, slow poke. Old Man Bernie likes to lock up early on Fridays."

I pause, a little surprised to learn Lucien's so well acquainted with the janitor. I can't blame him, Bernie is a great guy, and I enjoy our chats about his granddaughters.

"Oh, really?"

"Yeah," Lucien says. "Gives me shit for it all the time. It makes him late getting home to the missus." He mimics Bernard's deep southern drawl with impeccable ease.

"He's married?" I sputter, turning to face him after flicking the overhead lights and leaving the copy of the key I made after the fiasco with Tiffany, on top of the emergency fire box.

"Thirty years," answers Lucien, tapping his stick ardently against the wet mat in front of the push doors.

Guilt worms its way inside, unexpected and unbidden. I've stayed well past my allotted time, practicing until my feet bled or I threw up from over exertion. I'd never even thought to speak to the man until I started waiting for Lucien after his practices and yet he's been enduring my crazy schedule for almost a year. He never said anything either. Or if he did, I hadn't noticed—or I hadn't cared.

"Let's move it or lose it, we have a party to get to." Lucien waves in a circle, like a police officer ushering traffic.

Typically, I'd find his impatience annoying, like I do Bradford whenever he's in a hurry, finger snapping at me to pick up the pace. But I find Lucien's rush to whisk me away, extremely . . . sweet.

There's nothing sweet about him. The guy bit you. He's all spice and nothing nice. All bitter notes and too rich flavors.

I fight a wide grin that threatens to split my entire face open if I dare let it loose. The lingering guilt sheds away at the excited expression on Lucien's face, or at least I'm sure it's what he constitutes as excitement. He's not brooding or staring into space, he's vibrant and colorful even while swathed in all black.

"Aren't you going home to change first?" I ask, assessing him from head to toe with an arched brow.

He smirks, slamming the push bar with a brute force that has the shrill metal on metal noise thundering through the rafters. The door swings out into the vestibule in a wide arch, slamming into the adjacent wall. It's not an answer, but a clear demand to stop stalling and forge ahead. My legs shake and I trip on air, but I ultimately listen. Every willing step toward him is slow moving and sluggish, but every bit deliberate.

Running would be unbecoming.

Skipping would feel childish.

Step by step is the only way to approach a man like Lucien.

Lucien's eyes track me the whole way as he stands there waiting, propping open the door for me with a single steady arm. My eyes catch on the tattoos stretching across his bicep and my steps toward him slow even more.

"Go on, you were saying," he practically purrs as I reluctantly pass under his arm placed too low on the door frame.

"Nothing," I mumble, ducking beneath his thick arm.

"We're going to *your* house to change," he answers and my head whips to face him.

"What?"

"C'mon, I'll drive." He tips his head to the parking lot. "I'm parked up the hill."

"I—" This doesn't seem like a good idea. "I like to walk." I try to invoke a smile in my voice, but it doesn't work.

There's no way I can let him into my apartment. He'll figure it out, and then what? It'll be over.

"It'll be faster if I drive," he presses, his voice echoing as we walk through the vestibule.

My face must reflect my apprehension because he says, "Don't give me that look, I'm a great driver."

If only *that* were my primary concern.

I catch a glimpse of him out of the corner of my eye, and his teasing smile is infectious. I wish I could return it. To pretend this was our first day and not our last.

But the game of pretend isn't as appealing when playing against him.

"I really shouldn't," I say.

I feel his eyes on me like physical fingers. They grab, and pull, luring me to face him but for once, I resist the draw.

"And why's that?" he questions.

His tone of voice all but confirms my suspicions, he's all darkness and viscidity. And his question, sounds nothing like a lighthearted inquiry. It *sounds* like a dark omen, a premonition of what's to come should I choose not to heed it.

"Because . . . you're a stranger."

It's not my best excuse, but it's the best I can come up with at the moment. He *is* a stranger, we know very little about one another, and outside of what occurred tonight, that isn't changing anytime soon.

I sense it when Lucien stops walking. The ruffle of his bag stops swishing, his hockey stick stops making that clacking noise every time it hits the top of his skates hanging loose around his straps. But mostly, I sense the inevitable gravitation that keeps me wanting to stay in his orbit.

My feet stop moving. "Luc—"

In a flash, he's in front of me, backing me into the wall.

"Say that again," Lucien grits. "I don't think I heard you, Princess."

I lick my lips, rapidly blinking and wondering how and why he puts me so out of sorts. He's just a guy. *One* guy. What makes him so different from all the others? Besides the obvious, I can't understand why I lose my shit around him. Only him.

My mind blanks as my mouth goes dry.

"I— Y-You're a stranger," I rasp. The words taste funny, like a live battery on my tongue. It shocks me.

"That's funny . . ."

I tighten my hold on my bag, hoping it can distract me from the intoxicating scent wafting off him. Like it can distract from the throbbing between my legs and the tension in my belly.

"Stranger danger didn't seem to concern you too much when I was making you come." His lips are inches from mine.

I swallow roughly, locking my tongue behind my teeth to prevent myself from licking my lips . . . or his.

My eyes dart to the pouty lips attached to his face that appear softer than they have any right to be. I can barely see them past my nose, he's *that* close, but then they fly to his eyes when I realize what I'm doing: leaning in. It's fractional, but it's movement nonetheless and I have to stop it. My left hand rises between us, resting against his chest but no pressure at all is being applied.

"I . . ."

Yeah, I don't have a rebuttal for that one. That was reckless. I snap my mouth closed and try to will moisture into my dry mouth.

"Nor when you were stalking me," he continues, his hair brushing against my forehead as he leans in.

Point taken.

I try to clear my throat but it sounds more like a dry cough.

"H-haven't you ever heard of personal space?" I ask in a pointless act of defiance but it lacks its usual weight.

Lucien chuckles.

"If it's bothering you, then . . ." His fingers blaze a trail along my flesh, tracing my collarbone, then my shoulder, then elbow, "maybe you should let me go."

"Wha—?" My brows pinch.

Lucien's fingers pluck at my wrists. Sure enough, my fist is balled into his shirt, bunching and pulling the fabric tighter over his heated skin. He couldn't have pulled away if he wanted to.

"Sorry," I breathe, releasing my grip.

He huffs another laugh, shaking his hair loose before taking a step back.

"I'm not." His lips stretch into a wide grin. "So come along, Princess, before I bring you to the party in your cum-soaked leotard," he threatens, winking, then moving along towards the exit I should've taken all those months ago.

Because then, he'd still be a stranger.

CHAPTER TWELVE

SYDNEY

M Y FEET IMMEDIATELY START moving. The last thing I need is to remain in this outfit a second longer than necessary. If I'm being honest, it's already been too long, but I suppose receiving an orgasm from my heart's obsession is as good a reason as any.

Part of me wants to remind Lucien that I'm not a stalker. I just have an . . . obsessive personality. When I want something, I completely dedicate myself to doing everything I need to do to get it.

Ambition is a dangerous thing and it seems mine was no exception. It was dangerous to want Lucien from the beginning—and I did it anyway.

My steps mimic Lucien's as I linger behind, watching his back recede like I've seen countless times before, his hoodie slung casually over his shoulder on his hooked index finger.

He's here. Right in front of me. But now that he is, I don't know what to do. We are so far out of the realm of possibilities of what I thought might come out of watching a single hockey game in my entire college career. It's no shock to me that Lucien resides in the realm of impossibilities.

I know I'm setting myself up to be hurt if I keep dragging this out and I don't see Dad allowing me to come back here even if we did start up a relationship.

As if conjured by thought alone, my phone buzzes.

Dad 9:14 PM

> Don't forget the movers will arrive there a few
> hours earlier than myself. I'll be there around 11

to pick you up, but they will be there at 7. I'll be
checking in, so keep your phone on you.

Great. I have even *less* time to spend with Lucien if I expect to be up on time to deal with the movers, and I still have to finish packing. Luckily, I managed to bribe my driver to get started on my behalf, but no way he got it all done before Dad noticed his absence.

I lean my head back, trying my damnedest to brainstorm a decent solution to this cluster-fuck of a night. Unlike the movies I've watched and the books I've read, the answer doesn't fall from the sky.

We make our way up the outer steps of the arena, climbing toward the upper parking lot.

"You couldn't have parked any closer?" I groan.

"Nope. I had a little stalker to catch." Lucien's grin can be heard for miles, his satisfaction for 'catching me' a foghorn in the quiet night.

"I'm not a stalker," I grumble.

That aside, his logic makes sense. Had we exited through the east doors where the hockey rink is, his car *would* have been closer. This way, our trek is longer and, while under normal circumstances that would make me happy, I struggle to find the right words to fill the additional time.

So many of our chats were through texts or, until twenty minutes ago, with his hands between my legs.

I don't know how to talk to him like . . . *this.*

Ding!

I mentally punch the air at my social awkwardness around this man.

Ding!

I'm never awkward.

Ding!

Being social is my whole thing, my entire identity, I should be able to do this with my eyes closed.

So why can't I talk to *him?*

Dried blood lining the cuticle of my thumb stares back at me as I bring it to my lips, groaning at my inability to stop. This is seeming more and more like a bad idea.

Ding!

"*What* is that noise?" Lucien asks, finally turning around, and catching me just as I'm about to nibble my anxiety away.

"It's nothing," I rush out, quickly thrusting my hand behind my back. *"Disgusting habit."*

A habit I'll need to get under control when I'm back around my dad. He'll hate what I've done to my hands. *Men don't like a woman who looks more butch than beguiling.*

"Okay." Lucien drags out the word. "So, you're not gonna tell me."

If he were the sighing type, I'm sure he'd be doing it right about now.

I toss him a tight-lipped smile, but he doesn't react the way I expect. He just furrows his brows, but he doesn't push any further. "Alright then. I can take a hint. I'll leave it alone."

That feels unlike him, strange in a way, but I'm grateful for the consideration, until I catch him smirking, muttering beneath his breath, "For now."

I could share this one tidbit of information. It wouldn't matter if he knew or change anything if I told him that they're the telltale dings of my schedule being packed with galas, dinners, and lunch dates. But I keep quiet, wanting to reside a little longer in this realm of impossibility with him.

My phone calendar continues to fill with rampant beeps and chimes, as I receive invite after invite now that the word is out that I'm coming back home.

Where I belong.

Those words replay on a sad loop as we lug our bags in silence, reaching the top of the outdoor steps without another word uttered between us. And though I won't say as much to him, I *am* grateful for the ride he's offered.

Storing everything at the arena is a luxury I no longer possess. Tonight, it all goes home with me, and the carriage that awaits, will make it that much easier to walk away. For good.

"That's a lot of stuff you got there," Lucien notes, proving his superior conversation skills.

As psycho as his behavior has been, I've noticed he's a very observant psycho.

"Um, yeah, I needed to clean out some stuff," I say.

I don't know if it'll change anything for him if I tell him that tonight's my last night here. It may change nothing, but it could also change everything. He might decide there's no point in spending any time on a person who's leaving tomorrow. *He* might be the one to walk away from *me* once he realizes I taunted him only to disappear when it was all said and done. I don't see him taking that lightly or forgiving me. I can't afford for that to happen, not when I've already decided that I want this. I want him.

"Why do *you* have so much stuff?" I ask, nodding toward his bag.

He lifts his shoulder in a half-shrug.

"You heard Coach, they're thinking about suspending me," he says, trudging up the path at double my pace. To him it's like we're taking a nice stroll through a park.

"And that doesn't bother you?" I huff.

"Never said it didn't."

"So, you're a quitter then?" I question.

It gutted me when my coach told me I was off the team. I'm still reeling from the heartbreak even now. I don't know how Lucien can stand it. He seems so at peace and for some reason that fucking irritates me.

Lucien's steps slow, but he doesn't turn to acknowledge me yet.

"You've got it all wrong, Princess; it *bothers* me a fuck-ton, but it bothered me even more to hear that piece of shit talk about matters he had no business talking about. He won't be saying anything for a *very* long time now. I call that justice." He stops so abruptly I almost barrel into him, my feet stuttering before regaining balance. Spinning on his heels, he levels me with a glare, standing so close his breaths skitter over my lips. "And before you ask . . . I don't regret a single goddamn thing."

I scoff and adjust one of the straps on my shoulder. "Don't worry, I know enough now to not think better of you," I snip as fury builds in my belly.

He straightens.

"Judgy much?" He quirks a brow at me.

"Arrogant much?" I shoot back.

The other brow joins the first as Lucien asks, "And what makes me arrogant?"

"Thinking you were above the consequences of your actions, that you were above the rules. There were better ways to handle that situation. Smarter decisions could have been made. You didn't have to start a fight or risk your career. You're supposed to be getting drafted soon," I huff. "It was arrogant of you to think they'd keep bailing you out of trouble."

Lucien shakes his dark locks.

"Where is this coming from?"

"Hurting people isn't the answer to your problems!"

I'm no longer sure we're talking about him anymore, as a matter of fact I know we aren't, but I can't seem to shut up. Meanwhile Lucien stares at me, more confused than I've ever seen him.

"I've heard what they say about you, what they call you. But you don't have to be *Morningstar* all the time! You can just be . . . *you.*"

"Wow. So, the little stalker did her research. No surprise there. You know *all* about me, right?" He snaps his hand out, gripping my face. "I'm the fucked-up hockey player always causing fights and hurting people. I *must* be as dangerous as they say then. Maybe even a little *crazy.* Who knows? I could fly off the handle at any moment and hurt the sweet, innocent figure skater."

He takes a menacing step closer, and I stumble back.

"That's what you're thinking, right?" He leans in.

I shouldn't push him anymore; I should cower and play nice like I do with Dad and his *friends*, but for some insane reason, I don't.

"Well, you did say you were a painful fucker," I spit.

Christ on a stick. Must you be so bitchy, Sydney? He's going to say forget it and leave . . . or he might punish you. On second thought, that might not be so bad.

"And yet, you still chose to come with me." He releases my face, chuckling at whatever dumb expression I'm unconsciously displaying. "You still *want* me to fuck you. So, what does that say about the Little

Stalker Princess, hm? Isn't it a risk to *your* career to be associated with the likes of me? Shouldn't *you* be making smarter decisions?"

Not anymore.

I *should* have been smarter, *worked* harder but it's far too late for any of that now.

His eyes narrow into slits, his annoyance as palpable as his touch, but it's beneath that scornful glower that I recognize the smallest degree of disappointment and I want to curl in on myself and die for seeing such a look in his eyes, no matter the brevity of the moment.

Lucien turns away and starts walking again.

"We're almost there."

I nod, but his back is already to me again.

As if the wind is on *his* side, it kicks up, causing a shiver to run the length of my exposed legs.

I went too far . . . again.

Apologize, stupid.

"Hey, look I-I'm sorry, okay?" I stammer. "I don't know why I said all of that. That's not what I meant to say, or-or what I planned to say." My hand winds wildly in the air as if the right words will magically roll out with the gesture. "What I'm *trying* to say . . ." Jesus fucking Christ it's like I've never used human speech before. "I'm just a little out of sorts. This isn't me. It's been a *really* shitty day and I'm all kinds of messed up about it."

I try to laugh through the discomfort, but it trails off. Why am I being like this? This is what I wanted. Time with him, attention from him, so why am I self-sabotaging right now?

"So, I'm sorry, Lucien. I really am."

I let out a deep sigh.

"Look, I know I'm probably messing this all up, but I promise I'm not a bitch all the time."

He snorts and shakes his head, amusement back in his gait as he walks ahead of me though I can't shake the lingering stench of dissatisfaction he's left behind in his wake. I was myself when we talked under our monikers, not Sydney Sinclair. Not this person I've tried for years not to be. I don't want to be like Dad.

But I am. I'm just like my father, and that's probably why *she* left us both.

I squeeze the nylon handle of my bag, until it's digging into my palm, turning my knuckles white at the dredged memory of my mother. I bury the thought once more and keep moving forward. My dad might be hard on me, but at least he stayed. It hurts to think about, but right now nothing hurts as much as the thought of ruining this final night with Lucien.

I pinch the bridge of my nose, willing myself to be vulnerable for once.

"You weren't wrong, you know." I tell him, catching up. My thumbnail returns to its place between my teeth as I try to provide some sort of explanation for my behavior.

"I rarely am, but for the sake of clarity, enlighten me," he remarks without looking over at me.

I bite my lip to stop from smiling. He is such a cocky bastard, but damn it all if he isn't a loveable one.

"About the silver spoon," I clarify, wiping my thumb on my leg.

He peers back at me as he waits for me to continue.

I suck in a bolstering breath. "My last name's Sinclair."

Silence.

"My *father* is Syrus Sinclair . . ." Clearing my throat, I brace myself. "Of Sinclair Enterprises."

I peek open an eye, not knowing when they'd actually closed.

"No shit?" He doesn't even break his stride, and his tone sounds more sarcastic than anything, as though that explains nothing.

"I'm Sydney . . . *Sinclair.*" If it were warm enough for the crickets to chirp they would be singing.

I blink, waiting for him to react like others do when they hear about my background. But it doesn't happen. Most people freak out when I tell them that.

Most people lose their shit, but then again . . . he's not most people.

"You're kind of a big deal then, huh?" He responds lazily, glancing up at the moths ramming their fragile bodies against the light poles above.

I guffaw. "Uh, no. My *dad* is a big deal; *I* am a big disappointment."

This time his stride does falter, and we come to another abrupt stop. I don't catch myself in enough time and I run smack into his stupidly broad back with an audible *oomph*. "Can you *please* stop doing that?"

He ignores my complaint, turning instead to face me.

"You're *no one's* disappointment." He says it like he believes every word, pinning me with a feral glare steeped in warning.

"Yeah, well . . ." I shrug.

"Why would you say something like that?" His glower is off-putting.

I shrug and look ahead, afraid of what I'll see if I search his eyes for sincerity. I'd rather pretend he cares than admit it doesn't really matter. Or worse, learn he's only pitying me and that's why he cares. I couldn't handle either.

I pause beneath the street light.

"You're not the type to let things go, are you?"

Lucien's answer is swift. "Nope."

Sighing, I turn and explain, hoping he understands.

"My dad believes in power. There's no power in figure skating." I explain, "He succeeded in instilling a love of winning in me, but to his great disappointment, I fell in love with figure skating, not business or politics or industrialism. As a result, I'm 'wasting my potential.'" I mock, using my dad's deep inscrutable voice and finger quotes.

Lucien's stoic. I'd rather see nothing at all on his face than the dollar signs that shine in everyone else's.

I walk around him, taking the lead, but this time he walks in step with me, by my side. I can feel the warmth of his arms as we fight against the wind the remaining short distance to his car.

"Well, that's stupid," he grumbles.

My chest tingles with an unfamiliar warmth. I believe him when he says that. His candidacy causes a soft laughter to bubble from me.

"Yeah, you're right. But the Sinclair mentality is hard to break. That silver spoon afforded me everything I could ever want, just like you said, but it didn't spare me the hardships of never feeling good enough, you know? In our competitive world, talent trumps money. You have to be good at hockey to actually play it." I point to him, "No amount of money can cheat and make a bad player suddenly good. I have no clue how much money you make but I know you're the best."

He grins, "Yeah? You think I'm the best?"

I chuckle. "The best I've ever seen actually." I leave out the part that he's the *only* player I've ever seen. "But you have to understand that's a completely foreign concept compared to how I was raised. My dad and people like him look down on *everyone*. They wield their power and money over the weak and less fortunate. I'd like to think that I'm different from them, that I am a good person but . . ."

"Oh, I bet you're a very good girl," Lucien croons.

I scowl at him, though it severely lacks the heat necessary to burn.

"I'm being serious," I say.

"So am I," he answers.

His golden eyes almost look creepy the way they cut to me, hiding beneath his hooded lids and thick lashes.

"You have no idea. My dad and his 'friends' don't just want me to be *good,* they want me to be perfect. They push for me to look a certain way to set a certain precedent. It's exhausting living under that weight of expectation. To be who *they* want me to be. Figure skating was . . . *is* the only thing that alleviates that weight."

"While also being the cause of it, right?"

"Yeah," I breathe, though I can already feel myself choking up.

"It's worth it though." Lucien states it as if it's a point of fact and something I should know already.

"Yeah," I croak, trying to keep the emotion out of my voice. It *was* worth it. "It's just how all those guys in their position are, you know? They see something shiny and pretty, and they want it. They want to keep their shiny pretty things and lord it over everyone else's. But I'm a shiny pretty thing that doesn't want to stay in its case. I'd rather be on the ice."

"You don't belong to them," Lucien growls, his jaw tightening when I continue.

"I'd say that was sweet, but I'm quite literally the heir to a multi-million-dollar conglomerate who prefers figure skating to boardrooms. At least with figure skating, the only thing people want from me is the same thing I want from myself; to win," I say.

His bicep brushes against my shoulder as he continues toward the car, and that ferocity burns straight through my clothing. He's so warm.

"You're more than that though. You're talented."

I smile at his praise before chuckling to myself, "Good luck convincing them of that."

I stare down at my shoes, kicking a lone rock up the hill toward the edge of the lot as we walk. Lucien joins in, kicking it away before my foot can connect again.

"Well, fuck 'em. Better yet, set 'em on fire and dance on their graves, or triple lutz on their ashes forever doubting you." He kicks the rock as if it's a soccer ball sending it soaring so far out of my reach it's lost forever. "They can't have you if they're not breathing."

"What?" My head snaps up to Lucien.

"I'll bring the accelerant, and we can ride at dawn. Let's burn their whole world down."

I stop walking, stunned at the utter lack of levity in his voice. A humorless suggestion, he meant with sobering clarity and a vicious snarl.

"That's not . . . Are you crazy?" I shout.

He smiles eerily in my direction before pinching his fingers close together, revealing the tiny sliver of space where his sanity resides. Peeping through the hole he's created with his fingers, he winks before walking backward toward the car.

His car is the only car left in the distance. It dawns on me with frightening clarity how alone we are right now. Nothing around but barely contained sanity and lust.

I sigh, "You can't say shit like that."

"Why not?" he asks, continuing to walk backward with no fear of the unseen path behind him, his one hand tucked casually in his pocket as his bag bounces on his leg with each step.

"Because saying stuff like that is the kinda thing that gets you locked up in the looney bin," I say.

He untucks his hands and shrugs, palms up like a goddamn emoji.

"Aw, it's not so bad. It's actually kinda relaxing once you get used to it. If you tell the nurses 'I see dead people' they give you a lollipop." His fingers snap and I jolt. "Puts you right to sleep."

He adjusts the strap of his bag and turns back around, leaving me to stand there dumbfounded.

I can't tell if he's being serious, but I'm inclined to believe him. I blink, wondering if the additional second will allow my brain to catch up to his words.

"You're just messing with me, right?"

But he offers no further clarification, no explanations as to how he would know such a thing.

"Oh, Princess. I haven't even begun messing with you," he laughs, his shoulders shaking his bag and equipment in the process. A mad scientist cackle that jars me forward again.

"Hey, wait!" I shout.

"Keep up, buttercup," he shouts back.

I have to jog, but I eventually catch up to him. As we walk in sync, I feel compelled to clear up one thing. I may not *like* my situation, but I don't want to burn it all down either. And I certainly don't want anyone to die. I respect what my father has built, what he's managed to achieve. What *I've* achieved.

"He's a good person. *And* a good dad. He just wants what's best for me."

Lucien's silent for a beat, and I can't help but think he's probably wondering why I think he'd care about my life story or recent struggles. He just wants to play, to fuck, nothing more. So why tell him any of this? Who cares what he thinks?

You do.

"There's few things truly *good* in the world," he remarks, and I'm unsure what he means by it. I do my best to refrain from lashing out and demanding he tell me, though I'm well aware it'd earn me nothing good.

"I disagree. I'd like to think *most* people are good people, even when they are pushing me around. Sometimes . . ." I take a calming breath, suppressing the rising anger and need to snap at him. "It feels *good* to push back. It feels good to look down at others, so you can stand a little higher and not have to feel so low. And today . . . was a low day for me."

We finally arrive in front of an all-black muscle car that reminds me of Dominic Toretto's from that one movie, but before I know it, I'm being pressed up against it and Lucien's dropping his bag at our feet.

"What are you—" I start.

"Then I guess I better make this the best day of your goddamn life, Princess."

His lips crash against mine and to merely describe it as fireworks would be insolence. It's explosive. Atomic. Nuclear. I'm moaning so deeply into his mouth, I'm practically growling.

"Fuck, that's hot," he whispers against my lips. "Do it again."

I comply without hesitation, dropping the heavy bags from my shoulder too.

"So many delicious sounds," he muses.

I let my tongue explore the entirety of his mouth. I want to taste every bit of him, feel the tiny taste buds against his tongue. Trace the etches of his teeth, caress the feel of his gums. I want to remember the shape of his lips and solder the pillowy soft feel of them into my mind's eye. It's excessive, as is everything with me. I kiss him like I'm dying, like this is my last act on this earth before I'm swallowed into that deep pit of nothingness six feet under.

I'd feel embarrassed if Lucien's kiss wasn't equally consuming. He kisses like he fights: to win. It's brutal, yet there's a precision to it. Every stroke of his tongue has purpose, and his fingers claw at me like he's ready to rip my clothes off. He balls the fabric of my costume and pulls me in. True to his word, he elicits more sounds from me that come from a place I hadn't known existed. I wrap my arms around his neck. Our bodies are flush together and I can feel the evidence of what our connection is doing to him.

The kiss starts to hurt, but we keep going, the pain not a deterrent. It feels good. He *makes* it feel good. There's a sharp pull on my lip and I rear back.

"You bit me!"

"You bit me first," he retorts, smirking in response to my horror.

Sure enough, his tongue slips out and he prods at a small cut along the pink of his lower lip, fresh blood in the wound. He was right. Holy shit, I *did* bite him.

I'm poised to apologize, but he pulls me back to him, ravaging me again. I could die right now, and he'd still be fulfilling his promise. Kissing him like this . . . it's already the best day ever.

His hands grow more frantic, and my body moves of its own accord, seeking the pleasure hidden beneath too many layers of clothes.

"Mm, fuck, I want to keep kissing you," he says.

"Then don't stop," I practically plead.

His strong hands pin my waist to the door, preventing more movement and stalling our connection, but still we kiss.

"If we don't stop, I'm going to fuck you on the hood of this car and make you come all over the both of us. It will be quick, and dirty, and uncomfortable as hell." I'm not sure if he's trying to deter me or encourage me.

"I don't care," I breathe.

And I don't. The way I feel with Lucien, *about* Lucien, is a feeling unlike anything I've ever known before. It's a strange toxic mix of obsession and captivation with an intensity that burns through my veins. His hand grips my jaw as he descends on me again, holding me still as he devours my moans. I swallow harshly, barely able to breathe through the kiss. It catches his attention as the tension between us rises again. He clutches my throat in his grasp and another moan escapes my lips. I'm fully under *his* control now and it's a power I don't mind yielding to.

"Open," he commands. I'm not sure if he means my mouth, or my legs, but both accommodate him without thought.

"Seems I was right," he remarks, settling deeper between my thighs. His low voice and thick timber rolling through me as he speaks.

"About what?" I ask, his mouth trailing my neck before he bites me for the second time tonight. I hiss through clenched teeth then moan when he licks away the sting.

He pulls back an inch from the kiss.

"You *are* a good girl," he croons.

My tongue swipes over my swollen lips while I stare at the pink glitter gloss that stains his from our kisses. He seems unbothered with the sticky residue when he mimics the motion, savoring the taste.

"I guess I was right too. You *are* crazy," I say.

He glances toward the hood of the car and then back to me, flashing me a mischievous grin. His hands snake around my thighs as he hoists me against the side door of his car.

"Forget the hood. I should fuck you right here and show you just how *crazy* I can be," he threatens. I want him inside me more than I want air. It'd hurt like hell, but what's pleasure without pain?

Unfortunately, it's not up to me because loud voices interrupt us and rob me of the decision.

"Morningstar!" barks a random guy in the distance, slicing the shrouded tension of lust encasing us with one swift word.

"So, you have energy to fuck, but not to win games, huh?" shouts another guy.

"We had money on tonight's game. What the fuck was your problem!" says a third.

Where did they even come from?

"Yeah, you played like shit!"

I peer past Lucien's shoulder to see who would dare make such an outlandish claim. He scored three of the four goals they had. That's the opposite of a bad game, I would think. But one look at the one leading the pack tells me everything I need to know. He walks up to us with his friends on either side in triangle formation like some cheesy movie. They're a bunch of drunk guys itching for a fight, but they could still prove to be a hindrance to our night.

I glare at them for ruining our moment and talking nonsense. "Go away. Can't you see we're busy." I'm basically whining, but this is my first and probably last kiss with Lucien and they're ruining it!

At first, Lucien pays them no mind, he just trails kisses down my throat, alternating between nips and licks. His focus remains on me, and I try to fall back into the moment with him. It felt so good, it doesn't even bother me that they're watching, but then they're opening their big stupid mouths again.

"Look, bitch, this doesn't concern you. We'll let you suck our cocks later, but first we have business to handle with Morningstar," the tall one says.

"I don't know, boys, she's kinda hot. I say we put our business on hold so she can suck me right now." This from the ugly one. He blows a kiss at me and winks. I grimace, my stomach roiling at his gesture.

"I'm game," sneers the third.

Lucien sits me down and my hands tighten around his neck, fingers interlaced at his nape, instinctively seeking comfort in his arms as I stand there, offended.

I stare at them, slack-jawed at the audacity to speak to me like that, but I say nothing, refusing to resort to their level. They're just angry they lost money and are probably more than a little intoxicated too. By the looks of them they obviously don't go here, and they aren't worth the trouble of wasting precious time with Lucien, so I keep my lips sealed. I give them one disappointing shake of my head before directing my eyes back up at Lucien.

But the look on his face has me dropping my arms from his shoulders as I suck in a hurried breath, soaking in the frightening expression in his eyes. Though all too quickly I realize what a mistake I've made because he lunges for them, and I'm forced to watch in fascinated horror what Lucien unhinged is really like.

TIME-OUT

LUCIEN

Two months ago

Up here no one bothers me. The best part, it's noisy. The wind howls as we strike up conversation. It roars in my ears, and I listen. Some nights I roar right back, screaming into the void of my pain and frustration, but not tonight.

Leaning back against the cold ground along the cliff's edge, I indulge in one of my few private pleasures. Resting on my elbows, I listen to what the wind has to say tonight, what secrets it will divulge. I look out over the valley, leering at the school, illuminated and proud, off in the distance as it whispers across my skin and shouts in my face. It lulls me into a false sense of peace, and even though I know it's lying, it's one of my favorite pastimes. My legs hang weightless as I sit on the peak's edge like it's my own personal swing, except this is one I can't afford to jump off. I'm pretty high up and I'm *pretty* sure I wouldn't survive the fall.

Sleep does its best to evade me, but up here my body is relaxed and loose. Maybe sleep would find me easier if I just slept up here instead of back at the dorm.

I collapse my elbows and rest my back along the chilled lush grass. It's oddly comfortable, like the cold side of the pillow but better because it never grows hot, not up here. My lids stutter close to the sound of nature's lullabies. The soft quiet and cool nights are an illusion but it's one I can't help but come back to, if even for a little while.

The second the darkness wraps me in its hold, sleep beckoning, the illusion shatters and the memory of screeching tires, burnt rubber and rivers of blood assaults my senses, forcing me awake with a jolt. I jerk too hard though, rocking too far forward over the ledge, and slip. I catch myself in the nick of time, my hands braced on either side of my legs and clutched around the sharp peak's edge. The rough rock cuts into the skin of my palms and the pain yanks me out of my daze.

Blinking a few times, I swipe my hand over my face. It's wet, and warm, and it takes me a few lingering seconds to recognize I'm bleeding as I attempt to regain my focus. I turn my hand over and watch the dark substance spread along the life lines of my palm.

I should wipe it off or wrap it up.

I do neither, instead draping my hands between my legs, my forearms resting on my thighs, as I look far below where not even the trees can reach me. Falling would have been bad but I don't feel relief cheating death again as I stare at the base of the peak littered with jagged rocks. I feel empty and barren and the need to let go, and give in niggles at my brain. One little push from the wind and I could fall. It's a long way down, the kind of distance that could put an end to my miserable existence. I take a deep breath, scrubbing one hand through my hair while the other continues to drip blood over the rocks at the bottom. I could paint the rocks in red if only I'd fall. Satisfy nature with my demise.

I feed the rocks the blood it craves, watching as my hand drips slow steady drops from hundreds of feet above. It flows down my middle finger, pooling until gravity forces it to do what I wouldn't: fall.

Drip. Drip. Drip.

I stay like that for a while. Watching. Waiting. Until my conversation with the breeze is interrupted by a faint buzzing sound. I almost brush it off as another memory, or hallucination, but it sounds again.

This time I feel it, the vibration against my leg. It's my phone. My fingers slip, numb from the cold as I make several odd attempts to fish it out of my pocket. I'm tempted to chuck it over the side of the peak before it finally settles in my grip, the vibrations incessant and unhelpful to the current state of my mind. It takes a second for my eyes to adjust when

I bring it up to my face, but even through bleary vision, the username immediately catches my attention.

What the hell?

@BladeSpinner

> **Are you going to jump?**

I huff an exhausted laugh. I've thought about it. So many times.

@therealLucifer

> **Do you think I should?**

@BladeSpinner

> **If you want to.**

I squint, eying the message they sent. Well, that's different. I don't know what I expected their response to be but it wasn't that. I type back, despite the intrusive thoughts.

@therealLucifer

> **Do YOU want me to jump?**

@BladeSpinner is typing...

I wonder if they're aware that I can see the blinking dots. I grunt, staring at the screen disrupting the night air. Is this the part where they send me their manifesto or their plans for world domination? They'd probably push me off if given the chance. Too bad they won't get it. I'll thrust us both to our deaths before I ever let someone kill me.

@BladeSpinner

> **No.**

Something about the simple response makes me laugh out loud, surely startling the nocturnal creatures I typically spend my time with when I'm out here all alone. Except, I'm not alone. Not tonight it seems.

@therealLucifer

Lol. Did you have to think about it?

@BladeSpinner

I needed to check in with my feelings first.

@therealLucifer

And?

Bloody thumbprints litter my screen, but I merely wipe them away as I wait with baited breath for their response.

@BladeSpinner

What?

@therealLucifer

What did your feelings have to say?

@BladeSpinner

If it made you happy, it would make me happy.

@therealLucifer

That's a little fucked, don't you think?

@BladeSpinner

Well, it's a little fucked you want to jump.

I just figure you like fucked up things. *Shrug emoji*

They've got me there. It is fucked up. Then again, I'm a pretty fucked up guy.

@therealLucifer

Touche'

So . . . what else makes you happy?

@BladeSpinner

This

This? What about *this* makes them happy? Fucking with me? Taunting me? I want to ask but I know they won't tell me. It's the way they talk in circles. In riddles. Nothing is ever straightforward or as it seems with them.

@therealLucifer

Who are you?

@BladeSpinner

I don't know.

LUCIEN

Dr. Amelia Thatcher
Session Transcript
Audio Recording
Date: January 17, 2024
Patient: Lucien D. Morrow
Amelia: It's been a while.
Lucien: I've been busy.
Amelia: I heard. Congratulations on your win this week.
Lucien: I always forget how high up your office is. Everyone looks like ants.
Amelia: Have you been having any more unsafe thoughts?
Lucien: Doc, all of my thoughts are unsafe.
Amelia: Is that why you finally decided to show up?

Lucien: I'm only required to come once a month. I'd say this is progress that I'm here right now. Aren't you proud of me?

Amelia: It *is* progress and, yes, I'm proud of you. I'm always proud of you, Lucien. You've come such a long way, and I want to continue to see you improve. It takes true courage to face your fears as you have. I know it's been hard on you, dealing with the grief of losing your family, coupled with the survivor's guilt, and hero's guilt over trying to save the person who caused their deaths, only for them to perish too. It's a lot for anyone, especially someone at your age. I'm proud of every step you've made to receive the healing . . .

Amelia: How've you been sleeping?

Lucien: Like shit.

Amelia: Have you been taking the Olanzapine?

Lucien: No. They make my head feel foggy. I don't play well with that shit in my system.

Amelia: I can try writing you another prescription for some sleeping pills. Would that help?

Amelia: Are you able to tell me what's going on with you? You don't seem in good spirits today. Are you sleeping at all?

Lucien: Some.

Amelia: Has it been like this all week?

Amelia: Has it been like this for longer than a week?

Amelia: Well, we've talked about this in the past. When it gets bad like this it's important that you—

Lucien: I think someone's been following me.

Amelia: Excuse me?

Lucien: Yeah, I think I'm being followed.

Amelia: Have you contacted the authorities?

Lucien: I said, I *think*. I'm not exactly sure.

Amelia: Okay, let's start with why you think someone's following you.

Lucien: It's just a feeling I have. I can . . . I can feel their eyes on me, sense their presence, but I never see them.

Amelia: Are you sure this person exists? Are you hearing voices?

Lucien: No, they exist. It's not in my head. We talk sometimes . . . it's kinda nice.

Amelia: You talk in person?

Lucien: Online mostly . . . but sometimes they text.

Amelia: Yes, but you said you think they're following you. Why is that?

Lucien: I thought they might have just been a fan or a puck bunny, but that's seeming less likely now.

Amelia: How so?

Lucien: We don't talk about hockey or my games. They don't call me Morrow or Morningstar.

Amelia: Do you know if it is a male or female?

Lucien: I'm not sure.

Amelia: Do you feel in danger when communicating with them?

Lucien: Sometimes.

Lucien: They asked me if I was going to jump off the cliff at Werther's Peak. I asked them if I should do it and do you know what they said?

Amelia: What did they say?

Lucien: If I wanted to, I should.

Lucien: Can you believe that? No one's ever given me permission to do what I wanted before. It surprised me.

Amelia: So, you have been having thoughts of harming yourself again?

Lucien: No. I don't think I wanted to jump then. I think they just assumed I wanted to because they were watching me.

Amelia: Do you stand at the edge of the cliff often?

Lucien: Don't take that away from me, Doc.

Amelia: Look, Lucien, you know I'm on your side, but it's not good practice to tempt your demons like this. What if one day you're there and you *do* feel like jumping? What then? You won't have time to think through your steps if you're already at the edge.

Lucien: I'm *always* at the edge.

Amelia: Lucien, wait! Please sit back down.

LUCIEN

We won again tonight. I knew we would, those state kids didn't stand a chance against our defensive plays. I should be happy about that—I'm not. I'm restless. Physically and mentally. Everything inside me is itching and my mind is racing. Hockey usually centers me, but an easy shutout is not my idea of a great game. A great game is hard-fought. High stakes. Give and take. I want my win to *mean* something.

Everyone else is happy though. They high five, cheer red plastic cups full of foul-smelling booze, and fuck puck bunnies. *None* of those things appeal to me right now. There's only one way I want to celebrate after a night like tonight.

"Dude, are you good?" asks Chauncey. His hands, moving to mix himself a celebratory drink at the long folding table we've turned into a self-serve bar outside the eat-in kitchen.

"Dude. Do I *look* like I'm good?" My head rolls along the wall of the kitchen doorway to grace him with the eye contact he's so desperate for, though I suppose my bloodshot eyes and dark circles do little to ease his concerns.

"No, you're even more of a sourpuss than usual. You would think that being the *great* Morningstar," he sarcastically stretches his hand in an arc to showcase my infamous name, "*loved* by all, *feared* by many—you'd be in a better fucking mood, but you're not." *No fucking shit.* "You *look* like you haven't slept in days, and your eyes look fucking dead, dude." He waves his hands in front of my face when all I do in response is face forward again, staring at nothing.

"Earth to Lucien," Chauncey yells.

There's a game of beer pong being played outside that I can see through the cracked open window. Two girls are making out on the couch, sloppily sucking face and putting on a show. There's Jules, Ketchen, and Garcia playing rock/paper/scissors in the living room, but I'm looking past all of it.

I like Chauncey. He's one of those guys who doesn't have a malicious bone in his body. He's all good times and good vibes *all* the time, but I will gut him if he doesn't back the fuck off.

I grip his wrist mid-air on its fifth pass in front of me.

"Ah, shit, well, I see your reflexes are still intact," he jokes even through the pain.

Of course they are. My problem *isn't* that I don't have enough energy, it's that I have too much. I toss his hand away when I feel myself start to shake, shooting him warning daggers as I let go.

He rubs his bruising wrist. "Cranky much?" Chauncey grumbles.

"Leave him alone, Chaunce," a deep caramel voice warns, striding up to us to stand at my side. My shoulders drop as I take a deep breath.

Thank fuck.

Nursing his cocktail, Chauncey takes a step back, but of course he doesn't shut up. "All I'm saying is he should chill out, get laid and—"

"Chauncey!"

Trevor's glare holds more authority as he waits for Chauncey to concede and walk away before he's turning on me next. I beat him to the punch.

"The next words out of your mouth better be—"

"Are you okay?" he asks, the weight of his question holding the *exact* amount of sincerity I wanted to avoid.

My head hits the wall with a hollow thud as I throw it back and sigh. That's not what I wanted the next words out of his mouth to be at all. Not even close.

"Lucien?"

"Goddammit, Trev. I'm fine!" I shout loud enough to exhibit the complete opposite of the meaning. A blind man could tell I was far from *fine*. And the party goers give me a wide berth, avoiding me at all costs, unlike a certain six-foot-four defenseman who believes the power of friendship will heal my bad mood.

His arms fold, stretching his too-tight Henley even tighter. Stupid fucking D-man. I give a feral growl when he doubles down with a comforting pat to my shoulder. *Comfort* is not what I need right now. But he gently squeezes, and I don't bite his head off.

"Do you want me to . . . cheer you up, or something?" he asks, all the emotion of a concerned friend swelling in those puppy eyes.

"I said I'm fine," I grit, though I sound more exhausted than angry.

His features only soften. And if I didn't know him so well I'd say that look is pity, but it's not. It's something much worse. Regret.

A group of people walk by, toward the back door to join in the action in the backyard. I don't recognize any of them, but one of those fuckers knocks his shoulder into Trevor's back hard enough that he stumbles forward. I push off the wall, ready to educate them on their manners and let off a little steam.

But Trevor's arm brackets my chest, holding me back.

I glower at the offending party who doesn't even notice before shifting my focus back to Trev.

"You're just going to let him do that?" I seethe.

"Yes, Lucien, I am, because not every *accident* is worth getting worked up over," he retorts, ignoring the slight against him and letting the push slide—something I find much harder to do. I suspect this is why he took the hit in the first place. I'm too volatile. Too unforgiving. His stare deepens, his eyes flooding with earnestness, but they possess a fear I don't find pleasing.

"Are you sure there's nothing I can do?" he asks.

I give him an admonishing look, challenging his patience with me. "Are *you*?" I shoot back.

I know he's only trying to help, but involving him in my shit would complicate things. He doesn't need complications right now. We're both aware of it, but only one of us can admit it. My brand is violence, but unlike my own, Trevor's agent prefers he keep his squeaky-clean image untainted while his contract's being finalized. Like me, Trevor's already been signed to the NHL, but we both decided finishing college was important, so taking on my baggage, is not an option.

"Don't ask me that unless you actually want to make good on my request," I warn.

His Adam's apple bobs as he swallows. "I just . . . I know you're not sleeping. You're not acting like yourself. You're irritable, pushing everyone away."

"Not everyone," I mutter, canting my head to the side.

He doesn't take the bait.

"And I'm pretty sure I know why," he continues, shifting and then pivoting to stand against the wall with me. By my side like always.

"Then you know there isn't anything you can do about it," I lament.

He sighs.

"They're getting worse, aren't they? The dreams?" Trevor asks.

I can feel the weight of *his* stare on me.

"Well, I could—" he starts.

"Don't," I snap.

His stare deepens, hardens. We've known each other long enough that I can *feel* the loudness of his thoughts.

"They wouldn't want this for you," he says, his voice low in my ear. I want to tell him that what *they* want is irrelevant. My family's absence from this world all but renders their desires for me pointless, but that would only spur on his sympathetic nature. Sympathy is the last thing I need from Trevor James.

His shoulder bumps mine and I bristle when he shifts again.

Oh God, I think he's going to hug me.

And if he hugs me . . .

I shrug him off when he gets closer.

He sighs heavily, "Don't be like that."

"Be like what, Trev? *I'm* fine. *You're* fine. Everybody's fine." I throw my hand toward the crowd dancing in our living room and doing shots in our dining room. "Go on, enjoy yourself. Have *fun*. It's a fucking party after all and you only live once." I laugh but I'm convincing no one, least of all him. He settles back beside me.

"It's not very *fun* when you're in a mood like this." He tips his chin at me.

"You sure about that?" My arms cross as I eye him up and down. "I've been told I'm a blast," I say dryly.

He shakes his head, fighting a grin he ultimately loses to. His hand brushes over his curls and he assaults me with a wide smile I can't ignore.

"There he is," he beams, seemingly satisfied with himself.

Despite myself, my lips twitch to return his smile, but then I'm coldly reminded why I haven't bothered in all this time. "Look Trev, I'm—"

"Fine?" He finishes for me. "Yeah, so you've said."

I narrow my eyes, annoyed by his hero complex. "Like you, hm? Everything's *great* in Trevor's world. No need to fuck it up dealing with the likes of me, right?"

He freezes. And I feel like shit. "Sorry," I grumble. "I didn't mean that."

He arches a brow. "Wow, was that a real apology from Lucien Morrow?" He places the back of his hand to my forehead, and I promptly smack it away. "I don't know, this may be worse than a case of the grumps. The world may be ending. Someone better make sure Hell isn't freezing over." He juts a thumb over his shoulder. "Or maybe the polar ice caps melting. Should I go check?"

"Oh, shut up. It's not that I don't *believe* in apologies . . ."

"You just don't think you need to," he finishes.

We're both glaring at each other now.

"I *believe* they should be used sparingly," I say instead, staring at the tick of his bearded jaw because I'm too stubborn to take the hurt in his eyes. It doesn't help so I stare at the collar of his Henley instead. "I owed you that one. I shouldn't have taken a cheap shot at you like that. I'm just . . ." I run a hand over my face. "I'm tired, that's all."

"I thought you were fine," he teases.

Asshole.

He slides his warm hand to the back of my neck and squeezes, his special way of providing more unwarranted comfort. "So then, get some *sleep*, Lucien. If you need to, you can go upstairs and sleep in my bed. No one will bother you up there."

"Maybe I should take Chauncey's advice and get laid instead," I joke.

"Not if you're like this," he clips.

It's not hurt in his eyes when I look at him now. I see warning. The captain is right. It's not wise to play when I'm so riled up. They might break.

I huff, "Relax. I was only joking."

He steps in closer, speaking lower so only I can hear him.

"Look if you really need—"

"It's all good. I'm going to go out for a bit." I push off the wall and pursue the urge to escape with wild fervor. I need to get out of here. Out of this kitchen. Out of my skin. I need to run as fast as I can until the ghosts of the past haunting me go away.

"Please . . . don't do anything stupid," he pleads.

I pause, then turn away to leave before answering, "I make no promises."

"Text me if you need me!" he shouts, soliciting the attention of what I'm sure is the scrutiny of everyone at this party with his commanding voice.

I throw a two-finger salute behind me, acknowledging his words, but ignoring his plea. We both know I will be doing no such thing. I'm absolutely going to do something stupid, and if all goes according to plan, I won't need him tonight. I'll finally get some fucking sleep.

SYDNEY

MANIFESTATION JOURNAL

DATE: JAN. 26, 2024

Today I am going to talk to Lucien. He'll be speechless and as nervous as me, but I'll calm him, ensuring him there's no need. He'll say, "We should go get coffee sometime," and then I'll be like, "Yeah, any time. I heard the Bean Cup is pretty good." Maybe I'll bump into him off campus and we'll meet like two strangers passing in the night.

This is the first time I've followed him off campus and I'm regretting it. Luckily, I came prepared. I'm hidden in a two-sizes-too-big hoodie and dark sweatpants. Every time he turns his head—which is a lot—I duck behind a tree and hide in the darkness. The years of figure skating training aid in my ability to be light on my feet, and I'm grateful. Any louder and I'd be caught for sure. The game would end—I would likely get hit with a restraining order and serious repercussions for my actions. *We can't have that.*

We're in a wooded area with no end in sight, until we're striding toward a huge warehouse. The clearing is filled with cars, trucks, and what looks like spare auto parts. The air smells old and stale, like it has remained untouched by civilization for a while.

Bellemere is a huge university that sits on the edge of an abandoned town just across the way from Seattle. It's a perfect location for a college campus because we can easily cross over to Seattle in about half an hour and enjoy the city life or trek farther out to participate in the secluded bonfire parties and barn hangouts in the forested countryside of Washington.

This must be the latter because, though the sprinkle of buildings of this old town appears abandoned by society, it's flourishing with activity as lights stream between the cracked boards of the decrepit warehouse. Loud shouts and screams bleed into the once-silent night air.

I hang back and watch as Lucien talks to the two burly men manning the door. What the hell needs protecting in a building that's falling apart? He finishes his small talk and walks inside. I give him five minutes before following again.

"Password?" one of the security guys asks, his tone gruff and devoid of all pleasantries.

"Password?" I mouth. Shit. I hadn't thought this through. I have no clue what kind of place this is, let alone what the secret fucking password is.

Maybe they're just messing with me, testing me in case I'm a narc or whatever.

"Seriously? I just saw you let that other guy in," I retort.

The other security man shines a flashlight in my face, blinding me at first before chuckling.

"Oh, hell no. Look, little girl, get the fuck outta here. This is no place for you to be," he sneers.

"I was invited," I lie, folding my arms in defiance and cocking my hip out.

He's a scary looking dude. Big and bald with a cobra tattooed on his scalp. A giant bull ring is strung through his nostrils and I'm pretty sure the tattoo on his neck reads "Snitches Die." He looks me up and down, aware of my dishonesty.

"No, you weren't," he says.

"How do you know?" I snap. I have no clue where this sense of bravery is coming from. If I were back home, I'd be running and screaming at the sight of a man like him, but infatuation makes a girl do crazy things.

"Because nobody in their right mind would ever bring someone like you here." His laugh is boisterous and hearty like the thought is truly inconceivable. "And even if some nutcase did, there's no way they'd let you come alone."

What the fuck is this place?

I turn my attention to the building behind him when I hear more shouting and applause, but it's nothing like the roar of an arena crowd. This sounds like the violent cheering of a riot or a murderous mob.

"Look, I'm going to give you ten seconds to get out of here before I physically remove you," he drawls gruffly.

Eww. No thank you.

The silent one that stood menacingly at his side, though shorter in stature, is even more intimidating with a tattoo of a haunted clown on the side of his face.

Who are these guys? And what the hell does Lucien have to do with them?

"Fine." I hold my hands up in defeat, my oversized sleeves sliding down to my elbows. "I'm going!"

The shorter one licks his lips at the reveal of my skin. "Yeah, get a move on," he rasps, his voice hoarse and wet.

The words, a warning of the unfavorable alternative if I choose to stay.

Apparently, elbows do it for him.

I can feel them both staring as I trudge away, but once I'm sure I'm in the clear, I circle back, avoiding the front entrance and sneaking around to the western side. There's no entrance or exit to sneak through, but the building is so full of cracks, it's not hard to listen.

I hear an announcer.

"You know 'im! You love 'im! He never gives his name, but he always gives us a show! Ladies and gentlemen, feast your eyes 'cause it's about to get ugly!"

I'd give anything to see inside, but I spent this month's allowance getting rid of the Mary girl, so I don't have enough to even bribe the guys out front. Ugh, this is why you don't make financial decisions when you're emotional. Though, even if I did have the cash, something tells me money isn't what they would bargain for.

I rub my forehead with the sleeve of my hoodie, my makeup transferring to the dark material.

This was such an amateur move. I followed Lucien to this shady fucking place with no idea how to get back because I wasn't paying any attention to my surroundings. I don't even know how long he's going to be in there.

I hop up on the rusted hood of an old pickup that looks like I'd have a serious need for a tetanus shot if it so much as scratched me, but it's a solid sitting space while I listen and wait.

"Get him!" A shrill voice from the crowd shouts.

"Break his arm!" Another one yells.

"Yes! Fuck him up!" This from a voice that sounds like they smoke truck exhaust.

I can hear harsh blows being exchanged. I'd say it's obvious a fight is going on, but I can't believe Lucien would come here for fun. Then again, I don't know *what* he does for fun.

@BladeSpinner

What do you do for fun?

I wait for him to respond, but he doesn't. Even though he acts annoyed by the messages I send him, he has never *not* answered, except when he had me blocked for that brief time. But he's unblocked me since then, so what's his deal?

I tap my finger against the screen of my phone, my nails clacking against the glass.

Flopping back, I sigh.

This was stupid.

Group chat
Bellemere Figure Skating Team

Tiffany 10:37 PM

> Sydney, I hope you're okay. So weird that you missed practice. You're usually always here, so you must be sick or hurt.

Regina 10:37 PM

> We're all working really hard to do well at the upcoming competition. It's not cool for you to just not show up. Sick or not, you could have told us.

I roll my eyes. Regina's not even pretending to be sincere like Tiffany, but I start to feel bad when the other messages come in. Especially from Hannah who's finally feeling better after her own bout with illness.

Hannah 10:40 PM

> That's a little harsh, Regina. She must be feeling terrible if she's missing practice. Sydney never misses a practice, and she stays later than the rest of us.

Shane 10:45 PM

> I'm Switzerland, but I do agree it's ONE day. Cut her some slack.

Regina 10:47 PM

That's the exact opposite of being Switzerland, Shane.

Bria 10:50 PM

As long as she doesn't slow us down, I don't care. No offense, Sydney.

That's big talk when she's the slowest among us. I, at least, managed a pleasing enough score to secure a runner-up spot. She didn't even place.

Tiffany 11:00 PM

We're sending you well wishes, Sydney. Take however long you need.

It's ironic that Tiffany is the only one of them who rightfully considers me a threat.

Sydney 11:01 PM

Thanks

I lie on the hood staring up at the sky while I attempt to drudge up a fuck to give about what they have to say. I didn't mean to miss practice. We walked *forever*. I hadn't expected to be stranded this far from campus with no way of getting back on my own. I suppose I could try to find a way, but whatever Lucien's doing in there can't be too much longer.

I wake with a start. Astonished that I not only managed to fall asleep in such a precarious situation, but that I did it so easily. *Jesus.*

I rub my eyes with my sleeves and shiver. The temperature dropped as night stretched on into early morning. According to my phone it's three. So, *really* early morning.

Crowds of people are filtering out in droves, despite the late hour. I hop down from the truck and watch the faces of people who look nothing like the university kids I'm used to.

I wait another five minutes, my hands tucked into my sleeves like makeshift gloves as I rub my forearms, attempting to generate heat.

Come on, Lucien, where are you?

The lot is almost empty before a singular figure emerges from the warehouse. His gait is different from the ones who filed out before him. I know who it is instantly, but my feet don't move to follow him as quickly as these last few weeks. Something's off.

On most days, Lucien had a gravitational pull on me I couldn't escape. He was ethereal, fantastical even. His eyes an unnatural golden hue, his features almost elfin or animated in the way they were soft in some areas and sharp in others. The man was downright gorgeous with strong notes of darkness that hid beneath all that beauty. But right now, *all* I see is darkness, quite literally. He's covered in something.

Is it sweat?

No, it's too thick to be sweat.

Mud maybe?

Unlike *my* legs, his are moving at a steady pace, stretching the vast distance between us to the point I *have* to follow, lest I be abandoned here.

I'm careful to remain quiet, still unwilling to tip him off to my presence, perhaps even more so now than before.

The substance clings to Lucien's porcelain skin, painting him in filth. Yet he seems unbothered. In fact, he's almost tranquil.

What happened to him?

Shadowed branches reach out like claws of the night, grasping his shoulders and sweeping over his body. He presses on, never once turning to look back at me. It's odd. He's moving like he's entranced or sleepwalking. We walk for what feels like hours and I feel dumber by the second.

I'm swearing to myself that I'll never follow him this far out again when we finally approach the school entrance. I'm an on-campus resident, but I live in the athletics housing near the rink with the other sports students and sorority/fraternity housing. We should be walking in the same direction, but he veers toward the dorms. I consider this for a moment, looking both ways as I stand at a literal crossroad. On the one hand, I can go home and get out of this ridiculous disguise, take a much-needed shower, and make smarter life choices from here on out. But on the other hand . . .

Well, on the other hand, there's Lucien. Of course, he wins out. That pull I feel intensifies every day I keep this ridiculous farce up. But, I mean, I'm already out here, so I might as well see where he lives, right?

LUCIEN

Blood is stickier than people realize. It's itchy too. It makes my skin tingle after a while if I don't wash it off quick enough. Still, the most I do is wipe it from my face with the dish towel that hangs off the sink's ledge in the kitchenette of my single's dorm. I'm exhausted. Too exhausted to think. To dream. To remember. Just how I like it.

The next morning...

A few hours of sleep are better than none I suppose. I'm sore as hell and sticking to the sheets. It takes me a minute to adjust to the foreign space and remember why I came here. I crane my head to the side, a disturbing pop emanating from my neck that should be concerning.

I wipe my hand over my face. I still have tape wrapped around my knuckles, stained red from last night's fights, the blood crusted and dark. There's no telling exactly who it all belongs to.

I've achieved enough of a restful night to get me ready for practice and our upcoming game against Crestview. If any school could be considered our rivals, it'd be them, and I need my head screwed on right if I'm going to be of any help to the team. The fights take the edge off, but winning in the sport I love is what's proven most helpful. A *real* win.

I press my fingers into my eye sockets, rubbing until my vision unblurs, but it's not the blurriness that has me confused. I blink several times and scan the small two-hundred-square-foot room before I accept what is staring back at me is what I think it is.

At the foot of the bed sits a towel folded into the shape of an elephant, like the ones they put on the bed at fancy hotels. It's the bloodied dishrag from last night and, sure as shit, it's folded into an elephant.

The laughter continues to fall from my lips when I think about how I sought sleep so hungrily that I was too exhausted to hear my stalker follow me in here and gift me a fucking *elephant*.

I knew they were in the forest with me, but I stopped caring when I felt sleepy for the first time in days. I wonder if they even noticed or cared about the amount of blood on the discolored white cloth when they origamied my shit into a creative masterpiece.

I'm still chuckling to myself when my phone buzzes in the barren space, rattling against the empty nightstand.

Trevor 9:30 AM

> **Hey, you good? You didn't come back last night.**

I groan. Great. My hideout has been compromised, and my best friend is still mothering me.

Lucien 9:31 AM

> ***Thumbs-up emoji***

I flop back on the bed, arms spread over the comforter like a starfish, wondering why I'm not more pissed off by this before laughing again. A fucking elephant.

The sound of the whistle jars me into action. I push off at full speed as we scrimmage in preparation for this Friday's game. I approach the goal, running the puck up the boards as I skate toward it at breakneck speeds, but Ketchen, who we all call Kitchen, is an amazing goalie and he won't be easy to get past. Guy has the vision of a hawk. He won't be fooled by boisterous power plays and aggressive strong arming, not to mention Trevor isn't going to let me waltz into the defensive zone and get another shot on him. So, the only way to get by him . . .

I shoot the puck over to Chauncey—loud-mouthed playboy that he is, but most reliable and skilled winger I've ever known. The shot's wide, but he hooks the puck behind the net. Trevor's a few inches shy of slamming him into the boards before he's deking the shot back to our other forward who goes for a goal, and misses.

I'm not shocked, which is why I'm right there to take the rebound shot. Kitchen's hawk vision is obstructed by the flurry of bodies fighting for supremacy of the puck. Gomez slap passes it to me, and I sink the shot right over Kitchen's left shoulder. The sound of the buzzer is a cooling relief to the overheating of my body.

I chew on my mouth guard, skating up to Kitchen to bump fists as he smirks beneath his helmet. I may be a lead scorer, but the reason we win games is Kitchen. He's the best damn goalie I've ever worked with, and I always feel great when I get one over on him.

"I see you, Morningstar. Good luck getting past me twice though," teases Kitchen.

"Is that a challenge?" I skate around his goal. "Because you know I *love* a challenge."

"Careful, Kitchen. He's got that look in his eye," says Chauncey as he skates by.

Kitchen smirks, slapping his stick against the ice in a 'bring it' motion.

"He's not the only crazy motherfucker on this team. Bring it, baby!" Kitchen goads.

The rest of the guys join in laughing at our ribbing of one another.

"Don't worry, Kitchen, he's not getting past me this time," joins Trevor.

It's been weeks, but I'm finally feeling like myself again. I chuckle, hoping that this semblance of peace will last, even when I know the truth. It won't. It never does.

"We'll see about that," I jab right back, reveling in proving him wrong.

A few more plays and the sound of the whistle is breaking us apart once more. Our team ties for the scrimmage, but my teammates skate up to me and slap me on the helmet all the same. A tie is a good thing, it means that if we keep this up, the Crestview Wolverines are as good as dead.

The amount of howling and rhythmic stomping of the crowd is deafening. The Wolverine fans mimic their mascot while Titan fans pound their feet like soldiers on the battlefield summoning the gods of hockey. I fucking love it. This is the shit I live for.

It's a bloodbath. Metaphorically, unfortunately, but it is a shootout. We gain the lead by one, then by two, only for them to eat our lead by one before finally tying up the game again.

My leg is swept over the boards, ready to get back out there as I wait for my cue. The second my moment comes, I'm determined. Ready to steal and bring home this win, but I'm tired. I slept maybe a few hours before I was jolting out of another restless night's sleep. It didn't help that I stayed up thinking about the weird-ass texts I received in the middle of the night. I'm still thinking about them.

Unknown 1:19 AM

Can't sleep?

Lucien 1:19 AM

Is this who I think it is?

Unknown 1:20 AM

The one and only.

Lucien 1:21 AM

How'd you know I was awake?

Unknown 1:21 AM

It says you're online.

Lucien 1:21 AM

Of course you'd notice that.

Unknown 1:21 AM

I'm an observant person

Lucien 1:22 AM

You're a nosey person.

Unknown 1:22 AM

Does that bother you?

Lucien 1:23 AM

It surprises me

Unknown 1:23 AM

Why?

Lucien 1:25 AM

I've never been the object of someone's obsession before.

Me and Chauncey relieve Jules and the rest of the third line and get back out there. I skate harder, the puck glued to my stick as I tear up the ice, thinking about how my stalker teased, how they pushed. They're obsessed with getting under my skin and in my space, no matter how much I warn them otherwise.

Unknown 1:25 AM

Dude what are you talking about?

You have an entire fan club dedicated to you.

Lucien 1:26 AM

None of them text me.

Unknown 1:26 AM

None of them have your number.

Lucien 1:27 AM

YOU shouldn't have my number.

Crazy pants. They severely lack self-preservation skills or common sense altogether. My own teammates and friends even know to give me the space required when I'm too deep in the hole, too far in the midst of darkness, of insanity. But this person, whoever they are, it's like they want to drown *with* me. The further I go down, the more they follow.

Unknown 1:27 AM

Let's not dwell on the past.

We're here now.

Lucien 1:27 AM

Eye roll emoji

Unknown 1:30 AM

Has anyone told you you're kind of stand-off-ish?

Lucien 1:31 AM

Am not.

Unknown 1:32 AM

Are too.

Lucien 1:33 AM

Is that why you haven't revealed yourself yet?

Unknown 1:33 AM

I haven't 'revealed' myself because this is way more fun.

Lucien 1:34 AM

So you get off on danger?

Unknown 1:35 AM

What makes you say that?

Lucien 1:35 AM

The fact that you think provoking me is 'fun' tells me you must get a sick thrill from all of this.

Unknown 1:36 AM

Are you suggesting that what I'm doing is DANGEROUS?

Highly.

Devil emoji

Rubs hands maniacally. Muhahaha.

So what's the penalty? What will you do that's sooo dangerous if I don't stop?

I send the puck flying to Chauncey, a repeat of our play against Kitchen at practice, except when I skate up to take the rebound shot, I'm hit with the force of a truck and slam into the ice with a hard blow to my shoulder. The wind is knocked from me, and for once I'm taken off guard by the red haze of anger that's filled my vision, frustrated with the elusive person distracting me when they're not even here.

I haven't found my stalker yet. I just got hit. I can't fucking sleep, and I'm so fucking tired of holding back all the goddamn time.

Wrenching the helmet off the player who hit me, I punch and punch and punch. In front of the now-silent audience, I work out all my frustrations on the Wolverine.

You're asking the wrong question.

What's the right question?

How will you get me to stop once I get my hands on you?

Unknown 1:42 AM

Hmm. *thinking emoji*

I guess I better not get caught then.

Lucien 1:45 AM

You're too late.

A ref grabs my arm, pulling me off him before tossing me into the Sin Bin, a five-minute penalty. I hang my head between my shoulders, heaving big breaths as the conversation from last night lingers in my thoughts.

Lucien 1:46 AM

You wanted my attention.

And now you have it.

You're in my line of sight now.

It's only a matter of time.

So, run.

I'm going to find you, Little Stalker.

Most guys are upset when they're in the Sin Bin, but I can't help the smile that stretches across my face when I think of the unparalleled fight to come. Me versus *them*.

Little Stalker 1:47 AM

Only time will tell.

Goodnight, Lucien.

Sleep tight.

Don't let the bed bugs bite.

Devil emoji

The second I'm out of the bin, released from my cage, I'm out for blood. I'll win this game, and then, I'm going to hunt down a Little Stalker.

Lilith?
  Lilith, please.
  I'm sorry.
  Don't leave.
  Please don't go.
I startle awake.
"I'm sorry," I whisper. "I'm so sorry."

A few days later . . .

Dr. Amelia Thatcher
Session Transcript

Audio Recording
Date: February 3, 2024
Patient: Lucien D. Morrow

Amelia: Have you been journaling like I suggested?

Lucien: No.

Amelia: How come? We've talked about this, sometimes it can be helpful to get your thoughts out so that they're not stuck in your head.

Lucien: And I've told *you* that being stuck with a physical reminder of what's in my head is depressing as fuck.

Amelia: Then do you want to tell *me*?

Lucien: What's the point doc? It's the same thing as always.

Amelia: The accident, right?

Lucien: And everything that came after.

Amelia: Wait, do you remember now, what happened?

Lucien: No.

Amelia: Lucien, if you're remembering things, that can explain why you're having trouble piecing the dreams together. This is why I think you should be journaling.

Lucien: Trust me, they're not memories.

Amelia: How can you be so sure?

Lucien: Because in the dreams . . . I'm the one who kills them.

DREAM JOURNAL ENTRY

DATE: FEB. 3, 2024

They think I don't remember. Idiots. I can't forget. I remember everything. Every. Fucking. Thing. She left me and now I'm left all alone.

I can't sleep.

I *can't* sleep.

I. Can't. *Fucking*. Sleep

My head rolls against the sweat-soaked pillow, pungent with the stench of fear and death —things that once stoked anger within me, but are now only facts of the matter as I reach for my phone ablaze with notifications.

A comment was reported on this photo

A comment was reported on this photo

A comment was reported on this photo

A comment was reported on this photo

A comment was reported on this photo

Despite my shitty mood, my lips crack into a grin. I can't believe they reported all the thirst trap comments on my pictures. I rarely pay them much attention. Some are funny and some are even tempting, but a few scrolls on their profiles tell me everything I need to know about them. They'd fold in less than a minute and they aren't worth my time. They don't understand how bad I need the pain, the screams, and the fucking blood.

There are literal studies on all the ways I'm fucked up, but @BladeSpinner is doing their civic duty and ridding me of all those lesser beings. It's crazy, hilarious, and kinda sweet, if I'm being honest. I'm guessing someone's a little jealous, but they needn't be. Right now, there isn't anyone half as entertaining as this creeper.

SYDNEY

Breaking news. Tragedy has struck again here in Seattle, where four more bodies were found in an abandoned trailer this morning after having been brutally *beaten to death as well as multiple stab wounds.*

The victims were in their late twenties and found a little after 9 a.m. this morning, but authorities believe they were assaulted sometime between 2 and 4 a.m. this morning. Police do not suspect they were murdered where they were found and have started the search for the original crime scene.

When asked if the cases were related, SPD had this to say, "We do not believe this is the work of a serial killer, the pattern is too inconsistent and the method of killing varies greatly with each victim."

SPD is working hard to narrow down the list of suspects for all cases, but so far are without leads. They're asking all locals to please remain vigilant and to call the number on the screen below if you have any useful information that can help us apprehend this suspect. Eyewitness News 15. Gary, back to you.

The voices on the TV start off light, a far away sound that I'm able to ignore while I choose sleep over whatever humdrum story is being discussed over the airways. However, I groan when the ability to ignore it grows more difficult. I move and shuffle, tangling myself further in the sheets, annoyed that I'm being pulled from the most wonderful of dreams.

I've never dreamed of sex before, never wondered what it would be like to be stuffed full and begging for more. On nights that I do dream, I'm standing on the podium, a trophy in my hand with adoring friends and family cheering my name. On those days, I wake up refreshed, motivated, and ready to take on the day.

But the dream so rudely interrupted was filthy. Dirty. Downright debasing. And I fucking loved it.

I squirm in the empty bed, feeling the cool Egyptian cotton along my flushed skin. The sheets rub between my legs, swiping along my pussy, and I whimper. Damn him. I can't stop thinking about what I saw.

I squirm some more, replaying the image in my head again and again. I wish I could say the dream from last night was spurred by my imagination alone, but it wasn't. I saw something I shouldn't have last night. My subconscious tried to warn me not to follow him into the movie theater. It was my own fault I'd found myself in this situation.

Who the fuck does something like that in public and why did it turn me on so much? If I didn't know any better, I'd say he did it on purpose, but he didn't seem like he was aware of me at all.

I suppose this is what I get. I broke my vow not to follow him off campus anymore, and now I'm well and truly fucked. I'll never be right in the head again because last night I saw him come and I want to see him do it again.

My hand creeps down my chest, across my torso, slipping beneath my panties under my cocoon of sheets. I'm wet and it's all that hockey player's fault. I have classes and practice this morning. I need to get to the rink before the others, but I can't right now. I need to get off. I need to get his perfectly beautiful cock out of my head—or in my mouth. I cannot believe he had the audacity to jerk off in a movie theater!

Last night, I followed him to watch some old slasher film that's been out for months. I don't like scary movies, but I sat at the top, hidden from view. I snuck in after him, disguised in my oversized hoodie and sweats and walked in with a group of other couples who looked like they came to make out and pretend to watch the movie.

I was on edge the entire time, freaked out by his sudden nearness. The possibility of being spotted, and the movie itself, only aided in my torment. The premise was dumb. The motivation, simple. The whole movie was centered around a serial killer obsessed with this girl and compelled to chop off her hair. She spent the whole movie screaming for her life as he hunted her down relentlessly. But when he finally caught her, when she screamed for help as he straddled her, covered in blood and wielding a gnarly knife; I watched Lucien.

He, however, watched the scenes unfold with blind fascination, slumped in his chair, legs spread open and his hand down his pants. I hadn't thought he'd do it, but when he pulled himself free of his pants and held his cock in his hands, I almost screamed. horrified he'd been so brazen. His head lolled back as he stroked himself, releasing ropes of cum all down his shaft as the protagonist passed out and the antagonist walked away scot-free.

Her screams never gave way to help. She was left alone to the mercy of the villain, to do with as he pleased, never to be seen again. The screen cut to black and while I was shaken, I was also bemused by how . . . exciting it all felt. My senses were overloaded, and my attention could not stray from the look on Lucien's face as a sense of calm rested over him. He used a stray napkin to wipe the jizz from his cock, then tucked himself back into his sweatpants and walked away.

The release I chase as I remember how hard he came all but crashes into me. His own moans of pleasure were drowned out by the actress's screams. But there's nothing to drown out my whimpers now as my orgasm builds, nor the high-pitched moans as I let go, remembering the look of fascination on his beautiful face as he did.

As I lay here, spent with arousal-coated fingertips, my skin flushed, and my bed empty, I'm flooded with even more thoughts of him. I can't escape him, and for the first time since this all started, I'm starting to think that's a real problem.

CHAPTER THIRTEEN

LUCIEN

Present

"**L**ucien, stop!" Sydney screams, her cry an arrow through my psyche.

I pause, then turn.

It's a slow, calculated movement that I don't even feel myself making. My vision's still red, and my rage urges me to set the whole world aflame. But when I look up, I'm met with wet blue eyes that pierce through the haze and freeze me to the spot.

"Please. That's enough, Lucien," she pleads. Her voice a bell in the quiet air. Sydney's steps are cautious as she approaches, her hands out to show she poses no threat. I know she's not a threat. I've known it from the day she initiated contact, but it doesn't stop me from tensing the closer she gets. She must see the tick in my jaw because she slows her advance even further.

"It's okay. You can stop now."

I look down at my foot, poised above one of the assholes head before bringing my face back up to hers.

Her pupils are blown wide but they're on me. No one else.

I yield the moment I feel her touch again, melting into the warmth of her skin when her soft hands cup my face, and she swipes the blood of my victims off my cheek.

The three idiots are discarded at our feet, with varying degrees of damage but she doesn't even spare them a second glance. She doesn't yell at me or freak out; she just stands here with me in the silence and stares into my soul until everything stops looking red. The past remains where it is and there's only the present.

"Let's go, okay?" she whispers.

I nod.

"Yeah. Let's go."

I see why she wanted to walk. We pull up to her apartment in mere minutes.

She points out her apartment building and I pull into the nearest parking spot, but it's when the engine cuts off that the once-comfortable silence we'd enjoyed for all of five minutes, turns. Changes. The interior of the car fills with the scent of coconut and something sweet.

What should have been a warm breeze blowing from the car vents feels sweltering in the confined space. The hair on my arms stands at attention with an electric charge.

I pull the key from the ignition, but neither of us stir. We let the charge build, enjoying the pull. Sydney's eyes are transfixed on me, burning like lasers.

It's not entirely unpleasant.

She's been staring the entire drive. Most people would find that creepy, but me? I find it endearing.

I swipe my hair out of my face and drop my head back onto the headrest. Lolling it to the side to face her, I resume our unspoken staring contest.

Seconds pass. Maybe minutes.

"You're staring," I accuse, though the last thing I want is for her to stop.

"You're staring back," she whispers.

My lips curl into a crooked grin and I settle deeper in my seat as my eyes continue to bore into hers.

A beautiful shade of pink creeps up her neck as she maps my features, but she doesn't blink or move. She's not just staring; she's searching, and something about being found by her spreads a warmth I've long forgotten through me.

When the tension becomes too much, she blinks.

I win.

"Did I scare you?" I finally ask.

"Yes," she breathes.

My grin spreads wider, satisfied she's not lying to me again.

"Are you *still* scared?"

She turns her body toward me, tucking her ankle beneath her knee while a small smirk tugs at the side of her mouth. A very cute mouth.

"Yes," she repeats, more confident this time.

Interesting.

The back of my hand ghosts over her cheek, "Do you still wanna play with me?"

My knuckles are bleeding again, staining her pale cheeks as I stroke the skin. She doesn't rear back this time or sneer in disgust. She lets me touch and feel.

Her glittery eyelids flutter.

"Absolutely," she answers, gone to the sensation and relishing the contact. A deeper, redder blush highlights her cheeks now. It pairs nicely with the blood on her face, even more so when those blue eyes shine up at me.

I lean in closer, over the console and inhale the coconut scent of her hair. "Good," I whisper.

When her eyes flick to my mouth, I twirl my tongue along my lower lip, enjoying the dirty thoughts I imagine running through that head of hers. She tracks the motion, and her legs cross as she shifts in her seat. Her own tongue flicks out, subtly licking the seam of her dried lips. Her gloss, all but gone now thanks to our earlier make-out session against the car. Fuck, I can't wait to do that again.

"Such a brave little stalker, still willing to play even when you're scared. Still getting turned on despite the fear," I muse, more to myself than anything.

Sounds like my kind of girl.

I pull away abruptly, leaving us both reeling as I shift the conversation.

"Wha—" she starts.

"So, you weren't kidding when you said you lived close?" I note, looking up at the apartment building that's way too nice for a regular college student to be renting, but I guess plenty of people do since it is considered a part of campus.

Her eyes narrow at my sudden shift, but she doesn't question the change in pace.

"Yeah, um, it's super helpful to get to the arena and practice since I don't have a car." Her arms fold as she leans back against the door, legs still crossed, but more relaxed than before.

My eyes widen.

"What kind of rich girl are you? Why don't you have a car?" I ask.

"Sacrifices had to be made," she says dryly.

Sacrifices?

Something about that word bothered me. I didn't like the idea of her being sacrificial. A sense of protectiveness surges through me and I'm suddenly really fucking annoyed by her lack of transportation. I get that she lives close, but it's not safe to be who she is without a car. She could be robbed or taken hostage and held for ransom.

Fuck, don't these people watch true crime shows? Don't they know the world is a dangerous place? Tonight was a perfect example. What if I hadn't been there when those guys were waiting outside? What would they have done to her?

Granted, they didn't know who she was, but that goes to show how unsafe it can be even for regular college students.

The blinding rage sneaks up on me so fast, I almost miss her response to my question.

"A car is a *luxury*," she mocks, doing a terrible impersonation of an old English butler.

"Aren't you an *heiress*? Luxury should be your middle name, right?"

The furrow in my brows deepens yet she looks more amused than anything.

"I told you,"—she points to herself—"Disappointment, remember? Competitive figure skating comes at a cost." Her shoulder lifts into a shrug, as if it's the most inconsequential thing in the world.

"And I told *you* you're not a disappointment." I scowl, ready to throttle anyone who ever led her to believe she was a disappointment.

How can anyone be disappointed in someone as incredibly interesting as her? I've known her for all of an hour, and I'm fascinated. Drawn to her in a way I haven't been to anything or anyone in years. Who wouldn't appreciate everything this girl has to offer?

Her face scrunches with a somber expression before giving a sad smile. "Give it time," she sighs. "I'll disappoint you, too."

Before I can rebuttal that stupid statement, she's grabbing her bag and opening the door. Leaning over she says, "Wait here."

The door closes and she trots up the stone steps, her long braid bouncing along her back and her skirt blowing in the wind.

Yeah, fuck that.

I climb out of the car behind her, ignoring her little command. This is *my* game and we're only in the second period. Like hell I'm waiting in the car.

I catch up to her before she has time to unlock her door.

Her hand stalls on the handle when she hears me running up behind her.

Spinning on me, she glowers, "What do you think you're doing? I said to wait."

I smirk. I'm not sure what gave her the impression I would listen. She might be a disappointment to her asshole of a dad, but I'm still willing to bet Princess is used to getting what she wants. That staggering beauty of hers is the knife she wields to cut weaker men down. Despite what she says, she still carries herself in the same way most spoiled rich girls do.

I step forward, bracing an arm against the doorway and blocking her only exit away from me. "I'm not letting you out of my sight again, Little Stalker."

Her hand lingers on the doorknob and her lips part.

She huffs, searching my eyes for the punchline. "I'm not–"

I lean in closer, bringing my face down to hers. She sucks in a sharp breath, and I can feel the inhale against my lips.

"Let me in."

Her hand tightens on the doorknob, and she looks away.

"I shouldn't," she whispers back.

Her bottom lip, still swollen from our earlier kiss, tucks between her teeth. Pinching her chin between my forefinger and thumb, I pull it free. Then I sink *my* teeth in. She hisses in pain, trying to pull away but her back meets the door with a thud. The saccharine tang of her blood fills my mouth, and I lick at the bite.

"So fucking sweet," I groan.

She whimpers in response, but her body sings from the pain, groaning against my lips as she murmurs my name.

"Lu-cien."

Her left leg lifts, wrapping around my waist as she grinds herself against me. I slide my hands up her thigh, holding her in place as I kiss her again. This kiss is deeper, harder, and there's another thud when her equipment bag falls from her shoulder. If this weren't a corner apartment we'd be giving the neighbors one hell of a show. Even still, there's nothing stopping them from *hearing* us. More whimpering sounds when I squeeze her ass hard enough to bruise.

My dick hardens from the noises spilling from her lips, and the need to get her inside this fucking apartment before I lose all semblance of control grows.

"Let me in, Princess."

"I c-can't," she stutters between kisses and I'm not sure if she means she physically can't or isn't allowed. I have no idea if she has a roommate but I assume if anyone was home they would have come out by now with all of the knocking we've been doing.

"You *can*—and you will. I *know* you want to. So either stop fighting me or fight me like you mean it but either way, you're not getting rid of me."

I pull back, releasing her so she has to face me.

"I . . ."

We're both panting, unable to get enough air but our mouths draw closer yet again.

I press my forehead to hers.

"Open the *fucking* door, Sydney," I pant, my own desperation bleeding through. "Now."

What do you want

In life?

Seen

WTF. No

Haven't decided yet.

CHAPTER FOURTEEN

LUCIEN

THE KNOB TURNS, AND the door gives way. I move to close the space between us, ready to wrap her up and steal her breath, but then . . . her phone rings.

Sydney's pupils widen, and before I know it, she's turning her back to me, answering it before the first ring is even finished. It's a move that suggests she was expecting the call, but leaves me feeling somewhat rejected all the same.

"Hey, Dad. Yeah, I just walked in the door," she says.

She peeks over her shoulder to me, ushering me in and gesturing for me to be quiet.

I shake my head, amused by her frantic shushing, but ultimately listen. This time. After all—if even briefly— she surrendered, and invited me in. Okay 'invite' might be a generous word but I'm inside and that's all that matters right now.

Quickly adjusting my hard-on I scout my surroundings, looking around the lavish apartment. The shined parquet flooring and floor-to-ceiling windows are immediately some of my favorite features. The ten-foot ceilings are impressive, and the gourmet kitchen is huge. A bit overkill for one person, but she did say she was a Sinclair, so I suppose it shouldn't be too surprising.

"Well, there was a hockey game tonight, so it was a lot more crowded than usual," I hear Sydney say as she toes off her shoes and disappears down the hallway. I do the same, pulling my shoes off and leaving them at the entrance with her bags.

"Well, you know I had to walk," she says into the phone.

My ears perk at the sound of her lying again, but I do my best to ignore it. I don't follow the Sinclairs closely, but I'm aware of the wealth and notoriety they've acquired in recent years, though none of it is any good. They're worse than the Andersons, if rumors are true.

"I also had to carry my bags," she argues.

I note the magnitude of everything she has, from the massive bookshelf to the large sectional and gigantic island.

"It's a little over a mile's walk *uphill*, Dad." Her voice raises a bit to make the point.

Her apartment is grand and spacious, but there's also a coziness to it. I can feel her presence everywhere, see the little personal touches that give me more insight into who she really is.

"Yeah, no, yes, I understand. Okay, I'll be ready." Sydney continues scuffling about as she finishes up her call, attempting to stress clean by the looks of it. Leaning against the kitchen island, I watch her.

"I promise," she states.

"I love—" Her words cut short and her eyes close for a few seconds longer than a blink.

She lets out a defeated sigh. "Sorry about that," she says, finally addressing me.

"You changing apartments?" I ask, motioning a finger to the wall of moving boxes. The only thing unsightly among all the grandeur.

Her tiny neck bobs as she swallows. "Um, yeah. That's why I didn't want you coming up. It's a mess in here." She looks away, trying to shuffle some paper together on the island.

"You think I care about a little mess?" I tease. Her eyes roll when they cut to me, but she totally picks up on the double meaning.

I rest my back against the counter top, waiting for her to call me out on the joke but she doesn't. Instead she wrings her fingers, her discomfort evident with the fact that I'm here. In *her* private space. It's a bit ironic, but I won't bother dwelling on it. Soon I'll have her in all the private places, maybe the public ones too. My new toy seriously fucked up the day she decided to stalk someone like me. But it's like they say, good things come to those who wait. And I've waited a long time for a playmate like her.

No longer able to take the awkward standoff between us, she points to my folded arms. "You should let me take a look at that."

I look to where she's pointing and note that I never did wrap my knuckles from the altercation earlier. I was so busy marking her, it hadn't occurred to me again to wrap them. The skin around my knuckles is even more bludgeoned now that I'd been in another fight less than two hours after the first one.

That might be a new record. I typically avoid damaging my hands so much because of hockey, but since I was facing suspension, letting off more steam than I'm typically afforded seemed more than worth it. That'd come back to bite me for sure, but it was the least of my concerns now.

As it stands, my concerns lie solely in how quickly I can get my little stalker to take her clothes off. She's seen me stripped of all my protections and now it's my turn to have her just as exposed. I want to see the *real* Sydney Sinclair. Up close and in high definition.

I hold my hand out and flex it, proving to her I'm fine, but she shakes her head, turning away to reach above in her kitchen cabinet. She's a little taller than most other girls I've met, but she's still shorter than me and unable to easily reach the top shelf. When she arches to her tiptoes, I get a full view of her calves flexing. It takes everything in me not to jump over the island and bend her over. I never thought calves would be what did it for me, but I've never been so aroused. I clench the edge of the marble top, forcing myself to wait it out. It'll be so much better once she's begging me to fuck her.

"I don't have anything as fancy as gauze or medical tape, but I can at least clean it for you," she says sheepishly, holding a bottle of antiseptic and a bag of cotton balls in her hand.

She's already admitted I still scare her, and her request seems genuine, not a flagrant order like she made when she'd told me to stay in the car. So, I relent and step closer into the kitchen, purposely standing too close while I hold out my hand. She takes it shakily, blowing out controlled breaths as she rests my palm in hers. She avoids eye contact, choosing instead to fixate on our hands.

"You should be more careful. You could have hurt yourself," she admonishes.

Her warm hands are gentle when she swipes the wet cotton ball against my skin.

"They started it," I retort, relishing in the sting and yearning for more of her touch already. Even if it burns. Even if it hurts. Especially when it hurts.

"Didn't mean you had to finish it," she grumbles. "You could have scared them off."

My brows furrow, confused by her outlandish suggestion.

"You'd rather I let them go?" I grit.

The question is more accusing than I intended. Her thumb swipes over my hand in the briefest caress, though her focus remains trained on her task.

"I'd *rather* we kept kissing," she says softly, dabbing at a particularly bloody cut. She clears her throat, attempting to cover her slip up. "A few of these are going to scar."

The antiseptic burns, but I don't move a muscle, lest I risk *her* moving.

"They insulted you," I tell her, refusing to let her brush this off.

I can see her brows raise before she sighs, "It doesn't matter."

Her tone is somber, quiet. I half-expect her to finish that ridiculous sentiment with something stupid like 'violence is never the answer,' which is in stark contrast to everything she'd said in her messages.

I balk.

"Like hell it doesn't. They deserved what they got," I argue.

The tight corner of her lips curve into a smile, but she lets it fall away. It wrecks me, dawning on me too late this might be a really bad idea. The things I have planned for her might be too much, and whatever persona @BladeSpinner was, is a figment of my imagination. But then she's laughing again, stopping abruptly, then starting up again like a weird stuttering engine that can't decide if it wants to turn on or not.

"What's so funny?" I ask, not entirely sure what's happening right now.

"Nothing," she says, suppressing another giggle before she even gets the word out. "It's just, this is really fucked. I mean right? This is . . . this is *so* fucked."

Her laughter is uncontrollable now that she's done cleaning my knuckles.

"What is?"

"*This.*" She points between us. "You're in my house!" The last hour must finally be catching up to her.

"Uhh, yes?"

A bit of a delayed reaction, but okay.

She shakes her head, her laughter subsiding as she blows out a breath. "This is not how I saw my evening going."

"Really? And how did you think it would go?" I cant my head to the side.

Those soft lips of hers part. "I just mean, by all accounts, you should be furious with me," she admits, all sense of humor gone as she eyes me curiously.

I take a step closer.

"Who says I'm not?" She drops my hand, and I nudge her back toward the counter until her hips hit the edge. "Who says I'm not. Who says I didn't lure you here on purpose and force you to let me in just so I can have my way with you and see how *you* like to have your privacy violated?" I taunt, palming the countertop so she can't get away.

Her beautiful neck rolls with a slow, deep swallow.

"I'm—"

I place a finger to her lips.

"There'll be plenty of time to show me how sorry you are later," I say. "You'll *earn* my forgiveness like the good girl you are. Won't you, Princess?"

I give her a wink and lean back, allowing my words to sink in. I can tell the moment they register because her mouth instantly goes dry as she frantically licks at her lips. She turns toward the fridge, reaches over my arm, and practically rips the door from its hinges, before guzzling a bottle of Voss water.

The bottle shakes in her hands, her restless energy giving her away. I see Little Stalker for *exactly* who she is. That's not fear. *No,* that's adrenaline coursing through those veins.

She's excited.

CHAPTER FIFTEEN

LUCIEN

"WELL, THERE'S, UM, ROOM on the couch. I just need to go change, and definitely shower," Sydney says, her neck subtly craned toward her armpits.

I make my way over to the couch, settling in with both arms wrapped over the back, my legs spread. Sydney watches my every move with hawk-like precision, reminding me of a certain talented goalie, but when she notices me staring back she tries to scurry away down the hall.

"Come here," I call, stopping her in her tracks before she can turn the corner.

Her shoulders slump but she turns, her feet doing a light shuffle without actually moving closer.

"We're going to be late if I don't hurry up and get out of this outfit," she supplicates.

Oh, she needn't worry about that. Those clothes will be coming off shortly.

"This is *my* game, remember?" I croon.

She blinks once. Twice.

Had my Little Stalker Princess forgotten already? We were playing my game now and the rules were very different than they'd been before. "We're going to play a little game of Simon Says."

"Simon Says?" she questions. When I make no move to correct her, she says, "You want to play a children's game? What, are we five?" She practically spits the words.

"I can promise that what I plan to do to you is anything but childish. So, play the game Sydney . . . or forfeit and the game *ends*." I raise a brow.

"Do you mind telling me why we have to play right now? Can't it wait until I'm done showering?" she asks.

I pretend to think about it. "No."

"Why not?" Sydney puts a hand on her hip that now juts to one side.

I crook a finger for her to step closer before resting my arm over the couch again.

"It's important I know how well you take direction, Sydney." I keep my voice low and non-threatening.

She eyes me warily but her nails dig into her palm as she takes ten tentative steps toward me.

"Okay," she breathes. I nod my approval. I'll be taking the lead tonight and my sweet Sydney will follow like the stalker she is.

"Good," I say. "Now, Simon says 'take off your clothes.'"

She snorts. "Don't you mean 'Lucien Says'?"

That's the spirit, Princess.

"Oh, I *like* that," I tell her. "Okay then, Lucien says 'take off your clothes.'"

Her laughter settles and she gnaws at her mangled thumbnail as she shifts uncomfortably under my gaze. I'll have to break that bad habit of hers. Only *I* will get to make her bleed.

"What's the matter, Princess? You don't want to play with me anymore?" I pout.

Her hand quickly drops to her side. "No, I do!"

"Then what's the hold up?" I ask, gesturing to her overly dressed body.

She parts her lips to speak then closes them, shaking her head. "Nothing."

Without another word, she peels one side of her costume down her arm, revealing a muscled shoulder. We're barely past her collarbone and I'm already impressed with her body. Her chest is pink with embarrassment and my bruised bite mark on her neck has deepened to a reddish-purple shade. My smile only grows wider as her icy blue eyes darken. She looks back at me and I recognize her stare as my own. She wants this as much as I do.

Before I know it, her delectable breasts are on full display, and I have to grip the back of the couch to remain seated. The key is not to scare your prey before you go in for the kill, but fuck if I don't ache to make her kneel before me. I want to fuck those beautiful tits of hers, spit on them, and paint her chest in my cum.

Slowly, she drags the rest of her outfit down, revealing taut abdominal muscles that line her stomach with the cutest belly button. I rub the growing bulge between my legs, which is straining painfully in my pants right now. She hooks her thumbs under the bunched fabric and shimmies them side to side, taunting me with a peek of her sharp hips. Fuck, I think she's riling me up on purpose, that sneaky little . . .

"Lucien says 'turn around.'" My voice is hoarse, giving way to my true desire, but I need to keep control. I'm starting to forget why I'm not ripping her in half with my cock already. But then that sweet smile curls on her lips as she ultimately obeys me, and a rush of euphoria hits me straight through the veins.

With her back turned, her outfit and panties finally fall to her ankles, and she steps out, her pert ass plump yet firm. I hold my fist between my teeth to keep from taking another bite out of her. Her skin is perfect. Flawless. Save for my bite mark and the light bruise from when she fell on the ice, there's not a single scratch on her.

Oh, I can't wait to see her covered head to toe in reminders that she belongs to me. She'll be thoroughly marked by the time I'm through with her. The best thing about claiming a stalker, is that they're already committed to the chase.

"Lucien says 'bend over.'"

She doesn't hesitate this time, taking the initiative and spreading her legs slightly farther apart, gripping her ankles for balance. If I didn't know any better, I'd think she'd done this before, though her trembling limbs suggest otherwise. If I want her, I'm going to have to prepare her for what being with a monster like me is really like. Even if it takes all night long. I'll have her the exact way I envision. I cup my cock, rutting against my own hand as thoughts of all the ways I can contort Sydney's body to fit mine flit through my mind.

"Lucien says 'spread your cheeks apart' . . . and 'hold it.'" My voice is so gruff now I barely recognize it.

Again, she obeys, spreading her cheeks far enough her lips spread too, showing me exactly what I do to her. Her glistening pink pussy drips with arousal and I imagine what breaching those walls will feel like. Absentmindedly, I move my hand back and forth, lightly stroking myself, unable to resist the urge to take it out with her back turned, but at the mere sight of her, I'm ready to fucking blow. It's pure agony when her fingers start to slip from their hold, unable to remain spread with her arousal spilling over them. They twitch to rub at herself in kind, and I ache to watch her suffer.

She tries to look over her shoulder, no doubt for a better view.

But I don't allow it.

"Lucien says 'eyes front,'" I growl, jaw tight and predatory.

"You've gotten to watch me for months. An all-access pass to my torment. Well, now it's *my* turn to get my fill of you. To watch *you* to my heart's content. To see every unobstructed part of you. To see every hidden secret you possess. So, keep those fucking ice blue eyes straight ahead, and don't you dare steal another peek of me without my explicit say so, or you'll be punished, Sydney. *Severely*," I warn, my hand fully fisted around my cock.

She groans in protest.

"And before that rebellious streak of yours decides disobeying me might be worth it," I say. "I must warn you that my punishments are not for your pleasure, they're for *mine*."

She whimpers, but ultimately obeys, her head turning forward again.

"If you don't play my way, the game ends and you lose, understand?" I ask. The husk in my tone unmistakable.

I don't pull my pants farther down to reach the base, instead I rub a thumb over the sensitive head, edging myself into delirium.

"Yes," she breathes, "I understand."

I settle deeper into her expensive velvet couch, breathing in the scent of her home as a bead of precum leaks from my dick onto the costly material beneath me. I should fuck her on this couch and ruin the fine upholstery. I wonder what her dad would have to say about that. How would he feel to see the evidence of his daughter's defilement on her pricey cream couch?

I stroke myself again.

"Can you feel it, Princess? My stare on your skin?" I groan. "It's palpable isn't it, the feeling of eyes on you?" Her back ripples and she breathes a soft moan between her ragged breaths.

"*Yes.*"

"That's what it felt like every day you watched me," I reveal, my voice like gravel. "That's what it *still* feels like every time you look at me."

More arousal leaks from her pussy, dripping over her knuckles as she struggles to obey and keep spread.

Such a good fucking girl.

"Aw, Princess you're soaked. You can barely hold yourself open anymore," I taunt even as I drive myself further to the brink.

"No, no," she whimpers, "I-I can do it." She spreads herself wider for me, her tight hole stretching open, and I practically lose it.

"Oh, yes, look at that," I moan. "You're shaking. The anticipation is killing you, isn't it? It's the unknown. The undeniable curiosity."

I thrust up in my hand.

"Yes," she moans again.

"That feeling is intoxicating. I grew fucking addicted to it, Sydney." I groan as I choke the fuck out of my dick, fixated on how turned on she's getting by my words. "You will too."

She shakes her head, her loose braid swaying between her legs.

"Fuck, Lucien," she whispers.

"Even when you weren't watching, I'd imagine you were. I'd imagine your touch, your voice. I wondered what you felt like. What you smelled like. What you tasted like."

Fuck, I want to taste her.

"Touch yourself," I bark. She doesn't flinch.

"Does Lucien say so?" she asks, her cadence coy, but her words shaky.

Fucking hell, this girl.

"Yes. Lucien says 'stick those soaked fingers inside that tight pussy of yours and fuck yourself until I say stop.'"

Again there's no hesitation as she allows a single manicured finger to sink into her wet heat while her other hand spreads her lips apart. It's a perfect view. When she pulls her finger out, it's wet and creamy, a positive sign that this is probably the most turned on she's ever been.

"Fucking perfect," I murmur, stroking the head of my cock.

A feral moan rips from her throat as she tries to maintain her position and get off, but she's struggling to do both.

More precum spills from my own tip at the sight as I struggle to maintain my own control. She plunges in again, her pace slow and steady as she builds up to her orgasm. *In and out.* My grip tightens on my cock. *Up and down.*

She adds another finger, picking up speed, but not driving in deeper. Her thrusts remain shallow, not even knuckle deep. Her legs shake even more as she draws nearer and I'm conflicted on whether I want to let her come or not, but there's no stopping her because there's no stopping me.

I *don't* want her to stop.

I'm behind her in two large strides. Whipping my dick out fully, I shove my boxers down and jerk myself harder. She winces at the surprise touch of my palm to her back, but neither of us stops stroking.

"Lucien says 'don't *fucking* move,'" I growl.

My free hand slides down her spine and she preens like an animal, arching her back and spreading even wider for me.

"Lucien, please," Sydney moans. "Fuck, please."

She *wants* me to fuck her. But not yet, Princess. Not fucking yet.

I curl my fingers into the nape of her hair, palming her scalp when I feel the raised bump of a gnarly jagged scar. I'll have to ask her about that later, but for now I hold her tight until I'm sure she's not going to seat herself on my cock. The head of my dick rubs at her entrance, careful not to push in as I gather her wetness.

"Fuck you're so warm and wet," I say.

I pump harder, using longer strokes, spreading her wetness over the tip until . . .

She's gasping and moaning as I shoot my entire load on her ass. I watch as it dribbles down her back, between her cheeks and over her cunt. A carnal roar tears through me with my release. And she moans my fucking name.

It's music to my ears.

"*Oh*. Yes . . . Lucien," she moans. "Fuck. Touch me."

I smack her ass, feeling the sting against my palm since that is the only touching I'll be doing right now. It's exactly what she needs, because then she's coming, thrown right over the edge with me as she comes apart.

Fuck yes. Who's in charge now, Princess?

Her fingers finally slip, but I don't punish her for it. Taking her hand, I bring her fingers to my mouth and suck.

I moan around her fingers as she gasps. "Delicious."

I slide my other hand back up to the nape of her neck, gripping it before drawing her back to me. Her backside flushes against me, our cum sticking between us, and she squeaks in surprise. The feel of her breath quickening when I snake my palm to the front of her throat is enough to make me come again. A soft whimper falls from her lips when I apply a little pressure and my cock jumps in response, but I keep her steady, relishing the feel of her strained swallows against my palm. Her body shifts as she squirms, and I chuckle in her ear.

"Did you like that?" She nods and I squeeze harder. "Words, Sydney. You've been awfully quiet. I want to hear you *speak*." I nip at her lobe.

"Yes, I loved it," she moans, her breath ragged. "Di-Did I do well?"

She shifts from foot to foot, her body squirming against mine as I brush my other hand down the front of her body.

"Oh, Sydney. You did *so* well. Don't you feel like a winner?" I ask.

Her head bobs against my shoulder as she nods.

"Yeah," she whispers. "I fucking do."

"Good," I tell her, releasing her neck and turning her back around. Her cheeks are red and flushed, her hair is all messy, but a smile is in her eyes, even if she's holding back the one on her lips. She peers down, probably hoping to get a good look at my dick, but we'll have plenty of time for bodily exploration in the shower.

I grip her chin , forcing her head upward before capturing her lips in a painful kiss. She doesn't complain. She opens for me, and I swallow her squeals when I give her ass a quick slap and pull away.

"Now, Lucien says 'let's go take a shower.'"

CHAPTER SIXTEEN

SYDNEY

I WONDER IF IT'LL happen now. Will he fuck me? It might be good to let him fuck me now. I'm sure there'll be blood, and if we do it in the shower we won't make such a mess. I'd honestly thought he was just going to shove himself inside right there in the living room. Part of me hoped he would so I could be spared the embarrassing confession that I've never had sex before.

Boys were distractions from my goal and whatever sexual tension I typically had I used as fuel to make me a better athlete. I didn't feel this way about anyone else. None of my father's prospects for me came close to eliciting this reaction. Teenage fingers did little to break my hymen in the past and the few times it'd happened with Bradford had been so lackluster I'd barely come. It felt nothing like it had in the living room, and once again I'm reminded Lucien has hardly even touched me. A palm to the head and a smack to the ass and I was coming harder than I ever have in my entire life.

A small part of me screams to quit while I'm ahead. Turn the fuck back.

Letting him fuck me will just imprint him further into my mind. It will tie our souls in a way I'll never be able to untangle. Who in their right mind would bear that torment knowing it would all be in vain? I'd never be allowed to be with him.

Even if I wasn't leaving, my dad would never accept someone like Lucien. In all fairness, I don't know any sane parent who would accept him, but even if by some miracle my dad did, what chance would we ever have? He's a champion hockey player bound to go to the NHL and I'm a disgraced figure skater lined up to work for my dad's business as his legacy until the day I marry and produce my own heir. Lucien would be expected to bow and kiss the ring if he ever wanted to be a part of my family. But after everything *I've* seen, I know one thing for sure, Lucien bows to no one. Our futures are all but written in stone. So I should stop this before it goes too far, right?

But then again . . .

A Sinclair doesn't quit.

The water is warm when I step a shaky foot onto the tile and then the other. I sense his presence the whole time, like a ghost I only know exists because I can hear the soft thud of his clothes falling to the floor, but I don't turn around. I wait. I'm shivering even as the water grows warmer.

It's like he said, the feel of his eyes on me is a physical thing and Lucien's gaze is like razors slicing into my skin. He wants me to know how he felt all that time I followed him, but I can't bring myself to be regretful as his stare licks across my body.

After what feels like light years of imperceptible time, I hear the soft cadence of the water break, its trajectory obstructed. I take a deep breath, knowing what I'll see when I turn around, but also too cowardly to gaze upon it.

Lucien is next-level hot with his clothes *on*, a wet dream for those of us with the particular penchant for dangerous men, but without the barrier of clothing, well, he might just be too dangerous for consumption.

Come on, Sydney, there's no such thing as obstacles for a Sinclair. You want him to fuck you? Then you have to be able to stare at this man's naked body . . . preferably without passing out.

Pep talk completed, I suck in another lungful of air and spin around. Except the movement is too sudden and I practically slip and die on the floor of my shower before ever getting to marvel at his masterpiece of a cock. I just know it's as beautiful as the rest of him.

Quick hands whip out to catch me, and before I know it, an eyeful is the least of my worries. Our naked bodies are slick against one another as he smashes my wet body against his.

Oh, my God.

His cock rises between my thighs, hard and prodding. His abs flex against my torso and ribs. And I can feel his heart beating the strangest staccato rhythm against my breast, like it's just as insane as the rest of him. I should move. Bar myself from his hold. But my eyes can't stop taking in . . .all of him.

Tattoos adorn the front of his body, fewer than on his back, but still masterful. The script catches my eyes more than the images this time. They're like mosaic secrets to who he is written for those with the honor to see him bare–and an honor it is. One line in the center of his breastbone catches my eye.

Death is unrivaled, thus so am I.

My fingers brush over the lettering before I even give it conscious thought and his cock jumps up, tapping my pussy in response. I'm not sure that was with conscious thought either. I finally peek below his hips. That felt . . .strange. And not in the 'first time a dick has been near my vagina' strange. It felt foreign. Something metal and cold. My eyes are deadlocked with the offensive appendage as I stare at his cock, mouth agape. Sure enough, there are three silver bars speared through his dick.

I whip my gaze to his.

"You-How-*Why*?" I stutter.

I look down at it again, horrified.

"Doesn't that hurt?!" I screech, eying his dick with renewed curiosity. I know boys are distractions, but I'm not some stuck-up prude who doesn't know what a dick looks like or that sex—when done right—is supposed to feel good. I've gathered that much in my years of abstinence. What I don't get is how putting his robo-dick inside me with all of *that* going on is supposed to feel good for either of us.

His laugh is stomach-clenching and full, a fact I know because I can *see* his abs ripple the harder he giggles.

"No, it doesn't hurt." His hand wraps around my throat as he drags me closer. "But when I got the first one, it was *so* painful." He rolls his forehead against mine. "*Fuck,* you have no idea. I'm hard just thinking about it. I had to do it again and it felt just as good. So, I had to get it done a third time."

"Let me guess, you want another one," I rasp, because not even being choked will distract me from the fact that his dick has three silver rods pierced through it.

He shrugs.

"Someday, but right now I want something *just* as satisfying." He squeezes tight enough to make my eyes bug. On reflex, I grab his wrist, digging my nails in to abate his grasp. He leans into me, groaning as he slams me against the shower wall, but I don't push back. He holds me there while his eyes take their sweet time roaming every square inch of my exposed skin. My heart beats faster and my teeth sink into my lower lip.

It was one thing when I couldn't see him staring at me but now . . .

Lucien shakes his head, releasing some of the pressure from my neck.

"What?" I ask, craving the pressure again. It was grounding. Without it, I'm faced with how bare I am, and for the first time tonight, under Lucien's gaze, I feel the complete opposite of excessive, I feel inadequate.

"Don't do that," he whispers, his words almost lost to the sounds of the running shower.

"Do what?" I ask, though I can guess what he's thinking. I figured as much. He doesn't like what he sees in me as much as I like what I see in him. These past few months I've been a figure in the background of his life, a ghost over his shoulder. This up close and personal look is bound to come with some disappointments. I built up the mystique too much and fell short of expectations.

He gives me a pointed look, a crease forming between his thick brows, but he says nothing for a while.

I move to push him off.

"I know what we're going to play next." He grins, gripping me again.

Shit, did I make him mad?

I try to suck in air, but his grip is so tight, it's impossible to get enough. Adrenaline pumps in my veins and the whooshing sound of blood floods my ears. All the while, my pussy throbs, begging for the attention my throat's getting. I squirm in his hold, but it's not to get free—it's to create friction. He recognizes what I'm doing and shoves me back to force me still.

"Nuh uh uh . . . No getting off just yet. We have to finish the game first," he says.

I groan and he releases the pressure enough for me to speak.

"Okay, fine. What's next?" I ask with a huff.

"You'll like this one. It's called Seven Minutes in Heaven. You remember that, right?"

I nod, confused, but excited.

"Good girl." He lets my throat go and I suck in air—and water—causing me to cough. My head is loopy and fogged, but my body has never been more relaxed. The thrumming in my pussy grows stronger and I moan a muffled plea in response. I could grow addicted to his praise alone.

Grasping my hand, he wraps my fingers around *his* throat, granting me permission to squeeze in return. I'm shocked he'd give me this kind of control. Or at least the illusion of it.

My hand squeezes and he grins.

"You have seven minutes to explore my body in whatever way you want," he says.

I stroke my thumb up and down his Adam's apple.

"Why only seven minutes?" I ask, though I'm already stealing time, my fingers trailing his nape.

"Because that's the name of the game."

Of course, now he's being practical. I know he knows what I mean. He has to, right?

"I know that, but won't you . . . you know . . . need more time?"

I'm hoping he doesn't last only seven minutes. I want to really experience him, not just have some quick fuck in the shower. Seven minutes can't possibly be enough time for sex, can it?

A dark chuckle vibrates against my fingertips. "Oh, Princess, I'm not going to fuck you."

I drop my hand, side stepping him to glare at his entirely too beautiful face.

"What?" Jesus, I sound petulant, but his declaration surprises me. "You said—"

"I'm not going to fuck you . . . yet," he clarifies.

"Why not?" I quip.

Serenity, Sydney, serenity.

"Because . . ." His head tilts and his wet hair flops to one side. He'd be adorable if he wasn't looking at me like I'm his prey. "Right now, you'd break far too easily." He traces the edges of my collarbone with his finger. "I'd like to make sure you can handle me first, so I don't crush you." His finger drags up the column of my throat, then flicks my chin. "At least not yet."

I have no doubt that he'd be a bit much for any first timer, but he doesn't get it. It doesn't matter if he rips me in two, we only have tonight. He could break me a thousand ways and glue me back together and it still wouldn't change the fact that I'm leaving tomorrow.

"And playing these little games of yours will prove that I can *handle* it?" I ask.

He just shrugs, making me want to wrap my hands around his throat again and not let go.

The water beats against his back as steam bellows around us. Yet, somehow, he looks even more formidable, like not even the water can win against him.

"You can learn a lot about a person by watching how they compete. The game or task doesn't really matter, it's how you handle it that makes the biggest difference to me. So, if you can't handle *this,* well then, it's probably best we don't have sex." His hands tangle in my hair and scratch across my scalp, not the least bit hindered by my scar. He tilts my head up to meet him. "Besides, I don't need to fuck you to have fun with you. You've proven that already. I could ruin you without ever giving you my dick." He chuckles, the psycho look in his eyes bright as he threatens to withhold from me the one thing I desire most.

"Please, Lucien," I beg, unbothered with how I might sound anymore.

"Shh shh shh, I'll be taking my *sweet* time with you, Princess," he promises.

I whimper when he draws me closer, petting my head. His golden eyes reflect anything but sweet intentions.

"Now you have *six* minutes to touch me however you want."

"I thought you said seven"

He smirks.

"Clock's ticking, Princess."

I waste no more time. I have him naked in my shower for six minutes and I'm going to use every second to marvel at him.

Using the pad of my middle finger, I trace the outline of his face, swiping first over the bridge of his nose, then his cheekbones, then his lips.

I'm tempted to kiss him, but I'm not sure how I'll be able to stop if I start. Kissing him is my new favorite thing, but I won't let this moment go to waste.

Water cascades down his face, causing his hair to stick to his forehead. I lightly brush it away at first, but it flows right back to its original spot. He has a beautiful head of hair, dark and wavy. Though the water weighs his curls down, same as mine. Still . . . I wonder if I can cut a piece of it and keep it. Maybe I can make something out of it.

Jesus, this is why he thinks you're a stalker, Sydney.

I spend a moment longer than necessary fiddling with his hair before I rake my hands through it, straining on my tiptoes as I pull it back from forehead to nape. His low growl hums through my fingertips when I pull harder.

"Do it again." I whisper his words from earlier.

He grins and his neck cranes back the harder I pull, exposing his throat to me. I said I wouldn't kiss him, but I said nothing about biting him. I lick tentatively at first, allowing the warm water to slide over my tongue before I clamp down, savoring the bite. He moans and even that tastes delicious.

My hands glide through his hair again, before trailing my palms down his muscled neck to his shoulders and chest.

"Fuck," he mutters.

I tuck my lower lip behind my teeth, hiding the smirk that threatens to reveal his effect on me.

"Careful, Princess," he warns, a wicked smile on his lips.

"I don't think I will."

Lucien's brow arches.

"You'd said "to my heart's content."" I glance at his chest then back up. "I have a big heart."

His laugh is infectious, "Oh, of that, I have no doubt."

I continue tracing every rivulet, blemish, and freckle his body possesses. Every mole, scar, and vein, but once more I am drawn to his smattering of tattoos that complete his rebellious appearance.

My eyes snag on one in particular: a word beneath his left pectoral.

The single word is jagged, a little crooked and uneven, almost as if he did it himself. It lacks the appearance of a professional tattoo, more homemade or prison tat if anything, but still, it is beautiful, as if handwritten, an autograph transcribed especially for him.

My lip quirks, smiling as I re-read the word only for the sour taste of jealousy to churn my gut at the realization he has another girl's name immortalized on his skin. I want that. I want to be something permanent to him.

"Tick tock, Princess." Lucien looks down at me, the water glistening over his skin. "Better get a move on." His wet fingers hold me in place, gripping my chin as he speaks into my ear. "Time flies when you're having fun."

I press a palm to his chest.

"I still have three minutes. Turn around," I command, and to my surprise he listens. The only other command he seems to listen to is stop. The rest go in one ear and out the other but he allows me this.

My old friend *Luciens' back* stands before me in all its glory and again I rake my nails over the landscape of his tattoo. Tattooed demons smirk while beautifully shaded flames burn sinners alive in the intricate piece. It's not just Hell, but the whole landscape forms a dark skull in the palm of a large hand. It's so beautifully hidden.

Bending over slightly, I do what I've been dying to do since he first took his shirt off in that locker room. I take the flat of my tongue and drag a long desirous lick up his back, soothing the red scratches I've left. I leave kisses all over his shoulders while I grip and knead his firm ass. He startles, but then his forehead smacks against the tiles as though he's struggling to contain himself.

"Shit," he groans.

Looking around his waist, I see his hard dick jutting forward even as he phantom thrusts through my touching.

"One minute," he rasps.

"You sure? You seem to like me touching you." I reach around and trail a finger down his abs, but he grabs my wrist in a viper grip. "Fifty-five seconds."

It's barely enough time, but there's only one place left that I want to explore more than anything. I grab his shoulders and force him back around, grabbing his cock. He hitches a breath but doesn't force me to stop. I want to stare into those preternatural golden eyes some more, though first I need to understand his cock situation.

How can he stand to have that many piercings through his dick? Still gripped in my palm, I try to stroke it, but I'm afraid to touch the rods for fear of hurting him. Lucien senses my worry and reaches for my hand, guiding me from his base to tip. The jewelry pulls slightly, but they remain stationary, and he moans with each pass.

He drops his hand. "Harder," he groans.

No longer worried about the cock piercings, I take over the pace. Precum and water keep everything slick and even more spills out the more I keep going. There's about twenty more seconds before he's straining.

"Faster," he rasps. Again, I listen. Following his orders to a tee and trusting his guidance as I jack him off, another first for me.

His dick is pointed right at my stomach, and I want to paint my skin in everything he's about to release on me. He reaches for my throat again and I'm tempted to let go, but he growls in warning. I let the fear drive me to pump even harder, even faster. We're right at the seven-second mark when I rasp, "Cum on me again."

I don't even make it to 'one' before he's releasing ropes of cum all up my stomach.

My greedy fingers pull at his hair as he kisses me hungrily, the last of his cum dripping between us while I moan his name. How the fuck am I ever going to let this go? How am I supposed to walk away when even this has me losing my fucking mind? I could go insane with lust if I allowed myself to get lost in him.

I fear it's already too late.

"You did so fucking good, Princess. Five gold stars," he huffs, twiddling five fingers in the air. You'd think I won a fucking gold medal the way I beam with pride. Winning has always felt good, but I'm rarely praised for my accomplishments. Pleasing Lucien means not only reaping rewards, but genuine praise. It makes me want to *keep* pleasing him.

I look down at his dripping dick and swallow. He clocks my intention, the sudden need to lick the underside of his cock and clean every drop of his seed. I'd lick it from these floor tiles if it meant getting a taste of him, but he denies me. With the pinch of his fingers, he tilts my chin up, glaring at me in warning. His grip is tight and serious, but I swipe my tongue along the edge of my lips all the same.

"If you want it. You're going to have to earn it, Sydney."

"Please," I beg. "Tell me how I earn it."

CHAPTER SEVENTEEN

LUCIEN

I WOULD HAVE LOVED to sit and explain all my needs to her, have her fulfill my every wish and command, but that right there is part of the problem. I can get that anywhere, it's half the reason puck bunnies exist. That's not what makes my Little Stalker Princess special. The thing is I don't want her to simply fulfill a wish. I want her to crave it, to need it as desperately and fervently as I do, and so far she's done more than prove that she does. I'm convinced we found each other for a reason. I just need to toughen her up a bit, that's all.

Increase her endurance maybe.

Test her willingness if you will.

I'd like to know she won't pass out when I stuff my cock so far down her throat, she chokes on it. I need to know she won't freak out when I slice open her skin and watch her bleed. I'd prefer it if she didn't struggle so much to escape when she inevitably does try to run from me.

I'd hate to have to drag her back kicking and screaming.

A grin spreads across my face.

I'm kidding.

Of course I want her kicking and screaming.

Her precious giggles pull me from my thoughts of ruination.

"Are you going to walk around here naked the whole time?" She teases as we walk out of the bathroom and into her bedroom.

"Are *you* going to remain covered the whole time?" I retort, yanking her towel away.

She gasps, slapping an arm over her tits as she glowers at me. "Give. It. Back!" she growls. I dangle the towel just out of her reach above her head.

"Why? It's not like I didn't just spend the last fifteen minutes in the shower with you *naked*," I tease.

Her cheeks burn the prettiest shade as she holds up her full chest and stares down at her baby blue rug. I love that it's blue like her eyes.

"I mean, yeah, I get that, but . . ." Her shoulder lifts in a half-ass shrug, "it's different."

I hum, tearing her arm away from her chest before licking my lips.

"Different how?" I ask.

"Because . . ." she tries to cover them again and even one-handed, I manage to block her. "I don't know. I feel *exposed*."

She looks around for something else to use as cover, her nipples pebbled from the cold. She's still damp, unable to fully dry herself without the towel in my hand.

I drop her towel, and she eagerly bends to pick it up, her eyes rolling in defiance as she does. I take the opportunity and lunge for her, picking her up with her bare pussy pressed against my abdomen. Her legs automatically wrap around me. She's feather-light but her toned thighs grip me with the strength of an anaconda. *I bet her pussy would too.*

"I *like* you exposed, and I'm going to keep peeling back those layers of yours until I reach that ooey, gooey, center," I tell her.

Her nose scrunches up, the wrinkles along her bridge fucking adorable.

"Oh my God, please don't refer to my pussy as '*ooey gooey*,'" she whines.

"I was referring to your heart, but, yeah, sure, let's go with your pussy." I laugh, her body bouncing in my hold as I do, and she joins me.

"Yeah right, you're totally messing with me," she giggles as I turn to walk us past the bed toward her seating area. We came through the hallway entrance of the bathroom earlier, so I hadn't seen her room before now. It's a massive space for one girl with pops of blue and a monochromatic cream bedspread that screams luxury. But that's not what catches my attention. It's what's on the bed. Perched on the fluffy duvet sits a towel folded in the shape of an elephant. I laugh so hard she jostles.

Her arms tighten around my neck and it only drives me to laugh harder.

"Do you *seriously* think I'm going to drop you?" I ask.

Her laughter wanes and her expression grows more solemn. The shift in demeanor twists at my insides and I don't like the look in her eyes. I bump her chin up with my knuckle, urging her to look at me. And when she does, I'm gutted.

"I haven't decided yet," she murmurs.

My arms wrap tighter around her, a little nervous of what will happen if I let her go.

I sit us down in the large reading chair stationed in the corner of her room. Doing my best to shield my dick, I adjust it out of the way.

"Talk to me," I say.

She snorts derisively, brushing off my attempt at a real conversation.

"Is this a part of the game?" she jeers.

I draw her closer to me, her knees caging me in.

"Name one game where people don't talk to each other," I challenge.

She meets my challenge, easily rattling off a name.

"Seven-up."

Okay, was *not* expecting that.

"Name *two* games where people don't talk to each other."

She doesn't miss a beat.

"Charades and . . ." her finger taps at her cupid's bow, "Red Light/Green Light."

"Doesn't count. People talk in Red Light/Green Light," I retort.

"*One* person talks," she explains, holding up a finger.

"But there's no rule that explicitly states you can't talk," I argue.

"Fine," she relents. "Four Corners." She smirks, knowing she's beaten me.

Note to self: don't play trivia games against Sydney.

I'm tempted to poke further holes in her logic, but I settle with letting her win this round.

I swat her ass for being a smart aleck and she's a fit of giggles, squirming against me to get off my lap.

"You bring that pretty ass back here," I growl, playfully holding her to me. Her sounds of laughter are just as sweet as her sounds of pleasure.

I tilt her chin toward me, forcing eye contact again. "Sydney, I *want* to talk to you. And if you haven't noticed, I'm a great conversationalist. So just open up," I spread her legs wider, drawing her closer to me. "And let. Me. In."

She shoots me a droll expression for the double entendre, and I withhold my grin.

My thumbs rub soft circles into her hips, my palms still cupping her ass. At first, I worry I'm distracting her, but she calms, settling deeper into my lap.

Sighing, she looks away from me, her face cast down, tracing the outline of the tattoo on my ribs before finally taking another deep breath and revealing her ooey gooey center to me.

"I've wanted nothing more than to talk to you since the first day I saw you," she admits.

"So why didn't you?"

She shrugs, muttering, "You were busy, so I had to find the right time."

I nod, urging her to continue because there's no way she's just leaving it at that.

"I memorized your practice schedule so I could determine when you would typically do your private practice drills, but then I figured that doesn't really solve the problem of you being busy, so I had to catch you *outside* the arena. But *that* required learning your class schedule."

"Naturally," I deadpan, and she throws me a knowing glare.

"As you're well aware by now, we don't share any classes together. So, I had to determine what you did *between* classes. Then, I realized even if I could catch you, what would we even talk about? Outside of the fact we both skate on manufactured sheets of ice, we wouldn't have anything in common. *So* . . . I had to learn what you liked. What you didn't like. But then . . ." she pauses, taking a moment so long I think she's going to remain quiet.

"But then, what?" I push, loving every word of how her little obsession grew so out of control.

Her eyes flit back down to my tattoos before scrunching her brows in that adorable way when she's thinking too hard. I want to rake my tongue over the bundled skin and lick it smooth, but I refrain. I *do* want to talk to her, and putting my tongue on her again would surely distract from our conversation.

"But then I couldn't *stop*. I couldn't stop learning more. I couldn't stop following you. I couldn't stop watching you. I couldn't stop . . . *wanting* you," she admits.

"And the messages?" I ask.

She winces and shifts her weight. "I swear I was going to tell you who I was, but it became kinda fun watching you squirm. I *liked* the anonymity, it felt like I could be anybody. Somebody with control over her life, but more importantly . . . it felt like I could be myself." Her gaze leaves my chest to rest on my lips then finally my eyes. "Telling you would have ruined that. You'd have taken one look at me and seen another fake copy of a pretty girl."

She's not entirely wrong, it's possible I've walked right past her on campus and didn't give her a second glance.

"Mm hmm. And the gifts?" I raise a brow, knowing she doesn't really have a great excuse for that one.

"It's my love language?" she offers with a half-hearted shrug, her voice an octave higher than usual.

I huff a laugh. "So, you're in love with me?"

"No," she snaps, eyes panicked. "I didn't say that. I'm just saying it's all I really know in terms of showcasing affection. I . . . I don't know any other way." She looks away bashfully. *Oh she's totally in love with me.* "As for the *nature* of the gifts . . ." she clears her throat, nervously tapping her index fingers together, "*some* people like shiny things, *some* people like things with a common theme, like collectibles and such. *I* like . . . ugly things."

"Ugly things?" I repeat.

"Little, creepy, handmade things. It's a bit hard to explain." She huffs, pressing her fingers to her forehead.

"Try," I push, amused that she's somehow managing to justify the headless gingerbread man she made me that one time.

"It's exhausting trying to be perfect all of the time and I'm a shit artist but I like doing it and gifting them to you was I guess my own special way of showing you the ugly parts of myself, the parts I don't show anyone else."

Her words are more meaningful than she realizes as we quite literally sit before each other naked and bare.

"And still, you didn't reveal yourself to me," I state because it's not a fucking question. She still hid from me. I'd spank her ass all fifty shades of pink if I had any faith she'd survive the lashings.

"I played our potential first meeting in my head over a thousand different times, in a thousand different ways and none of it ever felt *right*." She peers up at me and that little twitch in her eyes appears again. "It felt right to just watch you from afar."

"Until today," I grin.

"Until today," she repeats, her voice melancholic.

I lean up, caressing her backside as I grip her body closer to mine. Our lips are inches from one another as we breathe each other's air. My cock hardens.

"Why *is* that? What made today the day?" I lick at her lips but I don't immediately go in for the kiss the way I want to.

She stutters a breath. "Because you caught me. Just like you said you would."

I bump my nose to hers, nuzzling each side before rewarding her with a chaste kiss.

It's my turn to confess now.

"You know . . . I saw you that day." She pulls back to regard my face, her eyes wide.

I clarify, chuckling a little at her petrified expression.

"More accurately, I *heard* you. The day you barged into my arena while I practiced. I was blowing off some steam when I heard soft crying." I thumb invisible tears away. "I thought it was the most beautiful sound I'd ever heard. I wanted to know who made you cry, and then I wondered how *I* could make you cry." I trail a finger from her cheeks to her chest. "Make you sob. Make you beg."

Her breath hitches in her throat, and she's once more made me *very* aware of our compromising position.

"Was that before or after you thought to yourself 'I'm going to fuck or kill the person who's stalking me'?" she teases, even as her skin pebbles beneath my touch.

I shake my head at her attempt to deflect.

"At the time it didn't matter. I could make you cry from pleasure or cry in pain. It was of little consequence to me which one you did." *It's of little consequence to me now.* "Like I said, I had steam to blow off. I was in a bad way when you found me."

"You were?" Her breath skims across my cheeks, as she struggles to maintain steady breath, my touch affecting her much in the same way *she* affects me.

"I was." My fingers trail between her tits then circle her nipples. "But then, as you kept coming back . . . as you kept watching." I palm her breast and lift it to suck on her left nipple. "And following." I lift and suck on the right. "I realized, I was going to have to make a choice. I had to get rid of you or make you a player in my game."

She groans; pleasure evident when her head leans back.

I twist and turn her nipples between my fingers. Her breathing picks up, but she doesn't stop me. She holds onto my shoulders, gripping into the muscle.

"But you see, the more you stalked, the more intrigued I became. I thought to myself 'what kind of person would think this wise?'" I pinch harder and her pained squeals stirs my fucked up desires, even as her breast pushes further into my hand. "I thought surely they must be out of their mind if they think I won't retaliate. Then I wondered if they were as out of their mind as me. Were we kindred spirits, twin flames, or soul mates?" She moans against my touch, seeking more, searching for more friction as her hips begin to move. "Or were we sworn nemeses, alien vs. predator, perhaps mortal enemies?"

She gasps when I pinch again.

"Are you my enemy?" I ask my lips brushing against her cleavage.

"No," her broken whispers are music to my ears and her fear is a decadent appetizer for the meal to come.

I nip at her jaw and I feel the shivers that ripple beneath the skin as my teeth graze her chin. "You see, I'm quite good at camouflage. People see me as a hot head at worst and an asshole at minimum but I'm really,"—nip—"really"—nip—"really"—nip—"dangerous, Sydney." I lean back in the chair, and stare at her, letting her see a glimpse of me *without* the camouflage. I tap my temple. "There's something broken inside here and the things I want to do to you are not for the weak my dear princess."

She scoots forward, pressing her naked chest to mine and wrapping her arms around my neck to bring me closer. "Well then, it's a good thing I'm not weak," she breathes.

I instinctively palm her ass with both hands as she grinds her pussy against me, her arousal spreading across my lower abdomen as she does. My fingers flex, digging into her thighs hard enough to bruise while she continues to move. I'm not sure yet if I want to stop her or encourage her.

"You better be sure, Princess, because I was already crazy, but now, I'm crazy about you."

She grinds on me again. "Good, because apparently . . . I'm *crazy* about you too."

I suspect with her kind of upbringing something broke inside her too. With me something just snapped—an unfortunate result of the tragedy—but with Sydney, I'm willing to bet it was different for her, that she was twisted and bent until eventually she cracked under all the pressure. It's evident to anyone truly watching her, she's been doing her best to remain whole ever since.

Her forehead rests against mine, the warmth from her face seeping into my own.

"Kiss me," she whispers. I do.

She moans, thrusting herself against me like she wants to ride me. But I maneuver to the side, purposely keeping my hard dick *away* from her entrance.

"Aren't you going to fuck me?" she pants.

I pull back from her, holding her face away and squeezing her puffy cheeks in the process. "In due time."

She jerks away, her face no longer adorably squished between my fingers. "Tonight though, right?"

"If you're good," I tease.

Her eyes light up. "I'll be *so* good."

I pout. "Not *too* good, I hope."

Those baby blues roll as she sucks her teeth. *The little brat.*

"You're very confusing. You know that?"

"Well I don't want you to be a doormat," I joke.

She scoffs. "I'm *no one's* doormat." We look between each other knowing that—unfortunately—*that's* not true at all. She all but admitted that was her role to play among her father's *friends*, and I had no doubt she played it well.

I slide my palms up her thighs, resting when I reach her apex. I use my thumbs to stroke the curves of her hips, my hands unable to remain idle with her naked body wrapped around me like this. I can smell her arousal and my cock strains to the point of soreness, edging that fine line between pain and *delicious* pleasure. It would be so easy to fuck her but, the voices in my head scream that I need to wait.

"I know how much you like to win, but my game isn't just about winning or losing," that pouty bottom lip of hers pokes out again. "It's about learning your limits and setting you free. Don't you want to be free?"

The tip of my nose drags along her jawline, then her throat, nuzzling into her neck as I inhale the lingering sweetness of her body wash that sticks to our skin.

"I *want* to be yours," she breathes, the words the faintest whisper against her lips.

My fingers twist in her silky damp hair, unbraided and falling in loose waves that kiss the top of her ass. She's so fucking pretty.

She tries to lean forward to settle her hips in a new angle, but I keep my hold on her hair tight and shift my hips.

"Ugh," she groans, frustrated with my evasion. "Fuck me, Lucien. If you're worried . . . about . . . you know . . . I swear I've been tested." I think that God fellow is capable of miracles after all because maintaining a straight face could only be made possible with divine intervention.

"And if you want . . ." she stammers. "We don't have to use a condom. I have the implant in my arm." She points to a space along her bicep, under her arm. "And you don't have to worry about there being anyone else, just . . . please. I want you inside me." She rolls her hips against me again. "Just for tonight, let me have this."

Fuck me dead, I'm barely holding on here. She wants me to fuck her raw? I mean, that was already happening, but to hear her beg for it makes my cock weep tears of fucking joy. Despite what others *might* say, I do manage to wield an incredible amount of self-control.

"I know, Princess. Believe *me,* I know, but I promise you'll be rewarded if you're really good for me tonight and wait," I say.

"I don't *want* to wait," she pouts. Spoiled Little Stalker Princess, so used to getting what she wants. Even naked, straddled on my lap with arousal spilling on my dick, I've managed to do what no sane man has ever done: deny her. It's too bad I'm not sane.

"Aww, don't make that face. You'll get wrinkles." I rub my thumb between her brows and her forehead flattens out.

She smacks my hands away. "Nobody likes a tease."

"*You* do," I quip.

I lean back into the soft chair, another material I imagine ruining with all the fun we're going to have. I *will* fuck this girl, she needn't worry her pretty little head about that, but only when the time is right. My teeth sink into my lower lip as I imagine myself saying '*fuck it, no time like the present.*' She seems the type to catch on quick, why *not* let her ride me, break me in, and fuck me on this insanely plush chair while I station myself as the throne she's meant to sit upon?

I buck once and she bounces, her tits jiggling in the process. She tries to scooch closer, her nails scratching into my biceps while she drags that sweet heat closer to my cock.

I tighten my hold on her hips, holding her back again.

"You're the *worst*," she whines, though I get the feeling she's acutely aware of what that pouty face of hers is doing to me.

I grin.

"No, *I'm* the one your daddy warned you about." Her lips part, face slackened as those precarious wrinkles return to their spot on her forehead. "The big bad wolf sent to devour his precious little girl."

"So, what's stopping you then?" she whispers, her lips hovering over mine. "Devour me."

I underestimated her irresistibility and am losing the strength to deny her with every millimeter she moves closer.

"So little patience . . ." I pull away again. " I like to play with my food before I eat it." I boop her on the nose with a tap of my finger but she's none too pleased with the repeated gesture and playfully bites the air near my hand, snapping her teeth.

I pull my finger away just in time.

"Bad Princess," I admonish. "You bite me . . . and I'll bite you back."

Her lips curl at the corners but she shakes her head and pretends to scowl before leaning back, resting her hands on my knees. "You don't play fair."

My eyes drag from her wet center to her blue eyes. "Neither do you," I rasp, my voice a hoarse whisper, my lips parted. *Gorgeous.* I clear my throat. Reaching around, I grip her wrists, holding them behind her back with one hand while the other ensures she doesn't fall.

"Lucien . . ."

"How about this," I offer. "If you can come just from this, I'll let you get off. But you don't get my cock until I'm good and goddamn ready to give it to you, understand?"

She nods vigorously and I squeeze her ass harder.

"Yes," she grits out. "I *understand*."

I let go, leaving reddened fingerprints in my wake.

"Okay, be a good girl and grind on me until you make yourself come."

She smirks and repositions herself. Straddling my knee, she rides it like her goddamn life depends on it.

"I can't come like this," she whines.

"There's that word again. You're an athlete, aren't you? You can do anything you put your mind to. Including coming all over my knee like the greedy little slut you are, right?"

She whimpers, hating the use of my words, but loving how they make her feel. I'm not saying them to hurt her, but to encourage her. To get *there*. Luckily, she sees it that way too.

Her moans reignite.

"Come on," I say. "You can do better than that. You said you wanted to *earn* my cock, didn't you? You're not going to earn it like that."

Challenge issued, she grinds harder. Her pussy creams my thighs, and I want to do more than sit here. I want to help her achieve the orgasm she's chasing, but those aren't the rules of the game. If I touch her more than I am right now, I'm a goner and the game will end quicker than either of us want it to.

"There you go," I encourage. "You're Sydney fucking Sinclair, aren't you? You're not just going to let me win, right?"

"No," she moans, her clit rubbing against my knee. She's soaking me and her nails are digging into my flesh again. She wants to come for me, but maybe my princess needs a tiny . . . push.

"I thought you always strive to be the best? For more? Who better to give you that than yourself. Make yourself come all on my thigh like you wanna come all on my cock. Show me what I'm missing out on for daring to deny you."

She stares down at me while she continues her figure eight's, already putting her back into it with my provocation.

She grits her teeth through another moan.

"You're going—to regret—challenging me," she breathes, holding back her release even if she doesn't realize she's doing it.

I break my no-touching rule, resting both hands at her hips. This should be fine; I can stay in control like this. Though the rest of me is considering breaking all of my rules for her.

"Then let me hear you. Say 'I'm Sydney fucking Sinclair and I'm going to come just like this.'"

"I'm Sydney fucking Sinclair and . . . and I-I'm— Fuck," she grits.

"Go on," I goad.

"I'm going to . . . to . . ." she moans, teetering on the edge.

"Try *again*," I spur her on, moving my leg to give her more friction.

"I'm Sydney fucking Sinclair and . . . ohshitshitshit I'm coming." She screams, her nails pressing into my forearms.

"That's my girl," I praise.

I kiss her temple as she slumps against my chest, her juices leaking from her pussy along my thigh. She jerks and twitches in my hold. I'm learning what she needs to come and how her body responds to my commands. Now we're getting somewhere.

I know she wants to fuck me, and I know she wanted to show me how good she'll ride me if given the chance, but we've already spent too much time at this house . . . and she's still not ready. The night's still young, the excitement still fresh and she still hasn't even seen the worst of me.

Despite her claims, she's yet to see with her own eyes the truth of my devastation. I'll have to make sure she doesn't go running for the hills the moment she does. We're just getting warmed up.

What do you want

In life?

Seen

WTF NO

Haven't decided yet.

CHAPTER EIGHTEEN

LUCIEN

"THIS IS SO STRANGE," Sydney comments, her long legs draped over the glittering red vinyl booth seat, reminding me of her outfit from earlier.

I hum, taking in the sight of her absentmindedly fidgeting with the torn skin around her nails again. "What's so strange about it?" I ask.

Her eyes sweep over my features, assessing my seriousness.

"What's *not* strange about it?" she huffs, her foot tapping my leg as she vents. "At this point, you've basically kidnapped me, seen me naked, and now we're casually sharing a meal together." She ticks off each point before throwing her hand out, gesturing to the empty table between us. "I mean, who does that?"

I snort a laugh. She seems to be forgetting she started this game of ours.

I'm not too sure she realizes it's not the table leg her foot is rubbing against, but I make her painfully aware, reaching beneath the table to grip the back of her knee. I stroke over her muscular calf and hinder her nervous leg bouncing. She flinches at my touch, moving to pull away, but my fingers tighten around her.

"I won that bet fair and square, Princess. So, you are here, *with me*, of your own free will." I trail the barest touch from the inseam of her leg to the heel of her foot, settling it into my lap. "Besides . . ." I lean forward, resting my elbows on the table, eyes flicking to her chest that practically spills out of that gorgeous dress she's in right now with its plunging neckline. "I haven't seen *nearly* enough of you." Her throat bobs as she swallows whatever useless retort she was conjuring. I sigh. "And meals are customary around this time of day, or hadn't you noticed?"

Her eyes narrow into thin slits that are more amused than angry. Meanwhile, mine remain fixated on her dress, her posture, and the thick blue vein running up her neck that looks like it's working double-time to pump that frozen heart of hers. *Don't worry, baby, I'll thaw you out.*

The black and silver beads of her dress cling to her body and compliment her strappy black heels. The straps crawl up the length of her long legs. I explained to her where we were going, and this is still what she chose to wear.

It's baffling how someone like her went unnoticed for so long. This girl can't help but stand out in a crowd, though that'd probably reign true even if she weren't dressed to the nines. She could be in a burlap sack surrounded by a horde of five thousand in this diner and she wouldn't simply stand out; she'd be the only one in existence in my eyes.

"Ha ha, very funny," she retorts. "I am not so out of touch with reality that I'm not aware of dinnertime . . . it's just," her eyes dart around us, soaking in the intimate atmosphere, "this feels awfully like a . . ." She dips her head, staring at her hands as she tries and fails to keep from worsening the self-inflicted wound on her right thumb.

"Date," I finish for her.

"Yes," she admits, her eyes shifting back up to me, both accusation and questions swirling around in them. My mouth pulls into a grin. I haven't been on many dates, admittedly they've never been a prerequisite in the past, but I'm pretty sure this qualifies.

I purse my lips, saying nothing at first as I watch her grow more uncomfortable with every silent breath exchanged. Her throat bobs, her chest rising and falling as her fidgeting worsens. Her tongue slides over her teeth as she feigns annoyance that I've not confirmed or denied her claims.

The truth? I'm enjoying this far too much to stop.

I like watching her prissy facade crack and break right before my eyes. I like the awkward silence and her insatiable need to fill it with her soft whimpers and quiet moans. It's not nerve wracking like the *other* silence. The silence that eats at my soul, chewing away at my sanity like a fucking parasitic worm. This silence feels warm, like the tingling sensation one gets when they stick their toes in the sand of a hot beach. It's less than pleasant but then you remember you're on a fucking beach so it can't be all bad. That's what this feels like right now watching her.

"Good, because that's exactly what this is," I say, leaning back in my seat.

Her breath hitches before she's laughing it off, her derisive tone not entirely off-putting.

"You're still in sweatpants," she retorts.

I arch a brow. In what handbook does it say sweatpants negates a date?

"And yet here we are."

I sweep my palm over the table between us, displaying the full glory of our awesome as shit first date at the Highway 59 Dine and Dash. Who says romance is dead?

"We could have stopped by your house first. You know, where we could have found you *proper* attire?" she grumbles, reaching for the menu. Though it's more like she snatches it from its tucked position behind the napkin dispenser.

Its obvious appearances are important to this girl, but too bad for her, she's aligned herself with the likes of me. A small part of me questions why that is, but it doesn't require a large degree of intelligence to figure that one out. This girl has daddy issues with a capital *D*. Though, she's still sporting a blush that hasn't left her face since I made her come on my thigh. The way she humped my knee like a horny little slut tells me she could stand to be a little more reckless in life.

In truth, I would have loved to take her somewhere more special than this, and I *would* like to get out of these clothes, but we have more important matters to consider. Could this pampered Princess even survive someone like me?

How can I get to a second date if the moment I try to fuck her she's begging for mercy? I mean, I definitely want her begging, but what if she runs? I'll have to chase. Then there's no telling what I'll do if I catch her. It's all a very delicate balance. I have to prioritize the game. If she can play, she can stay. Simple, right?

"We'll go to my house *after* we share a meal. I'll need you well-fed if we're going to be spending more time together," I say, propping my menu up to hide my smirk.

"How do you do that?" she asks, a perplexed expression playing on her face.

"Do what?"

"Make everything sound so . . ." Her hand rolls in the air, as if conjuring the word.

"Dirty?" I finish.

"Threatening," she corrects.

"I'm a man of my word, Sydney. I don't make threats," I say. Like clockwork, Sydney's body reacts, telling me everything I need to know—she loves it. The idea of promises and threats.

"Yeah, well . . ." Her face scrunches in concentration as she scans her own laminated sheet. I feel the weight of her glare each time she steals a glance my way, just like I always can.

It's become oddly comforting, addicting even. You'd think I'd be used to being watched, used to the limelight as the infamous Morningstar, but when I play hockey, all I feel, all I see is the game. It's like that fucker Jake said earlier, I had no family in the stands, no loved ones, no one who actually gave a shit. It's all just white noise . . . except for her. I felt her stare the whole game tonight. With her eyes on me, I played the best I'd played in a long time. Even the hat trick I completed, was for *her*.

Her absence for those two days prior to the game felt like a missing limb and her re-emergence felt like my first real intake of breath in days. If I had it my way, I'd never want her to stop. I'd always want her eyes to be on me.

As if the heavens actually deem me worthy, her gaze settles on me again. Her mouth opens to say something then closes. I continue pretending I'm reading the menu, waiting for her to speak. I know exactly what *I* want, and I'll have it soon enough.

She tries again but her phone buzzes on the table, rattling against the Formica tabletop, interrupting whatever she was about to say. Sydney tilts the screen up, giving it a glance, then sets it aside with a scoff.

"So . . ." she starts.

"So . . ." I parrot.

"Hockey," she states, as though the singular word is enough to get us talking.

I cock my head. "You want to talk about *hockey*?"

The incredulity laced in the question is apparent.

"Yes," she answers.

My brows knit.

"Why?"

"Because you like it?" It comes out like a question, like she can't understand why I'm not delving into all things hockey.

"I love hockey." I zero in on her jumping pulse in her neck, the only real indicator to the state of her nerves. "But you don't want to talk about that." My voice lowers, a husky timbre I don't even try to hide, the sexual tension crackling between us. "Do you?"

She licks at her lower lip then clears her throat.

"Fine, we'll talk about something else," she shrugs. "How many tattoos do you have?"

She can't be serious. She knows exactly how many tattoos I have. If she wasn't sure before, she definitely knows the answer now. She was thorough back in the shower when she scanned every trace of my body with her dainty fingers, storing it in her mind for her future skittle bank pleasure.

I lean back against the cushioned seat, scrunching my face in faux contemplation. "Um, no."

She blinks. "*No?*" She huffs. "What, you're just not gonna tell me?"

"I'm not going to tell you what you already know." The vinyl seat squeaks as I settle even deeper into the booth, my sweat clad thighs spreading to make room for the hard-on she so easily elicits within me. "Ask me what you really wanna ask me. Ask me the things you couldn't find out on your own, Little Stalker Princess."

"I'm not a stalker," she mumbles under her breath.

"You're not a princess either," I retort. "But the name still suits."

She flops back against the seat, pulling away from the table and dropping her foot from my lap in a huff.

I can almost see literal wheels turning in her head as she decides what to say next. The brat is so used to getting what she wants from people, and I love being the antithesis of that.

A slow grin creeps across my face as she settles into deep thought, warring with herself over the perfect question to ask. It's amusing until she asks the question I least expect.

"Who's Lilith?" she finally asks.

My grin drops and my world tilts a little more off its axis.

"Pass," I clip.

Sydney scoots herself in the cushion to sit up straighter. "That's not fair. You said to ask what I wanted to know. *That's* what I want to know," she says.

"Ask another," I demand.

"*No.*" She cocks her eyebrow. "Answer the question."

My jaw clenches, my eyes closing as the name on her lips stir what I can only describe as emotional bile in my gut. I feel sick. Damn Dr. Thottie for encouraging me to feel things.

"Is she like a girl *friend* or like a girlfriend?"

The sick feeling worsens.

I open my eyes, preparing to glare at her to get her to stop but when I look up, she's peering down, picking at her thumbnail again.

"If she's an ex or whatever, that's fine, I just wanted to know more about her since her name is like tattooed on your—"

"She's not an ex."

Sydney's shoulders slump, her whole body deflating like some sort of sad balloon animal.

"Oh. So, she's—"

Jesus Christ she's killing me.

"She's dead," I blurt, because how the fuck else am I supposed to say it?

Her mouth falls open. "I— Fuck, I'm so sorry. Who was she? Was it your—"

She reaches for my hands, but I pull them out of reach.

"It's fine," I say. "Ask me another question."

"How did she—"

"*Not* about Lilith," I clarify.

Her mouth turns down at the corners and Sydney's face softens in a way I find I *don't* like.

"Either use your mouth to ask another question, or I'll put it to better use. You'll find it pretty hard to frown around a mouthful of cock."

The pressure in my body releases somewhat when her face morphs from one of pity to barely contained desire mixed with a good bit of anger.

"That's more like it," I smirk.

"You can't just say stuff like that," she whispers, looking around as if to make sure no one heard.

"Why not?" I goad.

"It's . . . inappropriate," she says, swiping wisps of hair behind her ear, appearing the picture of innocence when I know she's anything but.

"Says who?" I lean on the table and prop my chin on my hand.

She laughs. "Pretty much everyone I know. Where I'm from, people keep their debauched thoughts to themselves."

"Where's the fun in that?"

A soft grin plays on my lips as I tap the table top, maintaining the precious eye contact.

Her eyes crinkle at the sides, her white teeth nibbling at her lower lip. *Where did this girl come from?*

"I suppose that tracks. I've never met anyone like you before," she says, her tone hushed and distant.

"I could say the same."

She hides her smile again, pretending to turn away as she flags down our waitress.

When she turns my way again, I tilt my chin at her. "Go on, ask me another question. I promise to give you a real answer this time."

Her tongue swipes over her pink-glossed lips as she prepares to ask me another question, one I'll actually do her the honor of answering as long as it's not about my sister, but then her phone buzzes again and whatever she reads in the text has her noticeably upset. The type of upset only another man can cause. Her hands shake as her nails clack over the screen to text back.

She finishes typing, then lets the phone fall from her grasp onto the table with a loud *clank*. Rolling her eyes, she reaches to chew on her thumb again.

"Who was that?" I ask, working to remain casual.

"No one," she clips, though we both know she's a fucking liar.

"Was it your *boyfriend*?" I ask with all of the stealth she obviously lacked when asking about Lilith.

Her panicked eyes pop up so hard I'm surprised her neck doesn't snap from the force.

"He's not my boyfriend," she rushes, giving me a deathly glare.

I hadn't even seen the name that popped up on the screen, but of course she'd fall for the oldest trick in the book and snitch on herself.

"Then who is he?"

At first, I think I'm only turning her own line of questioning against her, but her reaction piques my interest. There's something else to this. I can feel it. I haven't even heard his name yet and already I'm poised to rip the guy's throat out with my bare fucking teeth. Fuck this guy, whoever he is. He's definitely someone who *wants* to be her boyfriend, which is probably why she's looking so damn guilty right now.

Her tongue traces her lips again as she nervously tucks a wayward blond strand behind her ear.

"I . . . it's not important. Can we please drop it?"

Her big blue eyes are pleading with me, but they all but turn black when her phone starts rattling against the table. She glowers at it, apparently trying to incinerate it with the blaze of her ire, but it's too late, I can see it with my own eyes.

"Your *boyfriend's* calling back," I clip, a dangerous cut to my tone as the letters BF blink across her screen.

"He's *not* my boyfriend," she snips, pointing her ire at me, but it doesn't have the effect she's hoping for.

"So, what is he, your bestie for life?"

"I wouldn't go as far as that," she mutters under her breath. "But . . ." Her tone is several octaves lower than our previous talks with no hint of superiority or brattiness. Right now, her demeanor is that of a small child ready to be scolded by a parent. Shame paints that beautiful canvas she calls a face, and my balls draw tensely in response to her fear as I strain to keep from coming.

I want to get rid of her boyfriend. I want to chop him up into tiny pieces and scatter him in the mountains for the wolves to feast on. I *want* her shame, but not over something like this.

"He is probably the closest thing I have to a friend. He's annoying, yeah, but he's the most tolerable person in my life currently."

"If he's so tolerable, why do you look like you're swallowing glass right now?"

"Because boys are idiots," she states, obviously lumping me in with her biased sentiment. "And Bradford Fontaine is no exception."

I spit out a laugh. "*Bradford*? You're dating a guy named *Brad*? Wow, that's even worse than Chad. You sure do know how to pick 'em, eh?"

"We're *not* dating and he's *not* my boyfriend," she argues.

That adamant nature of hers leads me to believe she's not lying, but the guilty expression still has me wanting to push for answers. I tilt my head, regarding her closely.

"Who is he then?"

She stiffens in her seat.

"Tell me who Lilith is," she retorts, though her confidence is a little shakier compared to earlier.

I don't miss a beat.

"My sister. Who's Bradford?" Her evasion only drives the need to know further.

"Wait, your sister died?" The pity tries to make a triumphant return but I don't let it.

"Focus, Sydney. Who's Bradford?" I repeat. A possession I've never known flaring to life with every denied answer.

"Does it matter?" She huffs, flustered with my unwillingness to let this go.

"No," I answer blandly.

"Then why do you care?" she spits back.

"I don't."

"Then what's with the first degree?"

I hold up a finger. "I don't care *because* it doesn't matter. It doesn't change the plans I have for you in the least, so stop stalling and tell me who he is?"

Frustrated puffs of air slip past her lips as she reluctantly attempts to explain.

"If you must know . . ."

I bring my fists to my lips, resting my mouth against them to keep calm. She watches me with rapt attention as I lean forward, bracing myself against the table and stealing her with an icy glare of my own.

"Yes, I *must* know."

With my gaze on her she slumps back some, her tension relaxing as she yields to *my* authority and not the other way around. I don't want her docile but she will get it through that pretty, fragile, little skull of hers that this *isn't* her game anymore. She's not the one calling the shots here and there's nowhere else to run.

She swallows.

"A family friend," she finally says.

"What *kind* of family friend?"

"The long-term kind. Our dads are business associates. Have been for years," she sighs.

Our eyes are trapped in one another's, inescapable and infinite as I process that bit of information. She's purposely being vague and my veins pulse with the need to correct her attitude. We're so enraptured with one another, we don't even notice when the waitress comes to our table. The spell is only broken when she settles a basket of fries between us.

"Oh, no, I wanted the salad," says Sydney, already shaking her head and pushing away the basket.

The woman chuckles wryly.

"Not from here, you don't," she says.

I stifle my snicker as I watch Sydney's face morph into one of utter horror, imagining what could possibly make a salad non-preferable to fries.

"Well, we didn't order these," Sydney attempts to argue.

"First basket's free for the table, hon," the waitress informs her with a sideways glance before she takes our food orders and walks away.

I take a few for myself and nudge the basket toward Sydney.

"Go on, have some. The fries here are delicious. And they're half off refills," I say.

I pop another fry into my mouth, taking my time as I chew.

"*Great.*" She plucks a fry from the top, eyeing it like she's never seen one before.

"You have had fries before, haven't you?" I ask.

Her fingers twitch like she's scared it's going to eat her instead.

"I mean, I have, but . . . "

Her face looks crestfallen as she puts it down on the table, staring at it like it offended her for smelling so good.

"But what?" I press.

I grab a couple more, dipping them into the side of ketchup it comes with, while she looks like she's dying inside. *Aw, don't die yet, Princess.*

"I've been on a strict calorie deficient diet since I was in the eighth grade," she shrugs. "It's been years since I've eaten a fry."

I suck the salt off of my fingers, slowly and salaciously, making sure to rub it in her face what she's obviously missing.

Why anyone would ever deny themselves pleasure is beyond me.

I chuckle when I swear I see drool forming in the corner of her lips. Whether that's over the fries or my sucking abilities, I can't quite tell.

"Well then prepare your palate to have the best fries you've ever tasted."

I push the basket closer to her with my free hand.

"I-I can't."

She shakes her head, pushing them away.

265

I drop the fries poised at my lips.

"What did you say?"

She twiddles her thumbs nervously.

"I said . . . I shouldn't."

I glare at her. "No, you said you *can't. Why?*"

"Because, I'll get fat."

She doesn't even blink when she says it, but I do. Multiple fucking times while I try to wrap my head around what the fuck she just said. I'm sure it's *my* face now that's taken on a horrified expression.

"What?" I grit through clenched teeth.

"I'm not allowed to have fries," she repeats, oblivious as to why that pisses me off to hear.

What's worse? Is how confused she looks.

Who. The. Fuck convinced her a few fries would make her fat? I've seen every divine piece of this royal and she's *perfection*. There's not an ounce of fat on her. She's strapped in muscle, especially her weirdly attractive calves.

Her commitment to figure skating is unquestionable and fucking french fries would never diminish her beauty in my eyes. She could eat fries every day for breakfast, lunch, and dinner and I'd still be obsessed with her. This blasphemy against fried potatoey goodness will not stand.

"Sydney." My voice is strained as I attempt to reign in my temper. "Eat the fries."

She shakes her head, her lips rolled inward in defiance like a goddamn baby who doesn't want to eat her vegetables.

"Eat, Princess," I coo, attempting to take the nice approach.

"You don't understand. *I can't.*"

"Eat the goddamn fries, Sydney. Or so help me, I'll sit you on my cock and force feed them to you while I use your cum as dipping sauce."

Her eyes blaze, pupils blown wide, as she debates my threat.

"I— You can't— Jesus, you're—"

I grin. "Come on," I croon. "You know you want to. They're magically delicious."

She laughs despite herself.

"That's Lucky Charms," she chuckles.

"Potato. Cereal. It's all the same thing. Eat," I say.

I point toward the fries again. She stares at the basket and then the small silver cup of ketchup, lingering before shifting to me.

Oh, she's definitely thinking about the dipping sauce comment.

I stare back, smirking.

"We're still on a date, crazy pants. Sustenance first," I tease, nodding toward the fries one last time because at this rate I'm going to eat them all.

"Fine," she relents, reaching for the fries at the same time I do. My fingers brush against hers. We both stall, but then she's pulling away sharply as though she's *stealing* the fries instead of *sharing* them.

I shake my head, allowing her the win.

She slides one in her mouth slowly, savoring the greasy potato stick, her eyes rolling like she's about to orgasm.

Well, shit, I guess I better get the dipping sauce ready.

As if knowing where my thoughts have landed, she pulls another fry from the basket, dips it into the ketchup, then licks the tip before chomping down on the end.

Fuck. If that's how she looks eating fries, I can't imagine what she'd look like when I'm balls-deep inside her.

I clear my throat, hopeful to get back to the topic at hand.

"So, if *Brad's* just a family friend, why'd you look so upset?" I ask.

She stuffs a few more fries into her mouth, buying time.

"You could tell me, or you could show me," I push, peering down at her phone. I'm fast enough to take it from her, but I give her time to comply.

Sydney swallows her mouthful roughly, the food not well masticated enough to warrant the premature gulp. Her tiny fist pounds on her chest as she reaches for the water the waitress brought by, slurping it down like the words can be found at the bottom of the cup.

"You know I don't actually owe you an explanation, right?" Sydney retorts, her attitude distracting me from my murderous rage.

"You're getting pretty defensive over a family *friend*," I spit back. "These are simple questions, Sydney. Not too long ago, you were begging for my cock. Said I could fuck you raw, if memory serves. I'd think you would owe me *some* sort of explanation." I tilt my head at her gob smacked expression. "Aww, don't seem so shocked. Pretty sure I still have your cum on my leg after I . . ."

"Okay, okay, fine. Just . . ."—she looks around the semi-crowded diner—"lower your voice," she hisses.

"Now Sydney, you wouldn't be embarrassed to be seen with me, would you?"

She stills. "No, of course not. I . . .I just don't need . . ."

"Everyone knowing what a greedy little slut you are for my dick?" Her cheeks flame and I smirk. She's so freaking adorable.

Her eyes roll, unamused by my antics.

"Could you *please* try to have more couth?"

"Well there's a word you don't hear everyday."

She scoffs, "Why? Is it *beyond* your comprehension?"

My eyes shoot to hers and she quickly corrects herself. "I'm sorry. It won't happen again."

I sigh. It's one thing to tease but Sydney only knows how to go for the jugular. That's the second time tonight she's tried to put me down, implying I'm stupid.

"Look I'm a fairly nice guy, Princess. I'm a hockey player so trust me when I say I can take the chirping. But I'm a bit sensitive tonight. So...the next time you're mean to me. I will show you just how much *couth* I have when I force you to crawl on your knees and beg for my forgiveness in front of this whole goddamn restaurant. And, believe me, you will beg prettily and enthusiastically." Her mouth gapes and I chuckle.

"Now, let's try this again," I say. "What's the deal with you and *Brad*?"

"He . . . wants to come and visit. He's been wanting to visit for a while. But I *don't* want him to come," she reiterates.

"Why's that?"

She looks at me with that same twinkle in her eyes that tells me exactly what I already know but I want to hear her say it.

"I'd rather be here . . . with you."

I nod my head, a smile growing with her confession.

"Now was that so hard?"

She looks back down at her plate of fries, but I see her slight grin.

"It was torture," she teases.

I smile wider.

"Oh, Princess, you don't know the meaning of the word."

@therealLucifer
Online

ere you in the arena last nig

Seen

Who the hell is this?

Seen

SYDNEY

CHAPTER NINETEEN

SYDNEY

I**T'S ELEVEN O'CLOCK**, I'VE eaten a shit-ton of carbs, we haven't made it to the party, my dad's already texted once, and Bradford's the cherry bomb on top. Now I'm hiding in a bathroom stall, trying to pull my shit together. This is *not* how I expected my evening to go.

Dad 10:34 PM

> Wear something nice tomorrow. We're meeting with Phil Anderson for brunch before we leave.

> Something white to play up your innocence.

> And wear your hair down.

Anderson. Why does that name sound familiar?

Sydney 11:09 PM

> Will Mr. Anderson's wife be joining us?

I don't know if he actually has a wife, but I take a stab in the dark. All these assholes have wives.

I re-read the texts from Bradford I was hoping I had misread.

Bradford 10:47 PM

> I was trying to surprise you, but I see that's kind of backfired since you're not home.

Seriously?!!

Where are you?

What the actual fuck? I take several deep calming breaths as I try to wrap my head around why he would do something so idiotic.

I am on a date with *the* Lucien Morrow and today of all days, Bradford pulls *this* shit. I specifically told him *not* to come, and he came anyway. It's just like him to do this. I should have known better; he never listens to me.

I brace a hand against my stomach, breathing through the nausea before texting Bradford back.

Sydney 11:11 PM

Bradford, I told you not to come. I'm out with some friends right now. We're having a last supper kinda thing.

Dad 11:11 PM

No, which is exactly why you'll be joining us. His son is supposed to be in attendance as well, but even if he isn't, you still have a job to do.

It dawns on me just then. The Andersons. The family that's out to get Lucien suspended from the team.

Shit.

Sydney 11:12 PM

What about Bradford?

Dad 11:13 PM

What about Bradford? He understands his role as should you.

Bradford 11:13 PM

Is that important?

I stare at both text threads, ready to flush my phone down the goddamn toilet. It almost falls *into* said toilet when I suddenly hear a group of girls loudly talking and giggling as they enter the bathroom.

"Did you see Morrow outside?"

My ears perk.

"God, even in sweatpants that man is delicious. I bet if he stood up, he'd be rocking a monster package," a sultry voice says.

"I don't get all of the hype, if I'm being honest. I mean, he's cute and all, but everyone knows he's crazy," another girl says.

"Who cares? I hear he's especially crazy in the bedroom," says another girl, apparently in agreement with the first. I listen intently as they take out different makeup items from their purses and debate Lucien's sanity.

My teeth clench and my acrylics claw at the fucking walls.

"You just have a thing for that whole bad boy look," one argues.

"Yeah, and you have a thing for football jocks who've been hit in the head one too many times. But you don't hear me judging," she quips back.

"'Bad' doesn't even begin to cover it. Did you see the game earlier? He's fucked. They're probably going to expel him this time."

I lean on the toilet to get a better look at the girls through the gap between the door and the stall wall.

"Whatever. They always let him back on the ice. He wins games," says the first, staring at herself in the mirror as she swipes the excess lipstick from around her lips.

"Seems like a lot to let someone get away with just for being talented," says the redhead that's apparently not his biggest fan.

"And hot. Don't forget hot. The pretty privilege is real," says the blonde fixing her ponytail alongside the first.

"Yeah, but did you hear what happened to the guy he fought?" asks the redhead.

A beat of silence.

"What about him?" asks the blonde.

"Well, *I* heard it was the school president's son and that he had to be medevaced to Seattle General for emergency surgery."

"Nuh uh," gasps one of the girls. "You're totally lying."

"I'm totally not. Christy heard it from Tonya, who heard it from Becca because her sister's boyfriend's cousin works at the hospital."

"No way?" Another jumps in.

Well at least that takes care of the brunch issue.

The other two gasp.

"Yeah, and he almost coded on the way there because he swallowed too much of his own blood *and* teeth."

One of the girls makes a gagging noise.

"Eww," at least three girls say in unison.

"Sure, you still want to fuck him after hearing that?"

"Yep," they harmonize again as they all head back out to the diner.

I roll my eyes and redirect my attention to my phone, which already has a return text from Bradford.

Bradford 11:16 PM

Does your dad know you're not home?

Sydney 11:16 PM

No.

Are you going to tell him?

I wouldn't put it past him to snitch. He loves being in my dad's good graces, he enjoys the perks that come with his approval. I can't really blame him; I do too.

Bradford 11:17 PM

> Of course not. Do you want me to meet you at the restaurant? Tell me where and I'll come pick you up.

Sydney 11:17 PM

> No.

> We're about to leave.

Bradford 11:18 PM

> Okay, cool. You wanna meet me at my hotel afterward?

I stare at the texts. How the hell am I supposed to get out of this? I can't afford for Bradford to find out about Lucien and I'm definitely not forfeiting *my* time with Lucien so . . .

Locking my phone, I thrust it back between my tits.

When I'm all cleaned up, I check my own makeup in the mirror.

Pushing the bathroom doors open, I turn the sharp corner back to our table but stop in my tracks. I'm seeing red. Red lipstick to be exact. The same girls from the bathroom are flocked around our table flipping their hair and batting their mascara-crusted falsies. *Oh, hell no.* One girl has her hand on his shoulder, pressing her stuffed boobs in his face.

I'm so busy seething over the girls; I completely miss the group of guys approaching from the opposite side.

"Sasha, what the fuck? Get away from him!" A big guy steps forward, whirling on Lucien, his finger pointing menacingly at his face. "Stay the fuck away from my girlfriend, Morrow."

Lucien moves to get up, but I park my ass right into his lap before he can push himself up. I'm staking my own claim. *He's mine.* For one night only Lucien Morrow belongs to *me.*

"Tell your *girlfriend* to stay the fuck away from *Lucien*," I snap.

The boyfriend peers down at me, taking a moment to admire my tits, before he glares over my shoulder at Lucien.

"And who are you supposed to be? His girlfriend?" he sneers, flicking his gaze back to me.

Lucien and I both tense with my newly appointed title but as has been established it's of little consequence who I am tonight.

"*I'm* the lesser of two evils. So, how about you kindly back the fuck off and leave us alone?" My smirk doesn't exactly scream evil like Lucien's, but it challenges him all the same.

"Morrow, you might want to muzzle your bitch before she gets you hurt," the asshole sneers.

Lucien moves beneath me, but I force him back down, bearing my weight and using every last ounce of strength I have to keep him braced to the seat. It's not enough. He's ten times stronger than me, but he won't throw me off— of that much, I'm sure.

"Move, Sydney," Lucien growls against my ear, but I can't afford to do that. He can't fight them all. We're grossly outnumbered, even if we exclude the girls, and though the thought of clawing out their eyes and pulling hair extensions is tempting, I'd rather not break a nail. So it's up to me.

I ignore Lucien's command. And then . . . I scream, forcing large crocodile tears to fall from my eyes as I do.

"Ah! Oh my God! I didn't do anything! Ah, please, stop, go away! Don't jump me! Oh, *Lucien*, please hold me!"

I cradle myself into Lucien's arms, burying my face into his neck. He holds me awkwardly, his movements stiff as he's taken just as off guard as everyone else. Out of the corner of my eye, I see patrons start to look our way, concerned and pulling out their phones should they need to call the cops.

"Yo, *shh*, you crazy bitch!" Our disrupter whisper-shouts, panicked by my outcry.

I cry more, harder. I fucking wail.

"Why would you say that?! I'm not a bitch. I'm a woman. We were just trying to have a peaceful meal, and you all came over to us. . .being so mean." I sniffle and dab at my eyes. My makeup may be ruined, but my performance is flawless.

"Are you being fucking for real right now?" the boyfriend hisses.

"We don't want any trouble! Why won't you leave us *alone*?" I bawl.

Our waitress walks up, and everyone starts to back off, a blend of scared and confused faces, not knowing what to do with the scene I've caused.

Too easy.

"I'm gonna have to ask you all to leave," says our waitress, addressing the gaggle of assholes in front of us. "These nice folks weren't bothering anyone before you came in causing problems."

The boyfriend sucks his teeth before looking back at us.

"This isn't over, Morrow," He jabs a finger at Lucien. When he looks to me, the corners of my lips lift. *Looks like I win.* He glares at me, malice dripping from his features, but when the waitress turns back, I'm hiccupping and trying to regain my bearings as I swipe away my fake tears.

After they're gone, our waitress returns to the table. "Sweetie, are you two alright?"

I nod my head, hiding my face with the rough napkin she hands me. I almost break character and laugh when I catch the *happy* couple arguing outside the window behind her.

"Aww, why don't you get yourself cleaned up? I'm so sorry for the disruption of your cute date. I hate guys like that. Your dinner's on us and I'll bring you guys some milkshakes. On the house, okay?"

I nod my head.

"Thank . . . you," I sniffle.

Her hand covers her heart before she walks away to get our free milkshakes and comp our meal. I unfurl myself from around Lucien.

When I'm sure she's out of earshot, I turn around to find him staring at me like I've lost my mind.

"That was . . . You're kinda insane, aren't you?"

@therealLucifer
Online

Were you in the arena last night

Seen

Who the hell is this?

Seen

CHAPTER TWENTY

SYDNEY

LUCIEN COCKS HIS HEAD at me, not overtly angry, but still obviously upset with me. I dab at my eyes with some clean napkins and pull out a tube of concealer and lip gloss from my cleavage. His expression grows even more suspicious like I'm more insane than he originally thought.

"What? I like staying hands free." I pad my ring finger under my eyes to blend the concealer back out and cover the mascara smudges. "As for my sanity?" I shrug, popping my lips when I'm satisfied with the gloss. "That's yet to be determined. After all, I am on a date with *you*. That has to warrant some sort of lapse in mental state."

I wink so he doesn't think I'm being mean again, though if I were, I would gladly take my punishment and crawl for him right now. It dawned on me some time after we left my apartment that I don't have to worry about little things like embarrassing myself. I'll never see these people again. So if he wants me to beg like a dog, well then, *woof woof*.

He softens beneath me the slightest bit but his voice is cold when he speaks again.

"You didn't have to do that. I had it handled."

I drag my eyes away from the napkin dispenser I'm using as a mirror to look at him.

"And when you say *handled*, you mean stab him with that steak knife I see in your hand right there?" I quip.

He looks down at his right hand beneath the table his grip loosening on the handle. Sparing me another glance, he sets it gently on the seat next to him.

"Clever girl," Lucien coos.

I roll my lips to keep from grinning like an idiot.

"My way was cleaner, and we got a free meal out of it. So, what I believe you're trying to say is *thank you*," I retort, twisting the top closed and shoving it in my bra with my phone this time.

I tense when I feel the brush of his lips along my shoulder then my neck.

"Why would I thank you when there are *so* many better ways to show my appreciation?" he breathes against my skin. "Besides, you didn't give *my* way a chance. The results would have been similar."

"The *result* would have been bloodshed."

"What's wrong with that?" he retorts, snaking his arm across my middle, not allowing me up from his lap even as I try to stand, to get away and think clearly.

"Aww, I was only going to scare him. I wasn't going to hurt him," he croons, a sinful edge to his voice that highly suggests otherwise.

"Why don't I believe you?"

His laugh is sinister.

"Because you're smarter than you look," he says with a wink.

"Gee, thanks," I mutter even as I feel his cock thickening beneath me.

"What I *mean* is you see things the others don't. You see me, even when the rest of them are blinded by what they *want* to see. I like that about you."

I shift my body to revere him more closely, my heart lurching at his last words.

He likes me?

I search his eyes for the lie, but when I don't find it a wave of confusion washes over me. "I *see* you, but I still don't understand you. You have this seemingly golden retriever personality but then you turn serial at the drop of a hat. I know for a fact you would have gutted him right here in this diner and not bat an—" I gasp.

The tip of the steak knife presses between my thighs, no longer settled beside him, but held in his grasp and devastatingly close to my pussy. "Oh shitshitshit. I'm sorry. I'm sorry," I plead, whispering to avoid another scene. Lucien in trouble, is the last thing I want.

"No, no, no," he coos. "Don't be sorry, Princess. You're right." He slides the knife up my thigh, grazing the skin as it inches deeper between my legs.

I stutter a breath, fear clawing at my insides that he might cut me, that he *wants* to cut me, but I'm also so turned on, I can't think straight. My body hums, a new brand of adrenaline streaking through my bloodstream like a drug I've never tasted and a potency that already has me hooked. I've never faced odds this dire before, but I think I like it.

"Do you know the difference between a golden retriever and a wolf?"

His voice is still teasing, but his movements are deliberate, calculating. He angles the steak knife so the tip presses into my skin, but he doesn't apply pressure. My spine straightens.

"One will kill you," I answer, shivering beneath his touch as his thumb rubs tender circles against my side.

"Evolution," he whispers, his teeth grazing along my shoulder blade. I squirm, yelping when the knife pokes into my delicate flesh.

"Stay still," he warns through my gasp, his warm breath tickling my neck. "I never quite adapted to domestication. Unlike most, I've always tended to follow my most basic of instincts. I think something, I say it. I want something, I take it. I'm hungry, I eat."

"But . . . you're so playful," I pant through the mixture of pleasure and pain.

"My personality does not dictate my needs and this is what I need." His tongue flicks out, swiping against my lobe.

"Why?" I groan.

"To keep my mind clear."

My shoulders shake as I hold back laughter.

"*This* is your mind being clear?"

"It is when my focus is *you*. You keep me one-tracked. You . . . quiet the noise in a way I don't hate."

My heart swells. I'm his focus? I mentally shake my head, unable to physically do so without jostling the knife.

I shouldn't think like that. More likely he had no choice but to focus on the person he thought was stalking him. I didn't really give him a choice but, then again, hanging out tonight, that was *his* choice, right?

"Oh. And that's a good thing?" I manage shakily.

"Yes," I feel him laugh against my neck, his face buried in the crook as he licks the bite marks he's given me. "That's a *very* good thing."

The knife moves away long enough for him to turn my body, facing me more toward him. For a moment I feel like I can breathe again but I whimper at the loss of his warm embrace. My lower lip pouts when he grabs my chin, pinning me with a look as he stares up at me. His face is so close he could kiss me. Though his teeth baring in that way tells me he's much closer to biting me than anything else.

"You know if anyone is hard to understand, it's you."

"How so?" I whisper, my eyes still trained on the knife he's wielding when he positions it back between my legs.

He tilts my face toward his, turning it to look into his eyes. They're mesmerizing. I still.

"You come off as confident, spoiled, entitled . . ." His eyes search mine as he continues slapping labels on me. "But you melt when I praise you, you question me when I compliment you, and you fight me when I try to feed you french fries."

I refrain from wrenching away but only barely.

"So, what's your point?"

"My *point*,"—he digs the knife in a little deeper and I suppress a helpless groan—"is that you have no idea how beautiful you are, do you?"

I want to lie, to play the role I know all too well, but I swallow it down. It's useless. He sees right through me.

"I do." My head drops from his hold. "I just . . .don't always believe it."

Especially when it's used against me.

The pressure of the knife lessons as he stares at me, waiting for more.

"Why not?"

I'm not sure he means to sound as accusatory as he does but he's not stabbing me so I continue.

"Because it's not enough," I say. "It's not enough to warrant love, to grant adoration, to garner respect. I've been nothing but perfect my whole life and I have nothing to show for it. I've yet to earn my own father's respect, let alone his unconditional love."

Lucien shrugs one shoulder.

"You're right, it's not enough," he agrees, pulling the knife up and setting it aside.

I move to get up, afraid he'll see the tears already burning to fall. I *won't* let him see me cry. Not real tears. But he jerks me back, forcing my attention back on him.

"You're not beautiful because you're perfect. You're beautiful because you're not."

I try to push him away but he's freakishly strong.

"That doesn't make any sense," I argue, turning to get up.

"It makes perfect sense," he retorts, grabbing my hips and pulling me back down on top of him.

"How?" I demand, my voice raised as I try my hardest to ignore all the times my so-called beauty was good enough to land my dad a new business deal but not enough that he ever attended a single competition even after landing perfect score after perfect score.

His hand comes up to touch my face, "You'll see. By the end of the night . . .Your perfect skin will be bruised and bloodied. Your perfect makeup, smeared." He strokes my cheek. "Your pretty hair, mussed and tangled. Tears will leak from your eyes, streaking those beautiful pink cheeks. Cum will drip from your pussy, your ass, your mouth." His thumb pulls at my lower lip. "Those perfect lips of yours will be swollen from my kisses and your cunt will ache for weeks by the time I'm done with you."

I suck in a ragged breath, my throat no longer clogged with emotion but shock.

He releases his hold on my lip, and it springs back up with a pop.

Fuck me.

"Beauty is in the eye of the beholder, Sydney." A long finger trails down my throat, his eyes following close behind. "When your sweet, soft voice is rasped, your throat fucked raw, and your mouth dry from all your screams. Then . . ."—he glances back up to my mouth— "Then you'll be perfect. That's what perfection is to *me*. I'm going to show you how beautiful you can be when you're a filthy, bloodied, squirming mess for me. I'll show you what real perfection looks like, Princess."

Where is the air in here? It's all gone, sucked from the atmosphere, my lungs, everywhere. I struggle to breathe. He can't say stuff like that to me in public. I swear I can feel a full body blush coming on as a dangerous thought formulates in the back of my mind, bred in the secret chambers of my heart. *Then will you love me?* The intrusive thought comes out of nowhere. A deep, hidden desire I wasn't sure I even wanted. Unfortunately, the thing I blurt out is just as intrusive.

"I-I'm . . ." I'm panting in earnest now, my blood pressure skyrocketing. *Just spit it out.* "I'm a virgin!"

The waitress chooses that exact moment to arrive with two of the most creatively overdone milkshakes I've ever seen. To her credit, she doesn't drop them at my outburst.

I stare at her, mortified. Though from the corner of my eye, I can see Lucien grinning from ear to fucking ear.

She clears her throat. "Um. Here are your drinks." She sets them down gingerly, a strawberry confectionery for me and Oreo chocolate for Lucien.

"I'm so—" I start.

She shakes her hands in front of her. "All good." She turns to walk away but changes her mind at the last second. "Look, I know it's not my business, but just remember that safe sex is the best sex. You seem like a smart girl, but I'm barely forty and I'm a grandmother, so you know . . ." She looks over at Lucien. "Strap up and no means no, handsome. Always."

His grin only widens. *"Of course."*

The way he says it sends a thrill straight down to my core. I feel his dick harden as his grip on my hips grows tighter.

"Thanks for the milkshakes . . . Millie," he says, reading her name tag.

The barely forty-year-old woman blushes at the smooth way he says her name. It's a small comfort to know even she can be affected by his unique charm.

"You kids have fun." She throws us a wink over her shoulder as she walks away to tend to the other tables.

That was humiliating but my pussy doesn't stop throbbing as Lucien leans forward, the heat of his body against my back making my skin sizzle when he says, "You think I should have told her you already offered to let me fuck you raw?"

I almost choke on my sip of milkshake.

"What?! No!"

My mouth was so dry from embarrassment I took a sip without even thinking about the amount of sugar that's probably in this thing.

Lucien pats my back as I sputter, his hand drumming against my spine as I hack up a lung.

"Aww, don't be embarrassed. I'd already guessed you were a virgin," he muses as though it was so fucking obvious.

I hate that he's right, that it's probably noticeable to *everyone*. I'm so used to playing the innocent card, I fear it's become my whole personality. My father's business associates love it when I play the purity role. They're so distracted by the idea of taking advantage of me, they don't realize my father is the one taking advantage of *them*.

"Is that so?" I rasp, wiping the cream from my corner lip with a finger before licking it away.

I'm relieved he knows about the virginity part. One less secret between us.

"You're not the only one who watches people, Sydney," he responds, a sexy grin on his lips that tells me if the roles were reversed, I'd be no match for him. He'd stalk me to the ends of the earth.

If only this weren't a game, I'd relish the chase.

"Plus . . ."—his eyes narrow—"A girl like you has particular taste."

A girl like me. I replay his word choice in my head. I hate that phrasing. I hated it earlier tonight when Asshat from the game insinuated I was no one special. I hate when my dad uses it to remind me of my place, to remind me that girls in my position must act a certain way.

But it turns out, I hate it most coming from Lucien. I plop the milkshake back on the table.

"A girl like *me*? What's that supposed to mean?" I spit, a little more than ticked off that he's using it against me now too. 'A girl like me' didn't used to be a bad thing. Hell, back home it's a great fucking thing. Girls like me are the cream of the crop, the social elite who pull the strings of weak-hearted men. But here, at Belle U, it's starting to feel like a disease I'm only now discovering I'm afflicted with.

Lucien chuckles.

"It *means* a fancy hotel and bed of roses after prom was never going to cut it for you, Princess. You wanted something more." His head tilts adoringly and his beautiful black hair sways from his eyes as he pierces me with another longing look. "You *need* something more, don't you?"

I swallow roughly, unable to disentangle myself from his gaze. He's got me there. If I wasn't sure before, tonight only proved it. I'm so much more messed up than I thought. Even now, I'm wet, thinking of all the threats and pain he's inflicted. I want more. I need more. His eyes promise so much of it, but I resort to old habits to stave the reminder that even if he means it, they're promises I can't allow him to keep.

"How do you know I didn't take matters into my own hands?" I retort.

"Because . . . the game's no fun if you cheat. And *you* appreciate the challenge."

Three months ago, he would have been right. But sometimes the game isn't all about fun, and not all games are played fair.

Lucien pays my attitude no mind, rather he draws tiny circles in my back with the pads of his fingers, provoking those dark desires. My body screams *he's the one* at his touch. The one that will rid my body of this increasingly unbearable tension. Like the feeling of thirst when faced with fresh water. Or hunger when hit with the smell of freshly baked bread. He triggers me.

"And you know, it wouldn't change the fact that you've never been fucked, Sydney." My name rolls off his tongue like another threat. His shallow breaths waft over my skin, leaving goosebumps in their wake. "Not by me"—he presses a kiss to my shoulder—"Not by anyone."—he breathes in the scent of my hair with carnal inhales—"And I can't wait to change that," he groans.

What have I gotten myself into?

I shift in his lap, pressing my legs together.

"With that said, we're going to play another little game," he says, sliding a hand over my leg to spread them back open, the steak knife present once again.

I shake my head. Of course he wants to play right now. My thighs might be quivering, my heart drumming and my clit aching—all signs that I'm enjoying this—but I don't want to know what game he has in mind that requires this knife between my legs at our local dine and dash for a date.

"But you'll like this game," he sing-songs in a creepy way that suggests I very much *won't* like this game.

I groan.

"It's so easy though, Princess. Here, watch. I spy with my little eye something white."

I huff a laugh because of course it is never so easy with him. This is a trap.

The knife glides higher and the tip pokes at my clit. I freeze. Flooded with fear that he's going to cut my most sensitive area. I feel lightheaded. What happens if I lose *this* game? There's no telling what the punishment is for that.

I want to move, to readjust so his aim is off, but without even trying, he already knows where my clit is. If that isn't a good sign, I don't know what is.

Focus, Sydney. It's not a good thing if he stabs it!

"Th-the table," I shake out.

"Nope. Try again."

Oh fuck, oh fuck. I search around the dining room for items, watching as people eat their food and chat. They're oblivious to what's going on over here, or more likely, ignoring us altogether to avoid any more scenes or disruptions.

"The, um, tiles. On the floor," I guess again, staring at the checkered floors like they'll save me.

"Ehh," he makes a buzzer sound in my ear that makes me flinch. "One last guess."

My eyes dart everywhere, but it's a fucking diner. There's a lot of white. White countertops, white plates, white napkins. I try to think. He said there was a point to these games. That playing with him would prove something.

"Tick, tick, tick," he whispers into my ear. My body is rigid as I white-knuckle the table so hard my hands shake. I stare at them. My knuckles, completely devoid of color.

"Is it . . ." I pause, second-guessing my line of thinking. Could this really be the right answer? "Is it, my knuckles?"

He pulls the knife away.

"Ding! Ding! Ding! Ding! We have ourselves a winner!"

I empty my lungs. Only when I'm sure I'm in the clear do I relax a fraction, the color returning to my face and hands with a sudden rush. *What would have happened if I had been wrong?*

"I spy . . ." he starts again.

My heart drops at the thought of another round of *that*.

"Wait, don't I get a turn?" I blurt. The least he could do is give me a chance at retaliation.

"No. I spy . . ." he continues.

I roll my eyes. That's not fair.

"Did you just roll your eyes at me?" he asks.

"Of course not," I lie.

The next thing I know, he's moving the knife again, turning it horizontally and settling it between my thighs. Great. Now, I'm being punished for lying. The new position makes it so if I try to close my legs again, I'll do a hell of a lot more than cut myself, I'll skewer my thighs together. I'm panting harder than before, trying to regulate my breathing, but relishing the soft breaths blowing from his lips with every uttered breath.

"I spy with my little eye something . . . pink," he says.

My thighs shake, nervous energy sleuthing through my veins as I strain to keep spread.

"Um, m-my milkshake," I guess.

He thumbs my clit through the thin fabric of my panties with his left hand, startling me.

"Everything alright with the milkshakes?" asks our Millie.

I snap my head up. When did she get here? Can she see what's happening beneath the table?

"Everything's great, Millie," answers Lucien, his thumb rolling deep circles over the hyper-sensitive bud between my legs.

I'm panting hard, the sounds fast and sharp as I try my darndest to think my way out of this horrific situation. If I come in front of this lady, I'll die.

"Oh, sweetie, are you okay? You look flushed," says Millie.

I shake my head. "It's fine." *Not.*

She narrows her eyes at me.

"Brain freeze," Lucien offers. "She sucked it down too fast."

I nod my head in agreement, though I know he's being funny. He worded it that way on purpose. Still, now it's my whole body that's shaking. Lucien thumbs my clit again and I release a soft whimper. I try to sit up, but his arms have me locked in place and Millie isn't batting an eye at the fact that I'm still sitting in his lap.

"Oh," says Millie. "Well, fun little trick I teach my grandkids: press your tongue to the roof of your mouth. Does the trick every time." She gives a thumbs-up.

"Thanks, Millie, we'll try that." Lucien turns toward me, his face nuzzling against my cheek. "Go on," he goads, "give it a try. See if it helps."

He pinches my clit and my legs almost slam close.

I cut my eyes to glare at him but ultimately do as he says. More pressure is applied to my clit, and I almost come on the spot. Squeezing my eyes shut, I press my tongue to the roof of my mouth for no other reason than it's all I can do. I'm inclined to believe it's working. Between the knife, the attention, the danger, the pressure, I'm going to fucking explode, but I manage to keep it at bay. More importantly, I manage to keep my thighs from closing.

"Yeah, like that," says Millie. I can hear in her tone that she's proud of herself, but neither of us are paying her any attention. My eyes are back on Lucien, who looks like he's having the time of his fucking life. I don't think I've seen such light in his eyes before. He looks happy. And my poor, dumb heart squeezes at the notion that *I* did that. I brought forth that light.

Millie must walk away after noticing our lack of response because Lucien repeats, "I spy something pink."

"My cunt?"

"Good try, but no. I'm *touching* your cunt but I can't *see* it. Tell me what I see, baby."

I'm reminded of how he stared at my pussy from behind, how I wasn't allowed to look back, how wet it made me to bare myself for him. I close my eyes, settling into the feeling of him watching me.

I'm warm all over, my skin feeling on fire with his hands on me. Even the handle of the blade gently caressing the seam of my thigh as he brushes it against me is setting me aflame.

My eyes pop open.

"My skin," I pant.

"Yes," he croons, "now you're getting it."

I beam with pride. But then he starts strumming my clit with renewed vigor, and I have to brace myself against my impending doom.

"I. Spy. Something. Beautiful."

I squeeze my eyes closed; my head bowed forward as my core clenches. My whole body brims with tension as tingles crawl up my spine.

"Shitshitshit. I'm coming." I try to whisper, but I'm not sure how quiet I'm being.

I groan when my legs push in, and I feel the burn of being cut, but I only come harder. And he doesn't remove the knife.

"Fuck," I strain, gripping the table's edge for dear life as I try to control the wash of feelings.

"That's it, baby. Come for me. *Bleed* for me. Call out my goddamn name," he growls against my ear.

"Lucien," I say on a breath. "Fuck, oh my God, Lucien."

When I finally come down, I'm panting, flushed and most definitely bleeding.

"Now, tell me what I spy."

I'm still catching my breath, but I don't hesitate to answer because for the first time I think I actually believe it.

"Me."

@BladeSpinner
Online

What do you want

In life?

Seen

WTF! NO.

Haven't decided yet.

CHAPTER TWENTY-ONE

LUCIEN

"Y OU LOOK LIKE I murdered your dog," I call over to Sydney who's slowly approaching the car with this kicked puppy expression marring her beautiful face.

"Maybe you did." She shoots back, not missing a beat and replacing the air of sadness with haughtiness as she picks up speed.

"Oh Princess, what kind of monster do you take me for? I would never kill a *dog*."

I smirk, pushing off my car and stalking toward her. For a second, awareness flashes in those cracked-ice eyes but then it's gone as quickly as it appears. She scoffs, "You're a lot funnier than I thought you'd be."

"Oh, I'm a barrel of laughs," I deadpan, moving faster to open the passenger door before she can sling it open herself.

Her pupils blow wide when she notices I'm already right in front of her.

Gotta be quicker than that, Little Stalker.

"I swear, dealing with you is like befriending Jekyll and Hyde," she grumbles, slipping past me so she can get in.

I chuckle, it's funny how quickly people forget, at the end of the day, Jekyll and Hyde were still the same person.

She's about to sling another insult when her phone buzzes in her hand. She brings it up to her face without even looking.

"Hi, Dad. What's up?" she answers, her voice painfully fucking cheery and out of place compared to what she sounded like a second ago. I glare at her in disbelief.

My stare only hardens as I listen to Sydney put on that fake smile and that fake voice to lie to her dad . . . again.

"Yeah, Dad, I just left. Out to grab a bite to eat with some friends," she says in an exuberant tone from the passenger seat of my car. I haven't even closed the door, but I can't stop staring at her long legs wrapped in the sandal straps as they stretch out from under her black dress.

I have to blink a few times and shake my head at her theatrics before finally moving to shut the car door, but then I hear it.

"Yeah, Bradford texted," she responds as if she was happy to hear from the prick.

The sound of that fucker's name on her pillowy soft lips drives me insane. Bringing him up to her dad as casually as she does confirms her earlier statement that he's a family friend, but it still makes me seethe with hatred. It's a foreign sensation. Even the trash I like to take out on occasion doesn't solicit such a knee-jerk reaction.

I hadn't lied to Sydney earlier. Brad *doesn't* matter and usually I wouldn't care if a hookup had an ex or another romantic interest. As long as there's communication, I don't give it another thought. But that's not the case here. Something about Bradford's existence sets off all of my alarm bells. It's a bleeding sound, ear piercing and head splitting.

I hate it.

I hate *him*.

She pays me no attention as she chats with her father about her precious fucking Bradford.

"Did he tell you he wanted to come?" she asks him, referencing the text she received during dinner.

Yeah, fuck that, if anyone gets to come, it's me. I open the car door wider, settling into a squat as she chats idly with her daddy dearest. She watches me warily, but my princess doesn't break character. I toss my hair from my eyes, tilting my head as she regards me slowly. She knows I'm up to something, and she'd be right. I don't like being ignored.

I rest my palms on her knees, turning her body to face me. Her strappy heels scrape against the asphalt as I drag her legs into position. She doesn't help me, instead letting me do all the work as she continues her conversation. Settling in, I draw her closer as I kneel between her soft, creamy thighs.

The moonlight provides minimal luminescence, but she and I have more fun in dark places. In this position, I hardly notice the coldness of the parking lot asphalt against my knees or the pinch of gravel through my sweats, but I do notice one thing above all: her eyes on me. My hands creep up farther, parting her legs more as I lean in, my face between her thighs. Her breath hitches and she grabs my shoulder for balance, but she quickly recovers.

"Yeah, I'm fine. I was invited out by friends on the team, you know, like a last hoorah," she assures her father.

It disturbs me how easily she fucking lies. One minute she's an obsessed lover and the next she's a raging heiress. If I wasn't looking up at her face, she'd sound so fucking believable. How many people has my Little Stalker Princess deceived?

My fingers squeeze around her knees, and she winces, but the cadence of her voice remains unchanged. I spread her legs even wider, and she easily adjusts, offering little to no resistance as I open her up before me.

We're in a public parking lot. Anybody could see what we're doing, but she doesn't seem to care and I sure as shit don't. I ogle her wounds from our game in the diner and with the most tentative of licks, I test a spot on her inner thighs. She gasps, but again she plays it off with a well-timed fake sneeze.

"Gesundheit, baby," I murmur against her skin.

"Oh, thank you." she says, practically moaning her appreciation. I pause, wondering if I've finally gotten to her, that she's talking to *me* alone, but then I hear, "Yeah, no, someone was saying 'bless you,'" she explains.

I guess he's not entirely convinced because she changes tactics.

"Would you believe we've never been to this restaurant before? Yeah, I know, Dad . . . yep . . . you know best."

My eyes roll, but so does hers—for entirely different reasons—as I lick a slow trail along the apex of her thighs up, up, up, and . . . stop.

She physically vibrates beneath my tongue, a shiver that wracks up her body and into my waiting mouth. It's mildly satisfying, but at least it's a reaction.

I do it again, but just as she settles into the feeling of my mouth being so close to her sex, I bite down, clamping my jaws into the surprisingly tender meat of her muscled thighs. She's fast though. Her hand flies to her mouth before she can scream, and her teeth sink into the skin of her palm to deny me the symphonic notes of her agony while her other hand tilts the phone away. She glares down at me before her body tenses, her back bowing over the console when I suck. For a second I'm worried she'll come from the pain alone, but not even another second later, she's bringing the phone back to her ear.

"I know, Dad. I only wanted to spend time with them before I couldn't anymore."

Well, that just won't do.

I suck as I bite, creating hickies as I move along her upper leg. She writhes, going as far as trying to kick me off, her sharp, red-bottomed heel digging into my shoulder, but I keep my weight on her legs spread in front of me. She squirms, but she doesn't move to close them. In fact, she grinds deeper into my touch, wanting more, chasing my tongue like the horny little stalker she is, but she won't get that from me until I have her undivided attention.

To anyone else it would look like I am devouring her pussy, but I don't reward bad behavior, and my princess is being a very bad girl right now.

"Mm," I moan, "such a naughty girl."

Taunting words spoken between her pearly gates; the only heaven I'll ever be granted access to. I peek above the expensive black material of her dress to find those cracked-blue eyes on me. I'm soothed by the hooded, lust-filled twinkle in them, even more so when her mouth parts to let out a silent whimper, her neck elongating as she tilts it back. *Fuck*. Why didn't we go with the throat fucking again?

Right, right, right. Patience.

Her bucking continues as she tries to get closer, my tongue lashings unrelenting against her tender skin, but her attempts are futile.

"Dad, I think they're calling me. Yes, I know. Yes."

I grin as I bite another area. She has a tiny scratch on the inner part of her right leg from when she flinched earlier, and a teensy stab wound on the left from when she failed to keep herself spread for me. They're not life threatening, but, God, are they sexy.

I kiss the wounds I inflicted. Lick the blood I spilled. My hands slide up and down her quads as I work her into a frenzy, avoiding the place we both want me to be. I expect her to get angry, to get off the phone and snap at me again, but she doesn't. Instead, she runs her long nails through my hair and pulls. My cock leaks as she maintains her firm hold, alternating between soft strokes and tense pulling. Her squirming reactions were instinctual, hard to prevent no matter who was in this spot, but this, this is a sign she's not forgotten me, that she's here with me. Even if it is while on the fucking phone.

I move closer, rewarding her acknowledgement of me. I leave a third hickey right before I reach her glorious center. I'm in the offensive zone now, going for goal. My shot already lined up, but then, "I'm sorry. No, you're right. I didn't mean to be rude. I apologize."

I clamp my teeth down and suck hard, realization dawning that he's not letting her off the phone yet. "Mh-hm. No, yes. You're right. I understand." Her voice is strained, but to normal ears she's totally in control, not the writhing mess she actually is right now.

I lick the bite marks near her pussy, not wanting to take an actual chunk out of her from biting too hard. Cannibalism isn't exactly my thing, but her shaking legs and twitching muscles do soothe the ache, a comforting salve to the need growing between my own legs.

I hear footsteps rounding the corner of the car, but I don't stop my assault on her tender flesh. Whoever it is can fuck right off. That is until the dickhead from earlier decides to make his appearance known and interrupts my meal.

"Well, looky here. It's Morrow and the bitch who got us kicked out before we could even order our food. I can't bel—" I cut off his useless words. Hopping up, I spin around and throw his head in a headlock.

"Shh . . . Can't you see my girl's on the phone?" I growl.

He flails and grunts, trying to shake me off, but it's hard to do when your blood flow is being compromised. He's bigger than me, but I'm stronger. I deal with big-ass defensemen all day, every day. If he thinks he'd ever take me down easily, he's as stupid as the rest of the dumbasses who assume I'm not as big of a threat as I appear. I squeeze, forcing him to garble as I cut his air supply. He scratches at my hands and pulls at my hoodie, but he's not escaping me this time.

"Get . . . off," he grunts.

Sydney legs snap close and she slices her hand across her neck in a 'cut-it-out' motion, but it doesn't have the same effect as her voice. Still, she remains on the fucking phone. What could be so goddamn important she can't hang up? Is she really talking to her dad? Or is it actually Brad on the phone? I narrow my eyes at her, and she at least has the forethought to mouth, "I'm sorry. He won't let me go."

Well, neither will I.

"Do you think I should kill him, Sydney? Should he die for speaking to you like he did in the diner?" I whisper, as the dickhead grows more desperate, flailing and grunting as I wrestle him into submission. He kicks at the cars, and shoves his weight around, but we're in a tight area, sheltered in our parking spot beside a big SUV. Had he minded his own business, we would have never crossed paths, but he came looking for trouble.

She shakes her head rapidly, begging me to spare him with those innocent eyes.

"Yes," I nod, directly opposing her stance. "I think I should." I squeeze a little harder. "Make his eyes pop from his head. What do you think, huh?"

He taps against my arm, as if he can simply call mercy and I'll free him.

Sydney waves her hand rapidly to deter me, but it's not enough. She could stop me with one word, but for that she'll actually have to talk to me. She grimaces knowing what it'll take to get me to let go. I grin at her displeasure. Even more so when the asshole starts to panic and fights harder to free himself. It's a chaotic scene. One that should rattle anyone, but not Sydney.

298

The football jock summons the last of his strength and pushes us back into the vehicle beside us, but the large SUV absorbs the impact.

Her dad must hear the disturbance we're causing because she says, "No, Dad, everything's fine. The restaurants' a little loud, and the cashier was asking me a question."

"You're still ignoring me, Sydney," I pout. "Will you pay attention if I snap his neck? Will that make you happy?"

The guy's blunt nails dig into my biceps and he desperately slaps at my arms and back in hopes of getting me to let go, but I maintain my hold on him. His face is turning darker and darker shades of red until he's basically purple.

I want Sydney to focus. To keep those eyes on me at all times, like she's been doing.

"I know, Daddy. I'll be bright-eyed and bushy tailed by morning. Everything's going to be fine." Her voice suggests a smile even as panic inks her features.

"Tell me what it would take to get you to hang up that phone right the fuck now?" I ask.

She gives me a hard stare as her legs re-open, wider than before as she arches her back and slips a finger between her legs, rubbing her clit in soft teasing circles. She tosses her head back, removing her focus from me entirely as she brings herself pleasure all while lying through her goddamn teeth to her dad. She sounds like the perfect daughter, the perfect good girl as she wraps up her innocent conversation, but her fingers are doing wicked things between her legs. It should concern me that she's this fucked up to be bringing herself to orgasm while on the phone with her father of all people, not to mention with another guy present. I mean he's passed out now, his head tucked beneath my arm, but still, it's not like we aren't in public.

My lips curl into a salacious grin, and I let the guy's body fall to the ground, unsure if he's actually passed out or dead, but I seriously don't give a shit either way. When he grunts upon impact, I accept his survival and shift my focus entirely onto Sydney.

She hisses a breath then looks at me with such carnality I feel ensnared, like I'm the one who's caught. "Have I ever let you down, Daddy? Of course I'm a good girl. I know what to do."

Fuck. She's turned the tables entirely. I want to sink back down to my knees and reward her for her dirty words, but that voice still rattles in the back of my fucking skull.

Not yet. Not yet. Not yet. Don't you dare fuck her yet.

My hands rest on her knees as I watch her pretty lace panties shift and move. She's not actually showing me her glistening pussy, but I can hear how wet she is. I lean farther in, needing to see, wanting more.

"Mm," she hums as though in deep thought, though I suspect the real reason is the stream of air I just blew against her fingers.

I admire the bruises along her thighs already deepening in color. They'll be gruesome by morning. God, she really does mark so beautifully. She'll be a rainbow of purples and blue by the time I'm finished, a broken doll that I'll be there to fix up and break all over again. I won't need anyone else, anything else. She'll be the perfect distraction to satisfy all my needs.

"I understand. Yes sir. No. I won't forget. I'll tell Bradford you said hi. Love you."

Her chest heaves and her body tenses. She's on the brink of climax, of shattering right before me.

I let out a breath, sighing.

As entertaining as this show has been, she disobeyed me.

She *ignored* me.

And bad girls don't get to come. Reaching out, I grip her wrist, halting her movements.

Her angry blue eyes stare down at me, her voice never faltering, never changing, "Goodnight, Daddy."

Fuck me. She might kill me before I kill her. Why was that so hot?

"Is that really what you're going to wear to the party?" Sydney asks, eyeing me with a soft smile that's both somehow pitying and eager, like she wants to take me home and dress me properly.

I shrug, amused by her reaction and the revelation to come.

"It was the only other backup outfit I had in my bag."

"We have time to head to your house so you can change," she offers, pointing a finger outside toward the street leading back to the dorms.

How sweet.

Little does she know *my house* is exactly where we're going.

The moment we pull up to the hockey house, the party is already in full swing. We're late, but who the fuck cares about that when I have her in my clutches and at my mercy?

Gripping my arm tighter than expected, Sydney grits under her breath. "Why did you have me wear this? I feel completely overdressed. Jesus even when I'm not trying to stick out, I manage to do it anyway. Every. Single. Time. *Why* do I do this to myself? Better yet, why did I let *you* convince me to do this? I shouldn't even be here right now," she mutters manically, wringing my arm in the process.

I smile down at the gorgeous girl beside me, watching her freak out. My beautiful princess needed to be dressed as one. The black sequin dress and heels that tied up her calves made her look like a fucking knockout. I don't want my Little Stalker Princess hiding in the shadows tonight. I want her shining like the royal she is.

"You look beautiful," I muse, draping my arm around her shoulders. Her body softens against me, tucked beneath my hold.

"Thank you," she whispers, a small smile creeping onto her face. Whatever worries were plaguing her before seem to leave her for the moment, until we walk through the doors of the hockey house to greet a very upset hockey team who are none too thrilled with me.

"Finally decided to show your face," calls a voice from the crowd. A voice that even when he's angry spreads over me like sweet caramel.

I grin, shrugging my arm off Sydney's shoulder.

Things are definitely about to get interesting now.

@therealLucifer
Online
Seen
Who the hell is this?
Seen
SYDNEY

CHAPTER TWENTY-TWO

SYDNEY

TWO THINGS HAPPEN AT once. One: I lose the warm embrace of Lucien's protective arm around me. And two: a man with dimples so deep it doesn't even matter that he's frowning approaches, cocks his arm back and punches Lucien square in the face.

My hands fly to my mouth as Lucien's face knocks to the side, but he doesn't move from his spot. He takes the punch. I've known him for all of a few hours, but it shocks me as weird that he'd just *let* it happen.

"You done?" Lucien asks, voice calm. Though he's already sporting a small cut on his cheek that has started to bleed.

"No!" the other man roars, his green eyes blazing with fury. "What the fuck were you thinking? You knew how important it was that we win this game. You knew how important it was to *me*. We didn't have to lose!" I'd be taken aback with how beautiful the guy is if I wasn't so horrified by what he just did. He hit Lucien. Shit. Is Lucien going to attack him? And if he does, will he be able to *stop*? This is a much larger group of people and I'm not sure if I'm going to be able to navigate this without someone getting hurt again.

See, this is why Lucien hasn't fucked you yet. Why are you being such a scaredy cat right now? Grow a set of tits and defend his honor.

But words die on my tongue and as the fight ensues, I'm pushed farther and farther back by the growing crowd.

"You're right, you didn't! So, tell me, Captain, why did you?" I hear Lucien yell back.

More punches and blows are traded, but I'm so far back now I can't see a thing.

"We lost, because of *you*. Because you didn't consider the team."

"I always consider the team. Where was my team when he was talking all of that *shit* about my family, huh? Where were any of you? Tell me where my goddamn team was *then*!" Lucien shouts.

The entire party goes quiet; the only sound heard, the base of the music and the soft hum of distant voices. I wasn't sure what triggered tonight's fight on the ice and, if I'm being honest, I'd assumed he didn't really need a reason. But it's clear it has something to do with whatever happened to his family.

It's very still for a long moment, but by the time the crowd dissipates, and everyone goes back to partying; Lucien is gone. Only one person remains in the foyer: the guy with the green eyes, the one Lucien called Captain. There's a small gash above his eyebrow and he taps it with the pad of his finger.

Blood paints the tip but all he does is scoff at it. He walks away too at the realization he's bleeding, but all things considered, he's come out of it in much better condition than the others tonight. I trail the long hallways searching for Lucien, first throughout the massive open first floor of the house and then the basement. The basement is full of stoners and paired-off couples tongue fucking each other while strewn bottles and lines of coke litter the tables. I'm relieved when I don't find him down there.

When fifteen minutes pass and I still don't see him, I'm ready to panic, believing he might have just abandoned me here. If so, we'd never see each other again and I'll die a virgin. The rational part of my brain that still functions tells me I'm being dramatic. I'm not going to die a virgin just because he doesn't fuck me tonight.

Lucien has the right to not want to, or even to ask that we wait. It's *me* that's forced us to operate on this time crunch he's still not aware of. It's not his fault he's under the guise that we have all the time in the world when I know we don't . . . but the obsessive part of my brain, well that part is ready to hunt. Him. Down.

I'm not leaving until I know where he is, who he's with, what he's doing, what he's thinking, how he's feeling . . . I know I'm spiraling, but that's what he does. He scrambles my brain. He makes me *crazy*. I tell myself I'll give it five more minutes before I'm literally kicking down doors, but I'm holding on to the last shred of my sanity for dear life. Resolving that I should at least attempt to calm down, I push past the crowd and head toward the kitchen to make myself a drink.

Lukewarm tequila burns the length of my throat as it slides down in one large gulp, but the desired effect is quickly achieved, so who am I to complain? I'm preparing to down another when a blond-haired blue-eyed jerk takes my cup.

"Hey!" I shout, reaching for my cup, but he holds it at bay, his long fingers stretched around the edge of the cup, fingers that are attached to a very big, very muscular arm. It takes me off guard for a second, but *only* a second. "Give it back, you . . . you drink thief!"

I hold my hand out expectantly, but he defies those expectations. His smile grows, amusement twinkling in his eyes when I reach for it again. He snatches it back and I suck my teeth. I could *really* use that drink, and my nerves cannot handle something as childish as keep-away right now.

"Thief?" he chuckles. "If anyone's stealing, it's you, pretty girl." I gape at him. I'm a lot of things, but I've never been a thief. "You see I live here . . ." he continues, swirling my cup around like it's a fine wine instead of the shoddy mix of bottom-shelf liquor it is. "And I can't say I've ever seen *you* around here before. So, it stands to reason . . ." he trails off.

"That's because I've never *been* here before. I'm..."—I try to find the right word—"visiting."

It seems the most appropriate term.

My fingers thrum against the linoleum countertops, wondering where the guy I'm *visiting* could be.

The new stranger peers at me over the edge of *my* cup, grinning like the cat who caught the canary. I expect him to drink my toxic concoction but instead he smells it like some kind of weirdo.

I lean against the corner of the wall and the counter, my hip digging into the drawer nearest me. He hasn't taken a single step toward me, but I feel backed into a corner all the same.

"Is that so?"

When his eyes leer over me, I don't get the sense he's simply checking me out, it's more like he's cataloging me, filing me away for a rainy day.

"And does the lovely lady have a name?" he drawls, his tone flirty and playful as he turns toward the bar.

I take in his floppy blond hair and V-neck shirt that exposes his thick chest, and the gold chain wrapped around his neck as he pulls down some shakers and stirrers from the cabinet above me. "Or doth the lovely lady prefer *other* terms of endearment?" He teases in a posh accent that's fooling no one.

"The *lady* prefers her drink back," I snide, reaching for my drink again. Once more it's pulled away.

"Well, milady, Chauncey Bridgers at your service, but I can't in good conscience let you have this drink back."

He tries feigning serious and it only serves to make him more intriguing, though still mildly annoying.

Reaching over me, his fingers dance over the bottles, twiddling above the tops, before he snatches one up from the middle of the group.

"And why not?" I ask, eying the bottles as he uncaps his liquor of choice. Have they been spiked? Is Chauncey saving me from getting roofied? That would be a hell of a karmic event if so.

Chauncey reaches to the side of me, careful to avoid skin contact, as he lifts open the cooler lid by my feet. I hadn't noticed it before now, but his flurry of movement shines a new light on the makeshift bar area.

"I believe I speak for the whole team when I say we can't let our esteemed visitor attend one of our parties and not have a decent drink." He leans forward, a little like he wants to share a secret and, like an idiot, I lean in to listen. "We wouldn't want to put a bad taste in your mouth, now, would we?" His playful tone turns seductive and while others could use that same line and I'd gag, this guy is kind of clever, and funny—and as it turns out— another hockey player. Makes sense I guess, he's certainly built for it.

"What gracious hosts," I respond dryly, realizing that all of his moving about is so that he can *fix* my drink.

The corner of his mouth curls into a sly grin.

"You can save the theatrics," I quip, waving my hand around his space.

"Oh, but theatrics are what I do best, sweetheart." He winks, drawing my cup away from within reach when he sits it down.

Oh, I don't doubt that.

I can't actually tell if he's being a tool or just a professional flirt.

"Did it ever occur to you that I might *like* drinking warm tequila?" I challenge. "Besides, I have a perfectly good drink, right there." I point to my cup on the other side of his workstation.

He laughs again, continuing to mix my new drink despite my protests.

"*Nobody* likes warm tequila."

"Maybe *I* do. I'm weird like that."

He chuckles, wetting his lips as he shakes his head at me. "I like weird . . ." He stops his pouring and turns to fully face me, appraising me again, ". . . but okay."

My skin grows hotter the longer he stares, and not in a good way. I'm feeling judged, like careful research is being conducted and I'm failing the test.

"Pineapple!" He blurts out.

I arch a brow. "Excuse me?"

"Yep. For sure, pineapple." He repeats, turning from me again and adding the pineapple juice.

"What, were you trying to guess my favorite kind of fruit or something?"

"I was using my superpowers on you."

And there go the gag reflexes. *Ugh.*

"Is that what you do to pick up girls?"

"Nope. What *I* do is work magic," he answers, smiling at me despite my snide remark.

He adds a splash of other mixes and a lemon wedge for garnish before stirring the drink with ice and finally handing it back to me.

I eye it cautiously, then meet his eyes again.

It's strange. He's definitely flirting with me, but not in a wholly discomforting way. I'm sure this schtick works well on other girls, but he's a devious one. This guy wouldn't just distract a girl, he'd take her whole breath away with relentless fervor.

"Try it and tell me it isn't better," he says, his tone cocky like he knows he's about to win me over the second I taste his creation.

I take a sip, and the involuntary smile that threatens to take over can't be helped. I try hiding it against the rim of the cup, but it's too late, he can obviously tell I like it because he shines perfect white teeth back at me.

I throw him a suspicious glare.

"*Magic*," he emphasizes, his equally cocky grin and spirit fingers telling me he believes in every bit of his own 'supernatural' talent.

When I take a second sip, I practically moan. It's fucking delicious and getting the job done. My tension eases while I stand in the kitchen of my first college party—at the hockey house of all places—surrounded by peers who I've never so much as bothered to learn the names of before now. I'm pretty sure at least half of the business school is here as well as every major sport athlete.

I take another sip, while my new friend makes his *own* goddamn drink.

"This is *so* much better." I lick my lips, tasting the blend of sweet juice and strong liquor against my tongue. "Thank you."

God, I needed this.

"It's been my absolute pleasure, beautiful." He taps his cup with mine in a toast, and I guzzle another mouthful. He chuckles as he follows suit, scooting in closer. "Now that I've done my civic duty, why don't you tell me what someone as hot as you is doing here *all* by herself."

He sets his drink down beside mine, resting his arm above me against the upper cabinets, his biceps flexing. It's not entirely repulsive but . . .

"Oh, umm, well you see . . ."

He steps in closer, leaning down to speak in my ear. "Please tell me you came here alone."

"I . . ."

"She's with me." Lucien's voice cuts through the tension so deep I feel impaled, both with the relief that he didn't abandon me and the fear that he thinks I'm flirting back.

"You're back." The words ghost over my tongue like a whisper as I relish his return. I almost don't believe my eyes since he's clearly changed clothes. He's sporting a dark gray track jacket paired with dark distressed jeans, a plain black tee, and laced combat boots now.

Where the hell did he get clothes from? And why the hell does he look so damn good in them?

I clear my throat, attempting to move, when it dawns on me there's nowhere to go. I've made this corner my new home.

Chauncey's the one who steps back, releasing me from my cove, but I don't feel any less trapped. Not with Lucien here. With Lucien around, I feel bound. And whatever anxiety I felt about him walking away from me is only temporarily staved off.

"There's no way he's with a girl like *you*," Chauncey snorts. "A delicate thing like you doesn't belong on a leash. You could do a lot better than him. You should explore *all* of your options tonight," he admonishes, using the back of his hand to stroke down my arm as he speaks.

I flinch at his unexpected touch, subtly pulling away. And of course, Lucien notices.

"Touch her again and I'll rip your fucking tongue out, Chauncey," Lucien seethes, vitriol spilling from every word with an oddly relaxed demeanor. His arms are folded, but he doesn't look particularly angry. The anger clings to me instead.

Where does this Calvin Klein reject get off trying to tell me I don't belong with Lucien? I hold my drink out for Lucien to hold before stepping up to Chauncey, running my hands from his lackluster abs to his stubby cock. I don't know if it's actually stubby, and there's nothing *lackluster* about him, but that isn't very well the point. He insulted me first.

"I assure you I'm not *that* delicate," I say, squeezing his balls so hard he crumbles forward at my feet.

"Fuck fuck okay okay, please let go of my dick!" He squeals.

"Oh, is that what I'm holding? I was aiming for your balls. Are you telling me this is it? All that you have to offer me?" I pout.

I make a show of looking at my hand cupped between his legs.

"Fuck, you're crazy man," he whines.

I tilt my head, "I thought I was delicate. I think I'm doing you a service. Lucien wanted to rip your tongue out. At least this way you're getting exactly what you wanted right? Me, touching your dick?"

I squeeze harder.

"Look, I'm sorry. I was just joking, okay? You guys make a beautiful couple. Honestly. You have my full support."

I give him a bright smile, one equal to his oh-so-charming one.

"Aww, you think so, I was kind of worried you wouldn't approve. You sure you're okay with this?" I ask, my tone, frosted thickly in sarcasm.

"Ah fuck, Lucien, please make her stop." Chauncey pleads, looking over to Lucien who's beside himself with laughter.

Lucien is of no help to his teammate, he's laughing so hard his whole body is vibrating and he's keeled over, two seconds away from dropping my delicious drink made special just for me.

Chauncey glowers at a useless Lucien and I take advantage of his distraction.

"I have a confession, Chauncey."

"Oh yeah, what's that?" he grits through his clenched teeth, baring the pain I'm inflicting as he braces a hand on the counter.

I lean forward, my lips ghosting the shell of his ear.

"Your begging is turning me on," I whisper, pulling back to catch the look on his face.

My smile is wide, all teeth and venom, when he looks up at me with those Swedish blues, brighter and more luminous than my own. For a moment, those swimming-pool eyes I'm sure women find themselves backstroking in the longer they stare, look as though he'd gladly still fuck me. But what was once a carefree allurement slowly transforms into legitimate fear. I'm so startled by the shift I squeeze tighter.

"*Lucien*," Chauncey whines, dragging out the name.

Lucien clears his throat to stop laughing.

"Alright, Princess, let him go. Chauncey isn't so bad; he just made an error in judgment. Right, Chaunce?"

I loosen my hold, but don't let go completely.

Chauncey's head bobbles up and down, almost animatedly. "Please. I'm *sorry*. I didn't mean anything by it. I swear. It won't happen again, just . . . fuck, *please* let go of my dick."

It was fascinating, to be in a position of power, to see big powerful men cower and beg. To have *someone* suffer the consequence of underestimating me. I can't lie, I would very much like to see it again, but one arched brow from Lucien draws me back from that perilous edge and I let him go, feeling kind of guilty at my behavior, but mostly, I feel uneasy.

For the most part, Chauncey had actually been nice to me. He wasn't like the grubby old guys I was forced to mingle with back home, or the clout-chasing mama's boys who thought they'd use my status and body for their own gain. Chauncey is one of Lucien's teammates. I might have crossed a serious line by hurting him. Jesus, what is wrong with me? I don't hurt people, that's not me. *I'm a good person.*

Affixing a less sinister smile to my lips, I aim for contrition. "Sorry about that." I reach out to pat his shoulder as he straightens up, but he flinches away from touch. I can't blame him.

Taking a step back, he wags a finger between Lucien and I. "Yep, I change my mind. You two were made for each other," Chauncey chides.

My face heats and I work to stop the blush from creeping across my cheeks, I really do, but it's in vain. Based on the look they're both giving me, my cheeks are blooming bright red. I flit a sheepish look to the floor tiles, unable to hide my secret glee. Though I still feel bad, I love the idea of being made for Lucien.

Chauncey grumbles something incoherent as he slinks away, and Lucien starts laughing even harder, so hard he's the one doubled over now.

"I can't believe you did that!" Lucien chuckles.

"I'm sorry, it's just . . ." I huff. "He called me *delicate*."

Lucien's chuckles soften to a less hysterical snicker. "What's wrong with being delicate?"

Amused as he is, the guy still oozes sexual energy, tapping at my arms that have magically wrapped themselves around my middle. It shoots a spark through me whenever we touch and some of the tension falls away when I drop them to my sides.

"Nothing."

"It's not nothing. You're more twitchy than usual," he twiddles two fingers, gesturing between my eyes.

"I am *not* twitchy, I'm upset."

"Care to share with the rest of the class? I'm a great listener."

"No," I snap.

His glare intensifies.

I sigh, "Yes"

He moves in closer. Encroaching on my corner of the kitchen. He's even closer than Chauncey was, more blatant and a thousand times more tempting to boot but I don't move. I stand there frozen, afraid of what I'll do if I dare move even a centimeter.

His fingers swoop my curled tendrils behind my ear and I can feel his eyes on me while *I* actively avoid them. I thought I could do this, but it's only getting harder. When I'm sure I won't blurt anything out or go running to throw myself off the nearest bridge, I crane my neck.

"It doesn't suit me," I relent, tracing his sharp features, imagining the feel of him, before returning his gaze. "I am not some fragile thing that has to be handled with care."

I'm not sure which of us drew forward, but somehow, we're closer now. His scent of peppermint and leather enveloping me in a tight cocoon.

Nuzzling my hair, his lips trail a path along my forehead, and he leaves a kiss on my temple. I shudder beneath his touch, his affection. "God, Princess you have no idea how bad I hope that's true."

His whispers would be sweet if they didn't sound so ominous but I think this is his version of tenderness. God knows he's already put my body through the ringer, and there's surely more to come, but if pain is his love language then I want to be loved out loud. I'll take every lashing, every cut, every fucked up version of his love and hold it dear.

I clear my throat in hopes of clearing the tension.

"And where were you anyway?" I ask, pulling away from his embrace. "You wouldn't have had to threaten your teammate if you hadn't left me down here all by myself."

"I needed to change." He shrugs.

"You have clothes here?"

"I *live* here," he states it as if it's obvious. "This is my party. Or at least it was my idea. I suppose they could have canceled it on account we lost, but I'm a firm believer that you party hardest when you lose."

He holds his arms out like this is kingdom while some random guy fists bumps him on the way to the fridge.

My jaw drops.

"The party was at your house this whole time!"

In retrospect, I should have picked up on that. It's a hockey house and all eyes have been on him since we walked in. "Why didn't you just tell me?" I add, noticing for the first time the side-eyes and wary glares I'm getting from everyone at this party.

"Inviting you to a party, rather than telling you to come to my house significantly raised the odds of you saying yes," he says.

I scoff. I'm here because I lost a race, I would have walked away like I was supposed to had he not challenged me.

"Yeah, well, I never go back on a deal, so you could have told me," I huff.

It's both my best and worst quality. If I went back on deals and reneged on bets, maybe I could get out of this one with my father, but I'm almost happy I lost to Lucien and agreed to come out tonight. Fair and square at that. I tried to win, but so did he, which can only mean he meant it.

He wanted me here with him tonight.

I roll my lips inward to keep from grinning so widely.

"Stop doing that," he mutters, eying me in a way that makes my blood freeze.

I straighten, rolling my eyes a little at the reaction he solicits within me.

"Stop doing what?" I ask, because he's starting to give me serious whiplash with his hot and cold act. "What am I doing *now*?"

He doesn't answer. Instead, his arm reaches out and snakes around my waist, pulling me to him so quickly I stumble forward. Not expecting the public display of possession in front of all these people, I bring my hand to rest on his chest, stabilizing myself in his hold and trying to keep a distance. Looking around, I note everyone's stares, but his fingers wrench my face toward his. Fuck, those eyes.

"If I make you smile, then I want you to smile." He kisses the corner of my mouth. "If I make you cry then I want to see tears." He kisses the apple of my cheek. "If I make you feel good . . ." He leans into the shell of my ear, ". . . then I want to hear you scream my goddamn name."

I fucking melt. Never in a million years has a man ever felt so safe and so dangerous at the same time. I can't tell if my heart is ripping apart or ripping out but it's beating for him harder than I can contain. I open my mouth to speak but his gaze steals my breath . . . and his next words breathe it right back in. "Don't hide how good I make you feel, especially from me."

His proclamation makes me blush again, and I search the party once more. People are *definitely* watching us. I wasn't this conscious of them with Chauncey but all eyes are on Lucien which means all eyes are on me. On us.

"They're staring," I whisper to Lucien, though he acts like he doesn't even notice.

He holds me tighter.

"Let them stare," he whispers back, a resignation settling onto his face. I don't hold back my smile this time.

"Most of them are harmless anyway," he comments, unfolding his arms from around me and reaching for my hand.

"In comparison to you, maybe." I chuckle as he tugs me along through the crowd from the kitchen, down a long hallway, to a sitting area in the back of the house. "You're not wrong there." He winks at me from over his shoulder and I shake my head at his playfulness. In the corner of the room, there's a flip cup game going on. It's less crowded save a couple of guys already sitting on the couch in front of a large TV screen.

Lucien smacks one of their feet resting on the coffee table.

"Feet off, Garcia," growls Lucien.

"I think I deserve to break the rules, since they clearly don't mean shit to you," Garcia huffs, bringing his bottle of beer to his lips.

Lucien gives him a deadpan look, snatching his beer from him then taking a sip.

"Yeah, man, whatever," Garcia grumbles, rolling his eyes but ultimately moving his feet to let us pass. It's surprisingly the least hostile interaction I've seen Lucien have which makes me feel even worse that I assaulted his other teammate.

Lucien pulls me down into a chair with him, settling me onto his lap.

"So, you know . . . I really *am* sorry I hurt your friend," I mumble. I'd love to say he's making me apologize but the truth is I think I may have gone a little overboard with everything.

Again.

His shoulders shake with mirth as he laughs again.

"I know, Princess, but don't be sorry. He should have known better than to try and take what's mine."

He squeezes my hips.

"I'm yours?" Hope flickers brightly in my chest and I try my hardest to get the useless organ to accept there's no future past tonight for us but it betrays me. Taking root in that one little word, *'mine'.*

"Until I say otherwise, you're not getting rid of me that easily," he threatens.

"Never," I murmur. A vow my soul makes before my brain can warn against it.

His grin is wicked in its reward.

"Good, because I'm not done with you yet." He says voice lowered and etched in danger. "We're about to see just how *not* delicate you are."

I chuckle nervously. "So, what *game* are we playing next?"

He hums and the vibrations ricochet through every cell in my body.

"This is more like a *test* than a game," he says, absentmindedly stroking his fingers down my arm. "I wanna know how far you'll let me go."

To the depths of Hell if he willed it.

But I don't give voice to that thought. I can't. Instead I ask, "How are you going to test me?"

He gives me a wink and takes another sip of his stolen beer.

"You'll see."

INTERMISSION

INTERMISSION

LUCIEN

One month ago

@BladeSpinner

What are you doing?

Without removing my eyes from the ceiling, I slap around the bed until my hand reaches the phone. When I see it's them, I grin. Time to play a little game. I text back.

Why?

@BladeSpinner

I'm curious.

Well stop. Curiosity killed the cat.

Something tells me we're way past the stopping point though.

@BladeSpinner

Cats have nine lives. What's one more?

@therealLucifer

Too bad you're not a cat.

@BladeSpinner

You don't know what I am.

@therealLucifer

The same could be said for me. You have no idea who I really am.

The three bubbles that indicate they're typing flickers before finally their response comes through.

@BladeSpinner

I'm learning.

@therealLucifer

You're playing a dangerous game here.

@BladeSpinner

High risk. High reward. My favorite game to play.

@therealLucifer

Ohh when I catch you

@BladeSpinner

Run run as fast as you can you can't catch me I'm the gingerbread man

SYDNEY

@BladeSpinner

What if life as we knew it wasn't really like what we knew at all and everything we knew about the world was a lie?

What do you think?

@therealLucifer

I think you're high.

@BladeSpinner

I don't do drugs.

@therealLucifer

Why not, I hear they're life changing.

@BladeSpinner

What if I don't want my life to change?

@therealLucifer

You just said life as we knew it was a lie.

@BladeSpinner

I said what IF it was a lie.

@therealLucifer

Then I guess we could do as many drugs as we wanted.

@BladeSpinner

Touche.

If you could do one drug, what would you take?

@therealLucifer

Something that would knock me out and put me to sleep.

What about you?

@BladeSpinner

Something that would overstimulate me, like shrooms or acid. I wanna feel colors, and see sounds. I think it'd be kinda cool, to hallucinate a new reality. Don't you?

@therealLucifer

I think I'd be too pissed off when I was inevitably brought back to the real world and the dream ended.

@BladeSpinner

Way to ruin the thought experiment.

@therealLucifer

Shouldn't you be asleep?

@BladeSpinner

Shouldn't you?

@therealLucifer

I would if I could

@BladeSpinner

Having trouble sleeping?

@therealLucifer

Having trouble staying asleep.

@BladeSpinner

I can help with that

@therealLucifer

Is that a threat?

@BladeSpinner

It's an offer

@therealLucifer

Could have fooled me

@BladeSpinner

It's not my fault you jump to the worst conclusions.

I just want to help.

@therealLucifer

There's only one thing that helps.

@BladeSpinner

Which is?

@therealLucifer

Goodnight Little Stalker

SYDNEY

MANIFESTATION JOURNAL

DATE: FEBRUARY 14, 2024

Today I'm going to help Lucien. He'll see I'm useful and I'll show him that I really care. He'll be so grateful, he'll have to ask me out. Then this'll be the cutest meet—cute story for the grandkids.

"You can't be in here," says the new Bean Cup assistant manager aka the second victim of my plans to speak with Lucien. Seriously, this establishment is getting a shit ton of money from me as of late. I'm doing this blackmail thing all wrong. Dad would be disappointed.

I hold up a crisp one-hundred-dollar bill, newly withdrawn from my emergency account this morning.

"I need a favor," I tell the frumpy guy.

He stares at the folded bill between my fingers then me.

"What kind of favor?" he asks as he reaches for the cash.

I pull it back.

"First, you need to hear what it is."

I could easily be identified and caught if this guy really wanted to come after me, but the way his eyes are more focused on the money in my hand than my face, I'd say there's a good chance that's not gonna happen.

"What's the favor then?" he drawls, uninterested in who I am in the slightest.

I reach in my back pocket, swapping the money for the plastic item tucked between my fingers. Holding up the small baggie of crushed pills I got last night, I wiggle it in front of his face. "I need *you* to put this in Lucien Morrow's drink when he gets here in . . ." I sweep my wrist up to my face so I can check the time on my Apple watch, "ten minutes."

"The fuck? I'm not—" I slap my free hand over his mouth.

"Lower your voice," I grit. "Are you trying to get caught?"

We're tucked in the back of the shop and early risers are starting to fill the building. The coffee shop opened, and I caught this nitwit when he made the unfortunate mistake of leaving the back door open long enough for me to jam my foot in the door and sneak in. The door was heavy as shit, and I almost broke my damn foot, but here we are.

"I'm not trying to get involved in any of this," he backs away. "I don't know what the fuck your deal is but I'm not drugging the most popular guy in this school so you can do God-knows-what to him, you freak!"

"I am *not* a freak," I gasp. "And what would you do if he wasn't popular, hmm? He's a guy. A *regular* guy. You don't need to point out his popularity status. What are you, thirteen?"

The guy in front of me is, in fact, *not* a teenager but a grown man. I'd say twenty-six or twenty-seven, if I had to guess. He's a scrawny dude with glasses and a goatee that looks like he spent his whole life trying to grow it.

"No," he huffs, "but people are bound to notice a drugged-out hockey player if I give him whatever *that* is." He points to my hand still holding the drugs. "Jeez, what even *is* that? Are you trying to kill the guy or something?"

Anger zips through me. I curl my fist into a ball in his dingy brown apron, crinkling it along with his fresh-pressed white button down beneath. His name tag dangles, the name Will etched in block letters. Pushing him back, I shove him against the stock shelves. Various metal bowls and containers clang from the force, and he squeals like a schoolgirl.

"I would never *hurt* him. I'm trying to *help* him, okay?"

I will admit, our current positioning, with his shirt jacked up to his throat, doesn't help my case. The threatening look in my eyes probably isn't doing me any favors either, but I can't bring myself to let him go without getting this very important point across. I'm not like *them*; I don't go around hurting people. I'm a good person.

He holds his hands up. "Okay, okay, fine. You wanna help him, sure," his expression is scared and frazzled, and his eyes keep darting toward the office door. I know he's looking for an exit, but I'm just as anxious as he is. I have one shot at this. I nibble frantically at the corner of my thumbnail, checking behind me at the door.

"Look, he'll be here any minute. This," I pull my thumb from my lips and hold the bag up again, "is just to help him sleep. To you he may be some big hot-shot hockey player, but there are some of us who actually *care* about his well-being. You get me?" My brow quirks up, prompting him to respond.

"Yeah . . . Yeah, I get you." His arms are still held up in surrender and I roll my eyes and take a step back.

"Put your fucking arms down. You look stupid," I huff. "I don't even have a weapon."

His arms slowly come down as he seems to figure out how ridiculous this looks.

"So, that *isn't* going to hurt him?" he asks again, gesturing to my hand.

"No," I answer, handing him the baggie so he can take a closer look at it. "It's not cocaine or anything like that. They're just some *really* strong sleeping pills that I crushed up."

"And what? You want me to slip them into his coffee?" he questions.
"Yes."
"And they're supposed to help him sleep?"
"Yes," I nod.
"And the drugs wear off, right? They're not gonna fuck up our chances in the playoffs?"

"You care about that?" my face turns up at his question.
"You don't?" he retorts.
I actually hadn't thought about it.

"No . . . I mean, yes, I care, but no, they're not going to mess up his game performance."

I made sure these wouldn't hurt him. I even tested them on myself the other night. This is the second batch I bought since I had to prove I wasn't a narc after my first purchase. Only then was I given instructions and tips on how to properly use it. Who knew drug dealers had integrity and solid business practices?

"And you're sure about doing this?"

"*Yes*," I say, exasperated with his questions. I peer behind me at the door again. *He'll be here any minute.*

Will still appears wary but he seems more committed to the cause than he did ten minutes ago.

"How much you gonna give me if I do it?"

I hold up the hundred-dollar bill again, and somewhere in the last sixty seconds it seems he found a backbone in this stuffed storage office we're in.

Will eyes the money and scoffs.

"I'm gonna need more than that. This is *Lucien Morrow* we're talking about. I don't know the guy personally, but I've heard the stories. If he finds out I had anything to do with this, I'm as good as dead anyway and that's best-case scenario."

"Seriously, what's worse than death?" I ask.

"Oh, I dunno, taking drugs from some shady-ass chick who breaks into my coffee shop and asks me to drug a student, then going to jail if the guy keels over and dies." His finger jabs toward the ground as he drives home his points. "I'd be complicit to *murder!*" he hisses.

"So, what, we thinking three hundred . . ." I tilt my hands in a tipping scale motion.

"I'm thinking a *thousand*," he pronounces.

If I had water in my mouth, I'd spit it at him.

"A *thousand* dollars! Are you *insane*?"

"Are *you*?" he shoots back. "I don't know who the fuck you are or if what any of what you're saying is true. I'm just supposed to take your word and drug someone because you ask me nicely, which, by the way, you didn't even do." He's waving his hands around at this point. "You accosted me and then tried to bribe me with a measly hundred-dollar bill when you knew how high the stakes were."

Well, fuck, he's got me there.

Will cocks his head as he folds his arms, as if to say, *checkmate, bitch*. I check my watch one more time and secretly curse his name.

"Shit. Fine." Reaching into the pocket of my hoodie, I pull out four more hundred-dollar bills. "Here." I slap the money in his open palm. "I'll give you half now and half when the job's done."

He thumbs through the cash slowly and again I roll my eyes. He's flaunting it on purpose. Feeling pretty proud of himself, he holds out his other hand with a smirk.

"Yeah, whatever. You better not fuck this up." I place the baggie in his palm next.

"And you better not let this blow back on me," he quips, pocketing the drugs in his stupid brown apron. "Pleasure doing business with you." He twiddles his fingers in a sarcastic wave. "Now get the fuck outta my coffee shop."

I check my watch, annoyed I'm having to deviate from the plan I set. My plan was to do this in the morning and spend the whole day with him. Once the drugs wore off, I could slip out, make it to practice on time and no one would be the wiser. I lean against the door of a silver Camry while waiting for Will.

Meet me out back an hour after closing. — Will

P.S. Someone will know I'm out here, so don't even think about trying anything funny.

Sloppy.

How'd he know I'd come back? Way to keep it anonymous. Anybody could have found this. I hold the note up again and scoff when I read it. The car I can only assume is his is situated directly beneath the streetlight.

I guess I can't fault the guy for being overly cautious, but when he walks from the back door to find me leaning against his car, his mood shifts from cautious to overly annoyed.

"That was not pleasurable," Will says, shoving a small pink box in my face and holding out his hand. "Now, here ya go."

"What is this?" My nose scrunches at the frilly box as I grab it.

"It's a heart-shaped muffin."

My mouth drops open, a little shocked by the turn of events especially when the scowl he's been sporting hasn't left his face.

"Oh, um, that's sweet but, uh," I try to decline his gift.

"Ew, no, it's not for you. Honey, you are *so* not my type," says Will, genuinely repulsed by the idea of dating me. "This is for Lucien. I didn't have the guts to poison him to his face, so I baked you this and put it in the chocolate drizzle and strawberry filling. It should hide the taste better. And now *you* can give it to him."

"*Me*? Why me?" I screech, springing off the car.

"You're a girl and your chances of not getting *murdered* rank significantly higher than mine if he ever finds out."

"*That's* your reasoning?" I sputter because even though Lucien is scary, this man is an adult. He shouldn't be *this* scared of a sophomore in college.

He holds his now empty palms in the air, making it impossible to give him the damn box back.

"Look," he starts. "I don't know what kind of creepy shit you're into, but I did what you asked."

"You actually didn't," I retort.

"This way is smarter, and it doesn't blow back on me. So, take your little gift and give it to him."

His outstretched hand flexes in a gimmie motion and I slap the remaining cash in his palms.

"This better work," I mutter, shoving past him in the direction of the dorms.

He doesn't bother counting the cash this time. "Yeah, Happy Valentine's Day, creeper," he calls at my back.

SYDNEY

I had expected snoring, loud boarish grumbling, or nasally snorts of breath, though I suppose that's a more animated way of thinking. In reality, there were no such theatrics. Lucien's breathing is soft, even, and almost sweet. He slept with a boy-like wonder, sprawled on my lap, cuddled with innocence blanketed over his slumbered features. This is the closest I've ever been to him.

I stroke his hair, brushing it rhythmically to the timing of his breathing as I hum a lullaby. His whole body moves in time as though the rested breaths spread to every corner of his limbs. When is the last time he'd truly rested? When had I? The last few months have been such a blur. Without the aid of the "extra special" Ambien, I find myself equally exhausted watching him be at peace. Meanwhile, practice has been killing me. My body's rebelling at the lack of conditioning.

My phone chimes and I flip it over to read the messages scrolling up the screen.

Group Chat
Bellemere Figure Skating Team

Regina 6:40 AM

You're late again!

Hannah 6:44 AM

Hey, yeah, Coach is talking about giving you another demerit if you're late again. If something's wrong, I'd suggest calling her to explain.

Regina 6:46 AM

There's nothing to explain.

> I'm sure Sydney has a good excuse why she's leaving us hanging like this and doing her own thing. We should give her the benefit of the doubt.

> I'm not sure the rest of us would get the same benefit if we did the same thing.

Oh, fuck you, Bria.

I'm not typically a fan of early morning skate but I've never been late for it. Fuck.

My head bumps against the cheap wooden headboard as I think about what I'm going to do about upcoming qualifiers. I peer down at Lucien to ensure it didn't wake him, but he doesn't flinch, and his eyes are still closed. I sigh as I return to my thoughts.

At this rate Tiffany is still ahead of me. Her long program was cleaner than mine, though my short program bested her precision skills. We were neck and neck when we shouldn't have been. A year ago, I was already where she is now, one step closer to my dream of the Olympics, but I choked under the pressure, and I've been choking ever since.

If I can't nail this program, there's no way I can push myself to place higher than Tiffany in this month's qualifying competition.

The worst part is she isn't even the one to beat, she's the steppingstone I need to get me in front of the one who is: Keyshawn Reynolds. A sixteen-year-old prodigy who's already secured a spot on the US Olympic team and has already been invited to participate in the 2026 Winter Olympic Games. But then again, lately, I've been pretty good at removing obstacles. What's one more?

LUCIEN

What the fuck?

I wake with a long lock-jawed yawn, my mouth both loose and tight simultaneously. My limbs are like Jello and my head swims in a sea of fog rolling in my head until . . . Yup, nausea sets in. My body sways and I catch myself, my arm bolstering the majority of my weight. With my palms against the sheets, the first thing I notice is that they're dry. I brush a hand over the bed. There's no sweat. I cradle my head, the heel of my palms resting over my eye sockets as I groan. It doesn't help and my eyes squint against the light that spills into the room when I sit up. They're unfocused as I take in the space. I'm in my dorm, but why? And how?

I don't exactly remember coming here. Yesterday was a fairly good day, all things considered.

My stomach roils then shouts at me to feed it while I'm still in the midst of piecing last night together. One thing's for sure, only one person would be so bold.

The last thing I remember is a heart-shaped muffin and a stuffed gingerbread man with the head cut-off it.

"That mother*fucker*," I chuckle aloud. "I can't believe they did it. They actually drugged me." My legs swing over the side of the bed, and I sit on the edge. Pulling my boxers open, I check my dick. Nothing too out of the ordinary there. I give it a long stroke and sniff, caught a little off guard by the sudden musk smell, but slightly relieved by the lack of sex scent. So, I didn't fuck anything, great.

"Good to know they were respectful when they drugged me," I murmur, laughing hysterically that they not only followed through with their 'offer', but they managed to drug me at all. That is the *last* time I accept food packages from anonymous couriers. Clever Little Stalker. I wonder if this means I can return the 'favor' since they want to part from reality so damn bad.

I rise from the bed and pad to the window, noting the unlocked hinges. My lips curve into a smile. They were here. They stayed with me, and there were no nightmares. Shuffling over to the bathroom, I glance in the mirror, noticing how tousled my hair is. It looks like fingers have been run through it a thousand times. I run my own through it, but it doesn't conjure any memories or rogue feelings.

After a quick brush of my teeth and some water thrown in my face, I feel less drugged and more rested.

Leaving the bathroom, I flick the light switch, then catch sight of a single glass of water on my bare nightstand and a note sitting next to it, stuck to the glass with condensation.

Hope you slept well.

——Yours

I flip the card over, knowing there would be nothing on the other side, but eager to check all the same. They'd still not given me their name. I wanted to catch them more than anything but going about this the way that I was wasn't working.

The only time I felt good anymore was when I stopped caring about being good at all. It was time I put an end to these nightmares once and for all. I'll be the nightmare itself from now on. If my little stalker could go to such lengths to show me their true colors, so could I.

I read the note again. My gaze hung on the last word. Like a skipping record it repeats in my head.

Yours. Yours. Yours.

Mine. All fucking *mine.*

Dr. Amelia Thatcher
Session Transcript
Audio Recording
Date: March 3, 2024
Patient: Lucien D. Morrow
Thirty minutes into the session

Lucien: Haven't you heard, doc? I'm a psycho.

Amelia: You're not psychotic, you're traumatized.

Lucien: Not what the file says, doc.

Amelia: You know as well as I do, given everything you've been through—though it will have a lasting effect—it doesn't have to define you.

Lucien: I wouldn't worry your pretty head about it. I don't mind being crazy. I'd argue it's my best quality.

Amelia: You know I don't like that term, Lucien. And though I appreciate the compliment, you also know I'd prefer it if you didn't flirt with me. I'm your psychiatrist.

Lucien: What? Psychiatrists can't be pretty?

Amelia: Mr. Morrow.

Lucien: Oh no, she's using her formal voice. She must mean business.

Amelia: All jokes aside, I am happy to see you're in better spirits this week.

Lucien: Yeah, I've been filling my time with more . . . stimulating activity.

Amelia: That's great. And it's helping?

Lucien: Immensely, I am much better when I have my sights set on a particular goal.

Amelia: If anybody can achieve their desires, I have no doubt it's you.

Lucien: We're going to be parting ways soon, doc. You gonna miss me?

Amelia: We've been over this. Though our state-ordered meetings are ending, I highly encourage you to continue our sessions. The work we've achieved together has been pivotal to your overall growth and healing. I feel deeply that we can continue with our positive trajectory should you stay on with me.

Lucien: Nah, you've done more than enough. I don't need to be fixed, I just need to stop fighting it.

Amelia: Fighting what?

Lucien: My true nature.

SYDNEY

"Detective, why do you think you've been having so much push among the community when it comes to seeking justice for these heinous murders?"

"Unfortunately, Kate, the victims of these acts were not considered upstanding citizens. A couple of them had rape charges. One was a child

molester, and the others have been in and out of prison on domestic violence charges, sexual assault, and all were severe alcoholics with multiple DUIs. People haven't been motivated to come forward, but we must continue to do our job. It is up to our judicial system to enact justice, and it is our job to catch these criminals. We will not let these acts of violence go unanswered."

"Thank you, Detective Rothschild. Again, if you have any further information, please contact the helpline featured on the screen below."

"Can somebody please turn that down? I can't hear myself think," Tiffany whines.

It's on the tip of my tongue to ask her if that's because there aren't many thoughts in there to begin with, but unlike her, I am not needlessly cruel. Or at least I try really hard not to be. Tiffany isn't my enemy; she's an obstacle. There's a difference. I'm not going to go out of my way to be unkind to her, even if she is a bitch. We should be hitting the ice and perfecting our programs in our allotted time slots. Instead, *she's* insisted we have a team meeting.

"So, a lot of us have been talking and *we* think"—she nods her head in each direction to embody the whole locker room—"that only those of us without disciplinary warnings should get to go to the competition next week. It's an important event and only those who take this seriously should get to go."

"You can't *bar* people from competing, Tiffany, it doesn't work like that," I quip.

"*Sure*, they can compete, but why should the school fund the amenities for a team when not everyone's a *team* player?" she snarks. "If you want to compete, I'm sure you can afford it, Sydney. But it shouldn't be on our dime."

And there it is.

"So, what are you saying, Tiffany?"

"Oh, Sydney, don't misunderstand me. I'd be thrilled to have you come, you know me and you go way back. I'm just not sure it's in the best interest of the *team* to include you when you've been so absent lately."

"What team?" mumbles Kieran, typically the quieter type who ignores the rest of us.

Thank you, Kieran!

"Exactly, we're not a team. This is *figure skating,* not hockey. It's every woman for themselves," I agree.

"Or man," pipes Shane.

"That's yet to be determined," mutters Bria.

"Wow, so did everyone eat their cereal with piss this morning?" Shane quips back, sweeping an accusing finger across the room.

"Look I've had a lot going on," I deadpan.

Tiffany pretends to regard me, faux concern painted all over her face.

"Right, right, dating Lucien Morrow, correct?"

I almost fall out of my chair.

"Excuse me?"

Her fake-ass smile creeps me out, "Oh, you know, your boyfriend? The one you skip practices to go see?"

"I didn't know you and Lucien Morrow were dating," mentions Hannah.

Shane scoffs. "*That's* why you've been missing practice? I thought you were sick."

"Dick sick," snorts Regina.

"You're wrong," I snap. "You don't know what you're talking about." My ears ring, summoning more panic. My heart beats against my ribs, drumming up more anxiety. They're going to spread this weird rumor around the entire campus and then he's going to find out *I've* been the one following him around like some sort of crazy fan. He's going to tie me to the messages. *Don't freak out, don't freak out.* "It's not like that."

"So, what's it like?" asks Bria, obnoxiously chewing gum that we're not even supposed to have in here. It's partly why I chew my nail folds and not sugary confections. And exactly what I'm doing now as I attempt to get out of this situation.

"It's like *nothing.* I don't know what she's talking about," I press.

Tiffany puts her French-tipped nails to her lips, playing coy as she giggles. "Oh. Am I *lying,* Sydney?"

"You're *mistaken,*" I re-word. I know what she's trying to do, and it won't work.

"Hm, well," she sighs. "I guess that *wasn't* you I saw coming out of his dorm room this morning then. Sorry for the mistake—won't happen again. I suppose that makes sense though. I mean, what would *Lucien Morrow* be doing with *you* anyway? I'm sure a girl like you is too good for the likes of him, right?"

"I didn't say—"

"You have *so* many better things you could be doing with your time. Like, say, being on time for practices like the rest of us." Tiffany is rolling in bitchiness today.

"That's a little harsh, don't you think, Tiff?" Hannah asks. "Sydney's been a good team player for the—"

"So that means we should give her a pass?" Regina guffaws, cutting Hannah off.

"No, I'm just saying—" Hannah tries to defend me again.

"Yeah, if you girls are just going to be catty to each other, I've got actual ice time I wanna take advantage of," cuts in Shane.

We all pause when we hear footsteps around the corner. The clanking of Coach's whistles against her insanely large key rings, unmistakable.

"Sydney, in my office please," calls Coach, ducking her head around the corner before disappearing again.

"Oop, well, that's our cue, I guess," Tiffany smirks. "We've brought up our concerns with Coach, so we'll find out soon what her verdict is. *Good luck, Sydney,*" calls Tiffany over her shoulder while the rest of our so-called team trickles out of the locker room.

Hannah turns back, her hand resting on the large metal doors before they can close and gives me a sad smile. I try to smile back, but the truth is I'm over being a part of this 'team.' I'm here to be great, not to be *friends*. It's exactly what Dad is always trying to tell me. You can't make it to the top and still have your friends at your side, so why slow yourself down trying? It's best to leave them behind at the start.

The meeting with Coach does not go Tiffany's way, but it doesn't go my way either. I'm removing my guards from my skates and am about to step onto the ice when I hear loud whispers that are obviously not whispers at all.

"Don't choke," one voice carries.

"Again," finishes the other. The voices giggle loudly among themselves.

I sigh.

It's obviously Regina and Tiffany, but I don't say a thing.

"Don't worry about them," says Hannah and I almost jump out of my skin from how close she's standing to me.

"Jesus Christ"—my hand flies to my chest—"you freaking scared me."

Her face scrunches, as if tasting something sour. "Sorry about that. I've always been told I'm light on my feet. Guess that's what makes me a pretty good figure skater, huh?"

She nervously scratches at the one faint dimple at the corner of her mouth.

She's more than pretty good, but I'm not going to boost her ego two seconds before I'm supposed to hit the ice and outskate her.

"Yeah, sure, all good." I try to wave her off.

"That's a relief," she teases. "Can't go around giving heart attacks to my friends." She giggles and it's unlike the fake snickers I get from Regina and Tiffany. It's relaxing, the type of laugh you want to join in on when you hear it. "So, it looks like things went well with Coach if you're getting onto the ice? That's good." She beams at me, her smile precious.

I smile back. There's no wide showcasing of teeth or anything, but I don't want to be mean to her.

"Uh, yeah, it went fine," I say.

We may not be the best of friends or even close teammates, but she's always sweet like this and she's always defended me. Even when I haven't deserved it. I've dropped the ball and lost sight of what was important. That's on me. If I can find time to try to talk to Lucien, I can certainly find it in me to talk to Hannah.

"She decided to give me another chance," I add, hoping it's enough to smooth things over with her.

I could give her more details than that, in fact there's a desire there to talk all of this out with her, to have a real friend to share my burdens with. But I'm dying to get on that ice and prove I belong here. The more we stand here, awkwardly attempting a conversation at the mouth of the rink like this, the less time I have to practice. The silence drags on when I don't continue. Hannah takes the hint and steps back, giving me space to pass.

"Okay, well, I just came over here to check on you and let you know that not all of us feel the way they do." She nods her head in the direction where Regina and Tiffany walked off. "It's stressful for all of us, but I'd imagine it's even more stressful for you. You're only a few more wins from qualifiers." She beams, her tone animated and excited.

"You know my stats?" I ask.

She rolls her lips then leans in like she has a secret to tell. "I've always been a fan of yours. You're really talented, Sydney, and I think of all of us, you have a real shot of representing the US team in 2026."

I could cry at her admission. Shit, I think I am.

"Oh, no, wait, I didn't mean—" Her face turns to a look of shock when a stray tear kamikazes its way down my cheek. I brush it away with a delicate pass of my finger, blending the tear stain along my under eye.

"It's okay, that just . . .that really means a lot to me. It means . . . more than you know."

She stills. "Oh. Well, you're welcome," she smiles, waving me off as though it's no big deal.

Genuine kindness *is* no big deal to her.

I didn't say thank you. I should have, but I didn't. God, I'm the worst.

"Anytime you need a pep talk, I'm your girl." She points her thumb at her chest before leaning in again. "And don't worry, I won't tell anyone you cried." She tosses a wink over her shoulder as she walks away.

"Thank you," I whisper, but she's already gone.

Stepping onto the ice, I try to hold on to her kind words, to drown out the words of my father. It helps.

It doesn't completely keep them at bay, but I do a perfect run-through of my program. Then I do it ten more times until perfection is muscle memory.

"God, come *on!*" shouts a voice from the edge of the rink. "Your time is finished, it's *my* turn, Sydney. Or do the rules of the rink not apply to you?"

I roll my eyes. "I never said that, Tiffany." I skate toward her, ready to exit the rink, but she blocks my exit.

"You think you're so much better than us, don't you? Well, newsflash: you're *not.*"

I try not to react, but the words hurt. They sting like an open-handed slap to the face. She grins when she sees me flinch.

"Don't think for one second this changes anything. I don't care *how* good you are. Coach and everyone else will see you the exact same way I do," she hisses.

I don't bristle this time.

"Careful, Tiff." I smile wide, my eyes soft and friendly like Hannah's. "You wouldn't want anyone seeing those true colors of *yours.*"

Her eyes cast around me for a second when she catches on. Hannah and Coach are watching us from the other side of the rink.

"Less talking, more skating, ladies!" Coach shouts.

Tiffany's usual condescending smile reappears.

"Coming! Was just congratulating Sydney on her amazing set. Wasn't it beautiful?" she exclaims like she's *so* proud of me.

"Yeah, good job!" Coach agrees. "Now, come on. Let's see yours. I want to work on your run time. You're late on some of the cues."

Tiffany scowls but quickly adjusts her face before pushing past me, shoulder-checking me along the way. She doesn't deserve the spot she's coveted. She's everything I hate, a goddamn thorn in my side. Thorns are meant to be removed, cut out, and shaved directly from the stem. How else is one meant to enjoy the roses?

THIRD PERIOD

@therealLucifer
Online
ere you in the arena last ni
Seen
Who the hell is this?
Seen
SYDNEY

CHAPTER TWENTY-THREE

SYDNEY

WHEN HE SAID HE wanted to test me, this is *not* what I was expecting. Eyes bore into me from every angle as the crowd grows, an audience of bystanders that crave chaos and get off on violence, but this time it's not me being pushed to the back of the group, on the outer edges of the entertainment. I *am* the entertainment. Centerfold. They're watching *me*.

Several slabs of plywood are braced between me and the tree at my back. The jagged rings that I'm guessing were once painted red have now faded into a deep maroon.

Every muscle in my body is locked in place, unmoving as Lucien instructed, though I don't think I'd have minded so much if he chose to strap me down. Human target practice is a little macabre for my tastes, but I suppose that *is* the whole reason he called it a test.

Despite my better judgement, in only a few short hours I *had* grown to trust Lucien in some capacity; to believe he'd rather fuck me than kill me.

So, when he'd asked me to stand here while he disappeared back inside the house, I obeyed without a second thought, lost in that desirous gaze of his.

As one would imagine, I've caught the attention of everyone on the back lawn. People stopped their beer games and bonfire make-out sessions to leer at the girl in front of the target: me.

Then everyone on the inside who shared those same morbid curiosities joined them. I recognized some of them, and deep down I knew a few even recognized me. But I wondered if they knew what

I'd done, what happened earlier today? Maybe they were standing here tonight hoping I'd receive justice, that'd I get what was coming to me.

Maybe I would.

Goosebumps rise to the surface of my skin and jackhammers go off in my stomach. The dirt beneath my feet tickles as it slips beneath the toe strap of my heels and the heat of heavy stares starts to boil me alive. It's an uncomfortable, heady mixture of anxiety, fear, and arousal that's all for him.

My ears ring when the microphone interferes with the impressive karaoke speaker they've rolled out into the backyard.

"Alright, alright, alright. You know the drill. You wanna stay, you gotta pay. Phones in the bucket. And bets on the table. What do we got? What do we got?" announces a familiar voice and an even more familiar face, his drunken smile and chestnut brown hair the same as it was some hours ago.

Asshat.

"Well look who it is. Seems we have ourselves a challenger, folks!"

He's a lot less blue, but equally obnoxious. Same as before.

"Morrow versus . . ." He prompts me to give him my name, and though it pains me that *he's* the one emceeing this catastrophe waiting to happen, I reluctantly provide it.

"Sydney," I supply stoically.

"Morrow versus *Sydney*," his amused voice calls over the mic, a crooked grin on his lips that's all teeth and charm.

My skin crawls with the way he says my name, like he *knows* he'll be using it again. I'll be long gone before he gets the chance, but the thought isn't providing much comfort. His words about Lucien's 'leftovers' come flooding back and I feel sick that I'm only one of many who've tried and apparently failed to win Lucien's affections. It dawns on me with troubling clarity that this might be how Asshat secures his conquests; by comforting the girls who chicken out of Lucien's so-called tests.

As if able to read my thoughts, he grins at me, his arm thrust out in a display of showmanship. I toss him the fakest smile I can muster, full of sarcasm and snark, but he blows me a kiss all the same.

I inwardly recoil.

"Aww, don't be that way," he announces over the airways for everyone to hear. "We go way back, don't we neighbor? My money's on you tonight."

His face twitches in what I think is supposed to be a wink.

"I highly doubt your money would serve me well here," I state. I'm pretty sure he's betting against me.

The crowd snickers and murmurs, but he only riles them up further when he says, "Perhaps, *Sydney* . . . but I'm rooting for you, neighbor."

"I'd really rather you didn't." I roll my eyes and his face breaks into another self-assured smirk, an enigmatic twist of his mouth that annoys me as much as it makes me want to laugh. But then it changes, morphing into one of horror. It was a split second, a whistle of wind that I heard more than saw, but I witness the moment it registers to us both exactly what just happened.

Asshat's eyes slowly peel from me to his sneaker-clad feet. Next to his foot, in a patch of uncut grass, sticks a long blade, the hilt an obsidian black with silver skulls on it.

He slowly lifts his foot away, going two-shades paler when he sees the knife pierced through his shoestrings, pinning him to the ground. He stumbles out of his shoe, crawling backward on his hands like a crab, his eyes wide as he looks around, settling on Lucien's smug expression.

"Let's get this started shall we," booms Lucien.

It's my turn to smirk. I won't be losing.

@therealLucifer
Online
ere you in the arena last nig
Seen
Who the hell is this?
Seen
SYDNEY

CHAPTER TWENTY-FOUR

SYDNEY

THE CROWD WHOOPS AND hollers remind me of the roaring arena from earlier tonight. They only grow louder as Lucien strides toward me. They part for him like the Red Sea with a blend of worried gazes and feral anticipation. Their sweat-slicked faces and inebriated bodies gather around the backyard, apparently thrilled with this segment of the evening. Even though he's on the outs, even though they lost, they all still adore and praise him.

I'd kill for that kind of adoration, but I get a nice contact high from just being next to him. They shout my name, cheering me on as only drunken college students can. I pretend they're clapping *for* me and not secretly praying for my downfall and betting against my success.

They give a full round of applause as Lucien steps up to me.

"What took you so long?" I ask, grinning when he tilts my face up with one of his busted knuckles and gives me a wink of his own.

"I needed to grab some things," he says, skimming my lips with his thumb. "Can't leave you alone for two seconds, can I?" He tosses Asshat a death glare over his shoulder.

"Maybe you shouldn't leave a damsel in distress," I tease.

He chuckles, turning back to me with nothing but wicked intentions written on his face. I think I love it, that glare that burns down all my hesitations and fears. "You are no damsel. You're my little—"

"Don't you dare say it," I warn, though judging by the twinkle in his eye, I know he's thinking it anyway.

Lucky for him, he *doesn't* dare, but his laughter quickly ebbs away.

"You okay?" He tilts his head toward the onlookers and MC Asshat behind him.

I nod. "I'm fine. It's . . . a lot, but I'm not nervous."

His eyebrows pinch, but for once he doesn't call me out for lying. "Don't let them scare you. You got this. I wouldn't have asked you to do this if I didn't think you could handle it."

"If the *others* could handle it, then so can I."

His face falls, a flash of hurt in his expression if my eyes aren't playing tricks on me. I thought nothing could hurt Lucien, but maybe that's not exactly true.

"There are no others," he whispers, leaning closer. "Only you."

"Because they *failed*?"

"No."

The jeers of the crowd quiet, and all I hear are loud puffs of breath that I recognize moments later as my own breathing.

"Because you're already *mine*." He grips both my wrists, pinning them to the board as if I'm on a cross. His proximity scrambles my senses as his lips ghost my temple. "It's no contest, Princess."

A sense of pride flutters in my chest.

Even if it's only for a night.

Even if I *am* a human target for this psychopath.

I'm his.

I really *must* be crazy about him if I'm willing to go this far.

Lucien bends down to pluck an apple from the top of the pile in a bucket at his feet, presenting it with a magician's flourish when he rises.

"Hold the apple out to the side, balanced in your palm," Lucien instructs, running his fingers sensually across the inner part of my arm, then wrist, before flipping my palm up.

I still feel the stares we're getting. Hell, I even recognize some of their meaning. There's desire, jealousy, curiosity, and wonder, but they're nothing compared to the look Lucien's giving me right now.

Intense hunger. Deep-rooted obsession. Unhealthy fixation. Everything anyone normal would run away from. Everything I *should* run away from . . . but the more I think about running, the more stubborn my body becomes, because running from a man like Lucien is asking to be chased.

We're all bathed in flickers of orange light from the bonfire, but only Lucien looks godlike under the amber hues as I peer up at him. His scent cuts through the stench of booze and smoke, invading my senses, intoxicating me. The air between us crackles like the reflecting flames that dance behind his golden eyes. It's as if the whole world's gone silent and it's just me and him before he's bringing the apple to my lips.

"Kiss it," he commands, pressing it to my lips before I can think better of it. My lips pucker of their own accord as if placing a chaste kiss to his cheek. He turns the apple over, smiling as he admires the spot where my gloss sticks to the shiny red skin, then he gingerly sets it on my outstretched hand.

"It's very important you don't move, Princess," he murmurs.

I stutter a nod, straining to accept the dire implications of ignoring his warning. I understand basic logic, but I'm worried that my body isn't as resolved as my heart.

If I flinch, I'm dead.

If he misses, I'm dead.

Death is starting to feel like a *strong* possibility.

He must see the fear in my eyes, feel the thrumming of my heart, because when he straightens, he pulls an exact replica of the blade skewered to Asshat's shoe from behind his back and draws the terror out more. I stiffen and that fear ramps up several more degrees, just like he wanted. That thrumming in my heart, becomes a fluttering of bees.

He twirls the knife in his hands, whirling it around his middle finger, the hole in the hilt perfectly shaped.

"No need to be scared, Princess," Lucien murmurs. "I promise I won't miss."

"You can't make a promise like that," I choke out.

The blade stops and he grips it between deft fingers, holding it up until it's right under my chin, poking into the underside of my jaw.

Tilting my face up, he asks, "Aww, don't you trust me?" The glint in his golden eyes somehow shines brighter in the night. And what was a light breeze in the air, dusting the wisps of hair over my face and tickling my nose, is now a smoldering inferno that burns all my doubt away.

"Does it matter?" I whisper.

He chuckles darkly, "Honestly, no, it doesn't. I don't want your trust; I want your submission." His glare sharpens, training in on me in a way that tells me he's digging for something he knows I can't easily give. "That's a lot harder to earn, wouldn't you say?"

I take a deep swallow, the blade moving with my throat.

Yes, I *would* say. All things considered, I'm an obedient daughter and even an amenable lunch date, but submission? I've never in my life done that.

"So then, do it," I push. "Make me submit, Lucien."

He twists the knife so that it lies flat, dragging it from my chin and along my jaw as he speaks.

"So eager," he muses. "I told you you were no damsel. Don't worry, I have all night to make you submit to me."

"Promises, promises." *So many promises, Lucien.*

Lucien grins. "I *do* love a challenge."

There's a brief sting when he flicks the knife back. Without looking, I know he's nicked me, but his tongue's a welcoming salve as he licks up the base of my throat.

I suck in a shaken breath, my knees knocking. My pussy, wet. This is the second time he's pulled a knife on me tonight, the *third* time he's cut me, and I'm just as turned on and terrified as I was the first time. Even more so now that I hear the murmurs of our growing audience. Everyone can *see* I'm his and that whatever's happening between us isn't a part of their regularly scheduled program.

Lucien brings the blade across my cheeks to my lips, forcing me to kiss it, same as the apple. Except this time, when he pulls the blade away, he licks over the spot my lips touched.

I stifle a moan, ready to announce my fealty now and submit in whatever way he demands, but that's not the name of the game.

This is a test.

He takes a step back, then several more. More steps than I expect him to. The more the space stretches, the more my heart constricts. Can he actually hit his target from *that* far away? The crowd has more than doubled in size since I've taken my position in front of the target. They wait with baited breath to witness the outcome of my fate.

The large, mangled piece of plywood set up against the tree behind me should be evidence enough that quite a few things have been pierced against this wood. Glancing down, I see dark blood stains caked into some of the splinters. Those same splinters claw at my back, inciting my attention, but I'm not allowed to move too far from the target.

My last sliver of sanity rises to the surface, screaming at me that this is *not* safe. *Abort mission!* I don't need to prove anything to Lucien, I'm Sydney fucking Sinclair. I could be packed and vacationing in Aspen by tomorrow afternoon, with a *real* Calvin Klein model, cozying up in a hot tub, swiping Daddy's credit card and riding all the slopes and dick I want.

But who's to say the Calvin Klein model could even make me come, could even make me feel a fraction of how I've felt this whole evening with Lucien? The only other time I've felt this alive, is when I'm skating. And I don't mean in competitions. I mean in the cold air, on a frozen lake. No one in the stands and no judges critiquing me, just skating for me. It's been a while since I've done that. Since I've *felt* that.

A soft crunch echoes in my ears and twists my middle with a nauseating churn as cool liquid seeps into my palm.

My mouth drops open, ready to scream in pain, but the pain doesn't come. I dart my eyes to my outstretched hand where a knife sticks straight through the apple, embedded so deeply it's trapped against the wood.

I drop my hand in shock, then shift my gaze back to Lucien.

Did he even *try* to warn me, make sure I was ready before he threw it? *Of course not*, the stupidly pleased smirk on his face says as much.

Any *normal* person would be upset. Instead, I'm impressed. He didn't miss. Even from that far away.

Amazing.

He's a good fifty paces apart from me, and still, he hit the apple dead center.

"Another one!" Lucien shouts, gesturing with the knife to the remaining pile of fruit.

The people scream for an encore, piercing through my shocked haze. They holler and cheer at his impressive shot, begging for more.

Lucien only smirks at me.

"Did you see that, folks? The new girl didn't even flinch!" Asshat announces over the mic, fully reverted back to the asshat we know and tolerate. "Everyone who said she'd pass out or cry needs to pay up right now." He holds out an old paint bucket and though many people lost their bets, no one seems particularly upset about losing.

The crowd screams their shouts of praise and accolades, his blunder during the hockey game earlier almost totally forgotten, or simply forgiven.

I'd imagine it's his precision skills to aim so well that's made him a top scorer in the NCAA. I wonder who's all aware he uses human targets to hone his craft.

I look at the piles of apples at my feet, then pick up another one. He nods, looking so smug, so confident in his abilities and for a second I contemplate chucking the apple at his face, if only to get him to lose that cocky grin. It's no wonder he's such a good hockey player, why they win games, why his team must put up with his shit, because they *know* how good he is. They might be mad at him right now but they at least respect him. They believe in his abilities to win so profoundly that even if he does struggle to rein in his temper, it's worth keeping him on the team, worth being a champion.

My so-called team saw me as nothing more than dead weight. At the first sign of trouble they took the opportunity to cut me loose. Said I couldn't hack it, that I couldn't handle the pressure. They said that's why I did it. They accused me of becoming so desperate to win I did the unthinkable. I believe Tiffany's exact words were "it was about time they *trimmed the fat.*"

She made sure to slide that little jab about my weight in there. Girls like her are why body dysmorphia runs rampant among female athletes.

I should be grateful I'm no longer a part of such a toxic environment, relieved that I don't have to deal with the pressure of constantly failing them or maybe even a little bad for the danger I put them in . . . but I don't feel any of those things. I wanted to be a champion figure skater. I wanted to go to the Olympics. I wanted to win Gold. I *want* to win first place, to be the girl who wins Lucien's heart. To outshine anyone who's ever stood in this exact spot and challenged the demon himself. It's not enough to be the last girl standing. I want to beat Lucien himself. I want to win . . . win . . . *win*.

Tossing him a teasing smile, I place the apple on my head, balancing it on the center.

Let's see him hit his target now.

Soft murmurs buzz around me, but I quiet the noise. There's only me and Lucien. His eyes paralyze me. I've never seen Lucien accept defeat and I don't suspect he'll start now but for a moment he stares back at me like I'm his whole universe.

And then a blade soars right toward my face.

My eyes remain trained on Lucien as I feel the sickening crunch of the apple being pierced. If it were anyone else, I'd have passed out like those who bet against me predicted, or ran home but the pride on his face makes me feel like I can pull off a perfect quadruple axel blindfolded with my hands tied behind my back.

That's how invincible I feel. He may have hit his target but I stayed true. I endured and I didn't falter.

I submitted.

Except, I do falter when I hear a familiar voice ring out among the audience's jeering as they crowd around Lucien and celebrate the awesome shot.

"Hey, Lucien, do me next."

It instantly snaps my attention, the voice who dares think they're getting anywhere near *my* Lucien. I'm so focused on the voice that is undeniably Tiffany saddling up next to Lucien that I almost miss the second voice strutting in my direction.

"Well, well, well, if it isn't Sydney Sinclair. Surprised you're even here. I can't believe you showed your face after what happened today. You're *bold*."

Whispers immediately ratchet up.

"Sinclair?"

"The heiress."

"The figure skater?"

I take a step away from my position against the target, finally taking in the sight of the blade sticking right out of the apples center and once again planted deep into the wood. I wonder exactly *how* deep because, if need be, I'll need to use that blade.

I look from the bitch on a warpath to the knife, moving to grab it before thinking better of it. If Tiffany wasn't bad enough, her roommate and best friend, Regina, was just as bad.

"Poor thing. You're downright filthy," she mocks, swiping a finger along my forehead where I realize apple juice has dripped down my face. I try to brush her hand aside, but her sharp acrylics dig into my jaw, gripping my face with a punishing bite that keeps me in place. "I suppose it serves you right after what you did. So, what is Little Miss Rich Girl doing slumming it with the rest of us, huh? I mean, I heard you were having money troubles, but betting your life seems a little extreme, even for you," she sneers. "But I guess a life for a life, right?"

Those shouts of praises and excited stares I once felt not twenty minutes ago feel like judgment and disgust now as my dirty laundry is aired for all to hear.

Regina's eyes snake down my body and if I thought I looked ridiculous before, that repulsive glare she's displaying makes me feel like the naked emperor. Like I'm the fool who thought she was draped in expensive garments when in fact she was naked and arrogant.

Her head tilts, as if catching sight of something of particular interest in the black sequin dress and wrapped heels I'm wearing.

"Did you dress like that to prove you're better than us? Or was it to see which hockey god you could seduce next?" She shakes her dark hair. "Shame you snagged the attention of the crazy one."

"He's not crazy," I strain, unable to keep the raw emotion from my voice. All I want to do is scream and lash out while also wanting to cry and run.

You deserve this.

"I guess you weren't good enough to fuck anyone of real caliber." Another jab that lands.

"You don't know what you're talking about," I grit, but she keeps going, ignoring me in the process.

"Newsflash: you're not even good enough to stay on the team! Unlike you, the rest of us *earned* our spots."

I did *earn my spot,* is what I want to say but the words won't come.

It's all your fault.

"You're not one of us. You never will be," Regina seethes, her nails digging deeper.

It hurts. It *all* hurts.

"Get off me!" I swat at her hands, trying to raise my voice, but her grip on my cheeks is solid.

Regina's cackle matches her menacing tone. "Oh, how the mighty have fallen. You're a simping little puck bunny now? Can't hack it on the ice, so you're fucking the next-best thing, is that right? God, I can't believe Lucien's even wasting his time on you. I knew Tiffany was telling the truth. All those times you were *sick*, or *late*, you were just out fucking him. Must have been so beneath you to follow the rules like the rest of us."

"That's not true," I grit, though I know it's not all lies either.

"You really are pathetic, you know that? A little girl vying for attention and love from Daddy Bigbucks . . ." I try again to push her away, but I'm so bruised by her words that I'm uncoordinated, stumbling back and slamming into the wooden panel as I fall on my ass.

Laughter erupts from a few onlookers who watch the humiliating exchange, but they do nothing to help me. Even the girl from my *ethics* class turns a blind eye, though I can't even say she does that since she's opted to stay and watch. It's on the ground staring up at Regina's cruel face that I'm reminded she's absolutely right.

These people aren't my friends, they aren't my teammates, they aren't my anything. They're strangers I'll never see again after tonight, so why am I even bothering? Angry tears well in my eyes and I want to scream at her for being so mean and disgusting. But most of all, I want to scream at her for being so goddamn right.

I tried so hard to be a good person, to be *unlike* my father, but look what that got me. Maybe Lucien was right and there really is no such thing.

Regina smirks down at me, watching on in delight as I curl in on myself, drowned in thoughts of *what if* and *maybe*.

"No wonder Coach kicked you off the team; you can't even stay balanced *standing up*. Just look at yourself," she spits.

I don't though.

Instead, I look at the cold rough ground, riddled with rocks and weeds from improper lawn care. I burn all my feelings and hatred into the half-dead grass, wishing Regina was beneath it all. I want to put her in her place, to say something vile and unkind right back but then I'll justify why she thinks she hates me so much to begin with. I'll become the person she *thinks* I am. I want to destroy her, and that thought alone scares me. It's because of that line of thinking I ended up here to begin with. If I resort back to my old ways now, I'll never recover. I'll be forgotten and the Sydney I am with Lucien will be nothing but a fever dream, lost to the harsh reality of failed expectations.

She scoffs. "What are you going to do? Cry? I can't believe—" her words are cut off, garbled and strained as she tries to catch her breath.

I lift my gaze to find Lucien's hand wrapped around her throat. He slams her against the target with such a force, the wood cracks and bows. The heavy splinters mar her porcelain skin and Lucien pulls another blade from thin air, slamming it into the wood next to Regina's face. I'm frozen in place, watching it wobble while Lucien's hand drops back down.

Her chest starts to rise and fall at an unnatural pace, heaving for air she can't seem to get.

"Apologize!" Lucien's eyes have all but gone black. There's no more gold, no more light.

Sweat matriculates in heavy rivers down her brow, her skin clammy and devoid of color.

"*Apologize!*" Lucien shouts, drivel spilling from his lips as he screams in her face. Her lips part, opening to speak, to say something.

But she can't.

She *can't* speak.

"Lucien, p-please let her go. It's fine, okay. Let her go." I roll to my hands and knees.

"She wasn't being very *nice*, Princess. She *needs* to apologize." The words grit through his teeth like rough sandpaper. "She needs to pay for hurting you."

"I know."

I slowly rise to my feet, my dirt-covered palms shaking as I try to placate him like last time. "I know. But . . ." But this no longer feels like I'm approaching a lion, this feels immensely more dangerous, like walking in the dark, totally unaware of the real threat that lies within.

"She hurt you," he mutters.

I hear the people around us yelling, trying to figure out what to do, but since everyone's phones were taken at the start of this thing, they can't actually call for help.

They also can't record, which works in *my* favor. If any of this got out it would ruin us both, far past the damage we've both already caused. Lucien could end up arrested for assault or attempted murder. And me? I don't even want to *think* about my father's reaction to all of this.

"Alright, alright. Nothing to see here, folks!" Asshat's voice boasts through the speakers, though I don't actually see him anymore. "Everyone back inside so we can keep this party going. Ooouuu!" He howls, sounding even drunker than before.

Gratefulness is the last thing I thought I'd feel toward him, but the emotion sneaks up on me when half the party follows him back inside.

I briefly sweep my gaze over the rest as they watch on, stunned and curious.

I reach for Lucien, noting my shaking fingers, before I drop my hand to my sides. I just need a minute to calm him down again—*if I even can. Or . . . I could leave.*

I've done nothing but cause Lucien more problems. Every issue we've faced tonight rolls through my head like an old-fashioned reel of fuck up after fuck up. The parking lot, the diner, Chauncey, and now this. Regina's right, I *shouldn't* be here.

This is all your fault. This is what you do. You ruin people. You'll ruin him too if you stay.

Coming here was a mistake. Revealing myself to him in the first place was even more misguided. Like a wild animal, Lucien attacks first, lashing out before thinking of the consequences. Basically, the complete opposite of me.

The key is to never react.

It's easier to hide those feelings away, to push it down and ignore the pain until it's a dull ache you can no longer feel.

If I reacted to everyone I had a problem with there'd be no one left. Shit, look what happened when I tried. I ended up in *this* situation.

His teammates rush from the house to get Lucien off Regina, but they're only going to make things worse. Turning behind me, I see the green-eyed captain leading the pack, instructing some of the team to hold the remaining crowd back before heading right for us. I thrust my hand in their direction to stop them—to stop *him*.

I've got this.

Our eyes lock for a moment and there's a recognition that passes between us, an understanding. And to my surprise, he stops advancing. The group follows his lead and an imperceptible nod is all I'm granted.

Despite the situation at hand, I know Lucien's showing at least *some* restraint with her, otherwise he would have snapped her neck the second he grabbed her.

Lucien just needs to calm down.

I turn my focus back on Lucien and place a hand on his shoulder, squeezing slightly to let him know I'm here.

"Listen to me, Lucien. Listen to the sound of my voice," I whisper, running my other hand over the length of his arm until it reaches the hand that's wrapped around Regina's throat. "I know she needs to apologize, but she can't talk. You're holding her too tightly, see? You need to let go right now or she's going to die, and then we'll *both* be in big trouble. You don't want that, right?"

His eyes slide to mine and that murderous glare stings me. His dark eyes swallow the light, as colorless as the night sky but I don't leave his side.

"Please, for me, okay—let her go."

He grunts, but his eyes soften and he unclamps her throat. "Fine."

She drops to the ground with a harsh thud, but relief fills me all the same. It's sucked away when Tiffany comes barreling through the makeshift barricade of arms.

"Oh my God, you fucking psycho!" She screeches, running up to us as Regina's ragged coughs force her to throw up, her body violently shaking at our feet.

"You're finished," Tiffany spits, whipping her bleached blond hair about. That usually cool facade all but shattering to pieces now. "No one's giving you a pass after this. You can say goodbye to your precious hockey career and everything else you love. I'm going to end you for this, Morrow."

There's no more relief or fear, not even pity. There's nothing but frigid anger.

Tiffany bends down, muttering to herself more threats of ruining Lucien as she helps her friend. I squat down too, ensuring we're eye level as I get in close. I want them to *see* my eyes, to *heed* my words.

Regina's body is still shaking and I'm unsure if it's because of the fear or the force of her own hurling, but she slowly meets my gaze. Her bloodshot eyes are red-rimmed and filled with tears. Blood-stained splinters from the target board are stuck in her dark hair and a hand-shaped bruise is starting to color her neck. She's slumped in the dirt, an exact mirror of what I must have looked like just moments ago.

Leftover vomit sticks to her wobbling ruby lip and patheticism whittles her once beautiful features. Using my thumb, I swipe it away. The gesture is rough, it tugs at her lower lip, smearing her lipstick.

There was a time when I thought Regina was the prettiest girl I'd ever seen. I thought she was graceful in a wild, understated way, much like Lucien actually, until I saw all that ugliness she harbored inside. Looking at her now, she appears every bit as tarnished on the outside as she does on the inside. My only emotion is vindication.

"Listen up because I'm only going to say this once."

Tiffany screws her nose up in disgust, but draws her friend closer, who—for the first time since I've met her—has nothing to say. I wipe my thumb clean on Tiffany's dress, and she jerks back, looking like she wants to throw up next.

"You say a word about this to *anyone*, get him in trouble in *any* way, I'll make sure to put that Little Miss Rich Girl title to good use and *bury* you both. Am I clear?" My words are a whisper.

"But . . . you can't . . ."

Tiffany tries to speak, heaving clipped breaths as she tries to search my face for a lie. For once, there isn't one.

"Am. I. Clear?"

If ever there was a time to be a bitch, now is it. Unlike Lucien, I know the consequences should they choose to defy me, and it won't work in their favor. I won't have her ruin him, no matter the cost.

Lucien stands next to me, an avenging angel with his arms folded tightly in a shaky attempt to restrain himself. He's far from calm, but at least he's not killing her.

Tiffany's eyes flitter around, catching on to something behind me, before looking to me again. No one is coming to save her either.

"Crystal," she finally says, moving to help Regina up.

I look behind me to find the captain turning away.

"Not so fast. Your friend there still owes Sydney an apology," says Lucien, dragging my attention back to the girls.

Regina's still catching her breath, hunched on all fours and shaking again. Tiffany rubs her back, and that's when I notice she's sobbing.

"It's fine," I whisper.

"It's not. She *hurt* you," Lucien repeats.

"You *choked* her!" Tiffany yells back.

"She should be grateful that's all I did. Now, she has five seconds to apologize or I'm strapping her to my target board and aiming for *all* the vital spots. You've seen my aim. I don't fucking miss," Lucien seethes.

Regina sniffles.

Tiffany scoffs, "You're fucking ins—"

"Sor-ry," Regina rasps, cutting off Tiffany's whines, but Lucien's not satisfied.

"What was that? Could *barely* hear you," he taunts, cupping his hand to his ear.

"I said . . . I'm *s-sorry*."

Her voice cracks at the end and, if I learned anything about Lucien, it's still not good enough. I interject so he doesn't continue to push.

"Thank you. And you might not believe me, but I'm sorry too . . ." Lucien glares at me but I continue, "about everything. I didn't mean—" I stop myself from confessing too much. She's owed an apology, not an explanation. At the end of the day, she's just as responsible for what happened as I am. "As for your throat," I point to her neck that's already forming a nasty bruise. "I think we *all* just got carried away." I let my eyes narrow, looking between the two people I personally hold responsible for ruining what was supposed to be my escape, away from all the mess at home and attending my dream college. "So, we'll stay out of your way, and you'll stay out of ours." I let the lingering threat sit between us a beat and then usher us away. "C'mon, Lucien."

Reaching for his hand, I thread our fingers. I'm not sure if this is okay, if he's even registering the surging current that sparks between us when we touch like this, but he doesn't protest and follows easily. It feels good walking with him like this, like we could walk hand in hand through this world forever, but it's a wrinkle in time that comes and goes much too fast. His captain and other members of the hockey team approach us, and another dose of apprehension shoots straight into my veins.

"Give us a minute," Lucien tells me. "I'll meet you inside."

His hand slides from mine and there's a cool loneliness left in its wake, a premonition of life after Lucien. Before I can protest, he kisses the side of my head, nudging me away.

"I promise I won't be long."

I hate it, but I need to give him some time to smooth things over with his team . . . again.

I nod.

But when he turns to walk away, I let out a deep sigh.

So many promises, Lucien.

Some kind of way I managed to convince Chauncey, who had opted not to be a part of the 'reprimanding Lucien committee,' that I wasn't going to hurt him again and that Lucien definitely would *not* rip his tongue out if he'd make me another one of his special pineapple drinks. I wasn't sure I actually held that kind of power over Lucien to ensure his safety, but he believed me easily enough.

He stubbornly obliges at first but after a few minutes or so he's back to his charming flirty self. It turns out, he *is* good people and though he flirts, it's a harmless extension of his personality. Or harmless to those of us that are immune to his panty-melting smile. Chauncey Bridgers is just too good looking for his own good. Still, while he's distracted with his fancy bartending moves, I take Lucien's lead, apologizing again for being mean to him.

"I'm sorry I insinuated your dick was small."

"*Thanks,*" he trails off, looking over to me with skepticism.

"It's not," I rush out.

His hair flops side to side as he chuckles, unable to help the tiny smirk that forms at the corner of his lips from his ego being stroked.

"I know, but best we don't let Morrow know, yeah? I quite like having the use of all my limbs and bodily functions," he teases—or at least I assume he's teasing. I'm honestly not sure anymore.

There's no way Lucien is as bad as they say. But then again this is the same guy who doesn't believe there's any good left in this world. That nobody is ever really a *good* person.

But I swear I'm not a *bad* person, I don't think anyone is, it's just some people are more resolved with being exactly how they think they *should* be. By all accounts, I should be the rich stuck up mean girl, it's how I grew up—and sometimes I am—as proven outside. But I don't have to be that way. I can choose to be better.

I try *to be better.*

Chauncey and I share another skillfully made drink of his and I find he's surprisingly funny. He's also an excellent source of information as he regales me with stories of Lucien, telling me things I hadn't learned during my months of, erm, research.

My laughter is dying down from a joke he's shared that he swears brought Lucien to his knees when I ask, "Hey, can I ask you something?"

"Shoot, beautiful."

"Are you all actually afraid of Lucien? Like for real?"

He blows out an exaggerated raspberry, his lips flapping comically as he searches his mind for a suitable answer. I expect a simple yes or no but his response is thoughtful, calculated. "Uhh, hmm," He rubs at his jaw, smoothing a well-moisturized hand over a face that has fewer flaws than mine. "We're . . . afraid *for* him." He finally settles. "Morrow's a good dude with some scary demons. I like the guy. We're friends . . . I think." There's a contemplative look on his face though that says he's really not sure, but he quickly shakes the expression away. "We get along. We play well together, but the things I think he's capable of go *beyond* normal."

"Normal?" I ask.

"Yeah 'normal' and Lucien aren't exactly synonymous. Hockey helps. It gives him something to focus on, but sometimes . . ." He trails off briefly, finding his words. "Sometimes it's not enough and he withdraws into this really dark head space that no one but the captain seems to be able to help him shake. He's been withdrawn lately but he was coming out of it. Eventually, he always comes out of it. A few weeks pass and boom, he's back to his usual self. But that didn't happen this time."

"What do you think happened?" I ask, hoping he doesn't realize I'm fishing for more information. That I'm searching for the answer that scares me most.

"Dunno. Cap nor Morrow will talk to us about it. He seemed okay today—before the game that is. He'd seemed . . . better. But something must have happened on the ice tonight. We were all pissed to lose our shot at the Frozen Four, sure—some of us more than others—but most of us know underneath Morrow's a *good* guy . . . who will, yes, rip your tongue out." He pauses, lifting a halting finger in the air. "But he *chooses* not to." His shoulder lifts casually before he leans back against the countertop, grinning proudly. "That's real love right there."

A nervous bellow of laughter gushes out of me. "Yeah, I suppose it is."

And I suppose I might have my answer, that I could be the one to blame for his change of behavior.

Shit. I take a long swig of my drink.

I really do ruin everything.

CHAPTER TWENTY-FIVE

SYDNEY

WARMTH FROM THE ALCOHOL spreads through my chest and my limbs feel limp and relaxed. I don't typically drink. It's not good for training. But I'm not training for a competition right now. No, *I'm* training for Lucien, and the alcohol consumption feels necessary, vital even. It's lowering my inhibitions and preventing the onslaught of regret already formulating in my mind.

The pineapple rum drinks are the only thing keeping those regrets at bay while I wait for Lucien to come back. My body gyrates, moving freely and boundless as I do what I'm rarely given the opportunity *to do*; let loose. I'm not confined to my father's side or forced to have dinner with men old enough to *be* my father. I simply dance my heart out. I dance mostly by myself, but I sneak a couple in with Chauncey before he's distracted by some hot redhead. Turns out, he has a thing for gingers.

Who knew my new friend actually had a type? I just assumed he hit on anything that breathes, but he was the nice distraction I suspected he would be. Too bad I was once again without Lucien. I'm swaying to a sensual alt rock number that's playing, typing out a text to him when a different text comes through.

Bradford 2:11 AM

Are you at a party?

My spine straightens as I dart my eyes around the crowded makeshift dance floor. No one seems to be doing anything out of the ordinary. They're dancing, grinding to the beat of the music that reverberates through the space, but I don't see any sign of Bradford. He's someone who would definitely stick out, even more so than myself. Yes, I'm in an expensive cocktail dress at a college hockey house party, but I'm a girl and sometimes we do that, but Bradford? He's the type to go to a party in a fully tailored three-piece suit. And he doesn't just command attention, he forces it down your goddamn throat.

I text back.

Sydney 2:12 AM

No

Bradford 2:12 AM

Then tell me what you're doing right now.

Shit.

Sydney 2:12 AM

Walked into town to see if I could find some more packing boxes. I ran out.

Bradford 2:13 AM

This late at night?

I note the time. Double shit.

Sydney 2:13 AM

Yeah, all the discarded boxes should be broken down by now. They'll be picked up if I wait til morning.

There. That should keep him off my back for a while.
Except it doesn't.

Bradford 2:13 AM

Share your location. I'll pick you up.

I groan. Screw it.

Sydney 2:14 AM

I can't do that.

Bradford 2:14 AM

What do you mean you can't? Why not?

There's that word again, Princess. I try to shake the memory of Lucien's words away.

Sydney 2:14 AM

Because I don't need to be babysat.

Bradford 2:14 AM

Is that what you think I'm doing?

I'm trying to make sure you're safe.

That you're okay.

Sydney 2:15 AM

I'm not safe and I'm not okay.

Bradford 2:15 AM

So then let me help you.

Sydney 2:15 AM

I don't need your help.

And I don't want to be saved.

Bradford 2:16 AM

Sydney, what are you doing? This isn't you.

That's the point.

I shove my phone back into its hiding place. It's as the buzz I worked so diligently to create fades that I realize I never texted Lucien. I deeply desire another drink, but I decide to leave Chauncey alone since the girl he's with seems to be enjoying his attention and not using him as her personal mixologist. Meanwhile, Bradford continues blowing up my phone. I avoid it at all costs, deciding that looking for Lucien is the better use of time.

I make my way over to the windows and peer outside, but by the looks of it, he's not out there. Shuffling past the DJ speakers, I find my way into the hall where even more people line the walls. The party has grown in these last hours, which makes finding him even harder. I skip a line of girls to check the bathroom and am relieved when I find he's not here either, considering the bold offers he received earlier by girls who thought I wasn't looking.

I'm always looking.

I managed to get pretty acquainted with the house when I went searching for him the first time, but I never went upstairs. There are surprisingly few people hanging out on the steps with mostly everyone confined to the first floor, but they allow me to pass without any interference. The stairs creak as I ascend to the top and I pause to look back. Even from the landing, I don't see him anywhere.

It's darker up here, quieter too.

I peek into a few of the rooms, but each one proves useless. They're either locked or messy rooms with random hockey gear thrown about. Seriously, they need a maid in here. Ivanka, our maid back home, would have a fit if she saw the state of these rooms. Not a single one would receive her stamp of approval . . . with the exception of one.

I push open the final door wider. There's something different about this one—and I don't just mean the cleanliness of it. In *this* one, books are stacked neatly against a desk and the wood floors are clear of clothes, shoes, and hockey gear. A couch sits to the side in a small seating area and a large black iron canopy bed centers the back wall of the room. The bed looks more intimidating than comforting, but it's the energy of the space overall that compels me to walk inside. I step quietly, shutting the door behind me, and snuffing out the lingering sounds of music from downstairs.

It's so quiet, peaceful even.

Tentatively, I approach the massive furniture piece centering the room. There's something out of the ordinary about it, like it's not merely a bed. Walking closer to it, the gunmetal comforter set has a sheen from the soft bedside lamps that light the room. I take another step, touching the perfectly made sheets, my fingers coasting over the material. In a move that proves exactly how far I've fallen, I lower my face to the pillows, drawing in the familiar scent. It smells just like . . . *him*.

This is Lucien's room.

Knowing that I'm in his private sanctuary only kicks up the obsession meter a notch higher because I want to invade his space like he's invaded my heart.

Walking over to his closet, I swing it open, my grin growing ever wider. *Jackpot.* Like the true creeper it turns out I am, I bring some of his shirts to my nose and inhale as deeply as my lungs will allow. His scent envelopes me and my thighs squeeze closed as the familiar ache for his touch grows. He's made me wait all night and this is his *room*. His *real* one. I always thought it was weird that the other one was so barren. But this is his true inner sanctum. These are his *clothes*. I touched his *bed*.

I giggle when I spot his hamper in the corner, a discarded shirt sticking out the top. Grabbing it, I run to the mirror on the back of his bedroom door. I hold up his jersey, pressing it to my chest before I twirl around in a circle, like it's a ball gown, because on me it practically is. The heels are a nice touch too, and I smile, confident Lucien would like me in his jersey with nothing on underneath.

Maybe this was his plan? Why he wanted me at this party to begin with? After all, he did conveniently leave out that the party was in fact his own and being held at *his* house. Surely this had to be where he'd hoped we'd end up. It's where *I* hoped we'd end up.

My phone buzzes again and I snatch the phone from my cleavage, reviewing the multitude of missed calls and ignored messages I've received from Bradford . . . and a voicemail from my dad.

Fuck.

Voicemail from Dad

"Sydney, call me now."

Short and to the point. Perfect. I call him back and by some miracle, he doesn't answer.

Another text notification.

Bradford 2:30 AM

> Seriously, Sydney, I'm getting worried about you. You need to tell me where you are right now!

Sydney 2:30 AM

> I don't owe you an explanation, Brad. Stop texting me!

Bradford 2:31 AM

> Since when do you call me Brad?

> Why are you acting like this?

Sydney 2:32 AM

> Because you're not taking the hint. Leave me alone.

Bradford 2:32 AM

> You're leaving me no choice.

I scoff.

"Yeah, dude, whatever," I mutter. I'm about to be fucked within an inch of my life.

I don't text back, instead setting my phone on the nearby dresser where I find the rest of my things sprawled out. It's like Lucien said, we're already in trouble and I'm about to get in a hell of a lot more, so I'd rather beg *this* daddy for forgiveness because I've been a bad, *bad* girl.

I could surprise Lucien, lie across the bed and present myself as a gift, wrapped for him to have in whatever way he wants. I should have brought the blue bow he tied me up with earlier.

Then he'd see, @BladeSpinner and I are one in the same. That the girl from his texts was the real me.

I toss the jersey back into the basket then move to find a good position on the bed.

My pulse quickens when I hear Lucien's voice right outside the door. I scramble to move faster, but there's a second voice, one I can't immediately place.

Oh crap, he's not alone. Quick thinking has me running back to the closet and shutting myself inside just as they walk through the door—but, shit, my phone.

There's rustling and heavy footfalls as they walk deeper into the space, but I don't hear them talking anymore. I worry I can't hear them because my heart is beating too damn loud, or worse, my panting breaths are drowning out what they're saying. Leaning forward, I try to peek between the slats of the door to see if I can see anything.

"So, why'd you really follow me up here? Were you hoping for round two?" asks Lucien, leaning casually against his bed post. The second person, his team captain, seems unfazed by Lucien's tone, changing the subject of conversation entirely . . . toward me.

"Where's your new *toy*?" he asks, trying to appear casual, but he's not pulling it off as easily as Lucien seems to.

There's something about the way he says it that has me wanting to rip myself in half. One half can hear the condescension in his voice, it hears the insinuation that I'm just another fleeting pastime for Lucien, no one important and nothing special. The other half doesn't hear animosity. Or the negative connotation behind his captain's words. It hears jealousy.

"She's . . . *around*," Lucien says. "Why do you ask?" He smirks, unperturbed by his friend's odd behavior.

Uneasiness stirs in my gut, and I'm tempted to fling the door open and announce myself. I've been watching Lucien for months now, and in all that time I never once felt this kind of awareness around my actions–until now.

I've played Lucien's games. Endured his tests. But *this* feels like a trap.

It's dawning on me with frightening clarity that I *really* shouldn't be here, intruding on their private conversation or lack thereof because the green-eyed captain hasn't said a word. His jaw just keeps ticking, causing his deep dimples to ripple and shift. His eyes close and he hangs his head in a sign of defeat, fingers gripping his hips harsh enough to bruise his smooth brown skin.

"You're in a pretty good mood for someone who hates losing even more than me. I thought you'd be more . . . upset or something," he emphasizes, tossing his hand in Lucien's direction, though his words come off more like an accusation.

"So, what's the problem? Isn't that what you wanted? For me to *feel* better, Trev?" Lucien asks, his own hint of condescension present now.

His captain nods slowly as though he has to think about it first. "Yeah, it is." His teeth grit. "It's all I ever wanted," he says, his voice husky and deep as he rubs a large hand over his trimmed beard, like he wants to say something else.

But man, that voice. I bet he brings women to their knees with a voice like that. I could listen to him talk all day.

"Then tell me what you want," Lucien says. "What could the captain need from me now?"

"Don't do that," his captain croaks.

"Don't do what, Trev?"

His captain's chest expands and deflates, pulling his Henley taut.

"Tease me like that."

Lucien waits a breath before his facade cracks, his eyes smoldering.

"I'm not. That's your department, remember?"

Trevor steps forward, chest heaving and eyes on fire. For a moment I think he's going to punch Lucien again, but then Lucien takes a step forward, his defenses down, hands casually tucked away in his pockets. The only things that suggest his demeanor has changed at all is the sudden lack of a smirk and his serious tone.

"Lucien."

"Lock the door," Lucien commands.

@therealLucifer
Online

Were you in the arena last nig

Seen

Who the hell is this?

Seen

CHAPTER TWENTY-SIX

SYDNEY

I *SHOULD LEAVE.*

My pussy clamps on nothing but air at Lucien's authoritative tone, even when all he's doing is talking to his friend. Or arguing? I'm not sure anymore since neither man is yelling, but they appear equally angry and friendly if that's even possible.

Judging by the way he turns to leave, I expect the captain not to listen, that he's going to storm away and never look back, but as he reaches the door his large palm presses it close with a soft *snick*, turning the lock as told. With the click of the lock, he releases all of his tension, all of his worry, all of his concern. I watch it melt off him like warm butter as he turns to face Lucien again.

Whatever animosity they share lingers, and though it feels dangerous there's something else there too.

"Come here," Lucien orders, crooking a finger and pointing to the ground in front of him.

That uneasiness I felt festers, spreading from the point of impact to the fringes of my resolve.

I should leave.

My conscience implores me again and again that I should leave but my feet remain glued to the closet floor.

"First, tell me you're okay now. That you're good," says the captain, his back to the exit like its home base and the only safe space for miles around.

"I'm fine. Now come here," Lucien demands again.

"A-are you sure?" The tall hockey captain shuffles from foot to foot and I've never seen such a big guy look as nervous as he does right now.

Lucien isn't small by any means, but this guy has at least a few inches on him and twenty more pounds of muscle. With toasted brown skin, sweat slicked and glistening, he appraises Lucien a moment longer, looking every bit a Herculean god.

Lucien pierces him with a glare that strikes fear even in me. "Now," he repeats, finality in his voice.

This time the captain doesn't delay. Doesn't pause. Doesn't stop. He barrels straight for Lucien, until he's right on top of him, *kissing* him like a man starved, like he's been waiting all day for this very thing . . . and Lucien kisses him right back. With desperation and relief. Gripping the back of his neck and holding on tight like he's finally back where *he* truly belongs—with him.

I stutter a strained gasp.

There's no amount of resolve left inside me to prevent the onslaught of tears. They roll fast and heavy down my cheeks. I didn't see this coming. Lucien's always alone. Every time I followed him, he was *alone*. I didn't think . . . I didn't consider . . . I choke on a sob, clapping a hand over my mouth. I try to stuff it down, but I can't. It hurts too much, the pain is unbearable.

I knew this night would end in heartbreak—I just didn't think it'd end so soon. I didn't think it'd end like *this*. I mean, I know we aren't *together*-together. We're not boyfriend and girlfriend. We didn't swear allegiances. Hell, I'm not even sure we're friends to be honest, but we were *something*, weren't we? If even for a little bit, I was his, wasn't I? He said I was *his*. Shouldn't that have meant he was mine?

He took me on a date. We talked about things. Things I don't share with anyone else. He gave me all of that shit about Bradford, questioning his role in my life. Bradford might be an idiot and overbearing at times, but he wouldn't do this.

I bite my thumbnail, relishing the taste of copper as it glides over my tongue. I pace the small space as much as it'll allow. It wasn't all in my head. He said he was crazy about me. And I believed him, because I was crazy about him too.

I let him cut me open in more ways than one. I let him hold a knife to my skin and claim me as *his*. That shouldn't be something you can fake.

I let him . . . touch me, and . . . oh God, I told him I was a virgin. I offered him *everything*.

What if this whole time he's just been laughing at me? What if I've been some desperate horn dog so obsessed with his dick that I followed him around like a lovesick ferret vying for scraps of his attention? He's been calling me a stalker all night and like an idiot I took it as some term of endearment. I played a dangerous game of life and death all for the sake of his attention. God, I'm so stupid.

With my face in my hands, I cry a little more. I thought he was different. That he wouldn't use me like everyone else does. I thought I was going to be used in the way *I* wanted, that I was finally going to reap the reward I *rightfully* deserve, but I've stretched this out far longer than this was ever supposed to go, trying to fight a destiny that was never going to change. Maybe this was as far as I was ever going to get.

Maybe Bradford was right and I'm being ridiculous, going through some last-ditch rebellious phase. Some spoiled rich tantrum I threw because 'mean ol' dad' wouldn't let her have her way anymore. And now I have to get home and face facts. I'm going to belong to whoever my father says I belong to. I'm going to have my virginity taken by whoever *he* deems worthy. So, I need to pack and leave this place, for good.

Hand on the door handle, I brace myself to push it open. I'll walk right past them if I have to, but then I hear a long, slurred sucking sound.

"Oh, yes, that's it. Take me deep," Lucien moans.

My hand leaves the door, pressing to my lips as I watch his captain on his knees, with Lucien's dick in his mouth.

"That's it, Trev, just how I like it."

Lucien's head lolls back and he groans as his captain bobs his head up and down his shaft expertly, like he's done this before. Many times, if I had to guess.

My suspicions are confirmed when Lucien says, "Fuck, you've always been a natural."

His captain's hand grips Lucien's cock, firmly twisting up and down the length as he sucks it from base to tip. His beautiful dimples on display as he hollows his cheeks and sucks him deeper.

"Oh, *fuck*, you're so good at that," Lucien praises his efforts.

Rather than sadness, jealousy overtakes my system. He's sucking the dick *I* was supposed to suck, earning praises *I* was supposed to be earning. And why does he have to look so fucking beautiful doing it? Would I look so beautiful with Lucien's cock shoved down my throat, saliva leaking down my chin? Tears lining my eyes and mascara smeared down my face? Would Lucien look at me like he's looking at him? He said he would. He said I'd be perfect, so why is it *him* down there and not me?

"Deeper. That's right, choke on it. It's what you deserve after your little show downstairs." Lucien's hips rut into his captain's stretched mouth. "That hurt, by the way. It's only fair I hurt you back, right, Trev? It's our favorite game to play after all. You hurt me, I hurt you, and you fucking love it."

Lucien shoves in further, his captain moaning deep and growling in response to Lucien's punishing thrusts. It's the hottest thing I've ever heard. The sounds of their sordid pleasure chill the white-hot anger brewing inside and my breath quickens.

With shaky fingers, my hands dip between my legs, wetness seeping through the fabric of my thin panties in response to their sexual act. In response to his captain's eager moans and tousled curls as he nods to Lucien's songs of praise.

My fingers slip beneath the slim band.

Doesn't Lucien know how much it'd turn me on to make him feel like that? To have his balls drawn tight and his cum filling my throat?

I slide a finger over my slit, running along my opening. Back and forth.

Arousal coats the digit as I spread it over my throbbing clit, imagining it's me down there and not his fucking teammate.

But, fuck, he knows exactly what he's doing, bringing Lucien to orgasm with practiced ease.

I want to hate Lucien for what he's done, but the more I try, the wetter I become. I'm soaked.

Shit, even when I'm upset at him, he elicits this reaction.

I grind against my palm, bracing myself against the door frame.

The closet is drenched in Lucien's scent, every textile a reminder of what we'll never have. This is as close as I'll ever get to coming with him.

Trevor gags around Lucien's cock with no resistance, as I plunge a finger inside, slowly stretching myself before pulling back out.

My breasts press against the door, the slats rubbing against my sensitive nipples as I chase my orgasm.

I whimper, almost to the end.

But then Lucien pulls out of his captain's throat with an abrupt yank, moaning a curse before he's... laughing. "Oh, I *knew* tonight would be fun. Get out here, Princess, right the fuck now."

I stop strumming the sensitive bundle, flashing open my eyes, a little unsure of when they closed in the first place. I snatch my hands from between my legs and cover my mouth, afraid I'll make a noise and be found.

His captain's green eyes frantically search the room before he and Lucien both settle on the closet. Lucien's golden eyes smirk at me while the other glares.

"I know you're in there," Lucien singsongs. *Shit*, how did I ever manage to seek him out before? He's so goddamn perceptive.

Putting on a brave face, I swing the door open, doing my best to appear composed.

Fists clenched, I address Lucien first, compelled to explain the misunderstanding before he accuses me of stalking again.

"Look, it's not what you think." *Famous last words, Sydney.*

"Said no one ever," Lucien chides.

"It's the *truth*. I-I came up here looking for you . . . but then I figured I'd wait up here and surprise you. When I realized you weren't alone, I hid. I didn't expect . . . I didn't *mean* to interrupt your . . . moment." I spew the last word, throwing a hand in his captain's direction, still poised on his knees after sucking off *my* . . . whatever he is to me—*was* to me. Any attempts at keeping the attitude out of my voice all but fail. I'm furious, and he knows it.

Lucien chuckles, leaning back against his bed without a care in the world. "You didn't interrupt anything. I knew you were here," he says.

Trevor turns his glare on Lucien, standing to his full height that does little to intimidate Lucien, but instantly sets *me* on edge. He wipes his chin with a single thumb, smearing the wetness on his jeans.

"*Relax*," Lucien croons, tucking his cock haphazardly back into his pants. "She's not going to say anything, are you, Little Stalker Princess?"

He turns to pin me with a singular look that says, *I dare you to betray my trust*. I huff an astonished breath. It's comical really, considering he betrayed mine. *Why* shouldn't *I return the favor?* It's what a Sinclair would do and it's what he deserves, but the truth is I would never. I *could* never.

"I'm not a stalker," I grumble.

Lucien leans forward, cupping his hand up to his ear, pretending he's hard of hearing. "What was that, Little Stalker? You're literally still in the closet." He chuckles heartedly, his whole body emitting a frequency that stokes my insides. "You're so fucking crazy, I love it," he muses, leaning back against the bed, his arm spread over the neatly tucked comforter.

My temperature ramps up, and my arms fold in on itself as I remain closeted, afraid to leave this spot because otherwise . . . I'll fall victim to his words again. He'll suck me in and I won't escape his draw.

"It was an accident. I *panicked*. I don't even see how you knew I was in here," I sneer, hoping my bad attitude will keep him at bay.

But, fuck, it only fuels his steps as he stands and makes his way over to me.

He doesn't just eat the space between us, he absorbs it in three easy strides with pupils ablaze, a hazardous lust-filled gaze causing me to stagger. Trevor stands his ground, watching as Lucien reaches for me.

Holding my face in his hands, his left thumb strokes my cheeks with such tenderness I rear back in anger. How dare he be soft with me now? I slap his hands away but he's faster, stronger. His hand thrusts out again, wrapping around the back of my neck, practically dragging me out of my safe space—like he's been doing all night. He squeezes my cheeks in a familiar roughness I've grown accustomed to as he pulls me toward him.

"I *always* know when you're near," he growls, bringing his face so close to mine we share one breath. "I know the scent of you, the *feel* of you." I grab one of his wrists, my nails clawing into his flesh, drawing blood this time.

He doesn't let up, and I'm not actually pulling him off, just reflecting the pain I feel inside. "Plus," the pad of his thumb from his free hand swipes beneath my eyes, coming away with some of my tears. He licks them off and hums, "I heard those *sweet* cries of yours. I almost came all down Trev's throat as you stood there and cried for me." I pull my face away again, glaring at his precious Trevor who ruined what *was* turning out to be the best day ever as promised. But he stares back at me, in a way that suggests I'm the one who ruined *his* night.

"Why is *he* here, anyway?" I snap; my eyes trained on his *friend* and *captain.*

Lucien steps away, strolling over to lean against one of the iron bed posts at the foot of the bed again.

"Down, Princess, it's alright. We like Trevor. Trevor is a friend," he placates.

"He *hit* you," I remind him, gritting the words.

He just grins. "Yeah, I know. He's one of the select few I don't put it past to *give* as much as he *takes.*" His eyes twinkle. "But Trevor here is not our enemy, I promise." He holds up two fingers like a Boy Scout while Trevor smirks.

I roll my eyes.

"Know anybody else who could hit me and remain standing after the fact?" Lucien queries.

I mutter some choice profanities under my breath in response but neglect to give him a real answer.

He makes a decent point I guess. His other victims of the night haven't been as *lucky* as the captain but I'm past caring.

He wants to bloody his knuckles some more, fine.

He wants to get hit in the face and fuck his hockey captain, I'll let him.

It's not my problem—it never was.

He's not mine.

I look away, unable to stand the sight of either of them. I'm too angry that Trevor was with Lucien, *my* Lucien, in a way I haven't been allowed to have him yet. He's already gorgeous himself, he could have any girl . . . or guy here if he wants. Why did he have to take what was *mine*?

Of course, Lucien uses this awkward as hell moment to make introductions.

"Trevor James, meet my Little Stalker Princess I was telling you about. She's a little angry right now, but I promise she's a *really* good girl, aren't you?"

My mouth falls open and I look at Trevor in horror, unbelieving that Lucien just shared that with him, but Trevor surprisingly laughs, breaking out into a smile I wasn't expecting.

Blinding white teeth gleam at me as he flashes those sexy goddamn dimples that make me want to swim in the divots of his face.

"Nice to meet you," he chuckles, walking over to offer his hand for me to shake.

I shift back and forth, a little taken aback by his genuine expression. Like he's *actually* pleased to have met my acquaintance.

"Umm . . . You can just call me Sydney," I say, shaking his hand, albeit begrudgingly. "I'm *not* a stalker, by the way. This is just all one big misunderstanding."

I wave my hand in front of me in hopes of erasing the embarrassment I feel. I may not be Trevor's biggest fan right now, but that doesn't mean I want him to think ill of me.

"It's alright, I'm sure it's an exaggeration on his part. Lucien's the worst at nicknames," Trevor admits.

That voice of his runs smooth over the sound waves of my beating heart, thick and rich like. . . *caramel*, or chocolate. I smile at the immediate comfort it offers, a soothing balm over my aching heart.

"Am not!" Lucien retorts, disparaging Trevor's claims.

Trevor arches a brow at him. "You nicknamed your therapist, Dr. Thottie."

My brows scrunch as I turn toward Lucien. *His therapist?*

"No, that's what I call my psychiatrist. I call my *therapist* Mr. Penguin."

I turn back to Trevor, and he shoots me a droll expression.

"You see what I mean?"

The captain gestures to Lucien and now *my* brows are taking flight because *what the fuck?*

I stand there stunned as they both gloss over the fact that Lucien has a psychiatrist and a therapist. I wonder if everyone's right about him. Maybe he really is crazy.

"Fine, Toy?" offers Lucien, snapping me back to the moment.

"What? No," I answer, shaking my head. I don't mind being his toy, but I don't want that to be my sole identifier to him.

"Stalker Princess?"

I shake my head again.

"Little Stalker Princess Toy Doll."

"Ew, no," I grimace.

"Just pick one," Trevor groans, and I like him just a little more for being the voice of reason in Lucien's fucked-up head.

"I like it when you call me Princess," I lament. "Just . . . call me that."

He's leaving you for another man, stupid; he's not calling you anything but an Uber.

Lucien's head swivels between us before he relents.

"Fine." But the victory is short-lived. He sits back down on the bench in front of his bed, arms spread along the edge like he was on my couch earlier tonight, cock bulging in his jeans. His grin is sinful as he parts his legs, widening them farther.

"Get on your knees, *Princess,* and finish what Trevor started."

@therealLucifer
Online

Were you in the arena last nig

Seen

Who the hell is this?

Seen

CHAPTER TWENTY-SEVEN

SYDNEY

"I—UH . . ." I dart to look at Trevor, but he doesn't appear half as shocked by Lucien's request as I am. "But . . ."

"My game isn't over yet, so if you don't want to play anymore, you'd better tell me right now because I'm nowhere near done with you." His stare hardens. "Not by a fucking long shot."

I should say no, respectfully decline or something? Surely, I shouldn't let bygones be bygones and ride his dick anyway after all this should I?

But you want to. You really really want to ride his dick.

And isn't that like the height of feminist goals everywhere? It's my sacred duty to take back my power and suck his dick.

"Is he just going to watch?" I eye Trevor warily, a little unnerved by the smoldering look on his face. His honey roasted skin, caramel voice, and smooth demeanor make my mouth water. The man's a walking snack.

"No. He's going to help." Lucien tilts his head at the captain and throws him a cocky smirk.

Trevor pulls his shirt off, revealing a body that could only be cooked up by my imagination or a science lab. He takes a step closer to me . . . and then another . . . *and* another, until he's standing right over me. My chest heaves as he gets closer and the heat that started in my cheeks runs rampant across every surface, a phenomenon that Lucien doesn't miss.

Lucien bites his lip at my reaction and groans deeply in that way that at least suggests he's enjoying it, but I feel terrible, guilty even, like *I'm* betraying *him* or something equally as shameful even as he makes more demands for us to keep going. Is it betrayal, if this is what he wants? Is it what *I* want?

"Can I?" Trevor asks as he stands before me, but I don't know what he's asking, I'm too busy staring at his hard chest.

"Say yes, Princess," Lucien murmurs.

"Yes, to what?" I pant, shifting my gaze between the two guys who look set to take turns wrecking me.

"To *more*," Lucien supplies.

I tilt my head up to look Trevor in the eyes. They're kind, probably the nicest I've ever encountered. They're filled with vulnerability and understanding, traits I don't typically find back home.

I take it as a sign.

Slowly I nod, granting him permission.

"You're beautiful," he says, reaching out to skate his fingers over my shoulder, featherlight at first as I suck in a shaky breath. He traces around my collarbone to the other side, leaving goosebumps in its wake.

I try to clear my throat to speak, but it does little to prevent the scratched tone of my response.

"Thank you."

His fingers grip a little tighter as he trails behind me, pressing his bare chest to my back, his dick hard and already nudging against me.

I know I said I wanted to lose my virginity tonight, but never in a million years did I consider I could get two for the price of one.

Talk about a deal.

"You don't have to be scared." Trevor rubs my shoulders, urging me to loosen up. "Just relax. I'm going to help you."

"How?" I rasp, leaning into him for some kind of support, emotional or otherwise. Lucien stares at us while a million *other* questions flit through my mind.

"This is a trick, right? He's testing me again, isn't he?" I murmur behind me so that only Trevor can hear. "This is all some sort of fucked up trust exercise, isn't it? You can tell me. I'm right, aren't I?"

Trevor chuckles softly against my ear.

"No, pretty sure he's past testing you at this point," he supplies with the audacity to sound amused.

"Oh, really? And what makes you think that?"

"Because you're here with me."

I struggle to determine his meaning, but it's unimportant wording when he practically sings against my skin. "Now relax and listen to my voice. I'm going to tell you *exactly* what to do," he whispers, his breath ghosting my heated flesh, his lips just barely grazing the sensitive parts of my exposed throat and shoulder. "And if you're *really* good, Sydney, you *will* be rewarded. I promise."

I whimper in response, loving the sound of being rewarded and appreciating the commitment to pleasure. Trevor's hands rake over the sequin material of my dress, shifting new patterns into the ensemble before resting on my hips and turning me to face Lucien.

"Okay then." I nod; my eyes trained on Lucien. "Tell me what to do."

"Get on your knees." Trevor repeats Lucien's words, though *without* the authoritative command I've come to love from Lucien.

"What? Right here?" I ask. I'm at least a few feet away from where Lucien sits on the bench, too far away to reach.

To touch.

To please.

He nods. "Crawl to him."

I hear the command, but I don't obey on instinct the way I do for Lucien. *Is this really okay? Should I be doing this?* I barely know Trevor. I barely know either of them . . . and that's what makes this all so thrilling.

But then again, my time for thrills has passed and it's already so late . . .

"I'm waiting," Lucien presses, pointing his finger at my face then slowly dragging it down my body until it points to the floor. His gesture, as clear as his earlier command: *knees.*

Growing up, I've bowed to know one, haven't had to. In all my life, I've never even bothered to humble myself before anyone, let alone debase myself for them. Seduce, yes. Meaninglessly flirt, sure. But never more than that.

But now, he's asking—no, *telling*—me to get down on my knees in service to him; *in front* of Trevor.

It's his captain's presence that drives me to hesitate, but it also spurs me on. My knees shake, not fearful, but instinctive. They *want* to bend; to drop and feel the wood press into bone but I can *feel* Trevor's eyes. I can *smell* his scent.

He smells delicious, like fresh nectarines and cinnamon. Everything about him screams *he's* a good person. An angel amongst devils like us. A sweet soul tied to bitter creatures.

"You can do it," Trevor murmurs, one hand stroking my arm softly as he assures me it *is* okay. His other hand rests at the hem of my dress, his finger drawing slow circles along my thighs. "Try not to think so hard about it and just let go. We *both* need this." Is he talking about him and Lucien needing this or is he saying he and I need this? I'm inclined to believe it's the latter, but more likely that's the delusion talking.

I'm a toy tonight. Entertainment. A game. Maybe that's enough. This doesn't end well for me no matter what part I play, so I might as well play the one that gets me orgasms.

Heeding his words, I allow myself to bend, my body and my rules, because he made Lucien feel good, and if I follow his lead, I'll make Lucien feel good too. Better than good, better than even Trevor.

My bare knees dig into the wooden floor, palms flat to the ground, as one after the other, I crawl toward Lucien. My hips sway with the motion, hiking my dress up my thighs the more I move, sliding against my heated skin and exposing me to the cool air. I can sense Trevor's eyes behind me as vividly as I can Lucien's in front of me.

Double the attention.

Triple the intensity.

I'm fucking drowning in it. I make sure to hold my head high while I crawl, peering up at Lucien beneath long lashes that break up the sheer force of his gaze, his potent eyes already on me and predatory. When I reach the space between his legs, I stop, sitting up and resting on my calves. But he's not nearly as relaxed as he was with Trevor. He's a smoldering ball of intensity. Even more so when he slowly draws something from behind his back. It's the silver glint that catches my eyes first as he twirls that damn knife around his finger. His focus is on me and the fire in his gaze burns.

It's one thing if he's intent on hurting *me*, but I don't think I could stand it if he hurt himself. His lips curl into a grin as if he can tell what I'm thinking.

"Am I making you nervous?" he teases.

"Yes," I answer on a breath.

"Why?"

His gaze dips to my thighs and I swear the knife spins faster.

I lick my lips; my fingers twisted in my lap as I become aware of the perilousness around me.

"You're not being careful."

He hums, savoring my growing fear.

"Are you scared?" he croons. His head cocks to the side and his hair flops in his eyes like it so frequently does when he grants me that curious look. I itch to run my fingers through it. To pull on it again. But I don't dare move from my spot. I keep my focus on the blade spinning round and around and around.

"I'm terrified," I whisper.

A groan stirs from within his chest, bubbling inside as his breath blows out, as if he's expelling smoke. The air from it billows over my skin, rustling the wisps of hair along my forehead. It's a contented sigh. A gesture that tells me he *wants* me to know how much my fear turns him on.

"Oh, Princess, that's so fucking good. I want this night to haunt you for eternity. I want it to be celebrated as the night you willingly gave yourself over to the devil." His deep chuckle is soft and breathy but promises so much pain. "I can't wait to destroy you with my cock. Your screams of pain and pleasure will be so beautiful. It's going to be *epic*."

The knife stops spinning and he tightens his grip around the hilt, perching his elbows further on his knees as he leans in.

A shiver runs down my spine, but I remain seated at his feet.

He brings the dagger up to my face, tucking it under my chin and pressing close until I'm forced to sit up again.

"Spread your legs for me."

My body reacts before my mind can even process the command, obeying his call and giving in to selfish desires.

"Oh, Princess, I know you're more flexible than that." He taps my thigh with the tip of his boot before settling his own legs apart. "More. Spread those fucking legs for me so I can see if your pretty cunt is weeping for me already."

I obey, sliding my knees farther apart until each knee hits his boots. They're so spread I swear I can feel my arousal dripping through the fabric of my underwear. Lucien reaches one hand down between us and snatches the fancy La Perla thong I'd worn especially for this momentous occasion right off my body with such force I squeal at the sudden burn and snap of silk and lace across my ass.

"You won't be needing those," he muses, the blade still tucked beneath my chin.

"Hold on to these for me will you, Trevor?"

He tosses my ripped lingerie to the captain.

"It'd be my pleasure," Trevor smirks, but Lucien glares in warning.

"They're only yours to *hold*, not have, understand?"

Trevor's cocky smirk drops.

"Yes, *sir.*"

I expect his words to sound sarcastic, but they don't, they carry meaning and sincerity.

"Hey, Trev, I need you to confirm something for me," he says, though his focus is entirely on me. "Is she as wet for me as she claims? Princess here has a penchant for lying."

"I'm not lying," I moan as Lucien twists his blade so that it lines horizontally with my throat, more threatening than sexy now.

Trevor clears his throat loudly, looking to Lucien, but Lucien doesn't flinch, the gleam in his eyes shining bright.

"You should probably check, just to be sure," Lucien muses, his eyes daring me to pull away. I don't move a muscle.

I feel Trevor move as he kneels to the floor behind me, pressing in close again, his body wrapped around mine. I feel much more vulnerable this time with my panties ripped and discarded in his pocket, my knees spread apart while I drip onto the floor.

Thick, calloused fingers reach around me, tickling up my thighs and enveloping me in heat. It's hot, too hot. I'm an inferno when the light brushing of his finger swipes along my slit. He doesn't press deep. He teases, kneading it along his fingertips but not yet pushing inside. My thighs quiver, anticipating the intrusion, but it doesn't come.

"So fucking wet," Trevor moans, his exhales skating along my heated flesh.

"Let me see," says Lucien.

Like me, Trevor does as he's told. Lucien takes one look at Trevor's glistening fingers then opens his mouth. The captain offers his finger to Lucien and my insides constrict when he wraps his lips around them, giving them a long, languid suck.

"Mm, so sweet. You taste good, Princess. You know that?"

I shake my head gently against the knife. I've never tasted myself before.

"Oh, well then, you should get a taste too," Lucien says.

Trevor repeats his previous action, then sticks his finger inside my mouth. I lick it clean.

"Oh, fuck," Trevor groans.

I continue sucking even as Lucien trails his blade down my neck, to the crevice of my breasts, right to the edge of my dress.

"Now, should I cut this off or should I let Trevor do the honors?" Lucien muses.

Trevor pops his finger from my mouth.

"Please don't cut it," I whimper. I like this dress. It's one of my more expensive ones I actually brought here, and I've never gotten to wear it. I was hoping to keep it as a memento or trophy for when Lucien finally takes me. A fond memory I can look back on. I don't want it cut from my body, though not-so-secretly, I would love for him to drag that knife across my flesh and carve his name into my heart. "Please Lucien," I beg, though the glint in his eyes tells me he knows what I'm actually begging for.

I want him to take that which I don't know how to give. I hear the insane staccato rhythm that his heart beats again and my own joins in tandem. An equally insane organ because even with the knife poised at my chest, it beats harder for him. It bangs against the cage of my ribs like a wild beast, wanting nothing more than Lucien's hold around it. It's his to command, to have and own as long as he wants it.

"Let me take it off for you," Trevor whispers in my ear, dragging me back to the here and now.

Lucien pulls the blade away, setting it beside him, undoubtedly for later use.

I can't help but crane my head toward Trevor's touch. With his face against mine, I can feel his dimples against my cheeks as well as the tickle of facial hair. I smile at the sensation, and he returns it. His smile so deep and genuine. My eyes flick back to Lucien, expecting to see some sort of jealousy or anger in his gaze but it's not there.

"Are you sure this is okay?" I ask Lucien, my hands fisted into my dress as I anchor myself to this plane of existence. "You were ready to bite Chauncey's head off just for talking to me, but Trevor . . ."

Lucien's lips curl into a devious smirk.

"Chauncey didn't know his place. Trevor *knows* his place, don't you, pup?" Lucien's head tilts in that surveyor-of-souls way it does as he admires the scene before him, his eyes trained on his captain with pure respect, adoration, and ownership.

"Yes sir, I know my place," says Trevor.

I can hear the longing in Trevor's voice, the need that's already there. He's had it before, and he's desperate for it again. *I'm* desperate for it. If only for tonight, I want Lucien to look at me like that. Just once.

"I don't want you to be mad at me," I whimper, my body melting against Trevor's as he continues to tease the sensitive area between my legs, not quite touching me where I need.

"Aww, Princess, I could never be mad at you. You're my new favorite thing. I don't mind sharing my toys as long as the ones playing take good care of you. One scratch on your pretty little head and it'll be *Trevor* I'm mad at, not you." His eyes dart past me to Trevor, and whatever look they exchange causes him to smile even wider against me.

"It's not me you have to worry about scratching you." Trevor whispers so low in my ear that I don't even think Lucien heeds his words.

"I want . . . Trevor to take off my dress," I admit, voice a little shaken. I kind of like Trevor. Not how I like Lucien, but I feel oddly safe with him here, like nothing bad can happen as long as he's present. And besides, if Lucien trusts him, then I trust him. He's clearly getting something out of this too and I want Lucien to have fun. If Trevor helps with that, so be it.

"See? I told you she was a good girl. Now, are you going to be a good boy for me?" asks Lucien.

"Yes," Trevor moans, still running soft circles against my spread thighs. Wetness pools on the floor beneath me as I drip and I can smell my own heat. We're all mostly clothed still and already it smells of sex and sin between us.

"Good. Take off her dress . . ." Trevor lifts his hands to obey, but Lucien stops him. "*Not* with your hands. Use your *teeth*," he commands.

Trevor doesn't even think about it, he moves on instinct, lowering his head against my back, his hair soft and fur-like as it swipes teasingly down the ridge of my spine. I preen like a feral cat ready to come from just the soft brush of his hair. His teeth graze sharply against my flesh as he bites and licks the tab of the zipper, securing it between his teeth while simultaneously brushing a finger between my folds. My moans are resounding as I watch Lucien.

"So many delicious sounds," Lucien groans, fists clenched, and knuckles tucked between his teeth as he holds it to his lips. I like knowing it's a struggle for him to hold back like he is, but I can't wait to prove to him that he doesn't have to. I'm not the delicate flower or a shiny gold trophy. I'm his.

Trevor drags the zipper farther down, the fabric peeling from my body as he goes. It's agonizingly slow and I'm short of breath, only now truly processing what's about to happen. The dress zips from end to end, but Trevor's a tall guy and anything short of lying flat on his belly will limit his access to the end of the dress, so I lean forward, gripping Lucien's knees for support and poking my ass out for Trevor. The benefit isn't his alone. My face closer to Lucien, he leans forward in response, overtaking me with an all-consuming kiss.

"God, do you have any idea how hot you look right now?" he murmurs against my lips.

The corners of my mouth curve wickedly against his.

"Most people call me Sydney, but God works too," I tease between our kisses, recalling his words from earlier tonight.

"Oh, no, no, no, Princess. You don't want to be God." His tongue teases the seam of my lips. "I'm a sinner," he says. "A transgressor kicked out of Heaven for all my wicked deeds and evil ways. They call me Morningstar for a reason. So, if you're God, then I will have to be your reckoning. However . . ." He pulls from my lips and strokes my cheeks with the blunt tips of his fingers, more scratching than soothing. "If you're my Princess, then I can be something so. Much. Better. I can be your *redemption*." His eyes practically glow in the darkened space between us, the bedside lamps doing the brunt of the work setting the mood. Still, I hate how those mythical eyes can already tell I'm someone in *need* of redemption.

I gasp as my dress falls from my body, then gets kicked away by Lucien who latches onto my neck, sucking and biting. A groan vibrates against the cheeks of my ass where Trevor lingers and I mimic the sound, tightening my hold against Lucien as I push deeper into the vibrations.

"You're fucking dripping," Trevor comments, breaking the spell Lucien always seems to cast upon me. "Mm, can't say I blame you though. Lucien tends to have that effect." He flicks his tongue against my soaking cunt, and I practically buckle. But it's too fleeting. I need *more*. I whimper, and he makes it up to me, swiping again, but slower this time.

"Yes, like that. It feels so good," I say, my eyes closing as I relish the sensations of them both.

Like me, Trevor seems to enjoy the praise, the acknowledgement of a job well done. His efforts intensify, his large hands cupping my ass and spreading me further apart. I'm easily brought to the cusp with the additional stimulation of a second person, Lucien relentless in his own pursuits as he marks me yet again. God, this feels good. Why don't people do this more often? I mean, why have one when you can have *two*?

I almost lose it entirely when Trevor licks a trail up to my puckered hole, the surprise causing me to yelp and moan simultaneously.

"*Not* . . . yet," Lucien growls, releasing the skin on my neck with a pop. "She doesn't get to come until she successfully completes her challenge. Only then can she be rewarded, *understand*, pup?"

Trevor's tongue pulls away quickly and I can feel him settle away from me, his warmth retreating with him.

"Yes sir."

I crane my head over my shoulder to peek at Trevor and sure enough he does look like a scolded puppy, his big green eyes regretful for disobeying his master. He's supposed to be the captain, the one in charge, the leader among them, but in this locked room we're both just slaves to the madness of Lucien. Lucien will lead us to victory, to euphoric paradise, but only if we submit to him.

@BladeSpinner
Online

What do you want

In life?

Seen

WTF! No

Haven't decided yet.

CHAPTER TWENTY-EIGHT

LUCIEN

PERFECT TITS HANG FREELY between my legs like fresh apples ready to be plucked from the most forbidden tree. But it's like I told her. They call me Morningstar for a reason, so I will have this girl no matter how sinful the act. I'll have her screaming my name and roaring obscenities all night long. Tonight will be a night of transformation, where my little stalker transcends—and accepts—her destiny with me. Where she'll break the mold from the perfect picture of innocence into a dirty little slut just for me.

I even get a two-fer since, apparently, Trevor is in the mood to play today. It's been forever since he's let me play with him, but judging by the look of withdrawal on his face right now, he needs this too much to stop.

He needed this win tonight and I blew it. Fucking me when he's angry is a common enough occurrence, but even more so when's he's angry with himself and can't handle the stress load.

He's right though, I knew how badly he wanted to win this game, and I did kind of fuck him over on that one, so I'm more than happy to make it up to him now. More than anyone else, he's stuck up for me. Stuck by me. And he's the only one who I've actually talked in detail with about my family. All but the last detail of course but, the point is, I trust him enough to share in this little experiment.

He wouldn't be here otherwise.

Actually, this works out better because he'll help me determine if keeping her is even possible. To see if she'll live up to the fantasy I've built up in my head, or crumble like all the rest. For so long Trevor was the only one left standing, the one I thought would be there with me to the end, but he's made his choice time and time again, and it's never me. *Friends* is the extent of our relationship, but this is good too. Rare, but fucking good all the same. I guess now it's Sydney's turn. Will she play so nicely with me or will she cut and run too? Something tells me she'll exceed all my expectations and more.

"Open your mouth." I can barely contain the shaking in my voice, anticipation building up to near toxic levels when she obeys without question, her mouth opening wide to receive whatever I'm willing to give. My cock strains in my pants at the sight, but I refuse to free it again. With her tongue extended, pink and wet, chest panting like a trained pet awaiting its treat—not even my pup has ever managed to look so sweet and devious at the same fucking time.

She's a liar and a stalker, I know, but she's also a doe-eyed princess that could topple countries without ever knowing they were waging wars in her name.

"That's it, baby. Nice and wide for me," I murmur, sticking two fingers in. The second her lips wrap around my digits I almost lose what's left of my mind. Fuck the plans. Fuck control and breathing exercises. Give me chaos, carnage, and ecstasy. Give me her decadent mouth and timid tongue to use and fuck and . . . Sydney makes a sound in her throat that brings me back to reality. I pull my fingers back before pushing in again. Making sure I let her suck and reacclimate before shoving farther inside, slower this time. I test her gag reflex, being nice enough to give her practice so that I don't gag her on my length the first time she ever sucks cock.

I got carried away before—and it's likely to happen again—but just this once, I can go slow and steady *for her*.

Dead though they may be, my parents *did* raise me to have manners.

I can be sweet too.

Sometimes.

Sydney moans and that sweetness turns tart.

CRACKED ICE

"Who knew the best way to fix that smart mouth of yours was to make you open it more?" I tease when she starts taking initiative, sucking me all the way down her throat until I'm tickling her tonsils.

This time, rather than gagging, she glowers at me. And, fuck, I had no idea eyes so cold could burn so hot.

"Ah-ah-ah," I chide. "Don't look at me like that. Wouldn't want you getting lockjaw when I shove my cock past those full lips and so far down your tight throat, you're swallowing me whole."

She inhales sharply through her nose. A serrated gasp that makes me wish I *did* have my cock inside her.

"Don't sound so surprised," I coo. "I'm finally getting you all to myself . . . well, not *all* to myself, but double the trouble, double the fun, am I right?"

I look over her head and wink at Trevor, who bites his lower lip, looking as enraptured as I am with how her throat bobs to swallow. Though he patiently awaits his turn.

Such a good pup.

I grin down at Sydney and her forehead crinkles in that way I fucking love.

"Oh, don't make that face. You can't be mad at me, Princess. It'd break my heart."

She loses her focus and gags, before yanking her head away to speak. "Are you sure you have one?"

I grin, gripping the base of her skull and pulling her head back by her hair. She hisses, but her eyes remain trained on me like the good girl she actually is—sharp tongue aside—while her soft palms hold onto my thighs like they're her lifeline.

"Sure, I do. It grew three whole sizes, the moment I met you."

The corner of her mouth twitches before she's biting her lip. But her mouth reopens on a scream when I pull her hair again and shove my fingers back in.

"Now suck."

Her lips close over my fingers again and I let out a long groaning breath that feels more stolen than vital.

401

Who knew my snarky Little Stalker Princess, who teases and schemes, would be so good at following directions? She's pure sugar and sin staring up at me like that, her hair mussed, and her lip gloss smudged. I've never seen someone so perfect willing to break for me, shatter for me. I'm fucking addicted.

My eyes cast to Trevor, who's barely keeping it together himself. One hand resting on the peak of Sydney's ass while the other rubs absentmindedly over the bulge in his jeans that I've yet to permit him to free. He won't do it of his own accord because then he'd have to take responsibility for his own actions and there's no way he's doing that.

I tip my chin toward him, signaling that it's okay to touch himself. Similar to Sydney, he needs the instruction to keep going, to get *out* of his head and *in* this moment. His chest deflates with relief as he unbuttons his pants, keeping them on as he slips a hand inside.

I lean forward, whispering to Sydney. "Is *this* how you thought your night would go? Did you imagine you'd be kneeling before me while I train your throat to take my cock?"

Her soft whimpers spur me on further as she shakes her head, her hair falling loose as she lies through my fingers.

"You naughty girl, I bet you did," I taunt. "I bet you hoped and prayed and wished upon a star I'd fuck this throat."

She growls in protest, her teeth scraping against my fingertips. An adorable threat.

I tsk. "Let's not do that. There's punishment for biting, and you know who those are for, don't you?" She reluctantly nods. "Good. That's my girl. You see? I know how bad you want to be good for me."

I can feel her moan, and it's another tear in my fragile resolve. Not only that, it's the *way* she looks at me. She looks at *me* like I look at *her*. That same little twitch in our eyes that makes us a little different from everyone else. It's not psychosis, it's acceptance. A shared consciousness that allows us to accept the current truths, to accept what *is*.

What is abnormal.

What is broken.

What is *fucked*.

And as fucked up as it is, I'm so goddamn grateful I found her, because I don't think I have it in me to ever let her go.

I want to keep her forever . . .

and ever . . .

and ever.

My middle and ring finger strokes a line over her tongue, deeper and deeper down her throat, the heel of my palm anchored on her chin and my free hand holding the back of her head. She groans, letting her warm saliva gather and spill down the sides of her glossy pink lips as I thrust. I want that pink shimmery shit coating my cock by the end of the night.

"Stick your tongue out more and relax your throat, that way you won't gag so much," Trevor murmurs in her ear, coaxing her with his saccharine voice and tender touches. She should relish those touches, because I won't be near as gentle with her when the frays of my control finally slip. I'll be the one giving her what she really needs.

"I don't know, I kinda like the sound of her gagging on my fingers," I muse, driving in and out, compelling her to make those noises again.

"I have to teach her the *right* way, or she won't just gag when you let her suck your cock, she'll choke," Trevor insists, brushing the loose tendrils of Sydney's hair away from her face, then landing a chaste kiss to her temple.

Choke, not die.

I roll my eyes, and he glowers over her shoulder at me.

"Patience, Lucien," he soothes, stroking a hand down Sydney's chest. "You'll break her if you're not careful, and then all of our fun would be ruined, you don't want that to happen, do you?"

It's a bit of a trick question. On the one hand . . .

Sydney's eyes bug out and she tries to talk around my fingers. I laugh.

Trevor's only teasing, but he and I both know he's not entirely off base. It's why I'm glad he's here, I'd lack all restraint if he wasn't.

A shiver ratchets up Sydney's back and she moans around my fingers when he cups her tits, pinching her nipples between his fingers. She's loving every bit of this, and I can tell that at least *part* of her is glad Trevor stayed. She squirms at the reaction he's soliciting, her ass wriggling against him as he kneels behind her.

The beautiful panic in her dilated pupils, where fear and sadness fight to the death in her irises, is a sight to behold.

"It feels good having your body worshipped while I take your mouth, doesn't it, Princess?"

The way her tongue teases and strokes at just my fingers makes me hard as fucking granite. I'm ready to shove her to the base in one go but first . . .

"Trevor, stick your fingers in her cunt. I want another taste."

He does what I demand, relinquishing the control he doesn't want, while Sydney groans around my fingers again, even more so when I add a third. "There you go, baby. We have to account for width too."

Sydney whines and her eyes roll as Trevor and I stuff her from both ends.

Trevor pulls his fingers out first and my mouth draws open. Trevor—overachiever that he is—made sure to coat three of his fingers in her creamy juices. He stands up and drags them teasingly over my lips, painting me in her cream, before wrapping his free hand around my neck. Squeezing the sides, he slides his fingers down my throat, straight to the back, until I gag around them. That little cock tease. He knows this isn't about *me* feeling good, it's supposed to be about her. I want to suck his fucking dick right now. I eye his partially open jeans and swelling cock. Removing my fingers from Sydney's throat, I grip his wrist.

"All in due time," I taunt, licking my lips clean of Sydney's taste.

Focusing back on the star of this show. "Do you think you're ready for the real thing?" I ask Sydney.

"Yes . . . but . . ." she trails off, looking first to me, then Trevor. She swallows, and again the urge to slide in her throat with guns blazing, hitting the back until my cock piercings slides over her fucking uvula, is almost too great. "I want . . ." She clears her throat and sits up a little straighter. "I want to see . . . *you* do it."

"Do *what*, Princess?" I tease.

I know exactly what she wants, but I need to hear her say it. To admit she likes this part of me too.

"I want to watch you suck him, first," she says. "Please."

I scratch my chin as though considering it. Sucking that man's cock is a fucking gift I don't turn down often.

"You want to learn from the master firsthand? I'm flattered," I chortle, "I guess I *could* show you how it's done."

Her eyes peer up at Trevor as if seeking his permission. He grants it eagerly, smirking down at her.

"Have I mentioned I *really* like your new toy, Lucien? You should hang on to this one." Trevor drawls, the obvious lust contagious enough to get him high off it as he puts voice to desire.

"Okay, then. Watch and learn," I announce, reaching an arm behind me to pull off my shirt. I drop to my knees in front of Trevor, giving Sydney a front-row view.

She watches me as I fold down his jeans, his cock pressing against the unforgiving fabric. Gripping the edges of his pants, I slide them down his muscular thighs, leaving his underwear for last. When I get past his knees, I drop the bundle of denim to his ankles, allowing him to step out of them completely. I unconsciously bite my lower lip as I look up at him, taking him in. He's so goddamn pretty. I'll never understand why Trevor would ever limit himself to just girls. A gift like him should be shared with the entire fucking world. Though, ironically, it was the rest of the world that kept him from me in the first place. It was because the world was cruel that he couldn't bring himself to love me, the way I loved him.

"Don't . . . tease me . . ." he begs, panting like we just finished a two-hour practice drill.

Fuck, I love it when he does that.

I smirk devilishly up at him.

"Why shouldn't I?" I taunt, reaching for the knife beside me on the bench.

"It's not fair," he pants.

"Fair?" I swing the blade, cutting his briefs free. The swipe is quick and Sydney's mouth parts in surprise. She's even more horrified when she realizes I cut him a little with the motion.

Trevor hisses a breath, buckling forward as he grips my shoulders.

Dropping the knife, I brace my hands against his ass. "Mm, but teasing you is my favorite activity, you know that."

I run my tongue over the cut, soothing the hurt and staunching the blood.

Sydney looks stunned.

My lips stretch into a wide smile; one I'm sure Trevor feels against his split skin.

Now she's starting to get it.

She'd better—quite literally—have tough skin, dealing with a demon like me. I'm fucked up in all the ways she's imagined and more. Worse, probably. She never should have followed me because now, I don't think she'll ever find her way back. We're lost to each other.

My forehead brushes along Trevor's thick shaft as I nip and lick along his inner thigh. His legs shake and quiver while I make my way to where he really wants me. His dripping cock twitches, tapping me in the chin when it springs up to greet me, but I stall my movements. Picking up the knife again, I lightly scratch the blade along the deep V chiseled into his torso. Not enough to cut or bleed, just a trace as I admire the lines of muscle and flesh.

I'm tempted to cut him again. To hear him moan and lose himself to me like he has so many times before.

"You're . . . setting . . . a bad . . . example," Trevor moans, barely able to get out the words as I lick at the first cut again, making my way up to the underside of his length. "S-she might think she can get away with teasing you like this," he stammers as he does exactly as I intended and loses himself to my touch.

I chuckle darkly, wrapping his hard dick in my fist. "How else is she supposed to learn what the consequences are when she does something bad?" I lament.

Something between a laugh and a moan sounds from him when I stroke him firmly from the hilt to his fat, wet head, causing a long line of precum to string from his dick and plop right on my thigh.

"You're e-evil," he groans.

"That's right, keep talking dirty to me."

I suck him into my mouth, languishing his cock like it's my favorite brand of ice cream and look over to Sydney, who instinctively licks her own lips.

Running my hands over his balls, I give them a nice squeeze.

"Fuck, yes, harder."

Sydney inches closer, craning for a better view, but I don't stop. If she wants to learn anything from me it can be this: if she wants something, she needs to reach out and take it.

Trevor notices her apprehension.

"Come here, Sydney. Stand up."

She bounces up with a hop, relief showing on her face now that she's been given instruction.

He holds her to his side, his arm wrapped around her waist as he lets her look down at me sucking him off.

"He's so fucking good looking when he does that, isn't he?" he asks, his cheek pressed to hers while his jade eyes bore into me.

She nods, staring into my eyes too with my mouth full of cock. Even after everything that's happened tonight, she still looks at me like I'm her whole world, like out of a million worlds I'm the place she'd reside—I could get used to it.

Her obsession feels a lot like love. Or what I remember of it feels a lot like her.

"Feel how soft his hair is." He guides her hand to pet me, her small hands strumming through my locks. She's undeterred and my eyes practically roll out of their sockets at her touch.

She pulls slightly and I groan around his length.

"Ahh—fuck," Trevor groans in response and her hand snatches back so fast you'd think my hair caught fire and she was burned.

"No, it's okay Sydney, he liked it. It f-feels good . . . when he moans around me like that." He groans again. "He'll like it when you do it too."

His voice is huskier when he's on the verge like this.

Trevor grunts between thrusts, his hips undulating of their own accord. He's barely holding on as I glide my tongue up the vein of his cock. "He'll like it even better when the tears start running down your pretty cheeks. He l-likes tears—*fuck*, stop doing that," he whimpers as I graze my teeth over the sensitive part of his crown. Rolling my tongue over his slit, I savor his taste before driving him deeper to the back of my throat, forcing his moans once more.

A tentative hand swipes away the salted water that's gathered at my lash line. Trevor's not thrusting nearly hard enough to make me cry, too afraid of 'hurting me,' but it's enough for Sydney to collect at the tip of her thumb. It's when she takes it a step further and sticks it into her mouth that I practically lose it and groan again because she really was made for me.

"*Shit*, Lucien. If you do that again, I'm going to come," Trevor warns.

So, naturally, I do it again, sucking him as far back as my throat will allow and growling. He fucks my mouth in earnest with renewed vigor, and I prepare myself to receive every drop he's about to give me. What I'm not prepared for is Sydney reaching up and kissing him as he moans his whines of bliss into her waiting mouth. Gripping her head—and mine—he makes out with her whilst fucking my mouth, driving me to the brink. It's so fucking hot I have to use my free hand to re-release my own dick from my pants or I'm going to bust inside them.

The kiss between them deepens and with one final roaring thrust, he's coming down my throat and I'm swallowing it all. I'm savoring the last of his orgasm when Sydney bends to kiss me too, tasting of his lips and his cum.

It's everything.

I stand once more, towering over Sydney, who looks especially small standing between us now. Fragile even. Breakable.

I shove my pants and underwear down in one thrust, my cock fisted and pained. "Now show me what you learned, Princess."

CHAPTER TWENTY-NINE

SYDNEY

I THINK IT'S ANGRY with me.

Lucien's cock is red at the tip, swollen and dripping. The veins running along his shaft pulse, filling his thickening dick even as I continue to stare at it. It weeps in distress, precum beading and sticking to the metal. His cock jewelry shines in the dimly lit room, a wet sheen that reminds me of polished silver. It only serves to unnerve me.

I don't remember it looking so hostile in the shower, but my fucking God does it look like it could kill me now if it were sentient.

"Aww, don't worry. He won't bite. That's my job," Lucien taunts, waggling his dick in my face, that despite my best efforts, does little to tamp down my excitement.

Now it looks like it's yelling at me, a bead of cum flicking onto my chin with its angry movements. Without thought, my tongue extends below to lick it away. That seems to make it happy or considerably less enraged because now it looks acquiescent, submissive even, as it begs me to come forward. I shuffle closer, shifting my knees.

Even though the jewelry on his cock intimidates me, I push past my fears and take him into my mouth as far back as I can in one go. Lucien hisses in a breath, stiffening even more in my throat. The salty taste of his precum leaking onto my tongue fires off my taste buds one by *delicious* one. Lucien tastes slightly different than the cum I tasted on his lips. Trevor has a sweetness to his cum, whereas Lucien has a smokiness that's more savory. I want to drink him, until I'm filled.

Unfortunately, I'm overeager and gag, despite my best efforts not to.

Trevor squats beside me, his spent dick still half-mast as he lightly strokes a finger up my throat.

"Relax," he coos.

I listen, relaxing my throat like he showed me. I stick my tongue out flatter under the ridges of Lucien's dick, the cock jewelry rubbing strangely against my tongue. It feels weird yet satisfying at the same time. I've never sucked a pierced cock before. I've never sucked *any* dick before, but it's not as scary as I thought it would be. I thought sucking his pierced cock would feel like a serrated blade being shoved down my throat, but it's actually quite pleasurable. For him as well apparently because he looks down at me with such pride and admiration.

Finally. *Keep looking at me like that.*

I flick his jewelry with my tongue, nudging at it with the tip as I suck him harder. His head snaps down and his lips part. Those golden eyes graze over me like I'm the most beautiful thing he's ever seen. I'm still wetting his floors with the way my pussy weeps for him.

"You like this, don't you?" Lucien grunts.

I nod.

But he yanks me off by my hair with a resounding pop and I already know what he's looking for.

"Yes," I pant, "I love it. Give me more."

He leans his back up against the imposing bedpost, opening his legs wider, as he braces himself.

"I am *not* a gentle man, Sydney," he answers, his words filled with barely contained restraint. Lucien chuckles, a wicked smirk on his lips as those golden orbs meet mine. "I'm not just going to give you something because you look up at me with those innocent doe eyes. If you want it, then you need to take it."

Trevor whispers ghost my ear, sending an electrical current straight to my pussy. "Spit on it."

It's so filthy, so unbecoming of a Sinclair, but I want to be Lucien's dirty girl. He can play any game he wants with me so long as I get to be in the game with him.

I've never spat a day in my life. It's crude and unladylike, but I do my best to oblige, gathering spit and dripping it onto his waiting tip.

The small *pthht* sound makes me cringe, but it's doing the job as I massage it over his engorged head.

"Oh, Princess, you can do better than that," Lucien chides.

I deflate.

Not good enough. Suck his cock like you mean it, girl. Like you'll never get to again . . . because you won't.

I try again, and this time it mixes with his pre-cum, leaking down his shaft and over his balls.

"*Come on,* Princess, you've been salivating all night for this cock. Don't be shy now. Get me soaked." Before I can wrap my head around his next move, he's thrusting deep down my throat, holding me steady as drool collects in the back of my mouth, choking me. I gag again, but his hand on the back of my neck keeps me still, forcing me to take as much of him as physically possible.

It's a reflex when my nails dig into his thighs. There's so much pressure my eyes water, trailing tears down my cheeks. He grows impossibly harder.

Fuck, he's big.

My throat constricts around him, the jewelry resting against my esophageal walls, but I don't push him away. I don't pull off. I accommodate him. I make room where there is none, holding him there even as I struggle to fit him, to please him.

My pussy clenches, needing to be filled in the same way, and aching for a reprieve. Lucien's *not* gentle, but I'm loving every bit of it. He isn't giving me a choice. There are no bets. No deals. No responsibility for my actions.

The heady concoction of arousal and saliva, mixes with his scent and Trevor's light cologne behind me.

I breathe it in from my nose, but then Lucien's pinching it, cutting off my airway. More spit pools, drenching my tits as it rolls down my neck. I fight for air, my lungs burning, chest spasming. More tears stream down my face as I stare up into his beautiful demon-like eyes. The gold barely

KD CURETON

lines the edges of his irises now as the blackness of his soul bleeds out, staring back at me like I'm the answer, like I'm the light that could snuff it all out if I wished it. It's overwhelming pleasure and pain. I'm ready to come or pass out, unknowing and uncaring of which is going to happen first, but then he lets go.

Air rushes back into my lungs when he pulls out, a string of spit still connecting my lips to his cock. Blinking away the excess tears, I catch Trevor's hand wrapped around Lucien's wrist. A shared look passes between them before Trevor's pulling his hand away and Lucien is smirking down at me, his head tilting as he appraises his work.

"I told you I didn't mind messy," he says, his lips twisting into a prideful grin.

Yeah, so long as it's head. Lucien's spotless bedroom suggests he only tolerates the chaos in his mind, not his personal space.

Another moan slips between pants of precious air when I feel his soft breaths brush over the dampened skin of my chin. "Now make me come, Princess."

The spit adds the extra lubrication needed to slide him easily through my fists. "More," Lucien grinds out, already on the edge.

Trevor places his hand over mine, increasing the pressure as we jerk him together.

"Fuck, yes," Lucien whispers, staring at us both.

Trevor's thumbs slide over Lucien's piercings, rubbing them in tender circles. Lucien's eyes nearly cross.

Whispering into my ear, Trevor asks, "See how much he likes it?"

I suck him back into my mouth, groaning a garbled response when Trevor's hand moves to slide up my torso. He begins to play with my nipples again, pinching and twirling them with his fingers. It throws me into overdrive, driving me insane as I try to distract from my own impending orgasm. I want to come just from having Lucien in my mouth.

Unable to stave it off, I reach back to stroke my clit while Trevor trails kisses down my spine. But I'm thwarted.

"No touching yourself," Lucien growls.

412

I whimper in protest.

But then Trevor is licking up my thighs, over my folds until he's . . .

I moan around Lucien's cock, screaming as my body lights up. His cock twitches in my mouth and I grin, realizing he *does* love it, exactly as Trevor said he would.

Trevor's tongue swirls, reaching a place that has me nearly going blind.

"Oh shit, yes," I garble.

Trevor's licking my ass. *Holy shit.* The surprise sensation of his tongue against my back hole makes my jaws tighten and I suck Lucien deeper. I feel like I'm working for straight tens across the board and am close to my big finish. The pressure builds, heat radiating across my naked form. I struggle to keep with Lucien's satisfied expression, but then Trevor's sucking my clit and my eyes cross, blurring entirely when he flicks his tongue in just the right way. My whole body draws tight, tensing as an orgasm threatens to tear me apart.

"You can lick her but, *don't* let her come yet," Lucien grits, somehow warding off his own release and granting Trevor permission as he eats my pussy in earnest, like a man starved.

I whimper, barely able to suck in air as Lucien attacks my throat and Trevor wreaks havoc on my pussy, going so far as to shove his tongue inside, making my toes curl in my heels that neither of them have deigned to remove.

My thighs shake and it's a race of who's going to come first, but the game is rigged.

"I mean it," Lucien growls. "Not . . . fucking . . . yet." Trevor releases my clit with an upset groan. I can practically feel him pouting, showcasing those puppy-like green eyes. A sight I'm sure only spurs Lucien on. He gets off on the misery and helplessness of his victims. Sexual or otherwise.

I groan around him again, whimpering my cries even as he pounds into my throat.

"You're so fucking desperate for it, aren't you?" Lucien asks.

I draw back with a long slurping pull.

"No, I don't *do* desperate," I lick my lips. "but I am *extremely* motivated to get you to fill my throat with your cum. Give it to me, Lucien."

My eyes plead for more and I know he sees what I'm truly desperate for. I drop my mouth open for him to fill again, saliva dripping from my tongue. It's an offering. A demand he can't ignore.

His breath hitches, coming out stronger when he glares down at me like a queen at his feet. My lips curve knowing I'm having an effect on him. *Me.* I want more evidence of his pleasure. I need to know beyond the shadow of a doubt that I'm leaving a lasting impression behind, so he'll never forget me either.

"Fucking hell, Princess," he shoves me back onto his cock. "I'm going to give you *everything*."

The way he grits the word forces its true meaning even farther down my throat than his cock. His grip in my hair tightens, my scalp on fire and my eyes watering, but I'm giddy with anticipation.

If I succeed at this, he'll let me come. I twirl my tongue and relax my throat so much he's hitting my tonsils. Tears are rolling down my face again. My nose is running too while drool creeps down my neck, but I keep going, moaning and groaning until he's pulling out suddenly with an ecstatic pop.

No!

"Open," he growls. It's the only warning I get before he's shooting cum all over my face, my tongue, my eyelashes, my hair. He's . . . everywhere. And I couldn't be fucking happier.

"Jesus fucking Christ, Princess!" he roars, his hips still thrusting forward as he empties himself on my face. "That was . . . *fuck!*"

I beam so hard I'm practically floating until he says, "But, oh darn, you've made such a mess. Look at the state of you."

Lucien tsks mockingly, his chest heaving from his exertion, but his stamina is nowhere near hindered.

He swipes his hair back, his forearms bulging and glistening with perspiration.

I look down at myself, noticing the cum that paints my upper chest, his dick that's still dripping and the small puddle on the wood floor that sits right where my own arousal has leaked. We've *both* made a mess.

His shoulder lifts, and his eyes sparkle, a mischievous gleam in them.

"Ah, well, guess you'll just have to be cleaned." He trails a finger through the cum on my cheek, swiping it off and placing it on his tongue before wrapping his lips around it and sucking.

I shudder at the sight of him, then again when I feel Trevor repeat the motion with a spot on my breast where he's wiped it on my nipple.

"Fuck, I almost came again after watching you two," says Trevor.

"At least you got to come," I rasp, my throat raw.

Just when I think it might be over, I feel a tongue against my neck. And then another. They're licking, like savage dogs fighting over a bone. Trevor licks up my face and neck. Lucien at my chest and tits. There's even some on my ear that Lucien licks off, sucking my lobe between his teeth. Their hands grab and knead at my breasts, my hips, my ass.

"Yes, yes, yes," I moan.

"Fuck, you taste so good."

I'm not sure who that was for or which one of them said it, but I relish in it all the same. The attention, the buzzing, the sensations that are *everywhere*.

They both lick at my neck some more until Lucien is shoving our faces together, forcing us all to converge in the most beautifully chaotic kiss I've ever shared.

Finally pulling away, Lucien looks me over. "Oh no, seems we missed a spot." He points to the floor, toward the puddle of my own making. "It's your turn. Clean it up, Princess."

I look at the floor where our arousal sits and flash back toward him with wide eyes. I'll do it. I should be disgusted at how quickly I move to do exactly as he instructs, but something makes me pause.

"You . . . want me to . . . *lick* it up?"

He squats down so we're eye level, then smiles. I'm sucked into him, rendered speechless and docile, before he's placing his large hand on the back of my head, slowly applying pressure until my face hovers over the puddle.

"I want it sparkling when you're done."

CHAPTER THIRTY

LUCIEN

"**S**UCH PRETTY TEARS," I murmur, looking down at Sydney who looks every bit drunk, ashamed and horny all at the same time. It's fucking beautiful.

She's a far cry from the perfect doll she was some hours ago.

"Let me come, p-please. Lucien . . ." she rasps, on her knees looking up at me like she wants to thank me and kill me after licking my floors clean.

"You're aching to be filled with my pierced cock, aren't you Princess?"

"Yes," she admits. "I want you. I *need* you. Fuck me, please."

"Okay, I guess you've earned your reward."

Her eyes light up with relief that hits her so hard she looks like she's about to start crying again. She practically runs for the bed when I nod toward it. That's my little stalker, always running right toward danger.

She shuffles onto the bed and before she can even absorb what's happening I already have one cuff wrapped around her ankle.

"What are you—"

Trevor doesn't miss a beat grabbing the other one before we secure her to my bed.

"You'll be fine. I promise. Lucien's rewards are the best," he assures Sydney, but she's still looking at him like she's expecting him to save her. That fucker loves it.

He *would* save her, but no one is leaving this room unfucked. None of us are being saved. We're all fucked up.

"Since you've been such a good boy, I'll let you have a reward. But remember . . ." I whisper low into Trev's ear the rest of my plans so that

Sydney can't hear us. He nods in understanding. Bending down, his pert ass right in front of me, he dives into Sydney's pussy like he's a fish and she's the open sea.

I would fuck them both right here and now but there's still the little issue of Sydney being a virgin. I genuinely think she'd be down to try anything, but I'm not exactly sure we're there yet. She doesn't know what my punishments feel like. I wrap the second cuff around her other ankle and attach her to the bedposts.

I promised her orgasms and have delivered on that promise, but I still want to know where that carnality lies within Sydney. Though not for the first time tonight, I'm grappling with the real possibility I might actually scare her off, and that doesn't settle so well with me as much as it has in the past.

Before, if someone didn't work out, I'd let it go. Move on to greener pastures. But I don't think that's possible this time. I can't let this one go. I can't let *her* go.

"Fuck yes, Captain," Sydney moans, throwing her head back, neck exposed as Trevor devours her dripping pussy that's only gotten wetter with every degrading thing I make her do.

I can't wait to wrap my hands around that throat and squeeze while she chokes my cock with her tight pussy. But watching her back bow and her legs spread for him on command, is also a beautiful sight.

And Trevor's loving it. Usually, he's so in his head over everything we do, it's hard for him to fully enjoy these moments, even if we both know how badly he craves it.

I snicker a laugh. His blush is so red, even *his* ass is turning pink.

"You *like* that she's calling you captain, don't you, pup?" I coo in his ear. His spine ripples against the tips of my fingers as I drag them towards his backside.

He nods, lapping and sucking on her clit.

"You wish that you could fuck her while she calls you Captain?"

"No," he moans, but I can feel him tense beneath my touch.

"You're lying, *Captain*." I dig my nails into the cheeks of his ass, no longer harmless or careful, and he whimpers like the *pup* he is. "You know

I don't like liars, pup. It's . . . rude." He bucks when my finger penetrates his ass without warning.

"Fuck," he groans into her.

"Tell me the truth. Her pussy is perfect, isn't it? It's worth going against me. Worth the punishment you'll receive if you defy me. Admit it," I rasp against his ear.

Sydney's thighs shake as he increases his pressure, swallowing every drop she gives him.

"Yes," he moans again, continuing to eat her with unabashed fervor.

He's such a good boy. I know how badly he wants to fuck her right now, yet I trust him implicitly to not even finger fuck her too hard.

Her innocence . . . is mine.

She shrills in pleasure as he attacks her pussy, her legs spreading wider every time she squirms. Her body's taut and every muscle flexes as she strains against her need for contact and overwhelming sensory overload on her clit. I can't help but to partake myself.

Leaning down next to Trevor, I lick along her pussy, my tongue grazing his, until we're basically kissing, swapping between pleasing her and making out. His kiss is soft and tentative at first, but like every time before, he relaxes when I let him take more. He's starving much in the same way Sydney is, except he denies himself his fill of sustenance. Sydney's different; she's a picky eater, sure, but when she finds something she wants, the girl is insatiable.

Sydney's thighs grip us both as she begins to grind into our faces,

"Oh my God." Her groans are guttural in their need for us both. I can feel the vibration of her screams against my lips. Trevor adds a finger to her cunt as he strokes and sucks.

"Yes, shit, I'm going to come," she screams, as I sink my teeth into the flesh of her thigh.

Her screams grow louder.

"Yes, baby, scream for me."

I bite again and again; her thighs already bruised from my earlier assault. All the while, Trevor fingers and sucks her pussy.

Tears leak down her face even as she looks at me so adoringly, my heart skips a beat. I've been looked at with want, with need, with anger, disgust, hatred, and yes adoration, but there's a genuine love and acceptance behind Sydney's eyes that breaks through and hits me dead center.

I climb up her shaking body to cradle her face while Trevor brings her home for me. We stare at each other, suspended in time for a moment before I close my hand around her throat and hold her there.

"I'm so fucking crazy about you," I whisper against her lips, kissing her with her own arousal still smeared on my lips. She moans against them. Pulling back, I turn her head to the side.

"Now fucking come," I growl against her ear. "I want to see you break."

And like the good fucking girl she is, she obeys.

"Oh my—fuck—shit—*Captain* . . . Yes, right there."

My chest heaves as I watch her come hard and uncomfortably with the bar between her legs, forcing her to remain spread and open. She pulls and grips at her restraints as she comes, but they don't give. Her whole body shakes and convulses and I'm rock fucking hard again watching her squirm and plead.

"Ahh"—she hisses—"it hurts—it hurts *so* good. Lucien," Sydney moans.

I slide my hand down, teasing at her clit some more while I force her to ride it out all the way.

"Ah, no, stop, I'm too sensitive. It's too much."

"I know. The pleasure is blinding, isn't it?" I leisurely continue my ministrations.

When she finally calms down, I straddle her tied-up body, my dick strutting into the air even as pre-cum leaks down my tip. This has all been well and good, but I need more, so much more from my Princess.

Retrieving my knife from the floor, I twirl it round and round, the light making it glint between us. Her eyes go wide, but she doesn't flinch.

Good.

"Tell me, how did that feel?"

"Amazing," she huffs out, almost in disbelief like she didn't expect it to be.

"Yeah, Trevor, gives *amazing* head," I muse, smiling as I line the blade to her jaw and softly graze it downward. I still smile when I see the panic start to grow inside her. I smile even when she pulls at the restraints. Grazing over the soft area of her throat, I smile when she moans and arches her back as I poke at her nipples with the tip of the blade.

"You wanna play another game?"

"I don't want to play a game, Lucien. I *want* you to fuck me," she whines, and I think this is the perfect opportunity to see if she's always so compliant. She's been good so far, but she's a Sinclair, as she loves to point out. I know she's not always good. I know that little part of her that attracts danger is itching to bite back at me. I want her to.

Bite me, baby.

"What will you do if I say no?" I tease; my blade paused right below her sternum.

"Lu–cien." She grounds my name like it's a physical task to restrain herself. "Fuck me right now or so help me God I . . . I'll . . . I'll—"

"Go on, tell me. What will you do, Little Stalker?"

"I'll fuck Trevor instead." Her eyes narrow, completely unfazed by my blade now. That admittedly gets me really fucking hard. I'd love nothing more than to dominate them both and get my fill from their pleasure, their pain, their screams.

She must feel my dick responding to her 'threat' because her eyes flick down.

When she notices it doesn't faze me as much as she was probably hoping she continues, unwilling to accept defeat, "Or better yet . . ." Her head cocks slightly. "How about I bring your friend Chauncey up here and we can have a *real* party. He damn sure wouldn't tell me no. In fact, why stop there? You have a whole team downstairs. All sad and hurt from their loss, surely they'd be interested. I bet I could make them feel better. I'd let every single *one* of them fuck me. I'd come on every one of their cocks and make you watch while I scream their names. I'm positive they'd all love to have their turn and you get *nothing*," she growls.

Her threat is completely empty but that stung a little worse than I thought it would. I share what's *mine*, what *belongs* to me. I don't freely give my possessions to anyone to do with as they fucking please. Trevor is here because I granted him *permission* to be.

"Is that so?" I growl back, digging the tip of the blade into her flesh until blood pebbles at the tip.

She screams in pain but she doubles down. "Yes! I've been trying to get you to fuck me all night and you've been nothing but a tease. *Why* won't you fuck me already?"

I smirk sardonically as she watches Trevor who'd started stroking my cock as she rambled. He rests at my back, relaxing his chin along my shoulder and watching the scene unfold as he takes what he needs and keeps me grounded in the moment.

Like a good captain should, he remains focused on both goals, running multiple plays in his head that ensures we all get what we want up here.

"Look if you don't want to, just say that. If this was all one big ploy to get back at me then fuck it, you win, okay, but *stop* being a tease. It's not fair," Sydney huffs.

Trevor chuckles against my neck, the movement sending signals to my dick that almost have me caving to my own desires.

"You're in for so much trouble," he chortles, his laughter growing louder as Sydney's brows furrow, her naivety appearing all the more appetizing as she grows heated by her own confusion.

"For what? *I'm* the one tied up, getting bit and cut but not penetrated," she pouts.

I'm grinning ear to ear now as I watch the spoiled brat in her come out to play.

Trevor smirks, "I've been taking his lashings for years. It's your turn now, *Princess*."

"But I've been so good," she whines, turning to me. "I played your game Lucien. I played them all. So, if you want me . . . *take* me. I'm yours."

This is her first try at outright seduction and, fuck me, it's so hot I almost lose my resolve but this is what I've been waiting for. All night. All month. Since the day I realized she was watching me—*this* is what I've been waiting for. Now we get to see what she's really capable of handling.

"I'm not the one to be bratty with Sydney." I lean away from Trevor, bending over Sydney's body, "I'll let you in on a little secret . . . I'm going to enjoy this whether you're a good girl or not." I stroke her face with the flat of the blade and my crazy Little Stalker Princess leans into it. "I'll have you begging regardless. I'll spank you regardless. I'll make you scream, and cry, *regardless*. So, you better figure out which you enjoy most, my rewards or my punishments . . . either way . . . I'm going to inflict it with a smile on my face, Princess." I place my middle finger on one corner of her mouth, my thumb on the other side, and spread. "A big 'ol *smile*."

I make sure to show all my teeth when I grin at the considerably less pleasant manufactured smile I've forced onto her face.

Her bare chest rises and falls, her sternum pink with blood slightly smeared over her reddening skin.

This is going to be so much fun.

@BladeSpinner
Online

What do ... want ...

In life?

Seen

WTF. No...

Haven't decided yet.

CHAPTER THIRTY-ONE

LUCIEN

"**G**ET HER UP."

TREVOR wastes no time obeying the order, as eager for his reward as Sydney is for hers. Though, if anyone is being compensated for a job well done, it's me. Not only have I not completely shattered one of them yet or sent them running, but these are two people who don't mind my twisted need to cause pain. Who are *willing* participants in my fucked up game to lessen my own burdens—to make the load a little lighter. Even if it is for their own perverse pleasure and need, they chose me. Trusted *me* to be the one to tear them open, fix what's inside and stitch them back up again.

Though tonight . . . my burdens are particularly heavy.

Their pain may not be enough to satiate the ache.

I might be losing hockey, my one *legal* outlet. All because I'm so fucked in the head, I couldn't bear another word from that fuckface Anderson on the ice tonight.

"Knife!" I bark forcefully enough to jolt Sydney from her disgruntled stupor, the brat in her momentarily forgotten, as the chains rattle against the iron bed railing. She flinches away from me, and I try not to take it too personally. After all, she should be scared.

Trevor flinches too, his response dutifully opposite of Sydney's, ready to end the game altogether before finally relaxing and passing me my favorite blade from my dresser as told. Though I'm sure Sydney hasn't spotted the difference from the one we played with downstairs, *this* one is perfect for carving.

"You good?" Trevor asks, his voice wary of my sudden mood change and his grip still on the knife's edge as he holds the grip out toward me. He looks at me, then Sydney, then the knife, tensing.

"I'm . . . fantastic," I grin, the smile conveying the only truth that exists. I don't know what fate awaits me tomorrow but here, right now, I have my little stalker caught and bound to my bed. "*Fucking* fantastic."

He rolls his eyes and lets the knife go.

I snap my arm out, grabbing him by the back of the neck and bringing him toward me so we're flushed. His dick is hard, throbbing and wet from his leaking tip.

"Do you wanna be strung up there with her?" I threaten. He shakes his head, groaning when I rub our cocks together. "Because if you're going to roll your eyes at me, there's plenty of room for you right next to her."

He smirks, even as he pants through the sensation. "I don't . . . know what you're talking about. Must have been the lighting."

"Right, because there's no way this puppy would ever be so mean to his master now, would he?"

"No," he pants.

"Good." I nod my head toward the special drawer next to my bed. "You know what to do."

He stares a moment longer, but I focus back on the trapped prey at hand, marveling at how those eyes shift so much in color. I swear they were as cerulean as the ocean a second ago when she was blind with lust, but now that there's fear involved, those baby blues look up at me in prayer, like an altar that'll pardon her for the sins we're about to commit.

Such purity, in those deceptive eyes.

They're wet and dilated, dark and wanting.

Don't kill her, I remind myself.

I slide her cuffed hands along the bed railing until I reach the top of the canopy. Her body is the perfect size to accommodate the canopy's height as she hangs suspended, struggling to keep balanced on her tippy toes from the too-tall bed frame. Trevor sits quietly to the side as he grabs what we need, but I feel his eyes on me.

Don't kill her.

Sydney's already wincing with discomfort, sweat beading along her forehead as she squirms.

My cock twitches.

Don't kill her.

This isn't a mantra I typically have to use. I've been able to be as rough with Trevor as I need for years now. And though I've tried seeking the level of release I need with *some* women, I've never gone all-out with a woman before. I've never truly sought the level of release I wanted. Imagine how messy that'd get if I went around inflicting severe pain on every girl I thought I was pretty.

Don't kill her.

I take a step forward, running my nose along Sydney's jaw, then brushing it against hers.

Her soft breath tickles my lips. It tastes of pineapple rum and Coke with a lingering taste of coconut; a specialty of Chauncey's he calls a Piña Colada Float. I can't even bring myself to be upset she went back to hang out with him. I'm kind of glad he watched over her while I tried to work things out with Trevor. I *still* need to work things out with him—but *this*? God, this is something I could do every day and never grow tired.

"Please," she whispers against my lips.

I palm her face to keep us steady, to keep from diving off the cliff of sanity and careening us to our deaths.

"God, please, touch me. Punish me. Do *something*," she pleads. Fucking pleads. How can I deny her?

I swallow, remembering where we are and why we all need this.

I pull back, taking a step away. Her startled eyes go glassy and for a second, I think she's going to cry simply for not getting her way. Or that she's faking it since I now know she can cry on cue. Either way, it's hard to hide the smirk that tugs at my lips.

"Well, since I'm God, are you ready to confess your sins to me?"

"What?" huffs an exasperated Sydney.

"Yeah, what?" says Trev, finishing up his own preparations on the other side of the bed and now visibly anxious.

I better wrap this up.

"Ah ah ah, here I'm judge, jury, and executioner. I'll be asking the questions. And I'll be running the show," I say.

"What's that make Trevor?" Sydney juts her chin in his direction.

I peer over my shoulder where Trevor obediently remains silent as his anxiety melts away. The only time his mind allows for silence is when he's being submissive. He *craves* the silence I chase away.

Facing Sydney again, I answer, "That's easy. He's the bailiff."

"The bailiff?" she scoffs.

"Yep. Now, let's start with something easy." I tilt my head at her. "What did you do to make your teammates hate you so much?"

She guffaws. "You said easy." I arch a brow, but she doesn't back down. Even tied up, this hellion still has some fight in her. "What did you do to yours?"

Though she's being sarcastic, I answer anyway.

"One, my team doesn't hate me. And two, I asked you first."

"But there's nothing *easy* about that question and what does any of it have to do with my punishment?"

I shrug, "You're naked and chained to my bed. What better time to get you to spill your secrets to me than right now?"

"Literally any other time, Lucien!" she gripes.

"But then how will I know you're being truthful?" I lean in closer to her ear. "Even now you're hiding something from me."

I pull away in time to see her eyes grow wide.

"I'm not," she huffs, "We're strangers. If there's something you don't know it's because we haven't had the time to get to know one another, not because I'm hiding some deep dark secret from you."

"Bullshit. You've been watching me for months and after today, you're no stranger to me. Not when I've gotten to know you so . . . intimately. Hell, in a few minutes I'm about to know you biblically." I flick her lips playfully. "So, c'mon tell me what you're hiding. I know it has something to do with those girls. Tell me, who could ever hate such an angel?"

She huffs a laugh. "I'm no angel."

"Well, ain't that the truth. But I heard something rather interesting during our scuffle with the she-devils."

I start to pace the room; noting our discarded clothes in separate piles and beautiful naked bodies in various positions of my pleasing.

"Oh yeah? What'd you *hear* while you were half-choking her to death?" she snaps, a little angrier than I expected her to be, all things considered.

"It doesn't matter anymore anyway," her voice barely above a whisper. "What's done is done. There's no point in looking backward."

"Sounds cold-hearted," I say. "And here I thought you were a *good* girl," I goad, tapping the tip of the knife against her lips. I thought I only wanted her body, but seeing her withhold information from me shows me I want something more. I want all of her to be open to me. Maybe I should stalk her in return and learn her secrets that way. It worked for her, why not me?

"I *am* a good girl." Her protests cause her to nick her lip on the knife, but I don't pull it away as she licks the blood from the cut and continues her pleas. "So, Lucien, please, stop punishing me. I've been good. I'll *be* good, just please put me out of my misery and fuck me already."

Fuck, her pleas sound delicious. I smile as I drag the flat side of the knife down her naked body, truly taking her in from pretty little head to dainty little toes.

She's fucking perfect.

"But I *like* your misery," I pout.

She scowls and, God, her face is especially cute squished between her arms like that. Her restraints are tight, and she has nowhere to go but where I allow.

"Fine. Answer me this," I relent. "Why'd you stop the game?"

My eyes flick up in time to see hers go wide, panicked as she struggles against her restraints.

"I didn't tap out. I said I'll play. I'm playing, Lucien, just like you said. Don't send me away," she whines.

"Calm down, I meant the game *you* started. Cat"—I point between her tits—"mouse"—my thumb juts toward my chest—"Or is it the other way around?"

"I told you . . . you caught me," she pants. "Isn't that enough?"

"Mmm, too easy."

"Says the *actual* cat," she quips. "I think maybe you've gravely overestimated my abilities."

"Well, *I* think . . . you're lying. And we know what happens to liars, don't we, Sydney?"

CHAPTER THIRTY-TWO

LUCIEN

"DO YOU KNOW WHAT drives a stalker? Psychologically? Do you know what makes them . . ." I bird whistle, swirling my finger in a circle around my temple.

Sydney's heated glare is adorable. "I didn't at first. *My* mental issues stemmed from a different tree, so I admit I didn't quite get it, but my psychiatrist explained it to me." I continue, trailing around the front of her. "Wanna know what she said?"

She tries to answer, but I place the blade to her lips to shush her.

"She *said* they're blinded by the idea of an unfulfilled fantasy. And I thought to myself, well what's so bad about that? If our fantasies are one in the *same* . . . then I can fulfill your every one."

She whimpers a pathetic moan against the steel and my balls draw tighter.

"So, Little Stalker Princess, did you fantasize about me? Make yourself come to the thought of me? Because I did. I fantasized about you every day. What I would do to you. How I would *fuck* you. You were all I thought about."

She nods and I move the knife away. "Yes, I fantasized about you."

"Did it look a lot like this?" I skate the knife along her collarbone.

She nods again. "Yes."

"Really? Are you sure?"

The blade nicks her skin when I skim it over her sternum, but I keep going.

She shakes her head, moaning. "This is better. *So* much better."

I rub my cheek with hers, her skin smooth and buttery to the touch. "I want you to remember you said that," I murmur against her.

"What?" She's in a haze, an adrenaline-filled rush spurred on by fear and lust, she'll either be coming or screaming by the time we're done here. Or my personal favorite: both.

"Ready, Princess?"

"For what?"

"To be claimed." I sink down into a squat until her quivering thighs and firm ass are at eye level.

"So beautiful," I muse.

"What are you doing?" Sydney asks, voice trembling as her body sways from the canopy, her bodyweight pulling her shoulders back from the strain.

"Left or right?" I ask, my tone giving nothing away while I present her options.

"Left or right, what?"

I open my mouth to answer, but she interrupts.

"Fuck, these things are tight, can't you loosen them some?"

"No. *Left* or *right*?"

"Lucien, you're being super vague," she whines.

"And you're being super disobedient. You wanna get fucked? Wanna prove you can *take* it? Then stop thinking so much and just answer the question, Princess. Follow me and I'll open up a whole new world for you."

"Is that an *Aladdin* quote?" she huffs, pulling at her restraints uselessly.

"Uh, probably. Hey Trev," I ask over my shoulder, "did I just quote *Aladdin*?"

"I have no idea, but there's a huge butt plug in my ass and I shouldn't be punished just because Princess chose to be bad," he pouts.

"Don't you worry your big biceps about it. My good boy will be rewarded for everything he does."

His dick leaks as he moans, his balls already drawn tight as one of my bigger anal plugs sits in his ass. He's good and primed for me, which leaves one last order of business.

"You promise? Because, fuck, Lucien, I need you, man. Nothing else helps . . . just, *fuck* . . . Can I please touch myself?" He whimpers for release, but I can't have him distracted. He has a job to do. He needs to make sure I show restraint.

"No. Not yet."

Trevor's whines sound more like a groan as he says, "Fuck, Sydney, *please* make a choice. He's not going to give you more information. Just turn off your brain and cease all thoughts. And if you can't, let him do it for you."

Sydney sighs.

Just then her phone rings from somewhere nearby and she blanches, her eyes bugging when she peers over to me. "I need to answer the phone."

I get up and move to face her again. Tapping her lips with the knife I was about to carve her ass with. "You answer that phone, and I'll make you regret it." My gaze shifts from her lips to her eyes again.

She says nothing.

Tilting my head, I give her one last chance. "Just say the word if you don't wanna play anymore. I won't *make* you play with me."

I expect her to hesitate, to break that final straw, but she doesn't. She shakes her head, her hair bun flopping side to side.

"Okay," I nod, moving behind her again to squat into my position.

The phone stops ringing and she relaxes again. Or at least as much as she can while strung up on my bed like she is.

"Left," she breathes.

I grin, grabbing a handful of her left ass cheek, pinching it until it's taut and all the blood is pushed from the surface, turning it white. Then I start carving.

Her screams are beautiful and bright crimson blood streams down her thighs, down my hands as I lay waste to any alternate reality where she thinks I don't own this ass. Where she thinks she'll let anyone take this away from me after all we've been through.

"Fuck, Lucien!" She screams, but there's quite a bit of blood and I have to lick the open flesh to continue my work.

Mmm, she's a gusher.

She hisses at the contact.

I only have letters *L* through *C* written and already I'm falling victim to the lust.

More.

I want *more.*

I spread the remaining blood that leaks over her ass, tempted by her virginal back hole seeking my attention. She gasps between what I now recognize as sobs then moans when my tongue licks between her cheeks, a filthy mess of cum and blood smearing her folds.

"I told you I would catch you. I *told* you the right question wasn't being asked."

She hiccups between gasps, but I keep going.

"How will you get me to stop?" I goad.

"I d-don't want you to s-stop. *Please.* Keep going," she says.

Thank God Trevor's here. I can't help but look over to him, noting that he's barely holding it together himself, but his resolve is stronger than us all. He'll call the whole thing off if he has to, but he holds, letting me have this. Knowing what it means to me.

I want to make this permanent. I want her ass wrinkled with age spots at the ripe old age of fucking ninety still sporting my name like a brand on her soul.

Sydney whimpers.

"Aww, what's wrong, Princess? You don't like it? You don't like me laying my claim, carving your ass and tasting your come?" I ask.

"N-no," she stutters. "I love it."

"Then why are you crying, baby?" I suck on her clit, rewarding her as I dot the *I.*

"Because it *hurts.*"

"Is it too much?"

"Yes."

"Are you going to take it anyway?" I push.

"*Yes,*" she screams.

"And why is that?" My tongue sweeps across her ass cheek as I place the final curve on the *N*.

"Because I'm a good *fucking* girl," she growls.

"Yes"—*kiss*—"you"—*kiss*—"are."

I stand at my full height once more, rounding the front of her body.

"C-can I please have my reward now?" Sydney whimpers.

My eyes dip to her trembling lip, her teeth sinking into the bottom one as she contains her pouting.

"Trevor, unhook the bar." As soon as her legs are free, I reposition her body, sliding her back down to the bed and flipping her on to her knees. Leaving her arms tied to the lower frame. I slide between her arms, my body between her and the bed, her face right by my cock as Trevor holds her taut.

"Let's start with ten," I say.

Sydney's face twists in confusion, but Trevor understands what's happening.

Leaning forward, he whispers to Sydney. "Eyes on him or we'll both be punished," he says, kissing her temple. "Don't be mad at me, okay?"

Her forehead creases, but it's the only warning she gets before Trevor's large hand slaps across her unscathed ass cheek. When she opens her mouth to scream, I shove my cock so deep in her throat, her screams get caught.

I pop her off with a loud suction and saliva pools from her lips.

"One. Say it," I instruct.

Those cracked-ice eyes darken and hellfire blazes in them. But when those lips part, she growls.

"One."

I follow the same pattern and by time we get to three, tears are streaming down her face. I lick each one away.

"Isn't this so much better than getting fucked?" I tease.

She glowers, mouth clamped shut, probably out of fear that she'd only make things worse.

I desperately want her to, because they can. They can get so much worse.

"I told you I didn't need to fuck you to have fun with you." More tears stream down her face and her eyes close, pained by the very idea of not getting fucked. I mean, this could just be the male ego talking, but her need for me just makes me want her that much more. Shame, she probably has no clue just how badly I need her too or why I'm going through all of this trouble in the first place. Because if she survives this night with me, I know I'll never *need* to let her go. She'll be with me, always. And I'll never have to be alone again.

CHAPTER THIRTY-THREE

SYDNEY

"Six," I gasp between sobs.

My ass stings, my throat is sore, and my arms are falling asleep. The only thing sobbing harder than me is my cunt, because the arousal from all this stimulation is building to impossible heights, wreaking irrevocable havoc on my psyche and forcing me into a sex-hazed delirium—minus the actual sex.

Trevor's hands are huge and cover a lot of surface area as he claps my cheeks. They jiggle from the impact, which would normally make me feel self-conscious, but Trevor and Lucien's simultaneous groans of pleasure erase whatever self-deprecation my mind can conjure. It hurts like hell, but then there's the feel of his palms soothing over the stinging marks or sometimes his tongue—licking like a remorseful puppy licking his owner's wounds.

He's sticking to the side of my ass that's not bleeding, always the gentleman.

I don't hate him like I thought I would, I'm grateful. But gratefulness doesn't negate what I'm really after and it's not the captain's cock that's evading me.

I hiss when Trevor strikes again, groaning as I attempt to breathe through it. Each slap is repeated on my right ass cheek. In the same spot. Over and over again. The pain is building, but so is the orgasm.

"Why didn't you just punish me yourself?" I grit, unable to hold back my lashing tongue any longer. "Why make your *captain* do it?"

Keeping to his word, the smile hasn't left Lucien's face. My anger doesn't faze him in the slightest. My tears only turn him on, and my screams make his cock harder. He really is a painful fucker. The wound in my chest is still bleeding a little, I think, but it could be sweat. I'm wet all over, sticky and quite possibly bleeding, and yet . . . I've never felt better.

I've been sweaty and bloody before, practicing drills until my feet bled, practicing my spins and jumps until my muscles were so sore they gave out, but this is different. This feels like my every doubt, fall, injury, loss was worth it. That all my hard work is paying off.

Figure skating didn't pay off in the end, but Lucien pays with interest.

Even if he is evil for putting me through this. I'm grateful for him too.

"You don't want *me* to punish you, Princess. I hit way harder than the captain, isn't that right, pup?"

I crane my head back at Trevor who's shaking his head, warning me not to do it, but this time I don't listen.

Facing Lucien again, I don't take my eyes off him.

"I can take it," I say.

He stares back for a moment, contemplative. If I didn't know any better, I'd think I saw a glint of worry in his eyes.

"Fine. Don't forget to count," he states.

After switching places, Trevor now sits below me, and I smirk because I really wanted to suck his dick, but that smirk falls after the first strike, right beneath my ass cheeks where my ass and thigh meet. It's a strategic location, one that'll have me feeling the sting of Lucien's hand long after we're done. I'm inclined to believe it would hurt less if he'd just taken his belt to my ass instead.

My screams are garbled around Trevor's dick, but I lick and suck him anyway, soothing him. His hands are tentative in my hair, less pulling, more petting. He looks to be in agony, but his mouth opens on a silent moan when I peer up at him through my lashes, sucking him deeper and swirling my tongue around his thick head. He's shaped differently than Lucien and he's obviously missing the three rings sticking out of his cock, but I groan when I feel him slide against the roof of my mouth, the taste of precum slipping from his tip.

"Eight," I whisper, my throat practically rubbed raw at this point.

The next strike is to the top of my ass where it meets my back. It hurts so fucking bad, I almost run from him even as Trevor slips his cock back in my mouth. I suck Trevor in, screaming around his length as Lucien drags me back into position.

"Oh, no you don't. You're breaking the rules, Princess. No running away, remember?" Lucien teases.

I pop off with a slur and Trevor groans.

"Okay, okay," my voice shakes. "Nine."

"Aww, where's all that bravado now? You wanted this, remember? Wanted me to fuck you *so* bad."

His finger runs down my wet pussy and I shiver.

"I'm s-sorry," I cry, but it's not enough for Lucien.

"I don't *want* your apologies, Princess. I want your screams. Now, last one, Sydney. Make it good."

I nod, trying to not think about the pain radiating from my entire backside.

The last strike sends us all over the edge when Lucien brings his hand down right over my pussy, the reverberations so strong I come on the spot, gagging and sucking on Trevor so hard he comes down my throat in salted spurts that fill me faster than I can swallow.

It spills from the sides of my lips and Trevor moans as he buries himself deeper and deeper down my throat. Lucien uses the opportunity to tease me further, raking the tip of his dick over my hole as I orgasm, releasing his cum all over my pussy. He even pushes in slightly to get some inside me. I scream from the pressure and teasing, coming even harder after he does.

"Fuck, you guys are wild," Trevor huffs, releasing from my throat almost cross-eyed from the pleasure.

"Get over here, Trevor," Lucien barks. Trevor doesn't object. Lucien reaches for a small bottle from the nightstand, uncaps it, and squeezes the clear liquid all over his dick.

"I'm not done," he growls.

I'm so sore and spent, it takes me a while to turn over, but without Trevor or Lucien to hold me in place, I'm able to crawl back up the bed and untwist my body to face them. My arms are still bound, and my ass hurts so bad I can only really bear laying on my side, but it still affords me the glorious view of Lucien holding Trevor's head down and pumping into his ass hard enough that Trevor's eyes are rolling back.

Lucien is vicious in his thrusts, but there's a smoothness to his long, deep strokes that makes him look ethereal. The deep roll of his hips as he penetrates Trevor's ass looks so delicious that it's like I can feel him in me too. Trevor looks up at me, smirking and biting his lip. His green eyes hold me in place, relaying how it feels to have Lucien inside him. We share a deep and visceral understanding as he grips onto my ankles, letting me feel the vibrations and thrust through him as Lucien pounds into him.

I whimper just from watching them and Lucien's ears perk at the sound.

"This is what you want, right? For me to fuck you just like this?" he asks.

I nod my head enthusiastically because yes, yes, a *thousand times,* yes.

"Fuck, Lucien, that feels good," Trevor groans.

"You see, Trevor loves it. He can tap out anytime he needs to, but he's my good fucking boy and he's not going to, are you, pup?"

"Never," Trevor moans. "Fuck, I'm going to come again."

I wouldn't tap out either, but I can see how Lucien's method of fucking isn't for everyone. Certainly not for girls like Tiffany and Regina. Or even the girls or guys I know back home.

Everyone I know would be offended at the way Lucien degrades. They'd call bloody murder at the pain he inflicts. They'd call the cops for pulling a knife on them and using it to cut them as they orgasm. But that's just the way he is, and it works for those it works with and doesn't for everyone else. Not everyone can fuck a monster like Lucien, but I can, and I will.

"I'm definitely going to fuck your ass first, so prepare for that eventuality." Lucien smirks and I grin back. I don't care how he fucks me, so long as he does.

"Come closer," I plead, wanting to feel them release, to feel a part of the moment they break.

Lucien releases his hold on Trevor, and he scoots closer up the bed to straddle me while Lucien re-enters Trevor. Trevor moves to release my arm restraints, and I wrap my freed limbs around his shoulders. I kiss him, holding Trevor as Lucien continues his thrusts. I swallow Trevor's moans, feeling the jolt of euphoria when Lucien hits a particular spot.

"Fuckfuckfuckfuckfuckfuck," he chants, face burrowed into my neck as I hold him and his cum sprays all over my stomach. His abs contract against mine, and I feel the release of tension in his body as he lets go. Lucien's stare on me is just as palpable, like hot lava as we gaze into each other's eyes and he empties every drop he has inside his captain's ass.

I smile when they both collapse onto me, all of us heaving exhausted breaths.

Chuckling, I ask, "You okay, Captain?"

Trevor's green eyes shift over to look up at me with those amazing dimples. "I should be asking you that. How's *your* ass?"

I laugh. "Sore!" But then with a more serious expression I look at them both.

"I've never felt better."

LUCIEN
@BladeSpinner
Online
In life?
Seen
Haven't decided yet.

CHAPTER THIRTY-FOUR

LUCIEN

Pulling out of Trevor, I reposition us so that I'm in the middle and Sydney is tucked into my side. Her body twitches beneath my touch as I rub soothing circles over her ass where she's already starting to bruise.

In my defense, she bruises easily, but it's possible I might've been a little *too* rough with her. I wish I could say I felt a little worse about it, but I don't. The only thing I feel is pride that she took it like the good girl she is. I'll have to remember to reward her later, but for now, these two need a break. It wasn't the worst of the worst, but at this point, if she hasn't run away yet, then she really is here to stay. I haven't minded being alone all these years, it really was for the best.

I don't think I would have gotten as far as I have in life if I didn't adapt to the loneliness. With the exception of good friends like Trevor, who has really specific needs and secrets of his own, it's always been best that I don't indulge too much with those in captivity.

Sydney is different. She's proven she can survive on my side of the fence. I don't have to be separated from her. I don't have to be alone.

"Lucien," calls Trevor's smooth voice.

I sigh, knowing what he's going to ask.

"Are *you* okay?"

Sydney looks at me, recognizing Trevor's tone of voice for what it is. Forever the concerned pup that he is.

"I'm better now." I don't even have the energy to give a witty remark. I think I came too much. There's still cum leaking from my dick as it rests against my stomach, completely spent. Jesus fucking Christ, it's been a crazy night.

"I didn't realize Anderson was chirping about your family," Trevor murmurs into my shoulder. "You should have come to me. I would have handled it."

Trevor's hand rests on my chest as he lifts to his elbow.

Sydney looks up at me, hauntingly beautiful, with her face blushed. She's equally worried for me, despite her own demons that are clearly haunting her. She's had this sense of impending doom circling her all night, but right now all focus is on me. I'm not sure what I ever did to earn the affections of two big-hearted people, but it's a blessing and a curse—or a cruel joke altogether.

I shrug.

"You're the captain," I chuckle. "We needed you in the game. Besides, it wouldn't have mattered, I snapped the moment he brought up my mom."

Trevor's arm snakes over my middle, squeezing me tighter.

"That asshole," he grumbles.

I chuckle, "I know, right? He was *so* rude."

We laugh softly, sadly almost, but then Sydney moves to get up. My arm whips out and I grip her hand tightly, halting her midway.

"Relax," she coos. "I'm not breaking any rules. Not running away. See?" She leans forward and kisses us both. "I just have to pee." I release her and she giggles, sauntering away to the en-suite bathroom, no longer shy about being stark naked.

I watch her pad away, handprint bruises glowing on her ass.

Trevor hisses. "Did you have to spank her so hard?"

More laughter bubbles from my chest. "She needed to learn her lesson."

"You know she was only baiting you so you would fuck her, right?"

I stroke his head as he lays on my chest and tell him the truth. "I know, but I'm so fucking crazy about that girl, it's unreal. I needed to know if something with her could last."

His head lifts from my chest.

"Seriously? You want something long-term with her?"

I brush his dark curls off his forehead, peering at those pretty green eyes. He's not asking out of jealousy, I can see that. He *wants* me to have someone special since we both know it can't be him. His strict Christian upbringing and self-loathing would make a relationship between us difficult, to say the least.

I was willing to fight for him all the same but after being kicked out of his house and his bed, I didn't want to risk being kicked out of his life too. He begged me to stop fighting, so I did. Not to mention he's two years older than me, my captain, and well on his way to the NHL. There's no future for us beyond friendship and random hookups where he hates himself the next day, but there's an actual chance for me and Sydney.

"I want forever with her if I can have it."

His dimples are prominent as he smiles at me.

"That's amazing. I think if there was anybody you could have forever with it'd be with her. She's clearly just as obsessed with you as you are with her. You're both kinda crazy," he teases, pressing a kiss to my lips. "And you're both amazing kissers."

"She's a great kisser, right?! I thought it was just me, but she's really fucking good at it."

His laughter is as rich and velvety as his voice.

"Yeah, she kisses like you."

His lips press to mine, and I grip the back of his neck. Our time is coming to a close. Taking her virginity isn't something that's going to be shared between us, something he's already aware of.

That part is all mine.

One final kiss and he's putting his clothes back on, looking a little ruffled, but his room's down the hall, so he'll freshen up over there like he always does.

Standing up, I throw on my boxers and tuck my dick away before I'm tempted to use it again. Then I walk him out like I always do.

I hate it when he leaves, and he *always* leaves.

Even though this time is for a good reason, it still never feels good to have people you care about leave you behind. Leaning my forehead to his, I give him some final praise so he doesn't beat himself up over this again.

"You did so well, *Captain*," I say, mocking Sydney's little nickname for him.

He chuckles.

"But seriously, you're alright, right?" I ask, seeking his reassurance once more.

I need him to be okay.

He nods and I hold him to me a little tighter. "It felt good, and you know there's nothing wrong with that. You *deserve* to feel good. Fuck whatever your family has to say."

Fuck every single one of them.

He nods again. "Yeah, I know. I've . . . never felt better either," he says, giving me a smile that reaches his eyes and deepens his dimples. "Maybe we can do this again sometime."

I chuckle. "Yeah, maybe."

The worry I felt eases. I hadn't dealt with losing Trevor very well, but at this point I think I'd fare even worse if I lost Sydney too. If she would have run away from me, I'm not sure what I would have done. Probably lose all sense of rationality and saneness. I'd burn the whole world down if I had to lose one more goddamn person. For the briefest moment, I was worried she really would run away when she learned about Trevor. I'm so glad she didn't.

"I'm going to see if I can talk to Coach, okay? I don't want you to be kicked off the team. Not over that dickhead," Trevor says.

"Thanks," I say, though I don't actually believe he's going to be able to save me this time. I love hockey and I don't want to lose it either, but I also can't change the past. I've learned that lesson the hard way, so it's out of my hands at this point.

Speaking of hands . . .

I hold mine out to Trevor and he smirks, handing me Sydney's underwear from his back pocket. I'm tucking it into one of my many pockets on these jeans when Sydney returns from the bathroom.

"Hey, you leaving?" Sydney asks, walking out, looking as beautiful as ever. Her face is clear of makeup and she's dabbing her hair with a towel. She must have rinsed the cum off her face and hair. It's taken her makeup off with it, but she still looks like a gorgeous princess. Her wet hair clings to her naked breasts, the cool air and damp skin making her nipples perk into sharp peaks.

"Yeah," he grins, staring at the same tits, "but now I'm seriously thinking I should stay."

I clear my throat, and he takes the hint, grinning his dick-hardening dimples. Maybe I will have them both again, but tonight it's me and her.

She giggles, crooking a finger at him. "One last kiss, Captain. Before you go."

Something about the way she says *last*, sounds an alarm that I want to react to but that I allow myself to ignore. She doesn't say it like it's the last of the night; she says it like it's the last in her life. The alarms only sound louder when she kisses him like it too.

She pulls back, looking up at Trevor with gratefulness before pecking a softer, more chaste kiss to his lips.

"I'm sorry if I was a bitch to you before. I guess I was kind of jealous but tonight was . . . amazing. You were right, I needed this." Her hand cups his face. "And I'm really glad Lucien has someone like you in his life."

Trevor rubs the back of his neck; a sign *he's* the one feeling guilty.

"I know what that must have looked like in the moment . . . but I want you to know I think you guys are great together. I wasn't sure at first—that you'd be good for him—but I think he's in good hands . . . with you. I mean that."

Sydney reaches out to embrace him again in a final hug, but she still looks sad, defeated even, when she looks at me over his shoulder.

"Catch you later, Little Stalker Princess," he teases, throwing a wink in her direction and his award-winning smile.

Her smile, however, is weak, barely reaching her eyes. She's not even bothering to correct him that she's not a stalker.

I want to question her about it but when Trevor opens the door to leave, loud cursing and yelling filters in from downstairs.

"Where the *fuck* is Morningstar?!"

CHAPTER THIRTY-FIVE

SYDNEY

TREVOR IS THE FIRST of us to get moving. He's halfway down the stairs before I can even locate my clothes, but I'm not far behind, eager to prevent another fight, another delay to the pounding *I* was promised. Lucien's clothes are quickly thrown on, while I struggle to get my zipper up my dress without assistance.

"No. You stay here," Lucien barks, noting my obvious effort to join the fray before he's flying after Trevor.

Yeah, like that's going to happen.

It takes a lot of awkward maneuvering with my arms behind my back in his absence but the second the zipper is drawn up enough to keep the dress on, I locate my phone and shoes, grab a hoodie from Lucien's closet and run downstairs, heels clicking in hand.

By the time I've padded down the steps, absolute chaos is erupting in the front yard as another team pulls up to the house. It's a battlefield.

Gripping the rails of the front porch, I frantically search for Lucien, or Trevor. I'd even settle for Chauncey at this point, anyone that can help me stop him. This is exactly the kinda hellscape Lucien would thrive in. He'd be lost to the darkness, lost to me if he keeps choosing this path. He'll be lost to me anyway but one day, this shit . . .

I squeeze the banister hard enough to thrust splinters into my palm. One day this inability to walk away will be his downfall. Except when I do find Lucien, he's of course fighting again. He's swinging his fist into a guy's face, this time with Trevor who's also bashing two other guys across the yard. At least thirty dudes in total are spread across the lawn fighting at once.

I groan. I could be spending my final moments in town being ravaged, but no. Instead, I'm wrangling a bunch of hockey idiots.

Red SOLO cups, half-empty Jello shot glasses, and cigarette butts litter the trim lawn and hulking bodies smush the flower bed someone had attempted to keep alive. Fists fly and blood coats the stone pathway. I push past all of it to get to Lucien, getting shoved in the process when some six-foot-something tank falls on top of me.

"Fucking hell, get your ass off me," I shout.

I crawl from beneath him as he groans and struggles to right himself. I'm dusting the dirt from my palms and Lucien's hoodie when my ears catch wind of a nearby argument.

"Mother*fucker*! You put him in the hospital!" The words roared between punches.

"He barely made it. He almost *died*, you dick!" another one shouts, backing up his teammate.

The first of them tries to throw another punch, but he's countered with an elbow to the jaw. A dance of beautiful golden locks swish over his opponent's forehead as he swerves another counter and places distance between them once more.

It's then I realize their opponent is none other than Chauncey. I skid to a stop.

"Shame. Seems Morrow held back after all," he taunts, dripping with confidence of a man who can back up his easy shit-talking nature.

I hadn't noticed it earlier because I was too busy torturing him for his 'delicate' comment, but Chauncey isn't soft. He's holding his own in this fight, kind of reminding me of Lucien with his joyous expression. Even with a bloodied lip, he's still smiling.

"The fuck did you say?" the human punching bag asks.

"You heard me," Chauncey sneers. "If Morrow wanted Anderson dead, he would be. Count yourself lucky, considering what he said out there."

"Yeah, asshole. You know what happened to his family was fucked up. Anderson should have kept his mouth shut." Another one of our guys joins in, the one they call Sink, or Kitchen, or something.

I'm amazed these guys are carrying on entire conversations as they brawl, even more so by how fiercely they defend Lucien's actions.

Chauncey throws a punch but this guy just takes it on the chin, spitting blood before he continues to toss insults at an obviously riled-up Chauncey.

"Anderson was just chirping. We all talk shit on the ice."

Blood lines his inflamed nostrils and he keeps scrunching his nose like a squirrel, but his hands are up in defense ready for Chauncey to strike again.

"You know damn well it wasn't just a chirp. Anderson hit below the belt, and you fucking know it," Chauncey spits.

"So what? Fucking 'Morningstar'"—he taunts, using finger quotes—"does it all the time. He's a menace on the ice and you all just let him do it. So, who's the real villain here? It was about time someone put that rabid dog you call a teammate *down*."

I didn't get a chance to know Chauncey well or anything, so he doesn't strike me as the type to get angry easily but that's exactly what he is when he swings a haymaker of a hit right at the guy's temple, bringing him to his knees.

"Well, that *dog* is still standing and your teammate is in the hospital," Chauncey points out, spitting a glob of blood into the grass as his knee makes contact with the asshole's face.

I start walking again, catching Chauncey's eye and offering a small smile. It's all I *can* offer him, and when he smiles back, I know then he's going to be okay.

Lucien is still a considerable distance from me, and I have to dip and dodge the slew of people fighting just to reach him. I cannot *believe* he's in another fight. It's like trouble finds this guy wherever he goes. That, or he's having even worse luck than me today.

I freshened up and everything to prepare for our time together and now I'm outside, barefoot, damp hair and freezing my ass off while he engages in another blow-for-blow exchange. This shouldn't be happening. He should be balls-deep and fucking me until I can't see straight.

Then I hear it. Police sirens.

"Fuck. You've got to be kidding me," I mutter.

If Lucien's caught fighting again, he'll get in serious trouble. Hell, they might even lock him up for the night.

There are only a few more hours until daybreak before it's well and truly over for us. I'm not ready for it to be over. I ball my fist at my chest as I try to ease the slow tear of my heart. I know heartbreak will come, but it'll have to wait a little longer.

Unfortunately, I'm so distracted by my stupid heart that I don't realize in the haze of bodies someone's grabbing me harshly as they mistake me for another fighter. I'm yanked back and thrown to my knees, scraping them in the process. My heels slip from my hands, tangling around my feet as I attempt to peel my hood back in hopes that if they see I'm a girl, they won't strike. Cold hands grip me by the nape of the neck, pulling me back. I claw at them, unable to see who's pulling at me.

"Get off me," I scream. I kick and scratch, slipping in the damp grass, barely gaining purchase to fight them off.

Like a trapped animal, I snarl as I'm being dragged away.

I search the lawn for help, to see if anyone is paying attention, but everyone is too engrossed in their own battles to notice my absence.

My fighting wanes, and for a second I resign myself to my fate, until I lock eyes with Lucien a few feet away. He knocks out the guy in front of him with a kick to the chest that looks like it might've broken a few ribs.

"Shit. Shit. Shit."

This is all so fucked.

He turns to head for me, but then right beside him Trevor gets punched in the face, hard. Lucien turns toward him, conflict evident on his face. Trevor's hit again, brought down to the ground where the guy is ready to unleash hit after hit on him. Lucien steps in my direction again, but I thrust my hand up.

"Trevor!" I shout, halting him in his tracks.

He needs to save Trevor first. I twist in my captor's hold, unable to get a good look at their face, but feeling around for something, anything to get myself free. Finally, my hand catches hold of a strap, the strap of my shoe to be exact. Fixing my hold on the shoe I spin without looking and drive the heel into the guy's foot. Their hold on me releases and I run back across the lawn in Lucien's direction, not turning back.

I dip and dodge a few more guys like I'm a goddamn running back before finally reaching Lucien who's now punching the face of the asshole who hit Trevor.

I'm here in time to help Trevor up from the ground, still reeling from a punch to the face.

"Are you okay?" I ask, cupping his face in my palm. Irritation boils my insides that anyone would punch him in his beautiful face, but even more so that he'd put himself in this situation. There's no need for any of this.

My own turmoil forgotten, I tend to him, checking his body for serious injury. I may not feel for Trevor what I feel for Lucien, but he's someone important to Lucien, and by extension, me. Lucien and I aren't close to people, we have that in common, but somehow Trevor defies that reasoning.

He grips at my hand, bringing it away from his face and flashing his dimples, despite his bruising eye and busted lip.

"I'm fine," he winces. "You guys gotta get going. The cops are coming."

"I know, I heard them too." I turn toward Lucien. "Lucien, come on."

But, of course, he's not listening, or more accurately he's not hearing me. He's not seeing me *at all*.

"You need to get out of here, Sydney. I got him," Trevor sighs, cracking his knuckle, and preparing to rejoin the fight. My teeth grit from the absolute lunacy of men solving problems with their fists

Lucien surges his fist forward and it cracks against his new opponent's jaw. Blood flows from the guy's lips and he coughs up a tooth of all things. The guy tries to protect himself from Lucien's blows, but his jaw is so swollen he can't even beg for mercy.

"S-st—" His hand hangs limp as he tries to scoot away but Lucien is unfazed at the half-assed escape attempt.

Trevor looks over his shoulder at me, brows furrowed. Chauncey's words ring like a bell in my head, *'we're not afraid of him, we're afraid for him.'*

I soften my features and smile. "I got him. I promise," I tell Trevor.

His eyes search mine for a second before he relents, granting me one last show of those beautiful dimples before backing away and heading toward Chauncey and everyone else to clean up this whole mess. If anyone can do it, their fearless, level-headed captain can. I don't know the full story of what he and Lucien are to each other, or why Trevor submits to him the way he does, but I'm glad Lucien has someone like Trevor in his life.

"Good luck, Captain" I whisper.

"Hey, Lucien." I try to keep my voice even and calm, but he doesn't respond. He just keeps hitting the guy. Blood splatters onto my cheek and coats Lucien's hands.

Cold mountain wind whips through the air, stinging my exposed skin and chilling the fury burning within everyone except Lucien. It only fans his flames.

"*Lucien.*"

My nerves frizzle and fray with the amount of built up sexual frustration that's burning through me. Every time I'm close to having my moment with Lucien and confessing my true feelings, I'm thwarted. I want him to feel better, to unleash all that fury on me instead, but he's no longer here with me. He's somewhere else entirely right now.

"Lucien," I try again.

Nothing.

"Lucien, fuck, you gotta stop. We have to go."

Again he doesn't hear me.

In the time I've spent with Lucien tonight I've noticed he showcases a different type of rage when he's personally insulted than when someone he cares about is harmed or insulted. Then, it's like nothing else exists and he's a totally different person. I let out a panicked breath. He's clearly upset, and I think I know why. Someone hurt Trevor. And someone tried to hurt me. He felt helpless and out of control, two emotions I now know he can't stand to feel. But even with that, we have to go. Now.

"Lucien, please. Come *with* me." I yank at his shirt, pulling on him a couple of times before he stops, the haze lifting.

Finally, he sees me.

He looks like he wants to protest but one look at my tattered appearance, bleeding knees, reddened cheeks and a rats nest of hair, he's grabbing my hand, and we're running. I stare up at him as we run, shocked by his sudden change in demeanor but he seems more like his regular weird self and less like the unhinged monster he was a second ago. Yet something pulls at me to reach out to him again.

"Let's go to my house," I say, the offer more timid than I'd like.

"Yeah, but we can't take the car. We'll get blocked in," he says, looking up and down Sorority Row that has cops flooding in from both sides.

Just great. We break into a sprint through the backyard and straight through the line of trees that lead to the forest. The conifers are tall and the brush thick so they're our best chance.

If we cut through them, we can get to the arena and from there it's a straight shot to my apartment. Sharp branches block our path and scratch at my thighs. They pull the hoodie from my head and tangle their claws in my hair, but we keep running. The wind howls and violates my body, thrusting a bone-deep chill to rattle me beneath the barely warm cover up. Twigs snap beneath our feet as we pound through the forest, the underbrush sticking to my bare feet and the mud sloshing between my toes.

Several minutes pass and the sound of sirens hushes to a whisper. Only the forest acknowledges us now.

After running for what feels like forever, our predicament truly starts to dawn on me.

"How did we get here?" I chuckle, laughing at the insanity of it all. I just wanted to have sex with a guy I'm pretty sure I'm in love with. Is that so wrong?

I stumble to a halt, bracing my hands on my bloody knees, and ready to curse the universe.

"Come on, we can't stop," says Lucien.

"If you haven't noticed I'm running barefoot in a dress through the goddamn woods!" I shout.

Lucien rests his shoulder against a tree, amused with my bereft state.

"Oh, c'mon, it's not so bad. You're actually faster than I gave you credit for. I'm impressed. But you know, if we're going to be fucking, you're going to have to build up your endurance," he taunts, hiking his brows up and down suggestively.

I glare at him even as I struggle to catch my breath.

"I'm an athlete too. I have *plenty* of endurance!" I huff.

"Oh, yeah?" He pushes off the tree, arms still folded. "Then let's play another little game."

"No! I'm sick of your games, Lucien. Let's just go *home*."

He smiles warmly at me, beaming so brightly that I wonder if it's for the same reason I warm inside: the idea we could have a home . . . together.

"But you'll *like* this game."

"Doubt it," I mutter.

"Oh, but you see, I know your secret."

I stop breathing.

"I know you *love* a challenge." Breath returns in a painful rush. "So, how about I give you that rematch you begged for? If you beat me in a race. I'll fuck you right here and now."

Fear aside, we grin simultaneously because he's right. I *do* like this game.

"Okay, one *last* game," I relent, meeting his challenge and biting the corner of my lip. "And then you're mine."

CHAPTER THIRTY-SIX

SYDNEY

THE CRISPY LEAVES AND pointed pricker briars are sharp, embedding themselves into the soles of my feet, but I run as fast as they'll take me.

The dense Washington forests can be thick in certain areas of the state and this one's no exception. I have to do a lot more dodging and crouching than actual running, but I'm making incredible time and maintaining my speed. I'm running so fast I don't even realize I've left Lucien in the dust.

I risk a glance behind me, but he's not there.

Did he let me win so he could fuck me? That'd be kinda sweet if it weren't for the competitor in me not wanting a win handed to me.

I stop running, pausing to check my surroundings, but I have no idea where I am.

I call out his name, "Lucien!"

Nothing.

"Seriously. Lucien, this isn't funny!" I shout.

More silence.

"You better not be trying to scare me! I will be so—"

What am I saying? *Of course* he's trying to scare me. This is Lucien we're talking about.

My heart rate kicks up a beat and sweat matriculates down my neck. I'm suddenly hyper-aware of everything, including the brief snap of a twig. I whip my head, straining to see if I see him, but there's nothing but trees.

Get it together, Sydney.

Just as I turn back around, my body hits the chilled forest floor with a jarring thud, and I get rolled around in the brush of a clearing.

A startled scream rips through my throat—my assailant more than pleased with the noise. It's just me and a depraved hockey player in the middle of the woods, right?

What could possibly go wrong?

"You almost gave me a heart attack!" I yell even as Lucien's large, veiny hands pin me to the ground by my wrists.

"I caught you," he sing-songs, grinding his cock against my pantiless sex. "Again."

I flail beneath him, trying to regain purchase, but there's no overpowering him. I'm pinned. We're in the same position from seven hours ago when this all started, and he had me splayed against the ice. I remember the intense cold and scalding heat fighting for dominance in my body and I shiver. Except now, it's the earth at my back and a monster on top. Everything's different now, he's not a stranger anymore, or the talented boy I found practicing alone. He's . . .

Not playing fair again.

"You said we were racing," I argue, squirming beneath him, albeit uselessly.

"I said that?" Lucien pretends to sound confused. "I meant Hide and Seek. Looks like I win. No getting fucked for you I guess," he taunts.

The growl I let loose would put grizzlies to shame because fuck him! This is *beyond* torture. I don't mean to be ungrateful, but I still have a goal to accomplish: setting my V card on fire with Lucien.

I don't want Bradford or some other guy from back home who curried favor with my dad and wants to use me. If I can take this one thing for myself, I'll be able to keep going. I'll survive those people back home because they'll never be able to take this away from me. Never.

"Lucien," I whine. "Don't tease me anymore. I can't take it at this point." I'm pleading, the emotion spilling out of me involuntarily as I whimper, raw need heavy in my throat. "I know I haven't been coy, or ladylike, but I do want you. I want you so fucking much it's driving me crazy. I'm *losing* my mind."

He hums, staring down at me, and for once I don't mind my appearance.

He sees me.

"You were already crazy," he says matter-of-factly, a knowing smirk on his face.

I sigh, ready to give another piece of myself to him. To tell him the truth or some part of it.

"Crazy about *you* . . . I'd do anything for you. If you'd just let me. Let me give you this." I grind against him, lifting my hips, my wet pussy undoubtedly creating a damp spot on his jeans. I can feel the outline of his cock underneath the coarse denim, and it only drives me further insane.

"Hmm, let me think about it," Lucien muses even as his hands trail my body, hiking my dress up my thighs. His fingers are firm and strong, but they tickle as they slide against my skin. I never want to forget this feeling of his hands on me. "Tell me why you want me, and I might give you what you want." Gripping my hips, he flips me roughly, forcing my sore ass against him, the leaves and dirt in my hair flying. My ruined knees press into the leaves beneath us.

I groan. "Fuck, Lucien, this is a two-thousand-dollar dress."

He ignores my protests.

"Tell me what you want, Princess, and I'll give you everything you're begging for and more."

I want to push, to argue and tell him I'm not begging, that this is something more than lust. This is my one chance to choose someone for myself. For the first time, I talked to a guy I actually wanted to hold a conversation with. Tonight, I went on a real date where a man went out of his way to convince me I was beautiful the way I was, who acknowledged my talent and accepted my dreams.

Tonight, I sought to claim a victory that wasn't assured. I stumbled and faltered, and, yeah, maybe I stalked a little bit, but it all led to me being here with him.

"I'm waiting, Sydney, tell me why you want me . . . please."

His lips travel over my neck and jaw, kissing me, setting my thawed heart aflame, but it's his uncharacteristic 'please' that ultimately has me folding.

I need to tell him. It has to be now.

I slowly turn back over, to face him again. Trailing my fingers along his thick arched brows that lowkey have me jealous of their perfection, I reach a small divot hidden beneath his hair. I choose to focus on it as I declare my confession.

"All my life there was only ever one thing I wanted. More than toys. More than money. More than friends. And that was to be a professional competitive figure skater. The moment I realized I wanted it, I didn't see anything else. I didn't *care* about anything else." My forehead crinkles as I think about how sad that is. I never had any ambitions outside of that dream, no close friends or hobbies, just figure skating. "That was true for nineteen years, until I saw you." Lucien's eyes pin me as sharply to the ground as the rest of him does. "You were the only other thing in my life that made me deviate from that goal. The only other thing I wanted just as bad as I wanted figure skating. It was different and it felt good, but it also scared me." My fingers slide from his brows to cup his face—he lets me. "*You* scared me—but not in the way you think. It was because you rivaled my dreams. I tried staying away, I really did. But the more I tried to flee, the more you drew me in. Until I couldn't go a day without seeing you. Then *something* happened, and I knew I had to stop. But today . . ." Tears line my eyes the longer I drown in his sea of gold. I steel myself with a breath. "You wanted to know why it was today. *Why* I revealed myself and ended our cat and mouse game?" A self-deprecating laugh signals my impending breakdown. "Today . . . I lost figure skating. I lost the dream I chased my whole life. I lost the one thing that was always mine. I let myself grow desperate, and I was kicked off the team, Lucien. It's over." Tears slide down to my ears. "And the worst part is, there's no one to blame. It's all my fault."

It was all I could do to not pull my hair out and scream at the stupidity of my own actions. My fingers claw at the dirt as I lie beneath Lucien who hasn't uttered a word. He only stares at me as I get this out. My dirt-covered hands claw at his shirt next to draw him closer.

"Without figure skating in the way, there was only one other dream worth having and that's you. You were the only thing worth continuing to pursue. You're talented, funny, surprisingly nice, despite your violent streak. You make me feel alive, invincible, like I can take on the world. So, if I can't have figure skating anymore, then at least I can have you . . . if you want me." I drop my hands as he regards my face. I look from his eyes to his lips, unable to ask the hard question with all that intensity directed at me. "Do you . . . want me?" I shrug.

Lucien takes a deep breath, moving his hand to grab my jaw.

"Fuck, Princess, you have no fucking clue, do you? When I say I'm crazy about you, I mean it. Don't ever doubt that. You're mine. Never forget that I've claimed you."

"Never," I vow.

He nuzzles against my cheek, a gesture normally perceived as sweet, but when his eyes meet mine again, they're full of animalistic carnality and I'm reminded what being claimed by him means.

"Take off the hoodie and get on all fours," he instructs. I waste no time obeying. The time for talking and truths are over.

A dark, mirthless chuckle spills from his lips and a trickle of real fear tingles up my back as my bare knees settle into the cold, damp ground.

For a moment he's quiet, and it's only the sounds of the forest in the still air. His own name sliced into my ass for him to see. It's a stark reminder of the position we're in and how dangerous this all is. Anxiousness sprouts when that quiet stretches on before I risk looking over my shoulder. He meets my stare and the adoration I find staring back at me is almost too much.

"Is there anything you *wouldn't* let me do to you?" he asks.

"No," I whisper, because honestly nothing comes to mind. I'll let Lucien do anything to me—if it means having him.

"Oh, that's right, you said you'd do *anything* for me." He relishes the term like it's something to savor. "That's a dangerous word for someone like me."

He's trying to be ominous, but there's no need for either of us to hold back anymore. I get it now. I see him for exactly who he is, and I don't care. I want him anyway.

"I mean it, Lucien, *anything*," I breathe, dropping my head between my shoulders, praying the earth keeps me upright.

"Well, we already know you'll let me cum all over your pretty face and perky tits. You'll let me gag you with my cock until you can't breathe. You'll let me spank you black and blue. You'll let me sink my teeth into you. You'll . . ."—a sharp sting lacerates across my back, and I bow with a moan—"let me *cut* you."

That last one is still surprising to me, but I don't think about the severity of what it could mean psychologically at the moment. I'm more concerned he has the knife with him at all. When did he have time to grab it?

"But you see, I really want to test your limits. What *won't* you let me do?" he taunts, tangling his hands through my hair and pulling me back so that I'm no longer on all fours but sitting on my heels. His fingers glide over the scar on my head lovingly as his fingers play across the raised flesh. He hasn't asked me about it yet, but I know he's noticed it with how much he loves petting me and pulling my hair.

"I don't know," I rasp, already loving the friction of his hard dick pressing into me. I don't even care that my ass is still sore from his brutal spankings and carved signature.

"Let's see . . ." He grips my hair, pulling hard enough to sting. "Would you let me spit in your mouth?"

Disgusting. Unsanitary. Delicious.

I nod. "Yes."

He holds my jaw open, thrusting my head back to meet his. I stick my tongue out, ready to receive him, ready to have him integrate with me, live on inside me. His saliva is warm as it slides down my throat, thick and coating. A pleased whimper passes my lips.

This can't be taken, changed, or undone. It's inevitable when our lips join together like two magnets. He bites down on my lip. We kiss like a couple of mad hatters, our insane hearts ticking against time.

"I'll never get enough of you," he moans.

"Never," I moan in agreement. I'll yearn for his taste again and again until the end of time.

Holding my throat, he nips down my jaw and neck, trailing more bites along my flesh. I swear, I'm going to look like the victim of an assault by the time he's done with me. But my body craves more. My pussy aches with anticipation that he will be inside me soon. Running his hands down my body, his fingers roam between my ass, being gentle near my scarring skin, down to my soaked pussy and back up again. I know he can feel how wet I am . . . again.

I'm not sure there's been a single time all night that I haven't been. It's just the reaction he solicits. Everything he does, turns me on, even when it hurts, because none of it will hurt as bad as when I'll have to leave him behind.

"I'm not convinced, Princess," he taunts. "There has to be *some* kind of limit, wouldn't you say?"

Lucien pushes me back on all fours and my fingers sink back into the earth, bracing myself for what's to come.

"Let's see . . ." His hand brushes down my back again until it rests against my reddened ass cheek. "Would you let me into your ass?" he asks, hiking my dress up my back and pushing a finger against the tight rim. My ass immediately clenches in response even as the sound of him spitting reaches my ears. The feel of his sputum warms my entrance as he swirls his wet digit around the puckered hole, coaxing it to open for him.

I groan. "I don't . . . it's so . . ." I can barely get the words out, or rather I can barely arrange them in a way that fully describes this intense sensation. I don't hate it.

"I can't hear you. Was that a yes? You'll let me take this ass?" He applies pressure, pushing in slowly as he uses his other hand to circle my clit.

Fuck.

"Yes!" I cry out as he finally breeches my back entrance, making me go cross-eyed.

It takes me a minute before I'm able to fully acclimate to even his finger, but then I feel something drip inside the hole of my ass. My guess is that he spit on it again to use as natural lube, though this time I didn't hear him do it. The singular digit moves steadily in and out until his entire finger can slide all the way in with minimal resistance and the uncomfortable pressure settles into something pleasurable.

"Oh, fuck, Lucien." I push back against his hand, seeking more. *Needing* more.

"Oh, wow, that was actually really easy. It usually takes people a while to enjoy anything in their ass, but you are loving it, aren't you, Princess?"

My arms shake as I continue to brace myself. No way in hell do I want him to stop.

"Yes, *please*, keep going," I beg.

I wiggle my ass against his hand once more, chasing the tiny flicker of an orgasm that's already begun to alight.

"Your wish is my command." His finger slides almost all the way out before gliding back in, the resistance all but gone now. I clench his finger greedily, chasing the fullness they provide. "That's it. Take it deep. All the way."

My legs shake when he adds a second finger, then a third, stretching me wider.

"One day I'm going to fill this ass and fuck your cunt at the same time," Lucien promises. "You'll be so full, writhing and screaming for a god that won't save you because the devil will already be granting your salvation. Would you like that, Princess? To be filled, owned, and at my complete mercy?"

"Yes," I moan.

"You promise? You'll let me do it?" he prods, teasing my clit in the process, my mind lost and my vision blurred as I submit to him.

I nod; coherent speech rendered more difficult with every swipe of his thumb and press of his fingers.

"Don't make promises you can't keep," he warns. "I'm a man of my word and a slave to my commitments. So, if you can't take it . . . speak now or forever hold your peace."

"God, yes, anything," I croon.

"I'll never grow tired of that little nickname. Those whimpered pleas when you call out for me is addictive."

We're both making promises we can't keep, but I'm too lost in the moment to care. Lucien deserves to know my feelings, and the truth right now is that I would love nothing more.

His fingers pump into me harder and my knees dig into the dirt, filth coating my scrapes and bruises as I begin to thrust my hips back, fucking his fingers. Sweat beads against my flesh and the wind slaps against my exposed limbs. I want more. Arousal slickens my opening while every muscle welcomes his intrusion.

"Fuck, yes, please!" I beg.

"You're so fucking ready for me. You want my cock right now, don't you?" Lucien sounds proud. "You want me to fuck this ass outside in the open like this, like an animal, where anyone or anything can see you."

"I don't care who sees me. I just care that *you* see me."

For the person I really am. This version of me that'll die when the sun comes up and burns me away.

"I'll *always* see you, Princess."

Dirt and debris cover us both from our time rolling around on the ground, but I've never felt more connected with the universe, the earth, and with myself. Being out here almost seems more right than back at the house. I don't care that we would be fucking on the forest floor of these woods in the cold night air so long as he would be fucking me.

"Lucien, please, fuck me. I can't wait any longer."

I literally can't. I think I'll die if he doesn't stick his dick in me right now. I'm too lost, abandoned in the wind, swept up in his tornado of chaos to feel pathetic about my actions now.

He leans over my back, palm flat on my spine before he whispers into my ear. "There's that desperation I was looking for. Doesn't it feel *good* to beg?"

And then he's shoving the tip of his cock into my ass. I groan first from pain, but then something warm and viscus drips where he's notched inside. I feel so full, suffocated by his hunger.

"I can't believe you thought to bring lube out here," I moan as he works himself inside.

Lucien's chuckle is amused.

"It's not lube."

My entire body clenches and it makes all his prep work for naught as he drives in deeper.

"W-what is it then?" I pant.

"My blood."

I don't even really have time to process that before he's pushing in a little more.

"You're bleeding? Why?" I try to stop his thrusts, but he palms my back, keeping me hunched before him. I feel the viscous coating along his palm when it connects with my skin, his bloody palmprint sure to leave another.

"I cut myself," he says as inconsequentially as possible.

"On purpose?!" I screech, attempting to glare at him over my shoulder, but his grip is relentless.

"Yes," he hisses through his teeth as he struggles to steady himself, already moaning and relishing in the feel of my ass.

Why must he say things like that? Like it's the most practical thing in the world. 'Oh, don't have lube? No worries, just let me use a little blood.' *Fucking psycho.*

"Why would you do that?!" I shout, angry that he would mar himself that way.

I love that Lucien's a little unhinged. Honestly, it's one of my favorite qualities of his– how completely unafraid he is of anything—but I never want him to hurt himself.

He pushes in deeper, and I groan.

"Relax, Princess. I didn't cut deep. I needed something to ease the discomfort for you."

Again, he says it like it's the most natural thing in the world and I want to smack his stupidly handsome face for it. My comfort shouldn't come at the cost of his pain.

I huff an exasperated breath.

"You were worried about my *discomfort*?" I breathe. "You, the guy who's been making cuts against my very flesh, biting me, and spanking me 'til I'm bruised and bloodied is worried about a little *discomfort*?" I bark a mirthless laugh, refusing to accept such an excuse. He reaches his bloodied palm toward my face and in the moonlit area I can confirm what he's done, but I don't flinch away when he brushes my hair from my forehead and cups my face.

"I want you to enjoy this, Sydney. It's still your first time and I want you to like it, so if I have to bleed to make that easier for you . . . then I *will*." His words are sweet, but his thrusts aren't, even as he shoves in another couple of inches. I feel every piercing as they skim past my entrance.

"Holy shit," I whimper.

"I know, baby," he coos, "but you can take it. We've got a few more inches to go, so you'd better brace yourself."

Lucien's hand leaves my cheek as he shoves in another inch, and I practically come on the spot. He's so goddamn big, not to mention the jewelry that's pressing against my inner channel.

"Come on, you're Sydney Sinclair. I know you can take it. Breathe through it."

I take his advice and suck in a deep breath.

For a moment, I'm relaxed. Then he tells me to bite down, and I know shit is about to take a dark turn. He shoves a nearby stick into my mouth like a horse's bit.

"I'm going to prove to you that you're good enough," Lucien grunts. "You've conquered everything I've given you. If you can win against me, you can take on the whole goddamn world, Princess. Now take this cock like a good fucking *slut*!" With the last word, he shoves fully to the hilt.

His hip bones slap against my ass, and I see stars. Constellations. Hell, galaxies. I think I discovered the meaning of life: anal sex.

"Fuck, yes, I can take it," I moan around the stick. "I'm a *good* slut."

He barely lets me accommodate him before he's riding my anus like I'm a mustang and I buck beneath him like the wild mare I am.

"Let me hear you say it," he demands. "Who are you?"

"I'm Sydney. Fucking. Sinclair," I growl around the stick.

"Fuck, if it's tight now, I can just imagine how tight that pussy is gonna be when I fuck it next," he groans, before slicing another cut into my back, this time near my shoulder, licking at his wound while he fucks me into the ground. "You're mine. All fucking *mine*," he growls.

All I can do is whimper as his words sweep across me like thousand dollar silk, his encouraging words and degrading actions melding into one mind-numbing explosion.

Everything burns. Everything hurts. But it also feels so fucking good. Synapses and nerve endings are firing off everywhere. I feel him *everywhere*. A second later, a moaning roar rips through me, dug from somewhere deep within my core. Tears flood my eyes, my vision blurring from the blinding pleasure.

"Oh my God, yes!" I scream to the heavens, coming harder than I have all night. The wooden bit falls from my mouth and my arms give out as I collapse to the ground.

A beat passes while we wait for our heart rates to slow and our breathing to return to normal, his body slumped over mine.

"You belong to me, right?" Lucien asks.

"Yes," I answer, my body languid and boneless as I come down.

He slowly pulls out of me, and I wince, feeling each nub of the rounded metal rods as they exit.

"Last chance," Lucien says. He draws in a long breath. "Is there *anything* you wouldn't let me do to you?"

"No." I don't even have to think about it. I prop myself back up to all fours.

"So, if I asked you to . . ." He pretends to think about something, but judging by his expression, he already has something in mind. "Would you let me pee on you? Would you let me mark you as mine right here in this forest so every living creature can know you've been claimed?"

"Yes." It's a soft whisper I'm not even sure I meant to say. But already it sounds more like the truth than anything else.

He moves to stand over me. "Speak up, Princess. Nice and loud, so the whole goddamn forest can hear you. Yes, you'll let me piss on you, or no?"

"Yes," I say a little louder this time. If I really thought about it, I'm sure I could talk myself out of it, but right now, at this moment, I want him to do it. I want every part of him I can get.

Staring down at me like he is, it's hard to discern his expression. He could be disgusted, intrigued, or turned on, but for all my efforts, I can't determine his face.

Shit, was he joking? Was this another test?

I open my mouth to take it back, but then he says, "Gotta say, I've never gotten to pee on a princess before. I'm actually kind of nervous." He cocks his head in an appraising way. "But I want you to really mean it, Sydney. If you want it, I want you to tell me you do. Beg for it."

That's so like him. Push you to your breaking point, then tell you to take one more step.

"Yes, Lucien—please, I want it. I want you . . . to pee on me."

Lucien stands up, his bloodied cock pointed at me. I bow my head and breathe through the haze of lust and deprivation.

If I thought I was a filthy whore before, I had no idea what I was talking about. Damp, tangled hair falls over my shoulders, cuts and bruises wrack my body, dirt sticks to my skin, arousal leaks from my pussy, and his warm piss trickles against my back, over my ass, down my pussy and my thighs to my knees that stick in the mud of our own making beneath me. I am *filthy*, but I am his, all fucking *his*.

@BladeSpinner
Online
What do
want
In life?
Seen
WTF! No
Haven't decided yet.

CHAPTER THIRTY-SEVEN

LUCIEN

WELL, FUCK ME SIDEWAYS and back. So this is how far she's willing to go. She actually let me piss on her. There's something so fucking sexy about that. I've never gone this far with anyone before, never wanted to. But having this level of trust, need, depravity swimming amongst the sea of intoxication between us is more than I can ever ask for. This girl was fucking made for me.

Sydney remains on all fours, looking out toward the trees. The moon is high, and her eyes glisten under its light, but she doesn't turn to look at me.

I crouch down to meet her gaze, only to find tearstains on her cheeks. It worries me for a second, but then I see her smile. I'm not used to feeling emotions like worry, because what's there to fear when I've already faced down death, when I've already lost so much, but she makes me feel things I never have before. She reminds me my life has meaning.

"That was perfect," she whispers, her blue gaze telling me I'm the reason her heart fucking beats.

"Aww, Princess, you did so fucking amazing. I'm so proud of you." Her eyes practically glow at my praise. They flutter closed when I cup her cheek, kissing her lips more tenderly than I've been with her at any point tonight, at any point in my life. She's worth being tender for.

"It's breathtaking," I murmur.

"What?" she asks. Her forehead bunches and it only makes my smile grow.

"How fucking beautiful you are."

She looks away, but I see the smile she's trying to hide from me. "Stop it, I look crazy," she says, trying to fix her hair when we both know she's only making it worse at this point.

"You look . . . perfect."

Her smile releases unbidden now as she picks at her tattered dress. She peers up at me, bites her kiss-swollen lip.

"Come on, let me help you." I tuck my hand underneath her arm and help her up, the unmistakable scent of urine flooding my senses and reigniting the heat between us. Every muscle in my body begs to sprint back to her place and reward all her efforts. I've won a lot of things over the years, but no victory has ever been sweeter than what I've accomplished tonight because now I get to fuck her and hold nothing back.

There's no masks, no hiding, just ourselves.

Sydney struggles to rise and I wince. Maybe I went a little overboard today with the games. I tuck my dick away, then crouching back down, I turn my back to her.

"All aboard the Lucien Express."

Her giggles crack something open inside me and the emotion that drips from the crevice almost brings me to my knees. I don't want to exist in a world where I don't get to hear that sweet giggle of hers. Where I don't get to see her smile.

I look over my shoulder in time to see her bend over to throw my official Bellemere hockey hoodie back on. Damn, I'm tempted to fuck her again seeing her sporting not just my clothing, but my fucking number that's etched on the sleeves and back of the hoodie. If I'm allowed to play in our next game, I'll have to make sure I get her in my jersey as well. Then there'll be no mistaking she's mine. I'll have her sit in my saved seats, and they'll no longer be empty or filled with strangers; they'll be hers. For now, the hoodie works. I'm glad she was smart enough to bring it, yet forgetful enough to leave her shoes. I chuckle as she climbs on.

"You'd better not be laughing at me," she gripes.

My grip tightens around her thighs like vices when she tries to ease herself off.

"Calm down." I bounce her up higher and she growls.

"I would never laugh at you," I say, my tone serious. The last thing I want is for her to ever feel ashamed of what she wants or what she likes. And I'll kill anyone who'd dare try and make her.

"So, what's so funny?" Her thighs are strong as shit and dig into my ribs as she tightens them around my torso. She swings her foot in a feeble attempt to kick me in the stomach, but I laugh at the fact that it's her bare feet that are trying to inflict the damage.

"I probably should have asked this sooner, but why the hell didn't you wear shoes out here? It's fucking freezing."

"Well, I hadn't exactly planned to be out here," she huffs. "I had them in my hand, but I guess I lost them with everything going on. Then I had to use them as a weapon to get that guy off me."

I go still, remembering how Sydney was in trouble, and I wasn't there to help.

"Relax, tough guy. Pretty sure they thought I was you or something since I was wearing your hoodie."

She waves her hand flippantly.

My brows fly up my forehead in a way that'd be comical if she could see my face.

"They thought I wore strappy Gucci heels?" I deadpan as I keep us moving forward.

"They're Louboutins," she corrects. "But I get your point. Either way, I had it handled. I totally beat that guy's ass!"

"Yeah, you sure did." I laugh again, harder this time. Harder still when she joins me, her earlier frustrations melted away, as we shuffle through the tall trees and brush.

"Thank you by the way," says Sydney, her lips whispering against the tops of my ear. It sends a zing through my body, the way her words touch me, even simple ones like 'thank you' soothes me as much as it makes me fucking hard.

"For what?" I'm so distracted by her breaths over my skin I honestly can't think of why she would be thanking me.

"For inviting me to the party. I had fun."

"Really?" I crane my head towards her, but she's not looking away like I expected. She's looking right at me.

"Yeah, back home I threw a lot of parties but I wasn't invited to many. Not since Maddie Jameson," she giggles.

"Who the hell is Maddie Jameson?"

Sydney's eyes narrow, amusement twinkling in her blue eyes.

"My real arch nemesis."

I face forward again, her laughter warming me as I carry us ahead.

By now it's not unexpected for us to fall into easy conversation as we walk. In the ten-minute span it takes to clear the forest, we talk about everything from the origin of the hockey stick to anime of all things. I open up some about my family and she tells me about her love of making things, which turns out is also something her dad hates about her.

I fucking hate that guy. I can't make any guarantees I won't punch him in his stupid fucking face if I ever see him. He's really done a number on her and, what's worse, she still talks about him with adoration, like she just accepts it because he's her dad. I hate hearing her talk about how her mom couldn't take it and left. She talks highly of her mom too, who apparently wasn't an awful mom before she left, just not up to the task of surviving their lifestyle and the people they'd surrounded themselves with.

By the time we're out of the woods, the street that leads to the arena is empty and quiet. The orange glow of the streetlamps barely illuminates the dark pathway, but we both know the area well, not that it would matter since Sydney is content with letting me carry her like the princess she is.

I'd happily be her carriage. Her footmen too, if she keeps letting me fuck her like that. She's no puck bunny, that's for sure. I'm actually pretty sure she doesn't even like hockey ,but a figure skater? Gotta say I did not see that in the cards for me. It reminds me . . .

"Hey Sydney," I start. "Don't take this the wrong way, but if competitive figure skating is something you've always wanted and loved, why are you giving it up so easily?"

Her body tenses against my back, but my hold on her remains firm.

"I'm not giving it up easily." She lets the word sit uncomfortably between us before speaking again. "They kicked me off of the team. I have no coach, no choreographer, no sponsors. Are you starting to get the picture? I didn't give up; I lost."

"So, do you need to be on a team? Can't you find your own coach or choreographer or whatever?"

"It's not that easy," she sighs. "You saw my practice; I'm not getting any better. After narrowly missing my shot at the Olympics a few years back, it's like I lost whatever magic I had left. I went from being the best, to hitting this plateau. And now . . . Now it just feels like I'm going backward."

"From what I saw, you were fantastic . . ."

"But?" Sydney pushes.

I hesitate, not wanting to kick her while she's down.

She sighs, jostling side to side to get my attention.

"Come on, I can tell when there's a but coming." I crane my neck to look at her. "It can't be any worse than what I've been told before."

I look back at the road, our turn coming up in a few blocks.

"But . . ." I continue. "There would be this moment of doubt in your head and fear in your eyes. You caved into it every time. You let the ice win."

"Yeah, you're probably right, but it doesn't matter anymore. It's over."

I want to say something else, to make her explain to me why it has to be over. If she wants to figure skate, she should, but it's then I notice the streets stop being so quiet. Swear to God, I don't have time for this shit. At this point I'm more eager than Sydney. I'm out of patience and I just want to get to Sydney's place and slip inside her.

I never cared that she was a virgin, it wasn't some deciding factor for me because I just love virgin pussies. What I do love is the concept of being her first, being woven into her life's story as the one she shared this memorable experience with.

But, we're about to get delayed again because I have a bad feeling about whoever is around this next corner. Stopping, I gently slide Sydney off my back.

"What's wrong?" Sydney asks.

"Stay behind me," I tell her, swooping her back with my arm.

I can tell she wants to ask more questions, but she clings to my back, understanding.

"Hand over your cash!" shouts a haggard middle-aged man, his hands mischievously covered in the pockets of his hard-worn jacket. I expect he'd like us to believe he has a weapon tucked away in that jacket of his, but instinct tells me that the only thing dangerous about this man is his body odor.

"You've got to be kidding me," I sigh. We're so close, right by the arena.

"I know who you are." He points the hand in his pocket toward us. "You're that hockey guy. I know you're loaded. Pay up."

I hang my head. I know I said no more hiding, but this might be a little too much for Sydney. She has a life, and now that I've decided to stay by her side, I do too.

"Sydney, I want you to run to the arena and wait for me," I say, keeping my eyes on the walking stench.

She fists my shirt, her nerves tangible in the chilled night air as she puffs heavy breaths. We both know what she's really nervous about. I'm a far bigger threat than this guy.

"But—"

"I mean it, Sydney! We're covered in dirt, it's getting late, and I will be fucking that virgin cunt of yours as soon as we get home, so I really really need you to listen and not fight me on this. Can you do that?"

My cock thickens when her mouth drops open, surprised that I said it aloud for our mugger to hear. If he weren't here I'd fill her mouth again for being so readily available to swallow me down but I need us back at her place as quickly as possible, so this unfortunate soul will have to be handled swiftly.

"Hey! I'm talking to you! This is no time for chit chat," shouts my newest victim.

"Okay, fine," Sydney huffs. "But don't take too long. I'll be in the locker room." She turns to walk away, but I grab her wrist before she can leave.

"Wait, why the locker room?" I ask her.

Even the mugger guy looks confused.

"Strangest thing," she retorts. "I let some guy pee on me in the woods. So, unlike you"—she pokes a sharp fingernail into my chest—"I'm covered in dirt and piss."

Her smart-mouthed tone is adorable when she's being sarcastic.

"What the fuck?" the guy mumbles.

I chuckle. She has a point there. I had no idea things would get so wild between us, but there are no regrets.

She starts taking a few steps toward the arena.

"Don't you need a key to get in?" I ask before she's too far away.

"Ah, shit," she mutters.

"It's fine." I toss her the key I keep on me and she catches it seamlessly in the air with one hand. Thank fuck these are my same jeans from yesterday. "I'll see you in a bit. I'm just gonna handle this one little thing and I'll be right there." I hold up a finger and Sydney rolls her eyes, eyes that beg me to do something about her little attitude. Her lips quirk into a sly smirk before she turns away.

"See you in a little bit," she echoes. "Try to behave yourself," she calls over her shoulder.

"I make no promises," I mutter.

I watch Sydney's hips sway from side to side as she saunters off, knowing that this dude is no match for me. I'm actually surprised she relented so easily since she's made it her new life's mission to prevent me from fighting any more, but I guess dirt in your ass trumps defending purse snatchers, or whatever this guy's supposed to be.

"Stop trying to be a fucking hero. I'll fuck you up!" The thief's voice wobbles even as he tries to sound menacing. He scratches at his face and alcohol permeates from his pores. My jaw sets, cracking as I work to keep calm.

I quickly assess my surroundings, searching the sleepy college campus that's quiet with all the activity happening up the hill. I stand with my hands in my pockets, peeking down one street, then the other.

"Look, I'm going to give you one chance, man." I warn, stepping farther into the alleyway. "I've had a very long night. I don't have any money and even if I did, I'm definitely not fucking giving it to you. So, walk away and I'll call us even."

"Not happening, Morningstar. If you don't give me something, I'm going to bring your little girlfriend back here and—"

He doesn't get to finish that statement. It's hard to spew threats when your vocal cords have been cut.

I step to the side to prevent the blood from spraying me too much but it's kinda too late. I sliced a major artery, so it gets everywhere. I heave a sigh as his body drops to the ground in an anticlimactic fashion.

Damn. I tried to warn him.

Wiping my blade on his pants, I return my blade to its holster along the back of my jeans.

Ah well, like I always say, you can't win 'em all.

But this might have to be my last win. My last kill. If I'm gonna be serious about keeping Sydney, and finally living my life instead of chasing death and sleep, then there can't be any more distractions.

I squat next to the dead bastard bleeding out at my feet, resting my chin in my hand. I give him one final study.

"Congratulations. You're my last," I sigh.

Standing, I give the street another quick perusal before heading toward the arena, whistling my favorite tune—Kill Bill.

ZAMBONI BREAK

LUCIEN

Four years ago

"JESUS, SLOW DOWN!" MY dad shouts at drivers who can't hear him. "Don't they know these roads can get dangerous at night? There's black ice everywhere. They should be more careful," he grumbles.

My mother rests a slender hand on his shoulder to calm him. "I know, sweetie, let's just get home before the kids die of hunger," she teases, looking back at us as if to prove we're withering away.

Of course, my little sister, Lilith, takes the opportunity to voice her demands,

"I'm starving," she whines, "let's stop and get McDonald's."

"Not this time, sweetie," my mom placates. "I'll whip up something special when we get home. The roads are getting dangerous and we're expecting to get a lot of snow tonight."

"Ooo! Snow? I *love* snow!" my sister exclaims.

I scoff, "What's so special about it? It snows here all the time."

It's already falling in chunks and sticking to the windows.

Lilith scrunches her nose at me, the tip as pink as the fuzzy ball on the hat she refuses to part with.

"Because it's pretty," she harrumphs, her tiny fists balled in defiance as she defends the weather's honor. "It's so fluffy and white and cold." She ticks off these things as though it somehow makes snow the most special substance known to man. Her wide eyes are in awe as she leans forward in her seat, watching it float down and stick to the trees. It builds quickly, melding with the snow that must have fallen the day before.

"It's frozen dirt particles that fall from the sky," I counter.

She sticks her tongue out and blows a raspberry at me. "Hmph. You're no fun."

"She's right, you know," calls my dad from the front seat. "That's a pretty cynical way of thinking, son," he teases.

"What we call cynical might be his version of observant," interjects Mom. "I'm glad you know something like that, honey. You learn something new every day," Mom grins over her shoulder at me and winks. I can't help but meet her grin with my own. That's Mom, seeing the good even in the cynical.

"Well, I love snow," grumbles Lilith.

I chuckle.

"I'm not saying you can't love it, Lil," I nudge her with my elbow. "Even dirt can be loveable," I tease.

Her head cocks to the side. "Are you trying to say I'm dirt?"

The whole car erupts into laughter.

"What's so funny?" she whines. "I wanna laugh too. What'd I say?"

I'm holding my stomach at her expression. She looks so confused. I forget how innocent seven-year-olds can be.

"You're not dirt, Lil," I chuckle.

"What am I then?" she pushes.

"You're *sweet*, like candy," I offer, ruffling her dark hair.

"Aww," my mom and sister say at the same time. My mom with her hand over her heart, and Lilith back in good spirits.

"My sweet boy, you're such a good big brother."

"That's my boy," my dad grunts in agreement, though I suspect he's just as choked up as Mom is right now. What is it about the holidays that makes everyone so emotional?

"So, does this mean you're going to play with me when we get home?" Lilith asks. "I wanna play Go Fish."

"Nice try," I call out, seeing her gambit for what it is. "I'm busy."

She huffs, flopping back into her seat with her arms folded. "You're always busy."

"I'm a busy guy," I drole.

"You just wanna stay up and play with Trevor. Why do you like him so much better than me?" she asks, her bottom lip doing that trembling thing that makes me uncomfortable.

Oh crap, she'd better not cry. Dad will kill me.

"I don't like him *better* than you," I say. "He's my best friend. You'll understand when you're older."

That seems to stop her from crying, but now she looks as if she wants to smack me.

"C'mon, play one game with your sister," Mom chimes in.

"But she cheats!" I exclaim.

"I do *not*."

"She's just a kid," explains my dad.

My point exactly.

"So, I should let her cheat?" I grumble back.

To his credit, my father is as patient as they come, especially when it comes to me and all my . . . quirks. Pulling up to a red light, he turns around in his seat.

"No, son, you shouldn't *let* her cheat, but maybe you could teach her how to play the *right* way, so she doesn't break all the rules."

I roll my eyes. "But I'm supposed to be on the game with Trev in like twenty minutes. We finally found a way to unlock the bonus level in the zombie's lair."

He blinks at me. Saying it out loud sounds really dumb and lame, but we're like *this* close to clearing the whole game.

"What is it with fifteen-year-olds and killing things?" chides my dad.

"Zombies deserve to die, Dad, they *eat* people!" I reason.

"Right, my bad. How could I forget you were ignoring your sister's wishes for the fate of the world?" he deadpans.

"That's not—"

He smirks, knowing he's got me.

Way to make me feel guilty, Dad.

The light changes and he shifts back around. He's about to drive forward again when a car swerves in front of us, honking and cursing out his window as he skids along the road, throwing up his middle finger.

My dad's bad mood returns ten-fold, and he grumbles some more. "*What* is the rush? Why is everyone in such a hurry these days?"

"It's Christmas," my mom shrugs, unbothered with the delay if it means spending more time together.

"You would think that'd mean people would slow down, take their time, enjoy the scenery." My dad thrusts his arm out, arching it to showcase all the current 'scenery.' Though, I don't see a thing but snow.

"Wishful thinking, sweetheart," my mom chuckles, her hand sweeping over his broad shoulder in small circles again as he gradually calms back down. The woman is half his size, but you wouldn't know it the way she gets the big guy to chill. My father would be a force to reckon with if his road rage ever left the car, but ask my mom, and she'll tell you he's her own personal teddy bear.

"Yeah, I guess you're right." He looks back at us to make sure we're okay and then does a double take as he leisurely travels at a safe pace down the single-lane street that leads to our house on the mountain. "Put your seatbelt on, son."

He always says that when we turn onto this street. It's a winding, curving road that leads up to the residential neighborhoods that are on the mountain. I'd never admit it aloud, but I like our winter cabin up here, and I like that we're going to be away from the city for a while. Mom and Dad will be home and they won't be working so hard. We can go skating on the lake like we used to before dad's new job, and I can show them how good I've gotten at hockey. I'm officially the fastest guy on my team, plus my goal average has gone up.

"What is this guy doing?!" Dad shouts, honking the horn at his latest road adversary. I go back to looking out the window, watching the bare trees pass by, and the crystallization of ice that forms on the corners of the window. It fogs as I breathe against the glass.

Everything mostly passes in a blur as I count the seconds before we're home and I can play the game with Trevor—and I guess a game of Go Fish too.

"What's that sign mean?" Lilith points to a yellow sign on the side of the road.

'BEWARE OF BLACK ICE' it reads.

"It's a warning sign about the black ice on the streets," I explain.

"What's black ice?" she asks.

"It's, um, a translucent ice that builds up on the roads when the temperature drops like this. It causes the roads to go slick and—

Everything is dark.

It takes a long time before I realize it's because my eyes are closed, and it takes even longer for me to open them. My eyelids are so heavy. I don't remember being this tired.

When they flutter open, I still see darkness, but a different kind. I see the night sky and floating white specks. Snow.

"Ah," I wince, jolting upright and looking down at my knee that's caked in blood, but staunched by the snow. I reach my shaking hand to my leg, wrapping it under my knee to hold it up. I can bend it, so it's not broken.

I look around, searching the unfamiliar area. Where am I and why is it so quiet?

After a brief sweep, I note I'm no longer in the car like I'm supposed to be, I'm at the bottom of an embankment. I reach out to push myself up only to hiss in pain when I feel something sharp dig into my palm. I draw it to my face for a closer look. Glass. It's embedded in my hand. I realize it's all over me, and the ground around me. A trail of it leads all the way to the top of the road that I can no longer see. Shit, I fell far.

My blood runs cold. I fell?

I follow the trail of glass, but panic as I stumble over rocks I can't see and hidden tree roots. My hands and feet clamor for purchase. I can't hear a thing. Why is it so quiet? And where is everybody? I hold my injured hand to my head and smack my temple. It creates an echoing slap, but at least that's something.

I finally reach the top of the hill, straining to stand before I shout, "Hello!"

But there's nothing.

Snow falls and the wind whispers, but it doesn't whistle or roar. I clear the trees, reaching the road a few short feet away only to find our car crumpled like a soda can. I limp to the wreckage, realizing too late I can't move very fast and fall onto the hood. I bring my head up, clinging to the car as I struggle to keep upright, and stare at the scene before me.

What am I feeling? Shock? Is this real? What *is* this?

This . . . this isn't right. This is . . . this is a . . . bad dream. Yeah, that's it. I fell asleep in the car and I'm dreaming. I'll just wake up. Lilith will wake me up like she always does, in the most obnoxious way possible. I won't even get mad this time because this dream sucks. It's a nightmare.

I close my eyes, allowing the darkness to free me from the light. The light is lying. It's showing me things that aren't real. I open them again and I fall back against the hood, lightheaded and sick.

They're . . . They're all . . .

Why do they look like that? Why do they look like *that*, and I look like . . . I focus on my reflection in the cracked windshield, shifting my view from what's on the other side to what's reflected back at me. Splintered pieces all showing me the same thing.

Why do *I* look perfectly fine? There's not a scratch on me save for my scraped knee and glass-filled palm. I'm . . . perfectly fine.

"Help!" a voice shouts.

My head snaps up trying to trace the voice.

"H-help," I hear someone slur, but the bodies in my car are unmoving. I peer around the broken vehicle I once shared to find a Civic with the passenger door hanging off its side. The driver's side door is completely gone. In the driver's seat sits a man in an ugly Christmas sweater with blood seeping from his nose. He's slumped toward where the door used to be and his throat bobs as he swallows. I hear him stutter for help again.

"Help-p," he drawls. He sounds funny. I walk over to his car, my feet moving of their own accord. I feel numb, like I'm floating or sleepwalking. I'm shivering too, but I don't actually feel cold. I don't feel *anything*. Even the tingles have stopped. The snow is coming down hard and I feel the sharp bite of the air nipping at my skin but none of it feels real.

"Oh, hey," he chuckles. "Evening, officer," he slurs.

His breath hits me with a sharp kick. He reeks of alcohol, and I can see barf on his ugly sweater. He tries to move, pushing himself up to get out, but his seatbelt is stuck over his chest.

As in, so embedded into his flesh it's cutting him.

His floorboards are covered in empty bottles and in his hand is a clear bottle of liquor that's broken at the neck, like his hand locked around it and he couldn't let it go.

My eyes reach his, and though he's breathing, I can tell this man is already dead inside.

I point to his car that's been rammed through by the guard rail, almost splitting the car in half.

"Did you do this?"

It doesn't even sound like me but it is. I sound like my dad when he reprimands us.

"Help me," the man groans, his tone impatient, like he's *expecting* me to help him and wondering what the holdup is.

"I asked you a question. Did you *do* this?" I look between the wreckage of our cars, from my parents back to him. "Is all of this *your* fault?"

His eyes are barely open, and I can tell he has no idea what's going on.

"I'm innocent, officer," he stutters. "He ran into *me*."

Fire consumes me, a red hot heat that engulfs me from the inside despite the freezing cold around us.

"*What* did you just say?" I seethe.

My dad is the world's safest driver. The man who *insists* on driving five miles under the speed limit and gets on my case every day about wearing a seatbelt. I'm almost sixteen and he still makes me wear a helmet when I ride my bike. He won't let me practice hockey without a cage helmet on, even when my friends get to. This piece of shit wants to blame MY dad?

I wrench the broken bottle from his hand and cut him loose from the seatbelt, throwing him on the ground with a heavy thud. He groans and he's bleeding from other places judging by the amount of blood, but I don't know where. I don't plan to find out.

He's laid out like a starfish, mumbling incoherently and gurgling.

I look at him with no sympathy, no feelings at all.

I should call for help, or panic. I should *do* something. But what can I do? The damage is done, right? I look down at the disgusting shit-for-brains below me. This is his fault.

"You did this. It's all *your* fault!"

I bend my unscraped knee and settle it onto his heaving chest. His eyes bug out and he's bleeding from his mouth. There's a soft hiss in the air from his car that I hadn't caught before, but the sound is swallowed by the night air. Snow keeps falling and it sticks to everything, burying this terrible moment beneath frozen dirt.

"This is all your fault," I repeat as I continue pushing, applying more and more weight. "Your fault."

He coughs and splutters, but he doesn't fight me or try to shake me off. I don't think he can anymore. I bring my face closer to his and his eyes lock onto mine as I pinch his nose.

"You can't be saved," I whisper, leaning down for him to hear. "I won't *let* you."

When he stops moving, I rise. Heading back to our car, I slip through the broken back window, and slide back into my spot. The empty spot I vacated when I was thrown from the car because I *didn't* put on my seatbelt like Dad asked.

I look over to my little sister, buckled safely like she's supposed to be.

"Lilith . . ." I reach over and tap her on the shoulder, but she doesn't answer me.

"Lil?" Her head rests on the back of the seat, her hair covering her face. I reach out to brush it behind her ear, but freeze, rubbing her arm instead.

"You must be freezing," I mutter, looking around for her fuzzy pink hat.

She doesn't move.

"Look, it's snowing," I urge her to look, but she doesn't move.

The silence is deafening. Mind-bending and ear-splitting quiet that eats away at me every second I'm forced to endure it.

I rub her again. "Hey, don't leave me, okay? Y-you still hungry? I can take you to McDonald's. We'll stuff our faces with all of the chicken nuggets you want. I won't even care if you slather them in barbeque sauce. I still prefer ketchup but . . ." I sniffle, laying my head on her lap. "We can get whatever you want, okay?"

There's no response.

"Okay?" I ask again.

"Lil, please say something." I scoff, working to see if teasing her will wake her up.

"C'mon, is this because you think I called you dirt? Because I swear I didn't mean it. It's the snow. The stupid . . . *fucking* snow."

I snivel, rubbing the snot from my running nose. "I'm sorry. I'll put a quarter in the swear jar, two, if you wake up."

My nose continues to run but it dawns on me too late that it's not just snot on my jacket. It's blood. I feel another trickle on my forehead and my vision goes blurry. I wipe my face with the back of my hand, staring at the bright red smear. I know for a fact that it's not me that's bleeding. Some of it is probably that guy's, but the rest of it . . . is hers.

More blood spills on me, soaking into my clothes. It's warm, comforting in a way as I lie here.

"I don't want to be alone. Please don't leave me alone," I whisper.

Tears, blood, and snot streak my face.

"You can't leave me here. No one understands me like you."

I force myself to laugh, "People suck and you're kinda cool when you wanna be. So how about it, huh? Let's get out of here."

Silence. "I'll play all the games you want, and I won't even complain . . . just please wake up."

More silence.

"Please . . . *please,*" I plead.

Not even the wind responds.

I blow a shaky breath. "Okay, okay then. How about this? If you can't stay with me . . . I'll stay with you. Take me with you. We can play then."

LUCIEN

Two days ago

I can't seem to find my little stalker. What's even more annoying is that they can't seem to find me. It's been radio silence all day. All day I've gone without them sending a GIF, sharing some weird trending video or asking me some existential question about life.

I've grown accustomed to their complete lack of boundaries and social awareness. I like their creepy little habit of following me to class every day and their uncanny ability to be more on time to my practice than I am. By the time my skates hit the ice during my private practice, I can feel their presence, my own guardian angel. Except today, I haven't sensed them anywhere.

Lucien 12:04 AM

Hello

@thereallucifer

Hey you there?

@thereallucifer

Come out come out wherever you are

@therealIucifer

You wouldn't be ignoring me, now would you?

Lucien 1:11AM

You up?

Lucien 10:36 AM

Have you been kidnapped?

If you have, I swear to God I'll go full Taken on their ass.

Wow, nothing? Not even an 'lol' huh?

Then I do something neither of us have ever done; I call.

It rings and rings. For a second, I swear I can hear ringing outside.

An obnoxious chime blares through the phone.

"We're sorry, the number you have dialed is not accepting calls at this time. Please hang up and try again."

Are they done with me?

I send one more text.

@therealIucifer

Why are you hiding from me?

SYDNEY

I need to leave him alone.

@therealIucifer

Why are you hiding from me?

He's better off without me. And if I want to dispel any rumors about us, then I need to keep my distance. I wanted a whirlwind romance, not to trap him into a relationship based on lies and rumors. That would have been step one if I was a conniving bitch like Tiffany, but I'm not. I'm scared.

I'm scared he won't want me like I want him. Even if he did, we'd be torn apart like we are now. I'm missing practices, and Father would *never* approve. I should let him go.

I walk across the quad, looking ahead as Lucien walks with his head down, his face in his phone. Someone calls his name and he looks up to give them a nod and a wink.

He's the big man on campus, so I'm not too surprised. But I wonder . . . can they see what I see? Can they see the bags under his eyes? Can they see the veins in his hands protruding as he grips his phone? Can they see the red in the whites of his eyes? He's fuming. Mere moments from shattering apart.

I know that look of being on the cusp. I continue walking in his direction. I'm not hiding in a hoodie today, not even a hat, just my regular puffer jacket, cute jeans, and my favorite pair of Balenciaga ankle boots. My shoulder brushes his as I walk past him, soaking in the last bit of contact we'll ever have.

"My bad," he mutters, when he realizes we've bumped into each other, but his focus is on his phone as he continues on, his fingers flying over his screen as he texts.

I pause, but my phone dings.

I see Lucien from the corner of my eye, whirling around, but I'm already walking away. With every forced step, I keep moving forward, leaving him behind.

It's only when I make it to the rink that I take the risk to look at the message on my phone.

@thereallucifer

If you're hiding, I'll find you. Prepare yourself, Little Stalker. I love this game.

I'm panting, sweat coating every inch of my skin as I fight for breath. I've skated harder today than usual, and my heart is pounding. But it's not enough. Racing across the ice, I go again, speeding through my cues, flying through my moves. It's sloppy, uncoordinated, and I'm too late in some areas while too early on others.

Not good enough.

I go again.

Sloppy.

I fall.

You'll never be enough. You'll never win like that.

I fall again, screaming in frustration when my ass hits the ice.

You'll never make it to the fucking Olympics.

I squeeze my head, trying to block out the noise, but it keeps coming.

Last chance. You're going to lose everything. It's not worth it. You need to be lighter. You need to be faster. You need to be stronger. You don't belong here. This is a waste of your time. It's too late.

Every negative thought has a different voice. It trades off between my dad, Tiffany, my coach, my trainers, Regina, and even my own voice.

"Sydney? Sydney, are you okay?" a soft voice that differs from all the others calls out my name. "Sydney, look at me. Breathe." I blink up to see Hannah staring down at me, her auburn hair strewn atop her head in a messy bun, several tendrils have fallen and are blown across her face like she ran here.

"What are you doing?" I ask, realizing she's helping me off of the ice slab.

She braces a hand under my forearm, gently lifting me before she softly glides over to the exit, holding my hand.

"What happened? She fall again?" Regina scoffs from the bench.

I glare at her as we step off the ice.

"Now, now, no need for us to be nasty," Tiffany chimes from next to Regina. "Sydney can't help it if she's clumsy. It's an unfortunate circumstance for someone who made it *all* the way to qualifiers when she was in her prime. Sadly, that time has passed, but we should still show her *some* sympathy. It's gotta suck being a has-been still struggling to get back on top."

"That's enough, you guys," says Hannah. "We all fall sometimes. It's normal to—" She throws up right next to their feet.

"Eww! What the fuck? Watch it, Hannah," gripes Regina.

Hannah gags again before running to the bathroom, and it's a miracle I'm not struck by lightning with the hope that soars in my chest. If she's sick again, I can compete at Nationals. I'll have my shot.

"Ugh, disgusting," Regina comments.

"Well, look at that," Tiffany snaps with a smirk. "Seems you might get your second chance after all." She turns to walk away with Regina.

I was taught not to leave anything to chance, so why settle for a *possibility* when I can have a *guarantee*? Tiffany has caused me enough problems. I'm sick of it. If she goes away, all my problems go with her. Without Tiffany in my way I can go to Nationals. I'll win and I'll never have to hear her disdain-filled commentary again. I relish the thought even as I finish showering and get dressed to leave.

An idea forms, taking root as I brace myself against the wall at the top of the arena steps. A certain peace settles over me when I hear her condescending voice echoing in the stairwell as she talks animatedly on the phone. I peek over the side of the top landing to make sure she's alone, that she's not with Regina.

The echoes of her footsteps grow louder, and my insides start to crackle. I'm on the verge of shattering.

But you're a good person.

I hear her footfalls slow to nothing.

Spinning around, I turn the corner with my hands out, bracing as our bodies collide. The collision is too fast and hard to stop. Her shriek echoes, burning when it hits my ears, and I hear a mind-numbing crack that makes me flinch. My heart beats a mile a minute but then stops, along with time and space itself when I hear a harsh smack against the concrete floors. Blood stains the blue and white steps of our alma mater and the building tilts as I sway.

I whip my hand out to grip the railing, white knuckling the bar so hard I almost slip and fall with her. Bile doesn't just rise, it spews over the side as I fail to contain my reaction to the scene below me.

Twelve steps below, where I expect to see Tiffany in a halo of blond hair and blood, I see auburn hair and chocolate eyes. Tiffany is nowhere in sight.

My shaking hand rises to my mouth, holding in the scream that threatens to tear with me.

You're not *a good person.*

I fumble to pull out my phone.

"Hello? 9-1-1?" I sob.

You're a terrible person.

"Please. Send help." My voice shakes as badly as my hands.

Fucking monster.

"There's been an . . . accident," I breathe.

@BladeSpinner
Online

What do you want

In life?

Seen

WTF. No

Haven't decided yet.

CHAPTER THIRTY-EIGHT

LUCIEN

Present

I REACH THE ARENA a few minutes later to find Sydney exactly where she said she'd be: in the shower. A part of me wants to take a moment to stare at her from afar, to linger and watch as she's done to me countless times. But before I know it, I'm removing my clothes and joining her, not settling for watching. I want to *take*. Need it.

She doesn't flinch at my presence as I slide in behind her, my bloody clothes discarded at the bench. My naked body wraps around hers. She leans into me, letting her head fall back and rest against my chest. I love that she's more comfortable than she was when we showered together earlier.

Eyes closed, lashes clumped, the water softly pelts her face. She's gorgeous. Unlike earlier tonight, she's unbothered and relaxed even as I graze my bloodied fingers across her wet skin, stroking up and down her arms.

"Did you knock that idiot out?" she asks, straightening up to push the water through her hair.

I do the same and the water runs red against the light blue penny tiles as if washing away my transgressions.

"Yeah, sure did," I say.

She laughs. "What's that make? Six guys tonight?"

"Somewhere around there," I mutter.

Not sure if death counts as a knockout, but I chuckle all the same that she's been keeping count.

She spins away from the spray, facing me with a smile so bright I'd swear the sun was jealous. Then she catches sight of me, and her smile turns upside down.

"Is that *blood*?" she screeches, eyes blinking rapidly and brows smushed together in concern.

"Well..." I don't want to lie to her.

"And why is there *so much* of it?" she questions. "Are you *okay*? Are you *hurt*?"

She's swiping her hands all over my body, trying to find the source, but it's all washing away. My abs clench as I try to keep from laughing. Her hands are so tiny. And I'm ticklish.

"It's not mine," I admit.

Her mouth opens to respond, but then she closes it, deciding against whatever it was she was about to say.

She stares at me for a long moment while questions tumble through my mind.

She breaks eye contact first. Pulling my hand closer to her face, she inspects the damage, much like she did when we were in her kitchen.

She tuts. "You've gotta be more careful, Lucien."

The way she pins me with those fucking cracked eyes, stuns me. There's so much feeling and I don't know what to do with it all. "I obviously didn't bother stopping you this time, but you can't fight every person you have a problem with, okay?"

I pull my hand back and rake it through my hair, rinsing out more blood.

"Why not?" I ask, the question genuine because I don't understand why she's been so adamant about this.

She searches my eyes with a sigh.

"Who would fight my demons if I lost you?" she asks.

I grip her chin and tilt her head back.

"You could never lose me."

She clears her throat, her gaze ping-ponging between my eyes as we stare at one another.

"I . . ."—she shakes her head—"I will if you get in more trouble. I want you to promise me you'll be more careful and think about the people who care about you before you do anything crazy."

I cock a grin.

"When it comes to you, I'm always crazy."

"Nice try." She smirks up at me, pointing at me with her chipped blue nail. She swirls her finger in a circle around me. "You were crazy *way* before me."

"Perhaps," I shrug, "but I'm crazy *about* you now, remember?"

"Smooth. Real smooth." She looks away, nibbling on her decimated thumb. "But yeah, I'm pretty crazy about you too."

Something like a shiver causes her to flinch and she drops her thumb, but she turns her face back toward the spray, holding it there as if she's trying to waterboard herself.

"Everything alright?" I try to bring her face back to mine, but she pulls away. I don't like it. I want her undivided attention.

"Hey, look at me. What's wrong?"

I turn her by her shoulders, but she resists.

"It's . . . nothing." Her smile is small and gentile but unconvincing.

"C'mon, Princess," I say. "Let me in. Talk to me. That's all I actually wanted from you tonight. So please, don't chicken out on me now. Not when I know how brave you really are."

She scoffs a derisive laugh, turning to face me, but her head is down, looking at my chest.

"I'm not brave," she says.

"Really? Because I've seen lesser men cry after everything I've put you through tonight." I grimace a little at the realization I pushed her really hard for her first time. I should have tried holding back more.

"It's not that," she says. "I just . . . I didn't expect to feel this way. I didn't expect this night to be so . . ."

"Crazy?" I offer.

"Perfect," she finishes instead. "*Too* fucking perfect." Her forehead rests against my chest, hiding what sounds like embarrassment, but I already knew her feelings were strong. As strong as my own. It's why it'll last with her.

"I'm not hearing the problem." She draws back and her eyes flick from my lips to my eyes—the connection I've been seeking, solidified—when she lets me see that yearnful look on her face. She arches to her toes and kisses me, her hands pressing against my chest. It's soft at first, a tickle on my lips before it deepens, turning ravenous, like she can't get enough, like she'll *never* have enough. She pushes me until my back hits the wall, the thud echoes, and the steam grows thicker as the temperature rises.

I'm about to hoist her up to straddle me so I can fuck her against this shower wall when she drops to her knees, fisting my cock that's been at half-mast since I walked in. Her warm mouth wraps around me, and I nearly go blind. How is it already so much better than the first time? She sucks and teases, swirling her tongue over my crown and using it to flick the jewelry. I look down at her wide-eyed, somewhat surprised by her skill.

"What?" She grins. "Practice makes perfect, and I don't half-ass my training. *Plus* . . ." She licks the underside of my balls, the perfect picture of sin if ever I saw one. "I'm a fast learner," she mentions before sucking me down her throat again.

Fuck, she feels amazing, the way she pulls and sucks, keeping her thrusts shallow and focusing on the tip. She's playing with me. I can tell she's not sucking in earnest, not yet.

I grab her head, roaming my fingers over the scar hidden beneath. She lets me. The soft strands of her wet hair weave around my fist, my fingers tangled as she bobs back and forth in slow, deliberate strokes that keep my orgasm teetering on a razor's edge.

"Now who's being the tease?" I jest.

I can feel her lips curling into a smile.

"Captain warned you about teaching me bad habits," she teases, sliding my head back and forth over her tongue, looking too confident for her own good. I fist the coil of hair in my hand and pull, loving the control it gives me as I fight to not give in to her sinful tongue.

"The difference between me and Trevor is I know how to *correct* bad behavior," I rasp.

She whimpers when I pull harder. But then her lips twitch upward into a salacious grin.

"Then tell me how you want it, Master. I aim to please."

Oh, fuck me. I'm a goner. I spin us around so quick her back smacks the wall and I shove my cock to the back of her throat so hard her nails dig into my thighs. I'm sure at least one breaks flesh, but I don't relent.

With her head pinned between the shower wall and my pelvis, I grip her wrists, suspending them above her head before I go to town fucking her throat. She chokes a little and has to adjust, but eventually she picks up the new rhythm, relaxing her throat and calming the urge to fight back. She submits and takes every brutal thrust until she's screaming around my cock and swallowing every single drop I pump into her.

"I can't wait to be inside you," I breathe. I'm going to be dehydrated with the number of orgasms she's elicited from me today.

She licks her lips, swiping a bead of cum from the corner of her mouth. It's the most seductive thing I've ever seen.

"Then I guess we should go," she retorts, rising to her feet with all the grace of a real princess. Probably due to those sexy calves of hers.

She places a chaste kiss against my lips, and I almost lose control and fuck her against these tiles anyway, but now that we're back at the arena—basically right back where we started—there's something on my mind that I can't get out. She's so much calmer now. More comfortable, less irritated, less burdened. She said that figure skating was over for her and that she felt she wasn't improving, but in the hours I've spent with her even I can tell she's not that girl anymore.

I kiss her again. "One last thing."

"No." She swipes her arms in an X motion. "No more things," she whines, coming off her tiptoes to rest beneath my chin.

"Please, just one. For me."

I manifest the best puppy dog eyes I can manage, mimicking Trevor as best I can. It must work because she relents. "What is it?"

Her little hip cocks out and her lips curl into a placating smile.

"I want you to try to do your routine again."

"Right *now*?" she squeaks, her smile falling.

"Yes. Right now," I nod, not bothering to hide my excitement. This might be the very best idea I've ever had.

Sydney looks at me like I'm crazy.

"But *why*?"

I want to prove to her she can do it. That she doesn't need to give up figure skating. That she can have both.

"I have a theory," I say.

"A *theory*?"

"Yes. Just, please, will you do it?" I'm not one to beg, but I *am* willing to compromise. "Come on, I'll even do it with you."

Her shoulders drop and I can tell I've won.

"You mean it? You'll skate with me?" she asks.

"Yes, of course I'll skate with you." It's been fun and games with us for the most part of the evening, but something about this feels significant. Like we'll be changed forever once we step out onto that ice together.

She contemplates for a moment, her tongue rolling inside her cheek, but she doesn't bring her thumb to her mouth which tells me she's not nervous to do this with me. She *wants* to skate with me.

"You know we're gonna get sick from all this exposure to cold air," she counters.

"So? I'll take care of you. I'll bring you soup and blow your nose, just come on. Trust me on this."

It's the brief sigh that lets me know I got her hook, line, and sinker.

"Okay then, fine." She turns off the water and reaches for one of the school's towels overhead. "But you're gonna have to help me break into Tiffany's locker."

"Why?"

I shake my hair dry, whipping my head back and forth like a wet animal. She squeals from all the water flying everywhere, "Because . . ."

she laughs, drying herself off while I wait for her to finish. "She and I wear the same skate size . . ." She holds out the towel for me to use too since I was too focused on joining her to grab one. "And because she's a massive thunder cunt who deserves to have her locker broken into."

Her arms fold like this is the final make or break condition to yet another detour.

I shrug, grinning at any opportunity to enact vengeance no matter how benign.

"Makes sense to me. Let's rob that bitch."

After some serious finessing, we finally get Tiffany's locker open, and Sydney all laced up in Tiffany's skates. Thank fuck I didn't have to break into Trevor's locker. I already had his locker combo so I welcomed myself to his hockey skates and a clean shirt. He'll get rid of the bloodied one.

We stand on the ice, almost in the exact place we were before. Though, by the way she's staring at my skates, you'd think this was the first time we've done this.

It's deja vu for me, but to her, it's like I'm sullying her rink. She points to my feet.

"You realize those aren't ice skates, right?"

"Yeah, well, they're all I got right now."

She groans. "Fine, but you'd better not slow me down."

I hold my hands up in surrender.

"I won't. You have my word. Best behavior." I pull my phone out and play the song I heard her playing earlier, making sure to connect it to the Bluetooth speakers over the arena since she destroyed her boombox.

I wonder what Old Man Bernie thought about finding a shattered boombox on the ice when he came in earlier.

"You know the song?" Sydney questions.

I set the phone on the ledge of the rink and skate back over to her. "Yeah, I looked it up after watching you replay it so many times."

Her face contorts. "How much did you see?"

I keep my face neutral, not wanting to plant any more seeds of doubt than she already has.

"Enough." I skate around her in large circles, letting the music play and float over the ice. There's nothing quite like skating over fresh ice. The Zamboni has made the ice smooth again since our time earlier tonight and it feels amazing.

Sydney relaxes, swaying to the music as well as she follows my lead. We don't dive right into her routine, and I don't change the music back when another song starts to play. I don't even distract her with more talking, I let the quiet in and focus on the sounds of our skates slicing through the ice and our heavy breathing as we skate around each other, beside each other. I've never felt more alive and at peace than I do now, skating with her like this.

She busts a few moves, feeling good enough to show off a little, and I do the same.

Her eyes brighten as she stares at me, shocked that I managed to do something to impress her.

"How are you so good at this?" Sydney asks, loud enough to echo as we keep our momentum.

"I would think it's essential for most hockey players to know how to ice skate," I retort, my brow quirking with amusement.

She skates circles around me.

"You know what I mean. Figure skating and hockey are different."

"I know."

I grin, captivated by the look on her face.

She looks fascinated, like she truly can't believe it. "Even in hockey skates you're . . . amazing."

I speed up and swing around her, leading her back by her hips as she follows in sync. I bring my lips to her ear.

"I never said I didn't know how to figure skate, you only *assumed* I didn't," I chide.

She brings her leg up, leaning deeper into me as she points her skates to the sky. Her calf is eye-level with me, and my hands grab at it instinctively. She doesn't struggle to hold the position and she's fluid when she turns out of my grasp.

I pull her back to me, hoisting her up then spinning her around a couple of times.

"Keep going," I rasp into the shell of her ear.

We didn't get to dance at the party, and we spent more time fighting and fucking than we did anything else. I like it better this way though, and something tells me she does too.

She does a small spin, a pirouette. I copy her and she gives me a look like she's impressed. We do it again in sync, landing on the ice.

"How did you do that?" she gawks.

I hum, thinking back to how often I used to ice skate as a kid with my mom and sister. I don't hate the memory this time. It's a happy one.

"I can't do too many difficult tricks in these, but I can do some," I respond, lifting my foot to gesture to my skates. They're not designed to do tricks without the toe pick, but it's a basic physics problem. One that can be solved if you know what you're doing.

"You have no idea how talented you are, do you?" she shakes her head, but her mouth is stretched into the brightest smile I've ever seen. She's having fun and she's happy . . . with me.

"That's what I'm trying to show you, Sydney," I explain. "Stop worrying about being good enough, or falling, or what your dad thinks, or your team thinks. If you want to be the best, then be the best. You know the routine and if you ever feel like you're going to fall, know I'll be there to catch you."

I skate a little farther away, making sure to give her plenty of room as I leave her in the middle.

Returning to my phone on the wall, I give her a minute to steady her breathing and get in the right mindset.

"Just skate," I shout over to her, tapping my thumb on the screen to play her song again.

Sydney postures in position, waiting for her cue.

Her eyes are so damn expressive, and like ice, one look is never the same. There's fear, yes, but determination too. When she starts this time, pushing off her toe pick with only the power and grace a figure skater can, there's no hesitation or doubt. If anything, there's fire and passion.

I watch her in awe, amazed by how she's moving. I could tell early on that her dreams of making it to the Olympics weren't a pipe dream. It's something she's actually capable of if she'd get out of her own way. If she only had someone believe in her.

"That's it," I shout. "Keep going. Skate with your whole fucking heart, your whole goddamn body. Let the ice take you, *feel* it, Sydney."

I'm so enamored in watching her move and keeping up with her that I don't realize I've ventured too close, and we're back to skating together. She doesn't mind though, and she doesn't stop. My body moves with her, and she moves with mine. In fact, she skates with even more confidence. I don't have her moves memorized or anything, but I ebb and flow as she does, anticipating her movements, and dodging her attacks. It's like fighting, or fucking, there's a communication between us.

And when we reach the point where she kept falling earlier tonight, I watch in pure amazement as she flies through the sky, spins four times and lands beautifully right into my arms.

CHAPTER THIRTY-NINE

SYDNEY

IT TAKES A WHILE for me to come down from the high of that performance. I'm so riled up that by the time my apartment is within view again I still have goosebumps.

"I can't tell you the last time I've done a performance that beautiful, Lucien. You don't know what it means to me that you skated with me like that. I thought . . . I really thought I lost it, you know? That whatever skill I had in the past was a fluke. I *convinced* myself that everyone who said I was good lied to me. That making it to the Olympic qualifiers was a stroke of luck and good timing. I lied to myself, telling myself that my dad was right and that I never should have pursued figure skating in the first place." I'm babbling, but I can't hold back my excitement.

Lucien grabs me by the forearm, only to slide his large hand into mine.

"You're *more* than good, Sydney," he says. "You could be the *greatest*. Don't ever let those who don't believe in your talent distract you. Next time there's a million voices in your head telling you that you can't do it, listen to my voice that says, 'Sydney Fucking Sinclair can do anything she puts her mind to.'"

I scrunch my nose and bite back a grin.

"Your voice in my head sounds like a nightmare."

"Whatever, Crazy Pants, you'd love it." He ruffles my hair, ruining the semi-slick bun I only just managed. I swat his hands away and he pokes my neck, tickling me as we reach my street.

"Jeez, that's an even worse nickname than before," I tease, laughing at his insane musings.

509

We're still laughing as we climb the steps toward my building and we're howling like hyenas by the time we reach my floor.

"Lucien, stop! I'm ticklish," I screech, skipping away as he nips at my chilled thighs. Before tonight, I don't think I've ever laughed so much in my life, but the laughter ceases when I drop my keys at the sight of the figure standing in front of my door.

"What are you doing here?" I question, wondering what the fuck is going through Bradford's head.

Bradford narrows his eyes.

"Waiting for you. What is *he* doing here?" He points directly at Lucien, who I can already feel boiling over behind me. "Is he your *boyfriend* or something? Is that why you haven't been answering your phone and ignoring me all night?" Bradford's voice grows loud, and I take an involuntary step back. I'm not afraid of him, but I'm taken aback by his anger. I've never seen him so upset, but then again, I'm not the one who put him in this position.

"Just stop, okay. I didn't owe you a response and I *told* you not to come!"

He scoffs. "I see why. Are you really with this guy?" His eyes shoot to Lucien, who's now made his way beside me. "Are you *fucking* him?"

Jesus Christ. I roll my eyes.

He says it like it's the most unbelievable shit he's ever heard. Though plenty of other people seem to get the appeal of Lucien, he *clearly* does not.

"*That* is none of your business," I shoot back.

"Your pussy is absolutely my business," he quips.

The hell did he just—

I don't have time to finish my thought. Lucien's already got Bradford by his shirt, holding him up against my door, his loafers barely kissing the cement.

"Sydney is fucking *mine!*" Lucien growls like a man possessed.

"Dude, this is Armani! Get the fuck off me!" Bradford shouts back.

Lucien doesn't flinch.

"Seriously, man, you're wrinkling it!"

Bradford's feet swing in an attempt to find the ground.

"Is this guy for fucking real?" Lucien looks over his shoulder, watching me as I rub my temples.

"Unfortunately, yes," I sigh. "Please let him go, Lucien. I promise he's not worth it."

Reluctantly, Lucien listens. I shouldn't be so surprised, but you never quite know with Lucien. He's unpredictable like that.

"Wow," Bradford retorts, his tone despondent as he smooths his shirt back out. "Not *worth* it? Well, I can guarantee I'm worth a lot more than *him*." He nods toward Lucien.

"That doesn't make you more likeable, and it *certainly* doesn't give you the right to judge him *or* my decisions," I say.

"Funny," Bradford retorts. "You weren't complaining about my likeability when you were being a fucking cock tease, telling me how badly you wanted to *fuck* me these last few months." He shifts his gaze back to Lucien. "Did she tell you that?"

My eyes bulge in disbelief. Utterly amazed at Bradford's total lack of self-preservation. Is he so self-absorbed he doesn't sense the danger here?

"It was the whole reason I came here, right? So we could spend *alone time* together."

Lucien looks to me for answers.

"Stop it!" This time I shove Bradford and Lucien takes a step back. "That's not what happened . . . exactly." I look between them. "I never actually agreed to fuck you. We *talked* about it, that's it." I try my best to save what little face I have in this fucked-up situation.

"Bullshit, Sydney," Bradford huffs. "That's bullshit and you know it. You wanted me and now you show up here with *him* after doing God knows what! You look fucking terrible by the way."

I rear back, feeling backhanded by his observation. Lucien's been praising me all night, calling me beautiful even when I let him do the most vulgar things to me, but Bradford throws that all into the fire.

I stand my ground, looking from Lucien to Bradford. He doesn't look too much better. There's a hole in his fancy shoe and dirt on his expensive slacks.

"You need to leave," I tell Bradford through gritted teeth. "I'm not doing this with you right now."

Bradford chuckles. "I mean, I knew you were upset with your dad for dragging you back, but I never thought you'd stoop this low. I've been the one there for you. Life is better with me because then he isn't breathing down your neck. I let you string me along by my dick, knowing it was all a game to you, but I *honestly* didn't think you'd go this low. It's pathe—"

"Enough!" I'm fucking done. It's less about his insults and more about what he might let slip if he keeps talking. "I have neighbors and you're making a scene," I say flatly.

"Does your dad know?" he snarks, ignoring my attempts at de-escalation. "That you're spreading your legs for a piece of shit like him?"

He nods in Lucien's direction, but his glare remains affixed to mine.

"Just leave, Bradford!" I plead, tears stinging my eyes. He's going to let it slip, he's going to ruin it all.

"Yeah, Brad, go before this 'piece of shit' guts you," growls Lucien, unable to keep silent any longer.

"What do you think he'll say when I tell him?" Bradford muses, continuing to ignore Lucien altogether.

"She said leave," Lucien growls.

Bradford doesn't budge, he holds all the cards. He can tear down our tower of happiness with one swift blow should he choose.

But Lucien hits first.

He punches Bradford again and again.

"Please. Please, Lucien, stop. You're only making it worse." I pull at his shirt but it doesn't help. It isn't until I rub his back in gentle circles that he calms, letting Bradford go.

Bradford's back slams against the wall and he drops to the ground in a heap with a bloody lip and an eyebrow that's already starting to bruise.

Bradford spits out blood and then . . . he laughs. What the hell is wrong with everyone tonight? Bradford isn't crazy like Lucien nor is he stupid, but he's confident. He knows none of this matters. He knows how futile my fight is.

"Bradford," I whisper. "Leave."

"Yeah, okay." He grunts as he sits up off the ground. "I'll be seeing you soon, Sydney. You can count on that." He winces, shuffling himself up the wall. His hair is disheveled, with buttons missing from his precious Armani shirt, but he doesn't look the least bit beaten. In fact, his smirk suggests he won—and it sours my insides.

"Is that a threat?" Lucien asks, lunging again but I stop him, holding him back by the elbow to keep him at my side. I'll be lucky if Bradford doesn't choose to press charges against him. I'll have to find a way to convince him not to when we get back home.

"You know . . ." Bradford smirks, wiping the blood from his nose with the back of his hand. "I almost feel bad for you. You shouldn't let the cute face fool you, she's still a Sinclair and she will hurt you. It's what they do."

I open my mouth to retort but what is there to say?

A small voice inside me says that Bradford's right, what I'm doing is wrong, but it's only sex. One night of fun. College kids do it all the time, right? Lucien has Trevor, coffee shop girls, and puck bunnies galore. He won't miss me.

"Get the *fuck* out of here," spits Lucien.

Bradford ambles to his feet, holding his hands in mock surrender as he backs away, a knowing smirk on his lips that keeps Lucien tense.

Bradford bops his head in my direction. "Hope he was worth it."

@therealLucifer
Online

Were you in the arena last nig

Seen

Who the hell is this?

Seen

CHAPTER FORTY

SYDNEY

THE DOOR SLAMS CLOSED with a harsh crack, and I flinch. I thought the atmosphere would be calmer inside. That we'd go back to laughing and having my legs tickled—or spread. But I was wrong. I'm left afraid in the darkness with Lucien.

He's going to leave me.

Lucien whirls on me, pressing my back against the door, his grip on my hips a painful burn like he's trying to sear his touch into my skin. My legs shake as we stand in the entryway, locked in place. His face is furious, but gloriously beautiful as always. It scares me most to see him this way, to see something so beautiful contorted in pain and fury. Like this, I'm forced to face him and the reality that he's two seconds away from walking back out that door, never to return.

My breaths come out in short bursts, and my heart beats a mile a minute.

"Are you going to touch me now?" I whisper, staring at his snarled lips.

He pushes off the door, releasing his hold on my hips, and my heart falls to my stomach, eliciting a reaction that's somewhere between sickness and heartache. He flees to the comfort of the living room, submerging us in a thick, tar-like tension. Lucien is far from the controlled stranger he was earlier tonight, who coerced my clothes from my body with a single demand and an amusing game. Right now, he's a tiger pacing the length of my Tahitian rug like it's his own personal cage.

515

I follow him partway, but stop short when he stalls to answer my question, eying me as if he's trying to decide if our time together has reached its end or not. I couldn't blame him if it had.

"No," he rasps, his chest heaving. "Not right now."

"Why not?" I ask, though I'm pretty sure I know the answer. Bradford succeeded; he drove a wedge between us, just like he wanted.

Lucien pokes at his temple repeatedly as he attempts to regain focus, groaning, "because my control is slipping and I don't trust myself not to hurt you for real. I'm a little . . . too riled up at the moment."

My eyes shine with excitement. If he's worried about hurting me, then it means he still wants to touch me, which means, it's not over yet.

"Are you sure?" I hedge, tracing along the rug as his previous pacing morphs into a slow stride. We look insane walking around my apartment like this. Like we're on a leisure stroll through the park, with him on the massive rug and me on the refurbished parquet, but it's nice. Comfortable. And after a night like ours we're used to looking crazy.

His hand circles his chest, like he's trying to dislodge all of the bad feelings he's keeping bottled up. But I'd rather he didn't. I'd rather he let it all out and release that brimming frustration on me.

Finally, he looks over to me, his hands firmly to himself– something I want to change.

"I won't see you," he answers, though his eyes are seeing me more clearly than they have all night.

His steps slow even further.

"Who will you see?" I risk asking. It doesn't surprise me in the least that he's seeing someone else. I've watched him fight blindly all night, without a care to his own well-being or reputation, so I wonder, who does he see when he looks at me?

"My . . . mom. My dad. My sister. Them drowned in blood. Painted with it; their eyes wide open and staring at me. And . . . quiet. So, so much quiet, and trees, and snow. I see snow."

The confession he's dropped between us squeezes at my heart. It's heavy, weighted, only made light by the airiness in his voice as he stands stock-still on my rug, entranced.

I gently cup his face. Choosing to touch him instead.

"Hey, look at me. Look, it's not snowing. There are no trees. Just me."

My shoulder lifts in an awkward shrug and his eyes track the movement.

"You're not scared?" He questions. Though his words are careful, intentional.

I shake my head. "No."

"You don't think I'm insane?"

There's a slight tilt to his head and his hair brushes across my fingers. I sweep my thumb along his cheek.

"I think it's terrible, whatever happened to them. But no, I don't think you're insane."

His brows scrunch.

Scoffing, he says, "I think *you're* insane. Crazy is just fine for me but utterly unhinged is a dangerous place, Princess. You should have run from me when you had the chance."

The corner of his lips quirk ever so slightly, a smirk that tells me he's okay now.

"You're not *that* dangerous. You're just a little"—I see-saw my hand back and forth— "misunderstood," I finally supply.

He flops onto the couch and I stifle my growing amusement.

"Oh, baby, you have no idea how fucked up I am. I'm capable of things you've never imagined. It's why I have to do crazy shit like this to keep me stable." He gestures between us and my mind rolls back to our unconventional evening.

Lucien sighs, sitting up a little when I sit down beside him. I wince, having forgotten for a second that I have his name freshly carved into my ass.

"Still hurts?" he asks.

"Of course, it fucking hurts," I snap. "You don't exactly have a short name." I try to readjust and end up hissing in pain. "Couldn't you have just done your initials?" I whine. The reality of what my body has been put through hits me like a brick.

Lucien stands, looking down at me with a blend of pride and concern.

"I didn't want there to be any confusion," he says before walking back toward the kitchen. "At least now no one can say they don't know you're mine."

His words echo through the apartment and even though I roll my eyes, I smile too. I hope it's true. I hope the next time some man my dad forces on me gets handsy, they feel the scar etched into my skin. I hope it scares them to know I've been with someone crazy enough to carve his name on my ass. I hope the guy runs away in fear knowing that someone else owns me.

Lucien comes back, carrying two glasses of water, the antiseptic I used on him earlier, some pain meds and a mix-match assortment of band aids, paper towels and other items.

"I could practically hear you rolling your eyes from the kitchen," he chastises, setting everything down carefully on the coffee table. "Keep it up and I'll carve my last name on the other cheek."

Don't threaten me with a good time.

Lucien sits down next to me, then thumps me between the eyes.

"Ow! What was that for?" I yelp.

"Let's press pause on the naughty thoughts and get you cleaned up before we add any new marks, Crazy Pants" he chuckles.

Shit, how'd he know what I was thinking.

I rub my forehead. "You don't know if my thoughts were naughty or not," I whine.

"You were thinking of being bratty, so I punished you anyway." He hands me the glass of water. "I know how much you like pain, but we still can't risk infection," he says, gesturing for me to lay on my stomach after I take a sip.

I tug the hoodie over my head.

"Is it going to leave a permanent scar?" I ask as he shimmies my dress up, exposing my ass to him for the millionth time tonight.

"Do you want it to?" he asks, swiping a damp paper towel over my cuts.

I nod, nervous about giving voice to the darker desires of my heart. We've shared so much tonight but not much has been admitted aloud.

"We can do something more permanent later," he offers, continuing to clean what I'm sure is dried blood away. "This will scar for a little bit, but it'll eventually heal and fade. I didn't want to maim you on our first night."

Lucien chuckles, but my heart sinks a little.

"Hey, Lucien?" I ask sheepishly.

"Yeah," he answers absentmindedly, pouring the antiseptic over the fresh wound.

I wince, but rest my face against my folded arms. "Why'd you cut me?"

"Because," he says, blowing air across my heated skin to dull the sting.

I'm none too pleased when he leaves it at that, providing no further context.

"Because, what?" I huff.

"Because it's like I told you—I'm fucked up. That's all there is to it."

I refuse to believe that that's all there is to it.

I sigh, "Tell me the real reason. Please." I nudge his bicep with my toes. "Lying is against the rules."

He tosses the bloodied paper towel to the side, grabbing the Neosporin next.

"Because . . . there's beauty in scars. We're not meant to be perfect. We're not meant to survive car crashes and come out completely unscathed while everyone else dies. That's not normal. We're meant to make mistakes and eat fries and fall and die. We shouldn't be striving for perfection, we should be striving for . . . more," he admits, dabbing at some of the deeper cuts.

"So that's why the cutting?" I turn slightly to look at him.

He shrugs. "That's what Dr. Thottie thinks."

I chuckle, shaking my head a little at his abysmal nicknaming skills, but quickly sober. "I'm sorry about your family. That must have been hard."

He says nothing for a long time, and I worry I've crossed a line. I look over to watch him as he presses a Hello Kitty band aid to what feels like the U in his name and a tiny Batman band aid over the N.

"It was," he finally says, pulling my clothes back down to cover me.

I start to sit up, but pause when he asks. "Do you have any siblings?"

"Uh, no," I shake my head, "not really."

Lucien barks a laugh. "Not really? You either do or you don't," he chuckles. "Estranged siblings count."

My lips quirk into a smile.

"No, I don't have an estranged sibling, or any sibling really, but I almost had one."

Lucien cocks a brow at me. "Well, this I gotta hear." He leans back into the couch, turning his head to eye me further.

Tucking my leg beneath me so that I'm not sitting directly on my ass, I regale him with my sordid tale.

"When I was around eight years old or so, my dad dated this woman with a kid, a boy named Kenny." Lucien snorts at the name, but lets me continue. "It wasn't his real name, but it's what I called him. His real one was something dumb and Kenny was easier to say." I wave him off. "You'd think I would hate the idea of a stepbrother, but there was something about him that I naturally felt connected to. As far as I was concerned, he was a part of our family and for those two years we were together I thought we were, but . . ." My shoulders slump and I reach for the glass of water on the coffee table.

"But what?" Lucien asks.

I play with the rim of the glass, rubbing my thumb back and forth.

"But over time, he stopped playing with me. He only ever wanted to spend time with my dad or his friends. It was like I stopped existing. Then his older brother came back home, who I guess my dad didn't know about, and it caused this whole big uproar. It tore a rift between Kenny's mom and my dad. Kenny stopped speaking to me altogether after that and then my dad's business went belly-up. It was one of his first big business ventures and it blew up in smoke—literally. It caught fire and he lost everything, including his relationship and our little makeshift family. I never saw Kenny or his family again after that."

"Wow. Do you miss them?" Lucien asks, handing me two ibuprofen pills.

I think about that. It's been a while since I have, and now that he mentions it, I can vaguely remember what it felt like to have a real family, if even for a short while.

"I was never really close to the woman or the secret older brother, obviously, but I was close to Kenny. I miss him sometimes. I barely remember the details of him anymore, but what I do remember is that he made me feel so safe, like nothing could get to me as long as he was around. He was a small kid in stature, but to me he was larger than life. Beautiful. Kind. Smart. I often wonder where he ended up, who he grew up to be . . ." I shrug helplessly. "But I guess I'll never know."

A strange look passes over Lucien's face that he tries to disguise.

"What's with that look?" I ask before chugging the water and tossing back the pills.

"Nothing." He tries to feign innocence. I glare at him as I swallow the last of my water.

Lucien grins. "It's nothing . . . I'm just a little jealous, that's all."

I slap his shoulder, guffawing. "Of what, an eight-year-old?"

He looks at me with a soft expression. "Your first love."

I stare at him, scoffing when I can tell he's being serious. "Maybe puppy love, but real love? I don't think I experienced that until much later." I peek up at him beneath my lashes, afraid to look too closely at him.

I watch his lip twitch and curve a little at the corners.

"Perhaps, but I think it still counts." I roll my eyes, but he glares at me before softening his gaze. "Until recently, I didn't think anyone would ever have any kind of love for me. I think that's why I was in such a dark place when you started stalking me."

My voice catches, understanding dawning that Lucien felt unloved and unwanted, and I preyed on him—stalked him. I made a mockery of his feelings by not being honest about my own. "Really?" I ask though I already know even if I can't admit it to myself.

"Yeah," he answers. "But playing with you felt better than drowning. Talking with you felt almost normal."

He leans in closer, our knees brushing as his fingers trot up my arms, and somehow I've missed how we ended up seated this closely.

"Would it surprise you to know how hard I got knowing you were out there somewhere watching me?" He walks two fingers along my thigh. "I loved every second of knowing I had all of your attention, all of your focus. Not Morningstar but me, the worst parts of me that aren't easily marketable. That people don't see. The fucked up part of me that sometimes wants to set myself on fire and take the whole world with me. Having your eyes on me felt like you would sit beside me as we watched the world burn, and I loved every second of it. Thinking of you drove my nightmares away. It gave me something to fixate on and kept me from losing all sense of control. It's why I didn't mind those eyes on me. Why would I ever give something like that up?"

I try to dislodge the lump in my throat but it's proving difficult.

"You're going to be mine forever because we're one in the same, you and I," he finishes.

"How?" I rasp.

How could I ever hold on to a man like him forever? A girl like me with someone like him, could never work. We wouldn't be allowed to. Or more truthfully, I'd be too scared to. How are we anything alike?

"Because you can see in the dark too."

We talk and flirt some more until the only type of tension left in the room is sexual. Walking me back to my bedroom, he leads the way, my hands firmly wrapped in his, making it impossible for me to let go, or run. He calmly guides me to the bed, and I sit. There's a stampede of nerves reacting in my body at his touch, at the realization the moment has finally arrived. No more distractions or delays. There's boxes and clothes piled in random spaces, but there's no longer regret or worry filling the bedroom.

The bed dips when he sits next to me and it groans when I edge in closer, fisting his t-shirt in my hands to keep him here, or keep myself steady, it doesn't matter which.

"Lucien," I murmur.

"Yeah, Princess," he breathes, his breath tickling the inseam of my lips.

"Thank you." My eyes stare deeper into his. "It really was the best day ever."

He leans forward, kissing me. It deepens until my stomach knots and pulls at the ignition cord of my body.

"The day's not over yet," he whispers against my lips. "I told you . . . I'm playing for keeps and there's still one thing I haven't claimed yet."

It's four in the morning, the day has been over for a while, but the claiming I've been waiting for is finally here. He's marked me in every way possible, but I want him to own me, body and spirit. My heart is his for the taking too, if he wants it.

"Then take me," I whisper.

In one swift motion, he rolls me on top of him, my legs straddling his hips. His cock strains against his jeans and I can't believe he isn't tired from all the fucking he's done with it today. I thought he was only teasing about the endurance thing, but I can't imagine many people would be able to keep up with his . . . appetite. He's insatiable.

His strong hands grip my waist and trail up my back. They brush up the sequin material, pressing me closer against him. Then he's ripping my dress apart, the fabric like paper against his strength and tenacity. I'd wanted to keep it, but after everything it's been through, I'm just happy it's off.

Laying back down on the quilted duvet, he rests his hands on my hips as I bracket his thighs, my bare pussy inches from his hard cock.

"Now, take it out, Princess. You've earned it."

Those freakishly golden-amber eyes are hooded as he looks up at me, longing and obsession exchanged in equal measure between our gazes. I drag my nails down his torso, over every muscle and ridge until I reach the edge of his pants. Fuck me, if there was some way, anyway, I could keep him, I would. I'd do it in a heartbeat.

I've barely packed, but as the clank of his buckle releasing chimes, the zip of his zipper buzzes and the huffs of our breathing churn the cadence of this room, it all falls to the wayside. The only thing that matters is that I have him now. We played a game for keeps today and in the end we both won.

My fingertips barely touch as I grip him in my hands and pump long, slow strokes up his massive length.

He's easily the biggest I've ever seen, and though that isn't saying much, it doesn't make it any less true. This man is going to wreck me with his cock.

"Fuck, baby, just like that," Lucien groans as I thumb the head.

"Touch me," I urge, and he obeys, bringing his calloused palms up to knead at my breasts.

I lean into the feel of them, all the new sensations that threaten to overtake me.

"Have I told you how much I like your tits?" he rasps; his voice tinted in desire.

"No, you haven't actually," I smirk.

He jostles them in a way that makes me giggle. I love his unserious nature sometimes.

"They're so squishy, like marshmallows."

His large hands grab two handfuls as he proceeds to honk my tits. I slap at his chest.

"They're not to be toyed with," I scold.

"Oh really?" He releases my breasts to lean up on his hands before taking his tongue and rolling a nipple into his mouth. My breath gets caught and he drags his teeth across the sensitive skin.

"You should pierce these," he offers before doing the same to the other side.

I groan, even as desire hums throughout my body at his suckling.

"Absolutely not, how about you pierce yours?" I retort, my arousal adding to the slickness as I try to keep hold of his cock in my hand. Precum spills from his tip as I continue to rub myself against him and stroke.

"I just might," he moans.

He brings one hand back up, gripping my other breast harder than before and I feel the sharp pang right between my legs.

More.

"I should have known you'd say something like that," I sass.

His teeth clamp down, biting my nipple so hard, I scream.

"Fuck!" I yelp, letting his cock go and bringing my hands to his shoulder so I don't fall off his lap. "I think you did pierce them."

"Oh, please, I barely broke skin," he admonishes, pulling off to suck on the other one.

"What?" I jolt, patting at my free tit to ensure my nipple is still there, though I can feel his mouth turn up into a grin around my breast.

I moan at the feel of my nipple encased in his warm, wet mouth and his cock twitches when I wrap my fingers around him again. I give it another slow stroke and more precum squeezes from his tip, rolling over my thumb.

"Again," I preen, rolling my hips and rubbing my clit against the base of his length, against the barbells of his cock, appreciating their existence now that I know how good they can feel.

He groans in response, continuing to suckle and nip. All night long he's been ordering and taking advantage at every turn, but now I'm in control. His cock is in my hands, and he's not made a move to hurt me or cut me; he's following my lead.

"Good boy," I praise, running my hands through his hair as he sucks.

He pulls off with a pop.

"There's not a damn good thing about me," he growls before he's biting me again.

There wasn't one true thing about that statement, but there's no way I would tell him that now. Not when he feels this fucking good.

"You sure about that?" I ask. "You feel pretty good to me."

That earns me a hearty laugh, one I haven't heard from him before. This laugh is boyish, all sweet sunshine and rainbows.

Despite everything, he's so fucking sweet to me, though I'm sure he'd never see himself that way.

And I'm . . . so fucking horrible.

So . . . so . . . fucking . . .

"Good," I moan, when one of his hands reaches between us again, strumming my clit as he sucks.

"No, no, no, don't come yet, Princess," he chides. "We're just getting started."

"I want you to fuck me, Lucien. Now," I whimper.

He lifts his head from my breast and uses the other hand to twirl a loose curl around his finger.

"It's going to hurt in this position," he warns, though I'm sure he's only telling me for my benefit, since I can feel his hips thrusting upward into my hand, chasing the very thing he's trying to warn me against.

I shake my head. "I don't care, I want it to hurt. I don't want you to be gentle."

"And why do you want me to hurt you?" he asks, adjusting his hand between my thighs to pinch my clit.

I groan.

"Why do you want to hurt me?" I redirect his question, grinding myself against him like I did his thigh, chasing the friction. He doesn't take the bait.

"I asked you first."

I cradle his face in my hands. "Because pain isn't easily ignored."

"Pain is proof of life," he answers in kind, tugging hard enough on my hair to make me flinch. "Only dead people feel nothing,"

My eyes flick down to his and all the teasing and amusement has fled from his gaze, there's only ferality and desperate want. It only coerces more truths to fall from my lips.

"I want to feel you. I want you to have me so that I can't ever forget you were the one that had me first. Fucking destroy me, Lucien."

Kill the old Sydney and make me brand new.

Untwirling his fingers from my hair, he gathers it all back until he's pulling, exposing my throat to him. It's littered with bite marks, hickeys, and bruises and he kisses each one softly, cherishing every mark.

Grabbing hold of his cock, he rubs the tip of his dick against my folds, smearing his precum and my arousal around, making me wetter.

"I love how wet you always are for me." He licks at the cut on my chest. "You're fucking perfect." He sucks on my breast again. "So fucking beautiful." He sucks on the other one, before lining himself up and looking right into my soul. "And all fucking mine."

A shrill gasp pierces the air as he pushes almost all the way in. I'm frozen for a minute, unable to fully process that he's inside me right now, how tight everything is. I don't even realize my mouth is open until he's kissing me, sucking my soul right out of my body.

"Now ride me, Princess. Take me deep like a good fucking girl."

I'm too scared to move, unsure of what I'm really doing until he lifts his hips. I moan again, still trying to reconcile the intense pain with the blinding pleasure I feel. He breaks our kiss to stick his thumb in my mouth, and I suck instinctively.

I yelp as he bites me again on the nipple. I clamp down on his thumb, tasting copper. "Fuck, I'm—" I don't get to apologize. He pops his thumb out, pressing it to my clit, rubbing the sensitive nerves back and forth as he pumps into me.

"So tight," he groans. "Fucking hell, you're going to own me."

Riding up and down his cock, the piercings hit a unique spot inside me that has me ready to come.

"Yes, come on baby, keep going. Milk my fucking cock with your tight-ass pussy."

I lift up to the tip before slamming my full weight down on him. He's stretching me wide, tearing me apart.

"God, yes, fucking ride me," he growls, slapping my tits so hard I'm screaming from the sharp sting.

"Again," I moan. I'm panting as I chase my orgasm to the ends of the earth, ready to come for him this second.

He smacks my breasts again and again. And though it hurts, my pussy grips his cock so tight I know he and I both are close to coming.

"Wait, no, slow down. I don't want to come yet. I don't want this to be over," I whine, trying to stall for more time, to extend the pleasure for as long as I can maintain it. I want to stay on the edge with him a little longer.

Lucien chuckles and it sends a spark through me.

"Over?" he asks, his tone amused and mocking. His hands move to my ass as he spreads my cheeks apart to take him deeper. "You listen to me, Princess. You're going to come for me right the fuck now, then I'm going to come, and after you've had your 'oh my gosh I can't believe I just lost my virginity' moment, we're going again . . ." He thrusts deep inside. "And again." My eyes roll when he thrusts even deeper still. "I'm going to fuck you all night long. So, buckle up, Buttercup, because this is going to be a long ride."

I grind up and down his shaft three more times, rolling figure eights all the way down like my pussy is skating down his dick, before I'm coming with such intense force I'm squirting all around his cock and onto the sheets. It's not even something I thought I could do, but the release is blinding. "Oh my God, I'm so—"

"Don't you dare apologize for soaking my dick exactly like I wanted you to," he growls, rolling us over so he's on top. He doesn't give my orgasm time to fall away. "Grip the rails," he demands and, like the good girl I am, I listen. He drapes one of my legs over his arm, then the other, and my stomach drops to my throat, awareness dawning on me that this position offers me little control and gives him full power to fuck me into oblivion.

He sees the fear in my eyes, and he smiles wickedly. Leaning forward, he folds me in half as he presses a kiss to my lips then pulls away.

"My turn," he groans, before he's driving in so fucking deep my whole back bows off the bed. My hands slip and I let go of the railings. "Don't let go," he reprimands with a smack to my unsliced ass cheek, and I scramble to find them again. Either my eyes have closed, or I've gone temporarily blind because I struggle to regain the position. Sparks flash across my vision and for a moment I fear I have gone blind. His cock strokes in and out with the precision of a skilled surgeon, hitting every spot I missed when I rode him.

So, this is what fucking Lucien feels like.

His hands grip my thighs tighter as he pounds into me, a wet slapping sound echoing throughout my bedroom as he moves. The intensity of it all has me looking for something to focus on, landing on my figurines and trophies still lining the shelf above, witnesses to my defilement. My eyes drag back to Lucien's, and I struggle to draw breath at the expression on his face. All that control is lost to him. Like me, he's struggling to maintain that spot on the edge, he's about to come with me. He's so impossibly deep. I feel so full.

"Lucien!" I cry out.

He pounds again.

"Oh, God."

"That's right. That's my name, call for your God and I'll answer all your prayers, Princess."

Fuck.

"I want you to come inside me," I moan. "Please. Let me feel you."

"Christ, I fucking love how filthy you are." He strokes once, twice, then he's screaming. "Come with me." We both fall apart.

His cum is warm and thick, filling me up so much I feel it leaking from where we're connected. My cunt clamps around his cock like a vacuum seal and he releases a guttural roar, coming even more. I drain his cock, feeling his warmth coating me from the inside out. Our hearts beat an odd rhythm, one that doesn't sync, but matches in tenacity.

"Thank you, Lucien, for giving this to me," I cry, tears streaming down my face.

He licks them away.

"Thank you for giving this to me." He releases my legs, nuzzling his face into the crook of my neck, though he remains buried in my cunt. "I know I can be a lot to handle sometimes, but I'm really glad you didn't run away."

Looking down the length of my body, I can finally see the mess we've made. The sheets look like a goddamn murder scene.

"What the fuck? Why is there so much blood?" I screech.

"It's a beautiful sight, isn't it?" he sits back on his heels, admiring the display of blood and fluid that smears my ruined Egyptian sheets.

"No, it's not. You murdered my pussy!" I yell.

"Oh, no, Princess," he mocks, faking concern. "I guess I'll have to do a little CPR and resuscitate her."

He spreads my knees apart, sliding a finger in and out to force the cum back inside.

"What are you doing?" My pussy is so sore that even his finger feels invasive right now.

"I'm checking for a pulse." He smirks down at me, and I bite back a smile.

"Stop that, cunt murderer," I chide.

He laughs.

"I kinda like the sound of that. I think I might like it even better than God."

I giggle through my moan. Of course he would like that.

"I will never call you Cunt Murderer during sex."

"Try it out and see. You never know, it might just . . . roll off the tongue," he says, licking a lazy stroke over my slit. A deep, breathy moan is my only response. It's like a soothing warm compress to my sore vagina the way he laps at my sensitive core.

"Don't do—"

"Don't what?" he interjects, his question mocking.

"There's blood—and cum—down there." I can barely get my words out the way he's going at it, like he's trying to prove a point.

He hums, chuckling to himself.

"If you haven't noticed, I like blood—and cum—and I especially like down there," he teases. He drives home his point by sucking softly on my clit, the motion causing me to grind into his face. It feels fantastic.

"Oh shit," I groan when my thighs start to tremble.

"Poor thing, I think we're going to lose her. I'm going to have to do mouth-to-mouth." He's not dropping the ruse, and his tongue moves rapidly over the sensitive bud until I'm gripping the sheets and moaning. He slides a long middle finger into my pussy, pumping as he moans against my center.

"That's it, come for me baby, all over my face."

"Lucien, get up, I'm going to drown you down there," I pant, as I try to hold my orgasm back.

"If she goes, I go. I've decided, this is how I want to die. My final resting place will be between these thighs." He spears me with his tongue, then sucks harder on my clit.

And I lose it.

The dam breaks and I'm flooding his mouth again, coming hard from his tongue that continues to lick and suck even as my orgasm deepens.

"Fucking . . . Cunt Murderer," I moan, grabbing his hair and pulling to get him off, but he keeps going. He keeps going until there's nothing left for me to give. Until I'm a writhing exorcist mess. I feel like a wrung-out rag.

Sitting back on his heels, he licks at his fingers and rolls his tongue around his wet lips. Panting he says, "It took some work, but I think we brought her back to life. She'll be A-okay." He throws up the okay symbol with his fingers and winks. I can't help but break out into laughter.

Sighing, I relax back into the bed, completely sated.

"What am I gonna do with you?" I smile lazily up at him.

He falls back over me, head on my tits like they're his personal pillows before blowing a contented breath over them.

"Whatever you want, Princess. Whatever you want."

@therealLucifer
Online

Were you in the arena last night

Seen

Who the hell is this?

Seen

SYDNEY MALONE

CHAPTER FORTY-ONE

SYDNEY

Y HEART BURNS AS I run my hands through what is now Lucien's very shaggy black hair—and it's not the pizza that he had to convince me to eat that's causing the ache. With no more product in it, his hair's fluffy and soft, dried into loose waves and spontaneous curls.

I couldn't bring myself to tell him it's not about what I want. I don't get what I want this time.

My father told me there would be a cost. He *warned* me. I thought I could pay it. I was *prepared* to pay it, I was. Giving up figure skating would gut me, it would leave me a hollow and shriveled version of myself, but I was going to do it. I *am* doing it, but if the true cost is Lucien . . . it's too great. I don't think I can do it. My hand accidentally pulls at his scalp as I try to reign in the sob that's sitting lumped in my throat.

"Don't worry, Princess. I'm ready to go again whenever you are," he murmurs, his head resting on my lap as we lie at the foot of my bed on the floor.

I try to laugh to cover up the fact I can't catch my breath.

My fingers comb through his hair some more as I try to cope with the barrage of conflicting emotions. Luckily, he's loving the sensation too much, groaning beneath my touch, and too distracted to notice my melt down.

He practically purrs when he speaks, his cheeks squished against my bare thighs.

"I've been meaning to ask you . . ."

I pause my petting and look down to find Lucien's face turned up at me, one of his golden eyes peeking from beneath the flop of his hair. "What happened?"

I narrow my eyes.

"Excuse me?" I ask.

He points to his own head but looks ahead at nothing in particular. "The scar . . . on your head."

"Oh." I clear my throat, figuring he'd eventually ask, and resume playing in his hair. "Um, well it's not a particularly grand story, but the short of it is that I tried partners skating for like a year, a couple years back, but, uh, we weren't a good match. We were clumsy, out of sync, and both too eager for the spotlight." A small smile stretches over my lips at the memory. "Needless to say, one day we were trying to do this one move, and we severely miscalculated somewhere. I ended up with a skate to the head and more than twenty stitches." I shrug. "I'm surprised my dad didn't make me quit back then, actually." I chuckle a little because what else can you do? Dad didn't even come visit me in the hospital. He was too busy wrapping up some deal he'd made in Shanghai or something.

Lucien sits up abruptly, startling me when he whips around to face me.

"Are you telling me,"—he enunciates carefully, his Hyde side making his appearance known—"there's somebody out there,"—he points in the direction of my window—"*alive* and *breathing* who hurt you so badly you were left with a permanent scar in your head?"

He narrows his eyes, waiting for me to confirm.

I blink.

"Uh . . ."

Shit.

"Who is he?" he snaps, jostling me when he brackets his tattooed arms on each side of me, caging me to my spot on the fluffy blue rug we've been relaxing on.

He seems to love trapping me. We're wrapped in my silk sheets, but where I'm cocooned from the chest down. The fabric falls from Lucien's waist, sweeping across his bare ass and defined abs, allowing his fully naked body to crouch over me in a display of animalistic prowess. He looks as if he's about to eat me alive, threatening *me* as much as he is my old skate partner.

"Why?" I whisper, barely able to focus with his dick already hard and pointing in my direction.

"He broke something of mine," he says, calmer this time, nuzzling my nose and whispering his own version of sweet nothings. "It's only fair I break something of his."

Pragmatic as ever.

"Like what? His legs?" I snort.

He remains stoic.

"No, Lucien, you cannot break his legs. He doesn't even compete anymore." I sigh with a roll of my eyes, but he's so pouty about it, he doesn't bother to adjust my attitude.

Shame. I quite like when he adjusts my attitude.

"He doesn't deserve to walk either," he grumbles.

My lips quirk into a smile.

"Aww, there, there," I coo. "Next time I take a skate to the head, you have my full permission to break the person's legs," I laugh, but then I'm reminded with morbid realization that he could and *would* do it. And I just gave him permission. "On second thought—"

"No take backs," he quips, shutting me up with a searing kiss. He tastes of oregano and pepperoni, but he might as well be fresh air. I pull back, staring at him for a few more moments, wishing time would stop.

I cup his face, using my thumbs to swipe his cheeks.

"Tell me a secret," I whisper.

His brows furrow, but he doesn't pull away.

"What kind of secret?" he asks.

Any kind, I think. I want to know something about him that nobody else knows since he now owns a piece of me that nobody else will ever have. I'd say it's a fair trade.

I shrug.

"What's the worst thing you've ever done?" I ask, unable to meet his eyes even as I ask it.

He ponders his answer.

"By whose definition?"

I drop my hands from his face, but he maintains our proximity as he hovers his face over mine.

"Let's go with overall societal standards," I offer.

He stares at me for a second, looking from one eye to the other.

"I killed someone," he admits.

My breath catches. It's not the context of the confession that surprises me per se, it's his complete willingness to tell me. Lucien watches me intently, waiting to see what kind of reaction he'll solicit from me this time.

I blink.

"What'd they do?" I whisper, because regardless of what people might think, Lucien wouldn't do something so heinous for no reason.

"Something terrible. Unforgivable," he says.

My battered heart drops and my sore throat catches. It feels impossible to swallow and I'm not sure if I'm breathing enough air.

Something terrible. Unforgivable.

"Your turn," he urges. When I don't say anything, he says, "Tell me your *secrets.*"

I let out a long-strangled breath. I'm not sure I want to drop this so easily, not after what he just said, but if I'm going to press about his secrets, I need to pay with one of my own.

"I'm *not* a good person," I mutter.

Lucien sits back on his haunches, sighing.

"I said a secret, not a lie, Sydney," he retorts.

"That *is* my secret." I stare down at my hands, scratching at a hangnail on my demolished thumb that's nagging me. "You asked me why I didn't fight back against Regina and Tiffany. It's because I deserved it." My nose burns and my eyes sting as I feel tears welling up.

I risk looking at him.

"I don't—" My finger presses to his lips, shutting him up so I can get this out.

"I did exactly what they accused me of." My voice cracks. "I did something terrible. Something unforgivable. And when it came time for me to receive my punishment, I called my dad and made it all go away, something I *swore* I would never do, but—but I fucked up, Lucien." A tear slips down my cheek. "I fucked up so bad."

"What did you do?" Lucien looks at me, concerned.

My wet eyes meet his and I take a breath before letting it all go.

"I pushed her," I whisper.

"Who?" Lucien's forehead wrinkles in confusion, but again he doesn't pull away. Instead, he drags me closer, cupping my face softly. "*Who*, Sydney?"

I shudder. "H-Hannah."

And then I'm sobbing.

Lucien rubs my head, pulling me into a hug as he lets me release the tension I've been carrying over the past twenty-four hours.

"That your teammate?" he asks, petting my hair gently, his touch soothing and grounding.

I nod against his chest, the slickness of it not even a deterrent.

He breathes in the scent of my hair with my head tucked beneath his chin.

"That's why you stopped messaging me, isn't it?"

I swallow, the bile threatening to come up as I try to keep control. "It was part of it, yeah. There were other reasons, but after that . . ." I trail off because *after that* there was no going back.

He continues stroking my hair.

"Why'd you do it?" he asks.

I sniffle, pulling away from his embrace. He allows it, but he doesn't let me get far.

"I thought it was Tiffany around the corner, but by the time I'd realized the person falling down the steps wasn't her, it was too late. What's worse, Regina saw the whole thing, but then sat on the information until today, until right before I was set to perform at

Nationals, so *she* could have my spot." I sniff, my anger starting to grow. "That sneaky bitch was more clever than I gave her credit for. The program we did back at the rink was supposed to get me to qualifiers. I was finally going to get my second chance at the Olympics, but the universe doesn't give out third chances and calling my dad was my one Get-Out-Of-Jail-Free card. So, you see, I'm *not* a good person. I'm a Sinclair and that's all I'll ever be." I let out a deep breath, releasing tension I've held back with my secret.

Lucien considers all of this, working out which part of the story to address first. I can see the wheels turning in his pensive gaze.

"What happened to Hannah?" he asks after a while.

I tell him. This wasn't supposed to be confession time, but here I am, admitting all my transgressions. Maybe he *is* God?

More like the devil.

"She, um, broke her leg in three different places and suffered a hairline fracture," I answer.

His eyes crinkle a little and I can't tell if he's disappointed, disgusted, or what.

"She gonna be okay?" he asks.

I grimace, the reminder of how badly she was hurt, a punch to the gut, "It's . . . complicated," I admit.

"How so?"

I look away, unable to bear the judgment that even someone like him would give.

"She's . . . pregnant. Or at least she was last time I checked." I flinch when I feel his grip tighten on my shoulder, but I don't meet his eyes. I keep mine trained on the loose thread sticking out of the corner of the sheets still wrapped around my body. "I-I didn't know she was pregnant at the time. I found that part out later." I pluck at the string, trying to pull it out so it stops being an outlier in my otherwise perfect thread count. "I like Hannah," I choke out. "I didn't want to hurt her, but I let petty rivalries and jealous girls push me to do something heinous. I don't know if I can forgive myself for what happened to Hannah or if something happened to her baby because of me."

"Why don't you get your dad to help her?" His voice is quiet, but that alone tells me he's not unaffected by what I've done.

"He is," I defend. "He's making sure she gets the best care possible, paying for all her medical expenses and the best doctors in the nation. I begged him, I swear. I made *sure* he wouldn't hang her out to dry."

An uncomfortable silence stretches between us. I try to breathe through it, picking at one of the cuts Lucien's given me. None of them are deep enough to scar, they'll fade with time and disappear beneath dressings to be replaced with healed flesh. If only *this* were like that.

Lucien nudges my knee with his, but I don't look up. I don't think I could bear his disappointment right now, or worse, his retaliation.

Lucien sighs.

"Stop," he breathes. "Stop beating yourself up. You made a mistake, and you feel bad about it. And better yet, you were honest." He tilts my face up to regard him again, "I've seen *true* evil, and Princess you're not it, so stop saying you're not a good person." He leans in closer, his body pressing mine into the mattress's edge. "You're a better person than most, better than me at least."

I search his eyes. "What makes you say that after everything I've done?" I bring my hand up to his holding to my cheek. I let his warmth run through me.

"Because unlike you, I don't feel bad for what *I've* done," he says.

I want to ask him who he killed, but I don't deserve his secrets any more than I deserve his sympathy. He can keep them both.

"You're gonna be okay. I promise, it'll get better," he assures me.

My eyes close and I inhale as big a breath as my lungs will allow. Who knew this boy would have this kind of effect on me? He didn't just distract me, he captured me, mind, body and soul.

"I never want this night to end," I breathe. "I want to stay like this forever."

"Then I'll stay with you, and we can be just like this. Always." He bumps my nose with his.

A pathetic snort slips past my lips. "If only we could, right?"

"I only deal in absolutes Sydney. Words like *forever* and *always*, I mean them absolutely."

His lips press to my cheek, then the corner of my mouth. Pausing, he looks at me, seeking permission to keep going—and I give it. I want to believe him when he says it'll be okay. I want to believe in 'forever' and 'always'. For a few more hours, I want *this*. *Us*. His hands sweep through my hair, holding my head while he kisses down my neck, to my chest and back up.

He kisses me everywhere that's not my mouth and I moan, "Please, Lucien."

Within seconds, the fire is stoked within me again, burning long after our night of adventure. By some miracle, I'm not tired and I'm not done. I still crave him. My arms wrap around his as he peels the sheets from my torso, peeling back layer after layer until I'm stripped bare and naked before him again.

CHAPTER FORTY-TWO

LUCIEN

W E FUCK THREE MORE times, or at least I think it was three. I lost count around orgasm number five and continued ravaging Sydney's body until it started to feel like my dick would literally fall off if I dared get hard again. The sun peeks over the horizon and through the trees. The sky's a pretty coral pink: the color of Sydney's pussy right now. Though, I suppose it's more like a reddish pink at this point . . . and a little swollen.

"No more," she groans, "or you really will murder her."

I chuckle. I don't think I've ever been prouder of my work before. I knew we would have a fun night and that she'd sate all my dark urges and desires, but I didn't expect to feel like this: settled and calm.

Even after baring our souls and confessing secrets, I don't feel raw inside like I typically do, I feel soothed. It's so rare for me to meet not only someone I can relate to sexually, but someone I can relate to *at all*. Hell, we do *more* than relate, it's like we were born having already met and are just picking up where we left off.

I stretch out over the bed, arms splayed as I lie on my back, tracking the dirt that clings to her ceiling fan. I'm so relaxed it doesn't even bother me.

"Don't worry, Cock Killer. I think I could use a break too," I mumble, yawning as sleep seeks me out.

Her laugh is light, though I can tell it would be more humorous if she weren't falling asleep in my arms. "Aha, Cock Killer . . . that's . . . funny," she trails off before small, even breaths brush over my chest. Wrapping an arm around her, I bring her in closer, holding her as drool leaks from her lips. I've never had a girl sleep on me before. Not one I was having sex with, anyway.

Though it feels like a lifetime ago now, my sister used to fall asleep on me. My free hand rests on my chest and I rub at the burn of the empty cavern that used to possess my heart. I haven't thought about my sister in years. Don't get me wrong, I think of how she and my parents died all the time. I think of them in my nightmares when they're sitting there bleeding out, dead. But I don't think of our life together often.

It's a testament to our relationship that I was able to open up to Sydney about them, but it's been a *long* time since I've acknowledged the Lucien from before. The Lucien that had a little sister who used to hog the blankets any time we sat and watched movies, yet somehow inevitably moved to share it—only to fall asleep right in my arms. No, I don't think about *that* Lucien at all.

But . . . maybe, with Sydney, I can afford to think of them a little more. *Maybe* I can let her see behind the curtain of my soul where all the truly dangerous shit lies. Never in my life have I ever been so enamored by someone who I'd even consider this. Especially someone I've known one fucking day! Talk about crazy. But that's what she does to me.

The sun has fully risen, but judging by the quiet streets and soft bird chirping, I'd say it's still kind of early. I only managed to sleep a few hours before hunger awoke me, violently at that, but what else is new? *At least the nightmares have stopped.* Meanwhile, Sydney is sound asleep like the beautiful princess she is. Even with her hair tangled and eye boogers crusting her thick lashes, she's only more perfect to me.

Light shines into the room, illuminating every mark, scar, and bruise that decorates her body. I peruse every inch, proud of the masterpiece I've created. She'll be feeling my presence for days to come. Possibly even more than that because we're doing it all over again tonight. Hell, probably right after we have breakfast.

My stomach growls angrily at the thought of food and I force myself to tear my eyes and arm away to make us something to eat.

For a rich girl, I thought she'd have something more than milk, an almost empty carton of eggs, and a half-eaten BLT in her fridge. Outside of the cases of Voss water, there's only condiments and a small container of shredded cheese. I'll have to get her some groceries today if I expect us to be refueled for another marathon of fucking. There's still so much I want to do with her.

I'm in the middle of chopping the ingredients from the remnants of her sandwich when there's an unexpected knock on the door.

Knife still poised in my hand; I walk over to answer it. "Can I help you?"

Three guys dressed in matching jumpsuits stand in the doorway, but I direct my focus to the one holding the clipboard.

"Hi. Uh, we're here to pack and load the truck for a . . . Miss Sydney Sinclair. This is . . . apartment 3C, right?" He leans back to peek his head to the side, ensuring he's at the right place before his eyes catch sight of the knife still resting at my side. "I'm, uh, Samson and we're with Sam & Sons Moving Company." His throat bobs and the two guys with him shift closer.

I have no intention of fucking up a great morning, so I don't let the tension sit long before I put the guy out of his misery and let him know he's at the right place.

"Yeah, you have the right door. She's still asleep right now, but you can come on in and get started." I smile and give a welcoming gesture to usher them in. Absolutely nothing could ruin my good mood today.

"Thank you, sir, we appreciate that." Samson visibly relaxes, settling his mouth into a proud customer service smile. "Alright, boys, let's get to it! We have a long drive, and I want us on the road before noon."

The two other guys are young and strapping, and I assume they are Sam's actual sons if the resemblance and company name are to be believed. Either way, they follow their orders as given, starting with the couch we didn't get around to fucking on.

I finish up the omelets while they work on packing the rest of the living room furniture. Walking back to the bedroom, I deliver the omelet to Sydney.

When I get into the bedroom, I set a glass of water and our plates on the mahogany side table next to her bed. She's still sleeping soundly, so I shut the bedroom door to keep the room quiet. I admire her for a second more before nudging her awake so she can eat her food while it's still hot.

Her nose crinkles adorably as her senses wake before the rest of her does. She drags in a lungful of air, smelling the food. One blue eye pops open, and then the other. Stretching wide and yawning, she keens.

"Morning," Sydney says with a bright smile. Her breasts jiggle as she lifts herself up, rubbing the sleep out of her eyes.

Good morning, Sydney's tits.

My grin is wide when I ignore my dick's greeting and respond in kind. "Good morning, Princess."

She looks around dazed before she asks, "Did you go out and buy breakfast?"

"No." I shake my head, amused at her question as I push my hair out of my eyes. It's heavy and oily. We're both going to need another shower.

Sydney's brows crease when she turns her head and locates the source of the smell.

"You *cooked*?" she asks as she picks up the plate and inspects the food.

"You look surprised," I note, though I actually love how easy she is to surprise.

"No one's ever cooked for me."

I quirk a brow. "No one?"

"Well, no one *normal*."

My mouth twists. "Not sure I fit that criteria either."

"That's not what I mean, and you know it." She slaps my knee. "The only person who's ever cooked for me is our chef back home. Not even my dad has cooked for me. I don't even know how to cook for myself." She laughs, but there's no real humor to it. It sounds pitiful, like she feels sorry for herself for not knowing a basic skill like cooking. I'd imagine, for someone like Sydney, who strives to excel at everything, to her it *is* pitiful.

I rest a hand against her thigh.

She takes a bite, and her sad smile brightens.

"This is *delicious*," she moans. "Where did you get the ingredients to make this?"

"I just used your leftover sandwich and repurposed it into the omelet," I shrug. I never did like the idea of wasted food. Even as a kid, I always finished my meal and if I couldn't finish, I liked eating leftovers, remaking them or reshaping them to my liking to make them good again.

"No way. This is even better than our chef's back home."

Pain etches her features when she sits up further, wincing again as she struggles to get comfortable. Now that the adrenaline and sexed-up hormones have subsided, I'm sure she's even more sore. I thought the pain meds would help, but it seems I was rougher than I thought.

"How's your ass? Better?"

She glares at me as she slides a bite of egg through her teeth, wrestling back a grin.

"A little," she draws out.

I trace my tongue along my lower lip. "Good."

My hands cradle her feet as I inspect them. They're a little scratched up from our romping through the woods, but when I press my thumbs into the bottom of her soles, she moans around another bite of her food.

"Nuh uh, nope. You can't serve me great food *and* give great foot massages. It's not allowed."

I ignore her feeble attempt to deter me. I may be brutal with my toys, but I always know how to take care of them. Her foot kicks out, but I only grip her tighter until she's squealing for me to stop.

I don't.

"Okay, okay, you win," she surrenders.

I smirk. "Damn right, I win."

She shoots me a cute little stink eye before muttering under her breath, "Cocky fucker."

I take my time massaging her feet, working my way up her whole leg while I'm at it. I'm careful of her skinned knees and am moving up to her thighs when she finishes her food. Good thing too. Any closer and we'd be enjoying round six, I think? Whatever, she'd be getting fucked again.

Sydney's tongue flicks out to lick the crumbs from her lips.

"Thanks for this," she smiles, distracting me from thoughts of initiating another round. But I can give her body a little more rest—I've more than proven I can be patient.

"No problem. I'll just take this back into the kitchen."

I gather her plate and napkins, sweeping the crumbs from her crumpled sheets onto the plate.

"You're the best," she sighs, content with life as we know it before she burps adorably.

Her hand slaps over her mouth and she looks like she could die of embarrassment from such a normal physiological response. "I can't believe I just did that."

Her dad must have really done a number on her if she thinks it's not even okay to burp after eating.

I hate that guy.

"Pretty sure we're well past the uncomfortable stage. You let me pee on you last night, I'm not about to be disgusted because you burped in front of me."

"I— Yeah, y-you have a point," she stutters. My laugh is hysterical before I peck a kiss to her lips and grab her discarded plate and fork. She's fluffing her pillows to lie back down when I shut her door and head back to the kitchen.

"Hey, sir, we were told everything would be packed and ready to go when we got here but most of the boxes are empty and the kitchen isn't even packed," says one of the sons, his thumb jutting over his shoulder toward the island.

I look around and notice they've gotten the bigger items like her furniture and TV, but many of the boxes around the room remain empty.

"Uh, yeah. We . . . had a long night," I mention, though I'm cautious not to divulge too much. Everything that happened last night filters through my brain and I have to strain to keep my dick in check. I clear my throat. "But, uh, look, how about I help you get everything packed while she rests a little more," I offer. "She could really use the sleep, and I want to avoid bothering her if we can."

"Sure, the more the merrier," he says. "Is the missus alright?"

"Yeah, she's fine, just tired." Truthfully, I'm tired as hell too, but had she not spent all night with me, this wouldn't have happened, so I guess I kind of owe her one since she chose to be with me rather than getting this done. Though, in my defense, she never mentioned she had movers coming. I would have understood and helped her a lot sooner had I known. I'm not a *total* monster.

It's a breeze when we pack her essential kitchen items. I'm working on the remaining books on her bookshelf when I find two manga comics hidden behind a stack of books. I'm beaming with pride to learn she really is an anime fan when she walks out wide-eyed and flustered.

"What's going on?" she asks, through a yawn.

She's running her naked body back inside the second she discovers we're not alone. Luckily, only *I* catch her bare ass running away, so it's easy to laugh at the embarrassing moment.

"Alright, boys, we're making good time," the older guy, Samson, rallies. "We just need to do the bedroom and then we should be loaded up and in Palm Springs by daybreak tomorrow."

My hand freezes.

"Palm Springs?" I ask just as Sydney rejoins us, a robe tied around her this time.

She looks beautiful as always, but the look in her eyes cracks me in half. "Lucien."

The way she says my name sends a current of fear down my spine.

"Why is your stuff going to *Palm Springs*?" I ask.

"Lucien, I need to talk to you."

She's approaching me like she did last night, palms up and steps wary, as though *I'm* the scared animal that's about to bolt or attack.

Maybe I am.

"Sydney. *Why* is your stuff going to *Palm Springs?*" I grit, no longer able to keep the rising frustration out of my voice.

"It's . . . complicated. You know, it's just . . . one of those things." Her hands twist around each other, no longer sure of what to do with them since the surrender gesture has all but lost its effectiveness.

"One of *what* things?" I growl, taking a step toward her.

"Is everything alright, miss? Are you ready for us to pack your room next?" asks the younger of the sons, who's staring at her robed chest like he's wondering what's underneath.

"Uh . . ." She hesitates to answer with our audience here.

"One of those *things,*" I mutter, anger already pumping through my veins.

She looks at me, wary of what *our* next steps will be.

Turning away, she addresses the young man. "Can you give us a minute?"

"Um, alright, but your . . ."

"Everybody get the fuck out *now*!" I bark.

The guy stares at Sydney like her tits are going to tell him what to do.

"Now," I growl, and they all scurry to go outside.

I'm pushing Sydney back inside the room before I even fully register my actions. The back of her knees hit the edge of the bed and she falls against it, fighting with herself to either touch me or cower from me as she struggles to sit back up. I'm pacing the room, trying to process everything and click all of the pieces together. Her words and expressions from last night finally beginning to make sense.

"See you around . . ." "No . . . you won't."

"One last kiss . . ."

"A night to remember . . ."

"You're leaving?" The words feel like hard rocks in my throat as I try to speak.

I grab at my hair and pull, hoping to feel pain anywhere else but in my chest as I pace back and forth.

Sitting on the edge of the bed, her hand reaches out, but she pulls it back when she notices my pacing is not stopping.

"Lucien," she starts. "Please just listen. My dad only funded my schooling because I made a deal with him that as long as I didn't cause him any trouble and I won competitions, I could stay. I told you he doesn't like that I figure skate, but he'd been at least supporting me financially so long as I adhered to the agreement, but I haven't been. Not only did I *not* make qualifiers, but I was also *disqualified* from competing in Nationals. I'm off the team, remember?" Her begging urges me to understand. "So, the deal is off. After everything happened yesterday, he ordered me back home. I was to pack my things and transfer to a business program closer to home."

"That's too soon," I shoot back. "No way he gets a school transfer ready in a few hours."

She sighs. "I had a standing invitation. My dad's friends with the dean so he was able to get me in."

"So, say no!" I growl, frustrated with such a bullshit excuse when there's an easy fix.

"It doesn't work like that with my father," she clips, her response automated.

"Why not?" I shout. Why is this perfectly capable, intelligent, fucking stubborn girl just rolling over and throwing us away?

"It just *isn't!*" she shouts back.

It's the first time she's truly raised her voice at me. She sounds as panicked as I feel. I thought she feared *me,* but the fear in her eyes right now is intrinsic, made from the very marrow of her bones. She won't defy him . . . not even for me. She's going to leave me. I'm going to be alone again.

"So, what was that last night, huh?" I push. "Sharing secrets, giving confessions, and exposing truths. You just, *what*? Wanted to tick one last thing off the bucket list before you snuck out in the morning and left me behind?"

"First of all," she snaps, "this is my apartment. I wasn't going to *sneak* anywhere. And second," her voice softens, eyes glistening, "you said this was a game. It was entertainment for you, Lucien."

Right, a game.

I snort a dejected laugh. I wasn't stupid. I recognized that she was out of my league, lightyears beyond what I deserved. Sydney might not be an angel, but she is far better than me. Her strength is what forced my own walls to come down and accept her as someone I could trust to keep in my life.

But now she's leaving.

"Yeah, well, all games have rules, right? And the rule was no running away," I grit.

I expect her to say something, to have some sort of snarky reply, but she doesn't, she keeps her lips sealed. Her full lips press together as she holds herself back from saying what she actually wants to. It's frustrating. This beautiful fucking girl frustrates the shit out of me. Even with her robe coming undone and her hair a disheveled mess, she still looks perfect.

I don't want to lose her.

"Don't do this," I plead. "Don't leave."

"I-I can't," she croaks.

Despair and helplessness snake around my ankles, feeling like they want to drag me under the floor.

"And I would never betray your trust," she adds, promising my secrets are safe with her, but it's not my secrets that worry me. She betrayed my heart.

"Yeah, you wouldn't betray me, you just wouldn't choose me, is that right?"

"I . . . I-I—"

"For once . . . tell me the *truth*."

Her lips wobbles and her eyes slide close as if pained.

"I can't choose you."

Indignation erupts through me, and I explode, whatever rage people feared in me, is nothing compared to what I want to unleash upon her now.

"You're not leaving me!" I push her down flat against the bed as I straddle her, the blade from my back pocket pointed at her chest. She's ripping my heart out of my chest. I thought it was long gone, so it's only fair I cut hers out as well. She *cannot* leave me. I only just got her.

In the middle of everything else, I've resolved that I might be losing the one thing that ever mattered to me. I might be losing hockey the way Sydney was losing figure skating, and like her, I thought if I lost it that it would suck, but at least I would have *her* in the end. She would be my shining light in the dark. *She* would be worth the loss, but she's leaving me to be alone again with nothing and no one. She belongs to me, and she can't leave with *my* heart while hers still beats in her chest.

Tears fill her eyes, but it's only when one drops onto her cheek that I realize it's me who's crying.

"Please . . . Please . . . Don't leave me," I pant. I'm trying not to lose control, but I can feel the blade slipping farther into her chest. I can smell the iron of her blood, and it only spurs the monster that rages inside me. I could do it. I could kill her and then she'll have to stay with me just like *they* do. She can join my family in my nightmares—and never leave.

"Never . . ." she whispers, tears sliding to her ears. I want to lick them away, but she's not done. "I wanted this night so we could be tied forever. So that wherever I go, you'll always be with me. And even though you're upset . . . I'm so glad I got to have that with you." Her voice chokes on her last words. Her breaths, ragged and her speech choppy as she attempts to bear the pain.

What about MY pain, Sydney!

"Don't go," I cry. "I don't *want* to be alone again."

Why does everyone leave me?

She says nothing, and it's about the worst possible choice she could make. Her lips roll inward, and she closes her eyes. I hate that she's hiding from this right now. I hate the silence that bleeds in, overbearing and blinding me to what's real and what's all in my head.

All I see is snow . . . and blood . . . and trees . . .

"You won't be alone." She breaks the silence, but not the feeling. "You have a life here."

My eyes snap to hers. "A life that was *crumbling*!"

Blood flows in rivulets down the crevice around her pillow-soft tits and through the valley between them, staining her robe and sheets as I push in a fraction deeper. I *try* to restrain myself. To think rationally, or rather not-so-rationally, because rationale is telling me to carve out her treacherous heart so she can be like me.

"You have Trevor," she offers, but she's still not getting it.

"Trevor would never be with me. I might be getting kicked off the team and he's going pro. He's my best friend, but there's no future for us. Don't you get it? *You're* my future, my everything."

"There's no future for us either," she rasps, emotion I can't reconcile caught in her throat. It could be from the pain she's enduring from the blade, or from the loss of us because apparently there is no *us* and I was only kidding myself if I ever thought there was. Maybe she's right and I *am* a cocky fucker because it never once crossed my mind that she wouldn't be mine.

"Why didn't you just *tell* me? Why blindside me? You just checked me into the boards with no warning . . . no defenses . . . just betrayal."

"I didn't mean—"

I cut off her lies.

"You *knew* I was falling for you, and you did nothing to stop me." I put my face closer to hers. "And we both know how *good* you are at stopping me before I go too far. Which means this was a path you *chose*," I snarl.

Faint noises from the other side of the door bleed through before there's a banging sound. "Miss? Miss, your father is calling, and there's campus police out here. They want you to open the door."

Neither of us move to get up.

"I didn't mean to, Lucien. I *swear* the intention was never to hurt you. I stayed to watch you play so that I could see you one last time. I figured the chance to check on you in the locker room was the last opportunity I was going to get to actually talk to you. I tried to push you away when you came and found me, but then you offered me a night of fun and games. The more I talked to you, the more I liked you. I wanted more time with you, and I just thought . . . that if I told you . . . you wouldn't waste your time on me. You'd find another toy to play with, and I'd be a forgotten memory you'd never even think twice about."

She still hasn't told me to stop; she just let me dig in a little deeper. Her hands rest on my wrists, but they don't push me away or pull me closer, they just hold me as I slowly stab her.

"I-I couldn't stand the idea of walking away from you sooner than I had to." She hisses a breath, coping with the pain as she looks me square in my eyes. "I'd have rather *died* than see you walk away from me." She shakes her head, resolution set in her eyes, even through the tears. "I don't regret . . . a fucking thing." I press in a little more. "B-because I'm—*crazy*—about you."

This girl will be the death of me, the death of us both.

I squeeze my eyes shut, frustrated and confused. I want to believe her, but it's been so long since I've felt this kind of loss. I never imagined I would feel it again.

"And I'm crazy about you." I force air into my lungs, sucking in enough oxygen to clear my thoughts. "So where does that leave us?"

Her face screws up. "We found each other once; we'll find each other again."

I memorize the hope on her face and trace every line, hair, and mark from the crown of her head, down to her neck.

Her cracked blue eyes capture my own and we breathe in the silence together.

Blood coats my hands and I stop pushing the blade in, but she doesn't move. She stays. She accepts her punishment.

"I'm not *them*. My heart will still beat for you, even when I'm gone," she says. "It isn't the same. Your family had no choice in dying. Death is unrivaled, right? But that doesn't mean you're alone. I'm still here." Her bloodied hand presses to my chest, leaving a palm print against my skin. "Even if I'm not in your life, I still exist. We could be . . . friends."

I huff, disbelieving.

She wants to be my fucking *friend*?

Friends don't fuck like we fucked. Friends don't build altars in each other's name and worship at their feet. Friends don't give over their whole body and spirit to do with as a fucked up soul like me pleases. Friends don't beg to be choked on the pierced cock of their *buddy* while she drowns in my cum. A friend wouldn't be poised to cut out his *bestie's* heart for betraying him.

There's another knock at the door, but again we ignore it.

"Do you *really* want to live a life without me in it?" I ask, resting my forehead to hers and stroking my busted knuckles over her wrists.

"No," she whispers.

"Then I should cut your heart out right now so you can't give it to anyone else."

The door pounds again.

My hand flexes but I don't push in any farther. I really am liable to kill her by accident if I don't stop but I'm not yet convinced I should. What's left for me on the other side of that door?

Nothing and no one.

Not hockey. Not my friends. Not my parents. Not Lilith.

"So do it," she goads, "cut it out. It won't matter how many times I fall in love or who I give my heart to; you're the very blood in my veins. It won't beat without you. There's no getting rid of you. I'm yours, remember? They'll have to take it out of your cold dead hands if they want it." The corner of her mouth curves into a sly smile even as she pants.

Leave it to her to not only be unfazed by my suggestion, but to agree. I won't lie and say this doesn't hurt, because it fucking does. It hurts like hell, but if there's anything I can believe in right now, it's that Sydney and I aren't over. Not even fucking close. So, I'll do what I always do when there's a tricky play, no room for a shot, and no one around to make the pass. I'll make my own way.

Another knock raps against the door, only this time it's louder and angrier.

"You can fall in love. Get married. Start a family. You can find God and become a nun. You can travel a million miles away and join a convent and you would still fucking belong to me," I growl, tossing the blade aside and gripping her face, my palms slick with her blood. "I don't care where you go or what you do, just don't let me go. Don't ever stop being mine. If I'm the blood in your veins, then you would need to flay yourself and bleed me out to get rid of me. Do you understand?"

"Yes," she sobs, grabbing my face and pulling me in for a kiss. I fall willingly into her, consumed by her. Addicted to her. We kiss even as her stab wound continues to run red down her sweat-slicked torso. We kiss even as the banging on the door grows louder. We fucking kiss even as I'm pulling my cock out and sliding inside her wet heat that chokes me tighter as she writhes and screams my fucking name. We don't *stop* kissing until well after she brings herself to orgasm, riding my cock and praying for forgiveness.

"God, please. You have to believe me . . . I'm sorry, Lucien. I'm so *sorry*," she moans.

I'm not far behind her after that.

"You better fucking be, because I'm your redemption, Princess. Don't forget that."

They're my final words before I'm flipping her over, fucking her into the mattress until I'm coming deep inside, cursing her name and spilling out her sunrise-colored pussy. We're catching our breath when a man's voice booms from the entryway with such undeniable authority, I know exactly who he is: her father.

@therealLucifer
Online
Seen
Who the hell is this?
Seen
SYDNEY

CHAPTER FORTY-THREE

SYDNEY

"**S**YDNEY!" MY DAD YELLS through the front door. "You open this door right now!"

When I thought it couldn't get any worse it fucking does. My dad never yells, he thinks it's a sign of weakness. He says a person that holds real power could whisper his demands and the world would go silent to hear them.

Lucien pulls his cock out and my pussy weeps either tears– or cum– from the loss but she's definitely not happy with the turn of events. Blood is everywhere, the cut beneath my breast bone still leaking. Fuck. That's what I get for breaking a goddamn psycho's heart. I'll probably need stitches for this one . . . but brightside, it won't fade so easily with time. I do my best to cover the gash with my hand, but the pressure only forces it to bleed more, not to mention it fucking hurts.

"Here." His hand reaches out to give me what looks like a bundled pair of black socks from one of my drawers. I can't really decipher his expression but it's nothing like he seemed a second ago. A large sinking feeling grabs hold of me, even more so than when he had a knife to my chest. It holds on so tight I fear it'll end me before the blood loss does.

"Lucien Morrow, this is campus police. We need you to come with us. If you do not come out, we will be forced to enter the premises by force."

My head whips to Lucien again and the expression I'd tried so hard to place locks in. He looks . . . *defeated*. When I gaze into his amber eyes, they no longer appear golden, or shine like the sun. All I can see glaring back at me, is defeat.

I'm shaking my head in protest before words can even form.

"Lucien?"

"I'm sorry," he says, a hoarse, rasped sound serrating the air.

He puts on his shirt in a blur, buckles his pants, then slips on his shoes. I don't think about putting on clothes or dressing my wounds. I just watch him.

I stand there and bleed while my heart breaks.

Sitting on the end of my bed, he drags his hands through his hair again before plucking his knife from the floor. He folds it in half and, to my surprise, hands it to me.

"I want you to keep this. Don't let anyone have it, okay? Just, hold on to it . . ." His shoulder lifts into a shrug. "Maybe I'll get it back from you one day." He chuckles a little, but he doesn't sound like he believes it.

"Lucien, wait. Please . . ." I grab his hand, wanting to assure him somehow that he's not alone in this world, but I don't know how. I couldn't show him if I wanted to because I'm just as alone, helpless and defeated.

"It's fine," he says, petting my hair with his free hand then placing a kiss atop my head.

I lean into his hold because I don't think I'll ever get to again.

"I don't want to lose you," I cry.

"I know, Princess. Me neither," he croaks.

The banging has moved to the bedroom door, pounding like dynamite exploding the bridge that once connected us.

"You have one minute or we're coming in," shouts the campus police.

"Stop being defiant, Sydney, and open this door right now!" shouts my dad.

"We're coming, just give us a second," I call, quickly grabbing some sleep shorts and locating Lucien's sweatshirt. I hide my stab wound by holding the sock to it to stop the bleeding, then tossing on a sports bra. It's a struggle to get a hoodie on, but I manage. Meanwhile, Lucien pulls the sheets from the bed in one swift motion, wadding it all into a ball and tossing it in the corner before we give each other one last look.

"Ready?" he asks.

"No," I whisper.

His lips twitch to smile, but that's all it is, a brief curl of his lips before he's headed for the door.

My eyes don't deviate from his retreating frame even as he opens the door to find the movers, campus police, my dad . . . and Bradford. They're all standing in my doorway. I pay them no mind, reaching for Lucien's hand again when he stops to look at my dad. They remain that way, staring each other down, until the campus police interject.

"Mr. Morrow, you're going to have to come with us. We've received several complaints regarding your behavior last night and you've been summoned by the school's president. He's requesting an audience with you at once."

Lucien says nothing, looking from my dad to Bradford, but he doesn't turn to look back at me. His hand lets go of mine and he starts to walk away with the officers.

"Wait!" I shout, seeking his hand again. I need to go with them, explain everything that happened. It shouldn't all fall on him. It's not like he's the sole person to blame for everything last night.

"Sydney, what the hell has gotten into you?" My dad scolds, but I push past him.

"I wanna go with him. I can help, I can *explain!*"

I look from the officers to Lucien's back, but still Lucien doesn't turn around. He walks ahead of them out of my apartment, taking the steps two at a time until he reaches the bottom.

I stomp after him.

"Lucien, stop! Please!"

He doesn't even pause.

"Stop walking," I huff, but he has the advantage of both height and speed.

"Lucien!" I call out when he almost reaches the street, a campus police car parked right in front of the building.

His steps falter, slowing just enough for me to catch up. All night he's heeded my call, so this should be no different. He'll stop for me. He'll let me make this right.

"Please turn around," I beg, pleading with him not to end things this way.

He stops and for a moment I feel like I can finally breathe. His back ripples as he takes a deep breath, his hand moving to sweep his hair from his eyes as he looks up toward the sky. His whole demeanor is one of pure agony and I can't stand it. I'm ready to run to him, to force him to turn around, to beg him to run off into the sunset with me and say fuck my dad, fuck Bradford, fuck the school's president, fuck Tiffany and Regina, fuck the Andersons, fuck anyone against us, but he doesn't. He only stands there, and I know if I make one wrong move, it's over.

"I'm sorry, okay!" The cold morning air slices my bare legs, still bruised in areas where he's touched me.

He doesn't say anything back.

"Did you hear me? I said I'm sorry," I choke out.

His head hangs, falling between his shoulders as he struggles *not* to face me.

"Please don't go. Not yet. I'm not ready yet," I cry, tears streaming down my face as I watch him fight the urge to stay.

The two campus police officers ignore me as they open their car doors, one of them standing near the back while he waits for Lucien to get in. Neighbors stand on their balconies watching the scene unfold down below, and the movers aren't actually moving anymore—at least I don't think they are as I stare at Lucien's back that shivers either from the weather, rage or his fight to remain turned away from me. My dad is uncharacteristically quiet now, and I turn to catch him scowling next to Bradford who's even more smug than usual.

I quickly look away.

"Please," I whimper, no longer caring about anyone else but Lucien.

I'll stay, I think, but the words don't broach my lips.

His head turns slightly, and for the briefest moment I allow hope to flourish within me.

"See you around, Princess."

He climbs into the back of the car, slamming it closed. Then he's gone, taking my heart and whatever hope I had with him.

6 months later

My heart squeezes like it's about to burst right out of my chest. I have to rest my hands on my knees while I catch my breath.

"Your technique is really good, Sydney, but I still want you to loosen up a bit. Relax. You were way too stiff on that last move."

I nod while huffing, desperate for air. Sweat drips down my brow and my spine straightens when I address her.

"I can do better," I pant. "Just let me catch my breath and I'll do it again."

The stern eyes of my new choreographer, Oksana, pinch further as she continues to score me. I know I can't take too much longer, or she'll start getting on me about my endurance. The thought oddly reminds me of *him*, and my heart squeezes for an entirely different reason.

I still miss him. I foolishly thought the memory of him fucking me would keep me warm at night. I thought continuing to pursue figure skating would ease the pain of losing him. But more than anything, I thought that one night together would be enough. I was sadly mistaken. I didn't consider how much I would miss talking to him. Yeah, he fucked my brains out, but he was funny and caring too. We didn't just connect sexually, we connected emotionally, and I didn't prepare myself for losing that.

I knew my heart would break when I finally had to let him go, but I didn't expect him to walk away with it. I didn't expect him to try to cut it out either, but that's my overly pragmatic Lucien for you.

My heart might as well have been carved out when I learned he did get kicked out of Belle U. I'm not sure what ultimately did him in, but the guilt ate me alive for almost three months straight before I ever even considered forgiving myself. I can't help but believe that had I never spent the night with him, he wouldn't have gotten into half as much trouble as he did.

I tried looking for him after everything ended, but as it turns out, my stalking skills have been grossly overestimated. I haven't been able to find him.

I considered asking Trevor, but every time I tried, I couldn't do it. It felt like I deserved to lose him and reaching out to his *other* lover to bring him back to me when absolutely nothing had changed seemed selfish. I still wouldn't be allowed to be with him, even with my new deal with Dad.

This deal is considerably shittier than the last. I'm pretty much completely cut off at this point, but it's something. I couldn't get into another skate program, but I managed to get into another school that wasn't the one my dad picked out. Ultimately, Lucien was right. All I had to do was stop worrying so much about failing and just skate. Now that I'm so thoroughly acquainted with failure, I don't fear it as much. It's still there, like an uncomfortable rash that breaks out on occasion, but for the most part, it remains dormant. Triggers like my dad and stupid hockey players tend to cause flare ups, but missing Lucien is my biggest point of contingency.

I want nothing more than for him to be on this ice with me again and make me feel like I could take on the world. With one more deep inhalation, I think of him and do the routine over again. This time, according to Oksana, it's significantly better.

We call it a day and I slip on my guards, swiping my sweater from the bleachers before I head to my locker, same as I always do, but something feels off about today. There's not as much attention on me here, something I've worked really hard to maintain at this new school. Yet today, it feels like the entire arena is watching me. It's not exactly unpleasant, but it's a feeling I can't reconcile. Whatever this feeling is, I'm not inclined to believe it is a good thing.

I tie the arms of my sweater around my waist and hoist my bag over my shoulder. A weird part of me no longer likes to leave so much of my equipment at the arena. Who knows how long I'll last this time? This is my *very* last chance. There are no more do overs after this. Weighted with that knowledge, I continue with my newly formed routine and head upstairs to the atrium. It's less commercial than Bellemere, but it's practical and their prices are affordable. Something I never thought I'd have to consider, but you learn pretty quickly what you can afford when you've been cut from funding.

There's a quaint C-store that serves instant coffee that's not completely terrible. I finish stirring my coffee and grab a lid for the Styrofoam cup. Next to the checkout counter, there's a spinning rack with trail mix that I slowly turn before settling on a two-for-the-price-of-one deal. I pay for the subpar coffee and discounted trail mix, pocketing one and opening the other. It's gone too quickly and I'm throwing out the package along with my instant coffee before I can even find a table to sit. I don't want to eat my second bag yet. I know I'll need it for later, but I don't want to leave yet, something in me screams for me to wait.

Against my better judgment, I pull out the second packet of trail mix and snack on that while I sit at a table and ... wait. I eat each piece one by one, creating a pattern of cashews, raisins, chocolate chips, and yogurt bites until the second packet is empty. I haven't even noticed that I've zoned out so much that I'm just staring at the back of some guy's head this whole time.

Whatever. His hair doesn't mind if I stare.

I rip the empty trail mix bag into tiny pieces as I look closer at the shorter cut in the back and his longer length at the top. There's a slight wave to it and it's dark, a deep black you don't come across often. It reminds me of Lucien's and again pieces of my heart fall away. I miss him. I miss him so fucking much it hurts.

I've only felt loss like this two other times in my life, but this wound is fresh, still bleeding and sensitive to the touch. The guy's skin color even looks the right shade, and the build is similar to. He's wearing a black long sleeve shirt and sweatpants. I can't help but crack a smile, reminiscing on Lucien and I's first and only date. It should have been a disaster, but I've never felt more desired. One of the food kiosks around here is serving French fries today and I swear I'm going crazy because if I close my eyes, I can remember the scent of peppermint and leather that coated his skin that night.

When I open my eyes again, the guy is rubbing his neck and for the briefest moment I can see rough knuckles and thick veins that stream all the way up to his wrist. When his hands move, I can see a sliver of ink peeking out from under his shirt.

No fucking way . . .

My feet are moving of their own accord, that sensation of being sucked into a black hole familiar to me once again.

It can't be him.

I'm an arm's length away from the guy, close enough to touch him, but my hand freezes, poised to tap on his shoulder but unable to commit. It's not possible. And even if it were, what would he even want from me now? Revenge, maybe? Or nothing at all? Which would hurt more?

I pull my hand away and take a step back, but I don't turn to leave yet. Instead, I lean in, smelling him as if that'll confirm my suspicions over simply asking the man to turn around. He smells divine, but it doesn't prove anything. Lots of guys smell clean and spicy. I try to get a better look at the tattoo crawling up his neck, but from this angle, there's no other concrete identifiers. He could be anybody and though he may look like Lucien, there's no replacing the original. I don't want a copycat. I want the real thing and if I can't have that . . .

I turn to walk away.

"It's rude to sneak up on people, you know? Bad manners and all that."

My blood runs cold. Or hot. Or both. I'm unsure, but I stop moving.

"*Lucien.*" The word is barely a whisper as I slowly turn back around.

It's not a question. Not quite a statement either. His name is like that of an ancient relic on my tongue, a powerful summons that draws him forth. I dare not speak it unless it were really him, in the flesh, truly in front of me. He still has his back to me, but I heard his voice, I heard what he said.

Logic refuses to bow to emotion though and forces me to hesitate. My footsteps suspend in midair before I dare attempt another step in the stranger's direction. I'm not sure I could take it if it *weren't* him. There's a strong pull that begs me to avoid the pain of disappointment and continue walking away, but Lucien's pull is stronger and begs me to run *to* him and fall into the void.

I almost collapse to my knees when the man turns around and I'm face to face with *him*.

"Hey, Princess. Did you miss me?"

Golden eyes rob me of breath, and with a smirk and a wink, I fall for him all over again.

The End

EPILOGUE

LUCIEN

FINDING HER THIS TIME proved slightly more difficult. I had to really think about everything I learned about Sydney Fucking Sinclair.

She lived in Palm Springs, California with her annoying father who—according to her—she constantly disappointed. As a result of that constant ire, she struck a deal and moved away to what she *said* was the best collegiate figure skating program in the nation, but she lied. Again. It's by far her least attractive quality.

The best program is in New York, and that doesn't seem like the kind of thing she wouldn't know. Couple that with the fact that she's a wealthy girl who's funding shouldn't have been an issue for her and that she has a weird soft spot for her father, and it makes sense to believe she chose Seattle because it was the best program that was closest to home.

The next-best program is in Detroit, but a team didn't work out so well for my girl last time. Sydney thrives on being challenged. She needs someone who won't let her quit on herself. She has a steep goal of making it to the Olympics, so she can't afford to start over.

This meant my search narrowed to schools with figure skating programs closer to the West coast with instructors who already knew of her skills, offered training without the need to be on a team, and had availability on their rosters. Not to mention that they needed to be less expensive than her last program, since I'm willing to bet Daddy Dearest isn't willing to spend more money just to see her fail again.

The most crucial part is that it needed to be a place that didn't believe the rumors from her last school. No university wants someone who was so afraid of losing their scholarship due to her family going bankrupt that they were desperate enough to push a teammate in hopes of keeping their spot on the team. At least, that was the rumor.

Yeah, I'm impressed with myself for finding her this time, but mostly I'm proud of her.

After everything we've been through, there was no way my princess would just quit on her dreams.

Technically, she quit on *me,* but I'm almost soothed by the notion that she didn't even try to make us work. She saw the end and only cared about salvaging the pieces she could keep when it all shattered.

"I-I can't believe you're here. *How* are you here?" Sydney stutters, her mouth agape as she tries to come to terms that I'm really here.

"I should ask you the same question," I say, masking my features with a look of equal shock. She doesn't need to know my stalking skills are superior to hers. And that I have no patience for the flight skills she's surely developed over these past few months. Six months I had to endure her being away from me as I embarked on a personal journey to adopt a whole new persona and become someone she *could* keep.

I won't risk it all now by telling her I followed her here.

Her lip quivers and a single tear falls down her cheek. The old me would have licked it away and smiled at her tears, but I resist. This time, I simply thumb them away.

She hisses a breath like my gentleness stung her, but she doesn't pull away from my touch. There's a long pause before she finally leans into it, those crazy blue eyes ping-ponging over my features, incredulous as ever.

"What's wrong Princess? Cat got your tongue?" I smirk.

"I just . . . can't believe you're really here." She shakes her head, her braided ponytail tossing side to side. Her hair looks duller, her skin less porcelain and fake, but she still looks amazing. Less plastic and doll-like, but breathtaking.

"I know, right? What are the odds?"

She looks away from me, shame or guilt evident on her face as she sweeps a few loose strands behind her ear.

"I'd heard you got expelled," she mentions.

Rubbing the back of my neck, I shift my weight. "I was . . . asked to leave and this was my runner-up school anyway, so here I am."

I hate the way lies taste, but I've gotten pretty used to its bitterness as of late.

"Oh. That's good." She looks disappointed, but I just stand there.

"Yep," I rock back on my heels, not leading the charge this time, but moving at her pace.

"So, how've you been?" she asks.

My brows hike, amused at her attempt at normal conversation as though the last time I saw her I wasn't fucking her senseless and trying to cut her heart out.

"*Good*," I drawl, doing my best to keep the sarcasm at bay.

She rears back from the understated answer and a flash of hurt shines in her eyes. Part of me relishes in her pain, but mostly I just don't want to rehash our bitter end when I'm trying to ensure we have a future.

"Better now," I add with a smile.

She doesn't completely warm up with my new approach, but she thaws slightly.

"I'm . . . sorry" Sydney says with a sigh. "I know it's been a long time and we never—I just needed to say it again. I *am* sorry." She finishes her apology before dropping her gaze to her shoes.

"Forget about it," I brush her apology away with the wave of a hand. *We're starting brand new.* "It's water under the bridge."

Her lips curl into a smile, no longer slathered in gloss, but moisturized and soft. "Yeah." Her eyes soften finally as she looks back up at me.

"*So* . . . What have *you* been up to?" I prod, hoping this time she'll be honest.

"I just finished practice." She jerks a thumb behind her, pointing to the stairs that lead to the rink below.

I'm already aware of what she's been up to, but I want to hear her tell me herself. I want to hear from her own mouth how she *really* feels after everything.

"Seems you didn't have to give it up after all," I tell her, nodding my head to her skates over her shoulder.

"Thanks to you," she gestures toward me.

I grin slightly, but shake my hair. "Nah, I'm sure that's not true."

Her shoulders slump as though I've hit her with another crushing blow, and I'm starting to lose faith in this plan. I think I'm really fucking this up.

"Well, let's see it then," I push, opening my arms in display.

"See what?" She looks around like she's confused.

"How you've improved."

"Oh, no." Her hands wave in front of her. "I don't know about that, I just—"

"Nuh uh uh, Princess." I take a step forward, closing the distance between us physically and mentally so there is no confusion about *how* we're moving forward. "False modesty is a form of lying and we don't do that anymore, do we?" My fingers tilt her chin up and her throat bobs as she gathers her wits.

"No," her voice a hoarse whisper as she leans in closer.

"Good." I lean away. "Lead the way."

She's just as beautiful a skater as she always was, but in all honesty, she's better now. She hasn't fallen, not once.

"Come on." She skates literal circles around me as I stand in the center of the rink with a pair of rented figure skates, since they offer that here. "Skate with me?"

In the correct skates, it's easier to copy her movements. She tries to speed ahead, but I grab her hand and twirl her toward me. Her leg wraps around my waist, and I dip her back, letting her long blond braid flow in the wind and kiss the ice. Her eyes are wide with wonder and surprise. I flash her a wink.

"Did you already forget I knew how to figure skate?"

She shakes her head.

"It's not that, I forgot how good it felt." Sydney's cheeks burn pink, and I watch the flush spread down to her ample breasts that somehow look fuller. God, I miss her tits.

I turn and skate away to prevent myself from squishing my face between them.

"You ain't seen nothing yet."

I laugh at her dumbfounded expression when I pull off a triple axel that I *know* she wasn't expecting. Her shock quickly melts away and she's skating toward me at full speed. It's my turn to be shocked when she jumps with no fear and complete trust that I'll catch her—and I *do* catch her, bringing her body flush against mine. There's no amount of control that could prevent my cock from hardening at her touch right now as I hold her close and she slides down my body. Her breath ghosts over my lips, and her hands cup my face.

"Sydney," I rasp, unwilling to quite cross that line yet. I can't afford to move too fast again. This isn't like last time. I'm not just playing a game for keeps anymore. She and I are for fucking life.

We're a whispered breath away from kissing, despite our strengthened defenses, but there's an applause that rips our focus away. We both turn to find our unexpected audience. It takes me an embarrassingly long minute to pinpoint the intruder before I see a woman I don't recognize skating over to us. My body partially shields Sydney, ready to attack, despite my efforts to remain calm and exercise more control.

"Who are you?" I snap.

She ignores me.

"My dear, that was absolutely beautiful. I've never seen you skate like that before. You were . . . magnificent."

Sydney's blue eyes shine with tears and it only sets me more on edge. Why is she crying? I swear to God, if this woman is making her cry, she's dead.

Sydney's hands cup her face as she shakes her head. "Thank you. Thank you so much. I—you don't know how much it means to me to hear you say that, Oksana."

Oksana?

She peels Sydney's hands away from her face. "I knew there had to be something special about you. That's why I agreed to train you." Her attention falls on me. "But now I see you've been hiding your secret weapon from me." She gives me a discerning once-over. "What's your name? I don't think I've seen you around before."

My eyes assess her for so long in return that Sydney has to answer for me. "This is my friend, Lucien."

The term *friend* gut punches me so hard I almost keel over. I don't know what we were classified as before now, but 'friend' just doesn't suit. It's a disgusting word I want to spit out and make her swallow.

She was the girl who was willingly to do anything for me, who was just as crazy about me as I was about her. To shrink it all down to us being 'friends' is laughable at this point, so that's what I do. I fucking laugh.

The woman is unfazed by my outburst. "You're a strange one, aren't you?"

"Guilty," I counter, my grin obviously unkind, but teasing enough to make her blush.

She sighs.

"I suppose it doesn't hurt. You're obviously talented. Do you train together often?" Oksana asks as she skates around us, checking out my physique without shame.

"Oh, no, we weren't training. We were just . . ." Sydney looks at me for confirmation, but I don't offer any assistance. I'm at as much of a loss as she is. I don't know what we're doing. I know what I *want* us to be doing, but I can admit I have no clue how to get us there anymore. "Having fun," she finishes.

It's even more of a punch to the dick than being called a friend. We shared a moment, and she chalked it up to *fun*? Is this how she felt when we were playing our games? Did she think it was all fun and games and I wasn't falling for her?

Bradford's words play on a stupid loop in my head. *You know . . . I almost feel bad for you.* I sensed it then, that he was actually being genuine and that only pissed me off more at the time.

I shake it off. It doesn't matter. I'm here now, and this time I'm not getting pushed away.

"You're telling me you just performed that piece on a whim?" Oksana perks up, stopping her examination of my body.

The woman's brows pinch before her eyes light up in amazement. She seems impressed with us. Meanwhile, I'm still reeling from the effects of 'friend' and 'fun' hovering my head, circling like cartoon birds and I'm the fool that's been conked over the head.

"Um, yeah, I guess so," Sydney shrugs. "It wasn't really a piece though. Just us goofing around, you know."

I hate how nervous Sydney sounds. It's nothing like the fearless girl she was a moment ago when she leapt into my arms, nothing like the snarky girl with the bad attitude and foul mouth from months ago. *Nothing* like she used to be.

I turn away from what feels like the imposter next to me and out into the arena. Without the distraction of Sydney or the Oksana woman, I feel the telltale signs of eyes on me. I can't see past the lights and the darkness beyond, but their stares are undeniable. Someone is out there. I strain my eyes, trying to see what's trying to stay hidden. The best I'm able to do is catch two tall shadowy figures. Two guys if I had to guess.

Typically, I'd be on edge about that, ready to fight, maim or kill whoever dared to pose a threat, but this doesn't feel like a threat. It feels . . . nostalgic. I know this feeling. I've felt it before with Sydney when I realized she was watching my practices. Whoever's watching us now, feels *exactly* like that. I peer over to Sydney, who of course doesn't notice, then back at the woman who's still chattering on about her assessment of us rather than paying attention to our surroundings.

Oksana looks between us some more and though it's a struggle, I refocus my attention because the next words out of her mouth changes the fate of Sydney and I once more.

"Sydney, have you ever thought of doing partner skating?"

CONTENT WARNINGS

Alcohol use
Anal play
Anal sex
Biting
Blood play
Bondage
Breaking and entering
Bribery
Bruising
Bullying
Childhood neglect
Childhood trauma
Cutting
Cyberstalking
Death of a family member (depicted)
Degradation kink
Drugging
DubCon
Excessive use of violence
Fear kink
Golden showers
Knife play
Marking
Murder
Physical assault

CRACKED ICE

Praise kink
Rimming
Scarring
Stabbing
Stalking
Suicidal ideation
Threesome
Unhealthy methods of dealing with poor mental health

ACKNOWLEDGMENTS

First off, I just want to say WOW! I can't believe we have a book. And I can't believe there were so many people who not only believed in me enough to give my book a chance, but who played integral roles in helping me make this happen so that it could be shared with others.

I want to extend a deeply special thank you to my PA, Emily, who told me she had two friends she thought would make great beta readers and that could give me the in-depth feedback I was looking for; Gia and Vanessa you were truly awesome and my absolute rocks. I can't wait to share my other stories with you all!

And though it was a last-minute thing, I couldn't have gotten myself organized enough to get this done if it weren't for you, Emily. So thank you so much for organizing my chaos.

I'd also like to thank Jessica who was my very first fan. She started alpha reading for book two, and when she was foaming at the mouth for more, I said, "Hey, I have the prequel mostly written, do you want to read that in the meantime?" Her enthusiastic *yes* pushed me to finish writing the whole first draft of Cracked Ice in just ONE WEEK so she wouldn't have to wait too long. It was insane, but so much fun.

Special shoutout to Alexis Payge who let me use her upcoming debut's—The Ember—hockey team, The Crestview Wolverines as the rivals for Belle U in this story. She came up with the idea of creating interconnected worlds using other people's hockey teams—since there are so many hockey romances now—and I jumped at the opportunity.

I also need to give a shoutout and thank you to Missy who was the best critique partner I could have asked for. It is because of her that Lucien's truly unhinged behavior shined the way that it did. You encouraged me to be detailed and descriptive and to really go all-out with my writing—and you were so right! Thank you so much for being such an inspiration and I can't wait to support you in your own publishing journey.

I want to give an extremely special thanks to my best friend Alyssia who I know I drove crazy with all my book talk and whining about not being sure if I was good enough. In true best-friend fashion, she gave me an ultimatum: she would refuse to read my book until it was published, so if I wanted her to read it, I *had* to keep going. Get you a best friend who pushes you like that, and you'll have someone special for life.

Last, but certainly not least, I need to give a huge round of applause to my editor Tiffani, who not only made sure I would have a decently written book with minimal typos and grammatical errors, but who ensured me on the daily that I was a good writer who could only go up from here. She believed in my story, and she believed in me, and she put up with my crazy mood swings. I'm a better writer today because of her. And don't worry, she's nothing like the Tiffany in this book; she's better.

To everyone else like my graphics designer Katelyn, my friends and family, those who've left reviews and shared my posts, and you, who's taking the time to read all of this, I can't thank you enough. I can only hope this is the start of a pretty great adventure because we have more stories to tell, so many more. Thank you.

ABOUT THE AUTHOR

KD Cureton writes spicy dark romance that walks the razor edge between pleasure and pain. Known for her emotionally charged, boundary-pushing stories, she creates characters who are raw, flawed, morally gray, and unflinchingly real—yet still deeply deserving of love. Her books don't just bring the heat—they drag you through the full emotional spectrum: angst, desire, heartbreak, rage, laughter, and everything in between.

Readers can expect to clutch their pearls one moment and cheer for redemption the next, because with KD, a time will absolutely be had.

A proud single mom with a "life-is-a-movie" level of chaos, KD weaves real-life experiences into her stories—but she'll never tell you which ones. When she's not writing, she channels her creative fire into DIY projects and home makeovers, living out her HGTV dreams whenever inspiration to write takes a coffee break.

Stalk KD's socials for more:

ALSO BY KD CURETON

Cracked Ice

Black Ice
Releasing 2026

New Project
Releases Summer of 2026

Book 3 in the F*cked Players Series
Releases Fall of 2026

Book 4 in the F*cked Players Series
Releases Feb of 2027